# LETHAL DEFENSE

## A NATE SHEPHERD NOVEL

MICHAEL STAGG

Lethal Defense

A Nate Shepherd Novel

For more information on Michael Stagg and his other books, go to michaelstagg.com

Want a free short story about Nate Shepherd's start as a new lawyer? Hint: It didn't go well. Sign up for Michael Stagg's newsletter here or at https://michaelstagg.com/newsletter/

❀ Created with Vellum

# PROLOGUE

THE FIRST TIME I SAW HANK BRAGGI, HE WAS COVERED IN BLOOD. He was walking out of a hotel surrounded by four police officers and his hands were cuffed in front of him so that I could see the blood that coated his arms, elbows to fists, like he'd just dipped them in a bucket of it.

He had a beard but if it matched his curly blond hair, I couldn't tell because there was blood dripping off it too, spattering the front of his shirt like someone had thrown a jar of red paint at him for wearing a fur coat.

For a split second, he looked up at the camera with calm, blue eyes. He didn't seem the least bit agitated or upset as he followed the four officers, all a head shorter than him, to a squad car.

I was surfing my way up the channels to SportsCenter so I didn't read the scroll at the bottom of the television screen; I didn't see the names Lizzy Saint or Dillon Chase or Hank Braggi, and I certainly didn't see a description of the murder. Instead, I clicked right past him to ESPN, where Scott Van Pelt was showing highlights of the Detroit Red Wings beating the

Minnesota Wild, and I didn't think about the name Hank Braggi for another two months.

# LOCAL COUNSEL

# 1

As I walked out of the Carrefour courthouse, I turned on my phone for the first time that morning. Twelve calls from a number I didn't recognize scrolled up my screen. No messages. These robo-calls were getting out of control.

A moment later, my phone buzzed again. Same number.

I answered. "Nate Shepherd."

"Mr. Shepherd, I need to hire local counsel."

I looked up at the domed courthouse. "Proximity is my best attribute."

"It's for a murder trial."

I sighed. I'd handled all sorts of cases at my old firm – malpractice, injuries from industrial machines, and disputes between businesses that had more money than sense. But no crimes and certainly no murders. "Sorry, I don't handle murder cases. You may want to call—"

"You worked at the prosecutor's office, didn't you?"

"Years ago."

"Then I have the right man."

I needed to fire the person who screened my calls. Oh, yeah. "I'm sorry. I don't think you do."

"It seems to me that a lawyer who's newly out on his own might want to expand his horizons."

I sighed. "I appreciate your interest but if you want to stay out of jail, I'm not your best bet to represent you in a criminal case."

There was a matching sigh from the other end of the phone. "Mr. Shepherd, you wouldn't be representing me in a criminal case. Obviously. You'd be helping me handle one."

"I'm not sure how."

"Did you handle the Reynolds case?"

Brain-damaged baby case. An awful one. "I did."

"And the Hanover-Rigson case?"

Industrial accident. Hot press. Gross and awful. It was also settled before word of it reached the paper. "There was no Hanover-Rigson case."

A chuckle. "You're definitely the person I need. Listen, my name is Christian Dane and I'm a lawyer out of Minneapolis. I've been hired to represent a client there in Carrefour and I need a local attorney to manage relationships with the Court and the prosecutor."

I shifted gears. I was dealing with a lawyer in Minneapolis instead of a criminal—excuse me, accused criminal—or a family member. "Christian, I could do that but one of the local criminal guys will have a better relationship with the prosecutor. Let me give you the number of—"

"It's in front of Judge Gallon."

Judge Anne Gallon and I had been friends since we'd served in the prosecutor's office together right out of law school. She was smart and fair. She was also scrupulous about not showing favoritism. "She's not going to cut your client any breaks because I'm on the case."

"I wouldn't expect her to. But I assume you know what kind of arguments will carry the most weight with her."

"I suppose so."

"That's what we need. I'll handle the law. You handle the relationships. I think you'll find the fees in the case are more than fair."

"How much an hour?"

Another chuckle. "Mr. Shepherd, your past is showing. We don't bill by the hour, we charge by the job. And the result."

"So what do we charge for the job?"

"For local counsel?" He said a number.

Sweet Jesus.

"Mr. Shepherd?"

"You just hired yourself local counsel."

"Excellent. We have a pretrial tomorrow morning. Judge Gallon's court, 8:30 a.m. I'll see you there."

"Right."

We hung up and, as soon as I did, I realized that I didn't know the name of the client.

It had been a long time since I'd handled a criminal case. Seven years at least. Maybe eight. Jumping back into that arena with a murder case for a client I didn't know didn't seem like the best idea, but I figured that easing back in as local counsel wouldn't be too bad.

Turns out that was optimistic.

## 2

As I pulled into my driveway that night, I parked my Jeep next to the Honda and noticed for the twelfth time that the Honda's left front tire was low. I'd left the porch light on accidentally that morning but other than that the house was dark. I didn't have to go inside to know it would be quiet too.

I sat there for a moment. I thought about going to the Railcar for a sandwich and a beer but I knew I had to be up early for the pretrial tomorrow. I figured I'd be better off going in, making an eggs and rice two-fry, drinking a beer, and going to sleep.

So I did.

## 3

The next morning, I was sitting in the Carrefour courthouse, a magnificently ornate building built back in the late 1800s. I was in the judge's office off of Court Room 1, the courtroom of Judge Anne Gallon.

Judge Gallon was the perfect judge for our community—honest, pragmatic, and whip-smart. She had short, light brown hair and sharp looks that were all angles. She wore glasses that I was pretty sure she didn't need but which softened the hard edges and a piercing glare. She was an altogether practical, skilled, and dedicated judge who, above all else, hated lateness.

My co-counsel, Christian Dane, was late.

Judge Gallon made a point of looking at her phone. "It's 8:30, Nate."

"It is," I said.

"Much as I enjoy catching up, that's when the pretrial that Mr. Dane requested starts."

"Yes, Your Honor. He's coming in from out of town."

"The trial is in *this* town."

"That is true, Your Honor."

"So he'll need to be here."

"Yes, ma'am."

She gave me a look and a raised eyebrow at the "ma'am" business but let it go. "Where is he coming in from?"

"I believe his motion said his office was in Minneapolis, Judge." That came from the prosecutor, Jeff Hanson, who was sitting in the chair beside me. Jeff was a heavy, jovial, self-deprecating assassin. "That is a long way but you know I made it, even with my breakfast." He chuckled and slapped his belly lightly on the side.

"Still live down the block, Jeff?" I said.

"Oh sure it's close, Nate, but I did have two helpings of eggs." Jeff smiled and the edges of his eyes crinkled as if he hadn't just poked at me. "I didn't realize you were still doing this kind of work."

"I haven't been," I said. "Civil cases mostly."

Jeff's eyes crinkled further. "To what do we owe the pleasure of this reunion then?"

"I'm just local counsel on this one."

"Seen the pictures yet?"

"No."

"Almost made me lose my appetite." He tapped his belly. "Me."

"I'll be sure to time my lunch."

Judge Gallon tapped the back of a pen on her desk. "As local counsel, I assume you'll tell your co-counsel that our local practice is to be on time."

At that moment, a man walked into the judge's office that I assumed was Christian Dane. He was tall, in his late fifties, and had thick, swept-back white hair. He wore a crisp navy suit without a wrinkle on it and looked as if a Hollywood agent had cast him in the role of lawyer and sent him over today.

"My apologies, Your Honor." His voice was as deep as you'd expect. "My flight was late."

"Perhaps earlier flights from now on?" said Judge Gallon.

"There will be no more flights, Your Honor. I'm here for the duration until trial."

"Where did you come in from?"

"Minneapolis, Your Honor."

"That's a long way to our little court. Are you licensed in Ohio?"

"No, Your Honor. My co-counsel will be filing a motion to admit me *pro hac vice*."

That was news to me but I kept it off my face as Christian handed me a motion. I saw the title of the case for the first time: *State of Ohio vs. Hank Braggi*. It seemed familiar but I didn't place it as I scanned the boilerplate language and signed it. I noticed that it was thicker than normal for what was usually a pretty standard motion to obtain permission for an out-of-state lawyer to appear in a case. "Here you go, Your Honor," I said, and handed it to her.

Judge Gallon straightened her glasses and flipped to the end of the motion to look at Dane's resume. "Ohio has strict rules about who's allowed to try a murder case, Mr. Dane." She looked at Hanson. "The State is seeking the death penalty?"

"Yes, Your Honor."

"And even stricter requirements for trying a capital murder case."

Christian pointed a manicured finger at the motion. "We've attached a list. You'll see I've handled a number of them, Your Honor. Including capital cases."

"Any in Ohio?"

"May I, Your Honor?" Christian put a hand on the back of a chair.

"Of course." The side of Judge Gallon's mouth ticked. "The scolding is over."

Christian Dane sat and somehow managed to keep all the

lines of his suit in perfect order. He crossed his legs and said, "One in Portsmouth and one in Akron."

"How does a lawyer in Minnesota wind up trying murder cases in Ohio?"

Christian picked a piece of non-existent dust off the cliff-like crease in his pants. "You go where the clients are, Your Honor."

"And the clients are in Ohio?"

"Sometimes." Dane smiled. "It is God's country here after all."

Judge Gallon looked at him sharply. "We like it here, Mr. Dane."

"I do too. I meant it."

Judge Gallon stared at him and then, apparently satisfied that he was indeed serious, nodded and continued. "The Court finds that your qualifications are sufficient and will admit you *pro hac vice* for this case but you must practice in association with local counsel."

Christian nodded. "That's why we've retained Mr. Shepherd, Your Honor."

Judge Gallon changed her focus to me and the look she gave me wasn't much kinder than the one she'd given Christian a moment before. "You've been doing a lot of civil work, Nate. Are you still qualified to handle a murder case?"

Barely but yes. "Yes, Your Honor."

"Then the Court grants the motion to admit Mr. Dane so long as he appears in association with Mr. Shepherd. You'll submit an order to the Court, Nate?"

I handed her one. She smiled and, as she signed it, said, "I take it you'll be filing a motion to discharge the public defender and take her place?"

Christian Dane pulled another set of papers out of his thin leather attaché and handed it to her. "Yes, Your Honor."

"Did you tell her, yet?"

"No, Your Honor. I'll call her when we leave here."

"Don't be shy about getting her involved again if you're in over your head."

Christian Dane gave her a look that was completely respectful of the judge and completely dismissive of the idea in a way that I would not have thought possible.

"Very well." Judge Gallon flipped through her calendar. "We're only thirty days from trial. I can give you a little bit more time but not much since he has to be tried by—"

"We're not seeking a continuance, Your Honor," said Christian Dane.

Judge Gallon put down her pen and crossed her hands. "This is a capital murder case, Mr. Dane."

"Yes, Your Honor."

"You'll be ready to go in thirty days?"

"Yes, Your Honor. My client does not want to be incarcerated any longer than necessary."

Jeff Hanson coughed as Judge Gallon raised an eyebrow. Christian smiled and his teeth were as white and as straight as his hair. "You have to keep an optimistic outlook in this business, Your Honor."

Judge Gallon didn't look convinced. "I suppose you do." She tapped the pen again. "I'm not going to grant you a continuance later, Mr. Dane. You ask for one now or not at all."

"I understand, Your Honor. We'll be ready in thirty days."

I kept my face straight because that's what lawyers do. Good ones anyways. But thirty days was going to be pushing it and I started mentally reorganizing my life.

Christian Dane seemed unconcerned about what he'd just committed us to. "I understand the Court set a two-million-dollar cash bond?"

Judge Gallon looked at Jeff Hanson, who nodded and said, "Mr. Braggi has spent the last three years touring the world with a rock band, Your Honor. We continue to believe that he's a flight risk. Given the brutal nature of the murder, we believe that he should remain in custody until trial. Your Honor compromised by setting a full cash bond."

Judge Gallon looked back at Christian Dane. My new co-counsel nodded and said, "Leaving aside the questionable constitutionality of a requiring a full cash bond as opposed to a ten percent insurance policy, we'll be posting the money this afternoon."

Jeff Hanson started. "If that's true, we'll want to file a motion to reconsider."

Christian Dane smiled. "And if the State is going to ask for bond to be reconsidered once we actually produce the cash, we believe that the bond is illusory and doubly unconstitutional."

Jeff squirmed because Christian was right. "The State would want community control measures in place, Your Honor," Jeff said.

Christian appeared unconcerned. "Again, I don't know if that's appropriate but we intend to use one of the people your court uses, Your Honor. I presume Mr. Shepherd knows some."

It had been a while but I did. One. "I do, Your Honor."

"Who?" she said.

"Cade Brickson."

Judge Gallon thought. "He's perfect for this. The Court agrees. Cash bond is granted in the amount of two million dollars as previously set by the Court." She smiled. "Better warn the county office though, Jeff. They're going to have a heart attack. Is there anything else?"

"No, Your Honor," said Christian Dane and Jeff Hanson together.

"Good. Then I will see you all in thirty days. And I mean it, counsel. I don't want a call three weeks from now telling me that you need more time."

"Understood, Your Honor," said Christian.

We all stood up, thanked the judge, and left.

As we walked out, Jeff extended a hand to Christian and said, "We had an offer of second-degree murder out to the public defender."

Christian shook it. "Thank you, Mr. Hanson. The only deal I'm prepared to accept is a total dismissal of charges."

Jeff smiled. "I'll see you in thirty days then." He shook my hand and nodded. "Good to see you again, Nate." And he ambled off.

When he was gone, I said, "Thirty days?"

"Our directive is to get our client out on bond and then dispose of this as quickly as possible. That means no continuances."

The name, Hank Braggi, was still niggling at the back of my head from somewhere. And the business Hanson had said about touring with a rock band sounded familiar too but I couldn't place it. "So what's the deal here with Braggi?"

Christian looked at me sharply. "You don't know?"

I thought for a few seconds then shook my head. "I've had a lot going on."

"Braggi was touring with Lizzy Saint. The killing happened after a concert."

That rang a bell. "Rock star, right? Had a concert here at the University and her sound man beat a man to death in her hotel room."

Christian nodded. "Hank Braggi is the sound man. And our client."

"What happened?"

"According to the reports, Braggi beat the man until he was unrecognizable."

I nodded.

Christian's face was serious. "That's not a figure of speech. The victim's skull and chest were shattered. Pulverized."

"What did he use?"

"His hands."

Yikes. "What's his explanation?"

Christian pointed at the jail across the street. "Let's go find out."

THE COUNTY JAIL IN CARREFOUR HAS A SERIES OF INTERVIEW rooms and by the time Christian Dane and I arrived, Hank Braggi was waiting for us in one.

Hank Braggi was big, not in a bodybuilder, musclebound sort of way but in a broad, tall, put a steer on his back kind of way. His light brown hair and full beard were longish and wild, except that both were trimmed all around so that they were uniformly wild, if there's such a thing. He wore an orange jumpsuit and his hands were shackled in loops that were strung through embedded rings on the bolted-down table. His bright blue eyes widened as we entered then his shoulders slumped as he turned to the guard who stood in the corner. "I thought you said my lawyer was coming?" he said.

"We're your new lawyers," said Christian.

"I can't afford a lawyer who wears a suit like that."

Christian put his attaché on the table. "No, Mr. Braggi, you can't."

"So my father's paying for it?"

That was enough confidential conversation in front of a guard. "Thank you, officer," I said. "We'll knock when we're ready."

Hank opened his mouth to speak but Christian raised one

hand and Hank stopped until the guard had left and the door snicked shut.

"Cost is not something you need to worry about, Mr. Braggi," said Christian.

Hank's fingers tapped the table between the shackles. "You have to get me out of here."

Christian nodded. "That's what we've come to do."

"I mean it. I can't be in here anymore."

"You'll be out tonight."

"Really?" Hank's eyes grew wide. "They said bond was two million dollars. Cash."

"It is."

"So my father *is* paying for it."

Christian shrugged. "You can stay here if you like."

"Don't even joke about that, Fancy Pants. When do we leave?"

"As soon as I finish the paperwork."

"And the bail bondsman gets here," I said.

"Bondsman?"

"There are going to be conditions," I said.

Hank waved a shackled hand.

"Whatever. Just get me out of here."

"We will."

"Then let's go."

"It will take a little more time."

Hank's eyes grew dark. "Get. Me. Out of here."

Christian looked at me and nodded and I knocked on the door.

The guard returned.

"Where can we wait while Mr. Braggi is processed?" said Christian.

The guard scoffed. "He's not getting out."

"He is—" Christian peered at the name tag, "—Officer Wing

and I would appreciate it if you would tell us where we can wait while you process him."

Officer Wing muttered a few rights and lefts that should send us back to the main lobby area.

Hank rattled his shackles. "You better not be messing with me, Fancy Pants."

"Just don't screw up between here and there, Mr. Braggi." Then Christian nodded and we left.

As we walked down the hall, Christian said, "Is this bond officer of yours good?"

I nodded. "He is."

Christian stopped and stared at me. "Mr. Braggi demands a high degree of...attention."

"What's your point?"

"Mr. Braggi's father doesn't want to see his son back in jail."

"Or to lose his two million dollars?"

"I'm sure that thought occurred to him too."

"So find your own bond officer."

Christian looked away. "We tried to use one of our own men but the Court insisted on someone certified locally."

"You don't say." I didn't offer any other assurance. Eventually, Christian said, "Fine," and started walking again. Rather than heading for the processing area, Christian walked right out the front door.

"I thought we were going to interview him?"

"Hank was in no state to talk to us."

"What do you mean?"

"You'll see once he's out. He's a whole different person. The confinement had him ready to explode."

"It didn't seem that way to me."

"It was."

"So what now?"

"If this bondsman is as good as you say, he'll take care of getting Hank out."

"He is."

"And we can make better use of our time, like getting set up at your office."

"Sounds good," I said. "Want to follow me back?"

Christian gave me a slight smile. "I have the address."

I thought about the state of my office and the fact that it was only set up for me and Danny. "I'll stop on the way back and pick up some supplies."

Christian gave me a slight smile. "My legal assistant is already there, Mr. Shepherd. I think you'll find that we have everything we need."

Christian stopped at a black Mercedes (of course) and climbed in. I hopped into my Jeep and followed.

By the time we left, it was late afternoon. We had twenty-nine and a half days until trial.

## 4

CARREFOUR IS A SMALL CITY THAT STRADDLES THE BORDER OF Ohio and Michigan, the same way Kansas City sits in both Kansas and Missouri. Founded by French trappers in the 1700s, you can get anywhere from there—originally by canoe, riverboat, and trail, and now by car, plane, and rail. Sitting near the airports in Detroit and Toledo, the highways and rails between Chicago and Cleveland, and the ships on Lake Erie, trade constantly passed through Carrefour because it was so easy to go from our city to somewhere else.

The city was equal parts Michigan and Ohio. Having a city in two states created all sorts of rivalries and jurisdictional issues—Michigan and Ohio police, Michigan and Ohio courts, Michigan and Ohio tax systems. Hank's crime had occurred on the Ohio side so we were in an Ohio court dealing with Ohio laws which, most importantly, included the death penalty.

As I drove away from the jail, I shook my head at being involved in a capital case again but pushed it aside by remembering that I was only local counsel and that the ultimate responsibility for convincing a jury that Hank Braggi shouldn't be executed fell to Christian Dane. I was involved to help manage relationships so that's what I decided to focus on.

Lindsey Cooper, the public defender who had represented Hank so far, seemed like a good place to start.

I called her. "Lindsey, it's Nate Shepherd."

"Hi, Nate," she said. "It's been a while."

"It has."

"Heard you've left the marble halls and joined the brave ranks of the solo practitioners."

"I have. I'm cheating though, I brought an associate."

"Good for you. What's up?"

"I'm calling to let you know that Hank Braggi is going to ask that you withdraw from his case."

"Really? I didn't think you were still doing this kind of thing."

"I'm not. I'm just in as local counsel. Hank brought in a specialist from Minnesota."

"That's a long way from Ohio."

"That's why I'm around. I'm sorry by the way."

"For replacing me?" Lindsey laughed. "Don't be. This was a public appointment, which means it's not paying me nearly enough to spend a week getting my ass kicked. I owe you a beer."

"Still, it's a high-profile murder case."

Lindsey chuckled again. "Sure it is. But I prefer to win those if I go to trial."

"It's that bad?"

"Have you seen the file yet?"

"No."

"It's that bad."

"Is there really enough for aggravated murder?"

"I'll let you come to your own conclusions, Nate. But yes. Besides killing Dillon Chase, he tried to kill one of his friends too. Murder plus attempted murder gets you the death penalty. That's why I told him to take the deal. Are they still offering second degree?"

"As of today."

"Take it. Hey, I'm walking into court, Nate. Thanks for the courtesy call. Just send me the paperwork to substitute us and I'll sign it."

"Will do. Thanks, Lindsey."

"No problem," she said, and hung up.

By then I was coming up on my office so I didn't have much time to think about what I'd gotten myself into.

PEOPLE HAVE ROMANTIC IDEAS ABOUT LAW OFFICES. THEY IMAGINE the high-rise skyscraper of a large firm, the charming converted house of a small-town practitioner, or the dilapidated office building of a man down on his luck. Mine didn't have the romance of any of those. It was a generic three-story building of glass and chrome that rented space to small groups of lawyers and doctors and accountants with a shared receptionist on each floor and quick access to chain restaurants for lunch.

I took the stairs to the second floor and went into the three-room suite with "The Shepherd Firm" written on the door, which is what you call your practice when you don't have a second partner. As soon as I walked in, my young associate, Daniel Reddy, jumped up, sputtering. "She just started moving things around!"

"Hi, Danny. The pretrial went fine, thanks."

Danny looked as if he'd witnessed a sacrilegious act of unspeakable violence. "She unplugged the computers and everything. Do you know how long it took me to get the wireless printer to work?"

One of the hazards of a small office—the youngest attorney is the IT guy. "A long time?" I said.

"All weekend! And she just—" He made hand-flapping gestures that I assume was the unplugging of a madman. Or a madwoman, in this case.

"Do they work?"

Danny sputtered. "I don't know! That doesn't matter!"

"It does and they do," said a voice. A woman walked in with hair that was such a deep, blood-red that I couldn't tell if it was real or dyed. She had a strong jaw and angled cheeks and wore a tailored business suit that didn't seem like the garb of an IT menace. "Everything is ready to go, Mr. Shepherd," she said.

I offered my hand. "You're the anarchist with no respect for existing networks?"

"I am. Cyn Bardor." She shook my hand in an exceedingly precise way and glanced at Danny. "I think you'll find that your network's performance has been optimized."

"Good. What did you do?"

She gave me the slightest smile. "Do you really want to know?"

Point. "I don't. Can it be put back the way it was when you leave?"

"If you want. But I don't know why you would."

"Fair enough," I said. I looked around and surveyed the wreckage of files, papers, and blowups from our last trial that were still strewn about the office. It did look like Danny had pushed the bulk of it out of the way against the walls, but I felt a twinge that Cyn was seeing the office like that. "Sorry about the mess."

Cyn waved a hand. "You obviously finished a trial. If it were clean, I'd be worried."

From what I'd seen of Cyn so far, I decided that I shouldn't tell her that the trial had been a month ago. "Well, we'll clear it out so that you and Christian have space to work." I peeked in the other office and saw that it was empty. "He's not here yet? He left before me."

"He's here," said Cyn. "He wanted to get to work right away."

"Where is he?"

"In his office."

I raised an eyebrow.

"We rented the third floor."

"For the two of you?"

"We may have some people in and out, but we needed to rent the whole thing since it was such short notice."

Danny's mouth was open. It was a good reminder to me so I kept mine shut.

Cyn handed me a key. "We're in 302 and 303. We have 301 cleared out for the two of you and the computers are linked to your network." She checked the slim gold watch on her wrist. "Christian wanted to get through the indictment and some of the evidence and then touch base before you go home. 4:30 okay?"

"You're the boss."

This time Cyn raised both eyebrows. "Mr. Dane is and we'll see you then."

Cyn left then and it was hard to explain how. Striding sounds too masculine and glide doesn't seem strong enough but she left and it was like a purposeful force went with her.

When I looked at Danny, his mouth was still open. I smiled. "Wait until you see her boss."

WHEN DANNY AND I WENT TO THE THIRD FLOOR AN HOUR LATER, the space was unrecognizable. Where before it had been an empty shell without furnishings or supplies, it now was set up with four distinct offices, each with a working tablet and printer, and a separate conference room twice the size of mine with pictures and working files already set up. It even had a magnetic nameplate on the door which announced that this was the office of "Friedlander & Skald, Ltd."

Christian and Cyn were standing by the conference room table, sorting papers and putting them into piles. Exciting lawyer stuff. Christian's concession to informality was to take off his suit coat, revealing a cuffed shirt that was somehow barely wrinkled. I introduced him to Danny and, to his credit, Christian treated him like an equal and then asked him a few questions about how he was finding the practice of law. After a few minutes, I said, "So, what's first?"

Christian glanced at Cyn, who nodded.

"I'll be wanting your input of course," said Christian, "but I don't want either of us to start by making any half-baked assumptions. Let's interview Mr. Braggi tomorrow at his place and make sure he's settled in. Now that he's out, he'll be more calm and he'll be able to tell us what happened. Then we can spend the rest of the weekend reading the file and when we come in Monday, we can put together a strategy."

"Sounds good." I stared at stacks of papers that seemed overly large for the nature of the case. "I'll help you copy the file so we each have one before we go."

"That won't be necessary. Cyn?"

Cyn walked into another office and returned with two tablets, one for me and one for Danny. "Everything's been loaded onto this. You can go through it at home and we can talk about it on Monday."

"You got the file in advance?"

"No."

"You scanned it in already?"

Cyn smiled.

I looked at Danny. "You need to step it up."

Danny looked panicked. "But I..."

"Don't worry, Mr. Reddy," said Cyn without a smile. "He can't afford me."

"I'm certain of that," I said. Cyn took a moment and showed us how all the files were organized in a way that made perfect sense.

"You two should go home," said Christian.

"I don't want to just leave you. There's a lot to do."

Christian smiled. "This is a big case, Nathan, but until we talk to Hank and get through the materials, we're just spinning our wheels."

I nodded. I gave Christian the address where Cade Brickson would be taking Hank and said, "9:00 a.m. okay?"

"Perfect. I'll see you then."

"Goodnight, Cyn."

"Goodnight, Mr. Shepherd."

"Nate, please."

She smiled but didn't say anything else.

With that, Danny and I went downstairs, gathered our things, and locked up. I waved good-bye to Danny, climbed into my Jeep, and headed home.

I PULLED IN NEXT TO THE HONDA WITHOUT LEAVING ENOUGH ROOM to open its driver-side door. I gathered the tablet Cyn had given me and the groceries I had picked up on the way home and went inside. I set the groceries and tablet on the island and went to our bedroom to change. I threw on a T-shirt and a swimsuit and went to the back patio to fire up the grill. I turned it on, grabbed a beer, and plopped down into one of the two patio chairs, facing the low sun.

The grill began to heat up and the smell of smoke was delicious. We had an in-ground pool, just your basic sixteen by thirty-two rectangle, and as the sun worked its way down the sky and the filter rippled the water, it was peaceful in a way that we always enjoyed.

I sat that way for a while, enjoying the evening sun after being forced to be indoors all week. I enjoyed it enough to go get another beer and left the grill to keep smoking. When the sun began to dip behind the trees and the temperatures started to fall, my stomach got the better of me and I put the steak on. If you know grilling, you know those don't take long, not if you like them medium rare anyway, and soon I was sitting on the patio eating a steak and a salad, drinking a beer, and watching a hummingbird dart in and out of the daylilies we had planted next to the pool. The tiny bird was a brilliant blue-green, almost metallic looking, and just hovered right above the yellow flower, its wings beating a million miles an hour while it stayed perfectly still. Then a squirrel made a commotion in one of the trees and the hummingbird flew away. I would've been disappointed except I was done with my steak so I grabbed my dish, went inside, and put it in the dishwasher since we didn't like a mess in the sink. I grabbed another beer, went to the island, and opened the tablet Cyn had given me.

When the tablet had powered up, I found the Braggi file right there on the desktop. Cyn had organized the materials into sub-files—arrest report, crime scene, witness statements, catalog of physical evidence, autopsy. I thought about what Lindsey had said, clicked on "crime scene," then clicked on "photos."

The hotel room was a suite, not a suite like you find in a Las Vegas hotel but a two-bedroom unit like you find at a midwestern Marriott. The body was in the main room. The first few pictures were from a distance, showing the body's placement in the room. As the focus grew closer, it became clear that both arms had joints where they shouldn't.

I played football with a guy named Zach Stevenson. As tough a middle linebacker as you'd ever find. One game, he dislocated his ring finger and as he ran off the field, half the team couldn't even look at it because the sight of that finger sticking straight out to the side gives you a visceral scraping in your spine that doesn't go away as long as the finger is out of joint. I swear the whole team felt relief after the trainer popped Zach's finger back in.

The victim's arms were like that, popped out and bent in a way that made cringing unavoidable. Only they were never popped back in. They just sat there on the screen, broken and wrong.

As the focus of the pictures came in closer, an oblong red object filled the screen. It took me a moment to realize it was the victim's head. The face was a bloody mass that, like Lindsey had said, was unrecognizable. I thought I could pick out an eye socket and I definitely saw broken teeth behind a ruin of lips, but I swear I couldn't find his nose, which must have been pushed up into his skull. Side photos showed indentations where a nose and jaw should have been. The wreckage was so bad, so brutal, that it didn't look like a person—it looked like a special effect from a bad movie.

The photos panned back out then to capture blood spatters. On the wall, on the chairs, on the table, and pooled on the floor after the body had been removed. It seemed to me that there was too much of it and that there were more smears than spatters, like the body had been slammed around the room.

Lindsey was right. The level of violence here was going to be a problem. A big problem.

I clicked to the next set of photos.

A syringe.

A rubber tube and a spoon.

A clear bag of powder with a heavy glob of blood on it.

I found that I had to shut the tablet so I did. I realized that my breathing was ragged so I exhaled, slowly, then took a drink of beer.

I saw the hole in the kitchen wall for the first time in days, right there between the phone jack and the pantry. I didn't much feel like fixing it but I didn't really feel like seeing it either so I got up, left the house, and went to the Railcar.

I Ubered home about five hours later and fell asleep on the couch watching SportsCenter

# 5

THE NEXT DAY, SATURDAY, I MET CHRISTIAN ON THE OHIO SIDE OF Carrefour at the house where Hank Braggi would be staying (meaning confined to) until he stood trial. It was a little unusual for someone who didn't have a permanent residence here to be released but Christian had convinced the Court that there were two million reasons why Hank would stay put. Cade Brickson and an ankle monitor made it two million and two.

Christian had parked his Mercedes in the street and got out as I pulled up. I was admittedly feeling a little on the rough side but his blue-gray suit and open-collared white shirt were so neat and finely pressed that I wondered if he'd slept on a hanger. We shook hands, walked up to the door, and knocked. Cade Brickson answered.

Cade blocked all view beyond the doorway. He was six foot four but stacked with muscle in a way that made him look stocky, with thick arms and legs and traps that sat like base-balls on his shoulders. He looked exactly like what he was— the most fearsome heavyweight wrestler Carrefour North had ever produced and his training since then had only made him more dangerous. By all accounts, he was the best bail bondsman in Carrefour and, if the rumors were true, a bounty hunter as well. His dark brown eyes that regarded us both with calm interest.

"Morning, Cade," I said.

"Shep," said Cade.

"Hank's staying with you?" That was unusual.

Christian Dane stepped around me and offered Cade his hand. "Mr. Brickson has been offered a sizeable bonus to make sure that Mr. Braggi appears at trial."

Cade shook it. "Sizeable enough that I want to keep eyes on him 24/7." He looked at Christian. "You want to see him?"

"Please."

Cade led us back to the kitchen where Hank Braggi sat at the table. Somehow, Hank looked even bigger in ordinary furniture than he did in the cinderblock interview room and it immediately made me think that you would need someone Cade's size to even slow Hank down. Hank was eating some eggs, which, to be honest, smelled delicious on my jumpy stomach.

Hank smiled when he saw us. "Well, if it isn't the firm of Fancy Pants and Friend. You boys have breakfast yet?"

"We need to talk about what happened," said Christian.

"I'll be in the front room," said Cade, and left.

"You still need to eat," said Hank. He pushed back from the table and went into the kitchen.

It was the first time I'd seen Hank standing up. He was huge.

"Thanks for getting me out," Hank said as he pulled a carton of eggs out of the refrigerator. "Small spaces aren't my thing."

Hank did seem entirely different now than the man I'd met in the jail. The hair was still wild and the eyes still glittering blue but now that glitter seemed good-natured rather than frenzied as he cracked one egg after another into a glass bowl.

"We're here to try to keep you from going back," said Christian. "So tell us why you killed Dillon Chase."

"Because he deserved it," said Hank and began to whisk the eggs with swift flicks.

"That's not much of a defense, Mr. Braggi."

"Then you're not much of a lawyer," said Hank. "And quit calling me 'Mr. Braggi.' I'm no jumped up twit in a suit. Er, no offense. Braggi is what my friends call me, seeing as how I have a gift with the language. Or Hank."

Christian re-crossed his legs. "Mr. Braggi, if we're going to go to trial, we need a defense. And 'he deserved it' isn't a defense."

"Isn't self-defense a defense?"

"Yes," said Christian. "That's not the same as saying he deserved it."

"Well, it was self-defense then."

"Did he attack you?"

Hank pointed the dripping whisk at Christian. "See now, I would've thought that a fancy pants lawyer from Minneapolis would've bothered to read my file on the flight before he came in to see me." Hank's blue eyes narrowed. "So that means that you're a lazy ass or that you're trying to see if I'm going to lie to you and I'm not sure I care for either of those." He poured the eggs into a pan, causing a spatter and sizzle as they hit the heat, then dumped in what looked like chopped peppers and ham.

"Who said I was from Minneapolis?" said Christian.

"You said you were from my father."

Christian was silent.

"Pretty easy to figure out who he hired. Now are you lazy or a liar?"

"Neither. If Mr. Shepherd and I are going to defend you, we need to hear what happened in your own words. Did the victim attack you?"

"He was no victim."

"Did the dead man attack you?"

"You know he didn't."

"Did he strike you in any way?

"Nope."

"Threaten you with a weapon? Draw a knife on you? Point a gun?"

Hank took a spatula and began scraping the bottom of the pan to keep the eggs from burning. "Not even his finger."

"So how was it self-defense?"

Hank's eyes lost their mirth. "I saw what he was doing to Lizzy. That was enough."

"I don't know that it was, Mr. Braggi."

"Well, it's going to have to be because that's what happened."

I held up a hand. "Mr. Braggi—"

"Braggi."

I compromised. "Hank, I've only seen the pictures. We're going to have an uphill battle saying Mr. Chase deserved *that*. Tell us what happened so we can defend it."

Hank appeared to be contemplating the cook on his eggs more than listening to us as he ran the spatula in around the edge of the pan but eventually he said, "Pretty simple really. We played at the University here. Good show. Lizzy sounded great, cracked it out for a full two-hour set. When we were done, we knew we had the day off the next day, so we all got pretty lit."

He arranged three plates next to the stove and scraped out three helpings of eggs. He brought them over, slapped forks and hot sauce in the middle of the table, and sat down. The smell of the eggs was more than my shaky stomach could resist and I'm not ashamed to say that I started to eat.

"Where?" said Christian.

"At the hotel. We had a bunch of suites and there were all sorts of people there. Lizzy had a crowd around her, like she always does, and Jared was following her around, like he always does, as if standing next to her on stage while he plays the guitar all night isn't enough."

"Jared?" I asked.

"Jared Smoke. Lead guitarist, boyfriend, shit-stick. Name tells you all you need to know about him—makes one up and pairs Jared with Smoke. Might as well have gone with Mort Reaper. Anyway, he's always hanging around Lizzy, which I can't fault because I wouldn't let Lizzy out of my sight either if I were him, but that night he had some other folks with him that I wasn't crazy about. So anyway, they all vanish and go back to her suite and I decide that I don't really like the look of those new folks much. So I go up to the room and I knock on the door and I hear music but no one answers. I knock again. Nothing. So I try the door and it's open, so I walk in and I see Lizzy, drunk as the moon is full, sitting in a chair with her head lolled back. Now we've all been there on more than one occasion so that's not something that I would worry about except one of these strange guys is kneeling down in front of her and Jared's nowhere to be found. So I say 'Hey,' and this little rat-shit starts and looks at me and when he turns, I can see that he's got Lizzy's arm tied off and there's a needle sticking in it. So I stopped him."

My fork stopped halfway to my mouth and then I set it down as it turned out that I wasn't hungry after all. I stared at the eggs a moment longer then, when I realized Hank had stopped talking, looked up at him.

Hank gave me a look of glittering, unrepentant menace. There was a joy to it, an exultation.

"You killed him," said Christian.

Hank shrugged and shoveled a mouthful of eggs past his wild beard. "Like I said, I stopped him."

Christian was sitting back in his chair, legs crossed, hands relaxed in his lap, eggs untouched. "You didn't tell him to stop," said Christian.

"No, *I* stopped *him*."

"You beat him to death."

Hank kept eating. "Seemed more efficient."

"You fractured his skull."

Hank winked at me. "Didn't want him getting up."

"You broke his arms."

"See now a man with broken arms isn't going to be able to inject a beautiful young woman with heroin, is he?"

I gripped the edge of the table. Christian and Hank didn't seem to notice as Christian continued. "There's evidence that you slammed the body against the walls and onto the floor."

Hank nodded. "That's quicker than breaking all those ribs one by one."

Christian flicked an invisible piece of lint off the crease of his pants. "So you shattered a man's skull, broke his arms and ribs, and beat his face until his own mother wouldn't recognize him. And it's self-defense?"

Hank leaned forward, his glittering blue eyes focused and intent. "He won't do it again, will he?"

Christian nodded. "Did Jared see him inject her?"

I consciously slowed my breath.

"*Try* to inject her." Hank leaned back and shrugged. "You're the Fancy Pants lawyer. Find out."

Christian shifted slightly. "So Mr. Shepherd, what do you think of Mr. Braggi's self-defense argument?"

I gathered myself and saw that Christian was assessing me as coolly as he had been assessing Hank a moment before. That pissed me off so I picked up the fork again and took a few bites, ignoring him, before I said, "I think proportionality is going to be a problem."

Hank grinned. "His face was a bit lopsided."

Christian sniffed. "That's not what he means, Mr. Braggi. He means that you, in defending Ms. Saint, can only use that amount of force which she could use to defend herself."

"Well, she couldn't use any seeing as how she was unconscious. That's my point."

Christian's face didn't twitch. "Mr. Shepherd is saying that you went too far."

Hank looked back at me and pointed. "Do you think I went too far?"

I kept a lid on what I thought and said, "It doesn't matter what I think. It matters what the jury thinks."

"And what's a jury going to think, Counselor?"

I thought about the misshapen mass of blood, bone, and teeth that I'd seen in the pictures the night before. "I think we're going to have a hard time showing that Ms. Saint would have done what you did."

"Of course she wouldn't have. That's what I'm for."

I didn't think bludgeoning was part of the sound engineer's job description. "It's going to be a tough sell."

"So sell it. I assume that's why Fancy Pants get paid what they do. We done here?"

"It appears so," said Christian and stood.

"We should talk about the deal," I said.

"Not interested," said Hank.

"They're offering second-degree murder."

"So?"

"So they charged you with aggravated murder."

"I'm a bit aggravated about it myself."

"So if we lose, you can be executed. Ohio still has the death penalty."

Hank grinned. "Good."

"With the deal, you could be out in twenty."

"Days?"

"Of course not. Years."

"No way."

"Hank, this deal isn't going to stay on the table."

"Good. I won't have to turn it down again."

I looked at Christian who seemed utterly unconcerned with Hank's position. "Christian?"

"He said he's not interested, Mr. Shepherd."

"But if we lose..."

Hank turned to Christian. "You're being paid to win, right?"

"I'm being paid to try the case," said Christian.

"Same thing," said Hank and looked out the window. "It's a beautiful day and I've spent enough time inside. You can join me if you want, but I'm going to the backyard."

I wanted to keep working on Hank but Christian shook his head. "We have work to do, Mr. Braggi. We'll talk soon." He shook Hank's hand, then I did the same. I'm not small but Hank's hand positively engulfed mine. It was not at all hard to imagine it snapping bone. Then Hank nodded to me and left.

Cade met us at the front door. "Let me know when the next court date is," he said. "I'll have him there. Oh, and I'm billing you for the food. He won't stop."

"Of course, Mr. Brickson," said Christian. "Don't skimp."

I nodded, we all shook hands, and Christian and I left.

As we went to our cars, Christian and I agreed that this was going to be a tough case, that we'd spend the rest of the weekend looking at the file, and then strategize Monday. I drove home, thinking about the case and what Hank had told us about what he'd done.

When I arrived at home, I decided that I'd get some yard-work done before diving back into the file.

The thing about mowing the lawn is that it occupies one half of your brain and lets the other half roam. I barely noticed the grass as I pushed the mower back and forth. All I could picture was Hank coming on the scene of a man injecting Lizzy Saint with her helpless to prevent it. The depth of that evil was bound-less and I can't say that anyone would have blamed Hank for beating the man to within an inch of his life. The problem was just how far past that finish line he'd gone.

I gripped the lawnmower handle, hard, and felt the sweat pour off in the heat as I walked back and forth. I kept gnawing at it, picturing it, as I worked. The beating. The broken bones.

The heroin.

I thought about someone injecting Lizzy Saint without her knowing it and the good fortune, for her, that Hank was there to stop it. I thought about the divine intervention or the random chance that had brought Hank down like an avenging angel to destroy the man who was trying to shoot a ravenous monster into Lizzy's life and send it creeping through her veins. I thought about what would have happened to her if there hadn't been anyone there looking out for her.

After I finished mowing, I trimmed, and after I trimmed, I decided the boxwood bushes were getting unruly. Of course, you can't get a precise cut with an electric trimmer, no matter what those Home Depot ads say, so I used the hand-shears and worked my way around the house.

It was dark when I finished.

# 6

SUNDAY AFTERNOON MEANT A COOKOUT AT MY MOM AND DAD'S place. They lived in the hills of Michigan on Glass Lake, about fifteen minutes northwest of Carrefour. My dad was a pathological fisherman and my mom was happiest when she was near the water and her grandkids. Their lake house brought them closer to both.

I have two brothers. My older brother Tom is the head football coach at Carrefour North High School. He's married to Kate, who teaches there too, and they have four kids. Their three girls are named Reed, Taylor, and Page, and if you know that Tom was a fearsome strong safety back in the day and that he's obsessed with crafting a fast, bruising defense, then his girl's names will make sense to you. If you don't know all that, it's easier to say that he named his girls after Ed Reed, Lawrence Taylor, and Alan Page and that he might be slightly over-devoted to his job. His only son, the youngest, is named Charlie because naming a boy Woodson is obviously ridiculous.

My younger brother Mark is a tool and die maker for Ford. His wife Izzy is in human resources for Lounge King, and they're one of those couples who keep track of their boys by starting all of their names with "J": Justin, Joey, and James. My younger brother is a practical man.

I don't have any kids. My parents don't ask when I will anymore.

We all get together a couple of times a month during the winter and spring but once Memorial Day hits, my dad has a barbecue every Sunday that runs all the way through the Super Bowl. My family are suckers for football, the sun, and the water and, if I'm being honest with you—which I am most of the time —it's the highlight of my week.

I'd missed last week because I was traveling for work so when I showed up that Sunday afternoon with beer, an inflatable paddleboard, and Mickey Mouse ice cream bars for my nieces and nephews, the first thing I got was a cluck and a hug from my mother.

"Look at you," she said after giving me a hug. "How much weight have you lost?"

I'd lost about five pounds during a trial last month but there's really no future in telling your mom something like that, so I said, "I've actually gained a little bit."

"Thirty-four years old and you still lie to your mother like a teenager. How do you live with yourself?"

I smiled. "With a clear conscience."

"I doubt that. Ice cream bars?"

"You won't let me bring any chicken so..."

"If you can convince your father, you're more than welcome to."

"Hence the ice cream bars," I said and handed them to her.

She took them and waved. "They're down by the water. The kids will be happy to see you."

"Thanks." I gave her another hug and wandered toward the backdoor. As I did, I heard a scream and the slapping of controllers. I peeked in the family room and saw two young boys sitting in front of the TV where they appeared to be orchestrating the destruction of an alien race.

"Hi, trolls!"

"Hi, Uncle Nate!" said my nephew, Joey.

I bumped the other one with my knee. "Looks like Joey's getting you."

"In his dreams," said Justin. Then he elbowed me in the thigh and unleashed a flurry of laser fire which, if Joey's screams were any indication, were effective.

I looked out the window. "Pops is letting you play video games?"

The boys never looked away. "He's got James and the girls out on the boat."

I chuckled. "Trolls are tricksy and false."

"That's hobbits. And yes." Joey looked away from the screen for the first time. "Don't tell him!"

"I won't, but you better put it up when the boat docks."

"Not our first campaign, Uncle Nate," said Justin.

An alien pod blew up and the two crowed. "Apparently not."

I went out the backdoor secure in the knowledge that humanity was safe for the next five minutes and headed toward the lake. My brother Mark was in a vicious game of cornhole with my niece, Reed. Mark's wife Izzy was sitting next to Tom's wife Kate, who was absently playing beach towel tug of war with three-year-old Charlie.

I know, that's a lot of Shepherds at once. The first family barbeque can be overwhelming. It gets easier the more you come. For now, just remember that the boys who start with J belong to Mark and Izzy, and the three girls and baby Charlie belong to Tom and Kate.

And that my dad won't let you bring chicken to his barbeque.

"Nate!" yelled Izzy. "Bring that tight little ass over here and fill this cooler up!" Izzy had frizzy blond hair and dark green eyes, and I was always amazed that she'd picked HR as a career field.

Kate turned without stopping her tug of war with baby Charlie. "The prodigal lawyer returns." She had short, athletically cut brown hair and a placid calm that served her well as the mother of four and the wife of a football coach. She yanked on the towel, making Charlie squeal. "That cooler's not going to fill itself, you know."

"It's good to be missed." I dumped the beer into the cooler to the slosh of water and ice. I cracked two in succession before handing them over. "Lady Isabella. Lady Kate."

"See Kate, I told you there was a reason we wanted him around." Izzy's eyes twinkled.

Kate nodded, smiling. "Still, last week was such a nice break."

"Nice to be missed," I said.

"Jesus, Nate," said Izzy. "Crack a beer already, would you?"

"Sorry." I smiled and did. "Been busy with other chores."

Izzy flipped a hand. "Well, you have to make time for yourself or no one else will." Her eyes homed in on me. "Speaking of which, my friend Jessica's going to the Dierks Bentley concert with Mark and me next weekend. Want to come?"

"Izzy," said Mark from the cornhole game.

Izzy's eyes were wide innocence. "What? He might not have plans."

"I have plans," I said.

She sipped her beer and said, "Liar."

"I actually do."

"You mean you didn't before?" This was somewhere around the eleventh time she and Mark had been going somewhere with one of her girlfriends in the past six months. For some reason, she was the only one who did it and the only one who could get away with it.

I took a sip. "Who's the lawyer here?"

"I can't help it. I have an evasive witness."

Kate stepped in. "Going out of town again?"

"No. New case going to keep me busy for a while."

Izzy snorted and Kate's eyebrow twitched. "You just finished one last month."

I shrugged. "Another one came in. Emergency."

Izzy shook her head. "There's no greater emergency than you going to that concert with us and Jess."

"Let it go, Iz," said Mark.

"He'll tell me when to stop. Won't you, Nate?"

I smiled. "Stop."

She pouted.

"Please."

Izzy smiled. "Okay. So what's so important that you'd deprive yourself of our company?"

"A new case."

"Duh. What kind?"

"A murder case."

"Ooohh. Juicy." She leaned forward. "I didn't think anyone had been murdered in Carrefour."

"Seems like we would've heard about it," said Kate.

"Oh my God, Uncle Nate," said my niece Reed from the cornhole boards. "Are you on the Lizzy Saint murder?"

I have a great relationship with my niece, Reed. She's smart, she's fun, and since she's my oldest niece, I've been playing with her for a long time. But she was fifteen that summer and I'd be willing to bet that she hadn't really paid attention to any serious conversation that I had been involved in for at least three years. But here she was now, mouth slightly open, holding two beanbags lax at her sides as if she knew exactly what case I was on and was shocked.

"You know about it?" I said.

Reed's eyes got bigger. "Oh my God, is that really the case that you're on?"

"Well, Lizzy Saint's not really involved, Reed."

"Holy crap, Mallory's not going to believe this!"

Kate looked from her daughter to me. "What's she talking about, Nate?"

I glanced back and forth between my placid sister-in-law and my animated niece. "There was a murder after Lizzy Saint's concert at the University a few months ago. They brought me in as local counsel. I don't know how Reed here knows about it."

We all looked expectantly at Reed who didn't seem to notice the bemused scrutiny at all. "Are you kidding, Uncle Nate? It's not just some murder. Supposedly her sound engineer beat a guy to death protecting her from being attacked. It's been all over the place."

It was uncomfortably close to the truth. "What do you mean all over?"

"Entertainment Buzz, YouTube, Twitter. Everywhere."

"Have they been reporting that? That he was protecting her?"

"Sometimes. Mostly they just show pictures." Reed shook her head. "It was amazing."

"Reed, you should not be looking at those pictures."

"I'm fifteen, Uncle Nate. I've seen way worse than that. Besides, it's everywhere. It's not like I can avoid it. So what happened?"

"I'm sorry, honey, I can't talk about it. Besides, I'm no big deal. I'm just the local guy. There's a lawyer coming in from Minneapolis that's going to handle most of the case."

"Oh, right. The Silver Fox."

There are times when keeping up with a teenage girl is exhausting. "You mean Christian Dane?"

"Is that his name? The sites just call him the Silver Fox. There's even a hashtag."

Kate looked at me, looked at her daughter, and decided that she'd heard just about enough of murders and silver foxes. "Why don't you see if Grandma needs help with those pie crusts."

Reed looked at her mother with daggers that the mother of any teenage girl would find familiar. "She won't let me."

"Check anyway. She's in there all by herself."

Reed stomped. Literally stomped. "That's because she won't let anyone help her!"

"Still. No reason for her to be lonely too."

Reed slammed her beanbags onto the board. "Of course. Your stupid conversation was finally interesting." She marched with a lamentation of injustice back up to the cottage.

Since she wasn't his daughter, Mark looked bemused at the scene and his aborted cornhole match. "I thought you didn't do criminal cases?" he said.

"I don't usually but they just need a local guy and the price is right."

"You just came off a trial you know," said Kate.

"I know."

"You can't just keep going from one case to the next. It'll catch up with you eventually."

"I know."

"You have to take care of yourself," said Izzy. "It'll be a pain in the ass to find someone else to fill the cooler."

"I imagine so."

"Take Reed's place?" said Mark, tossing a beanbag into the air.

"Yep." I pulled two more beers out of the cooler, took one to my brother, and proceeded to lose two out of three before we started a doubles tournament. Reed, who eventually escaped from her cottage confinement, actually wanted to be my partner and we proceeded to whip butt, five matches in a row, until dinner.

Having a good partner makes all the difference.

## 7

ON MONDAY MORNING WHEN I ARRIVED AT THE OFFICE, I FOUND Danny already working. Actually, working was too strong a word. He was in front of his office door, fidgeting.

"What's up?" I said.

"They're upstairs."

I set my laptop on my desk. "That's where their office is."

"They were here when I got in. The Mercedes was already in the lot."

"Trial lawyers work hard, Danny. You know that."

He kept fidgeting. "There's got to be a lot to do. We only have four weeks."

"That's what the calendar says."

"We should see if they need help."

"We will. Let me get settled and check my email first."

"Sure. Okay." Danny kept standing there, shifting and twitching.

"You can go up there now if you want. I'll be up in a minute."

"No, that's okay. I'll wait."

He stood there as I sat down. He kept standing there. "Danny."

"Are you ready?"

"I'll come get you."

Danny realized what he was doing. "Oh, yeah, right, I'll be..." He pointed over his shoulder.

"I'm sure I'll find you."

I waded through the emails that had piled up over the weekend as Danny clattered around in his own office. Finally, after he'd rattled the coffeepot, knocked over a file, and kicked his chair, I stood up. "Shall we?"

Danny tumbled out of his office with a couple of notepads and a pen. "Bring the tablet she gave you," I said.

"Right." He scrambled back into his office and, as he took the tablet off its docking station, knocked over his cup of coffee, sending it spilling across the desk.

I went to our makeshift break station and grabbed a few paper towels. Danny muttered something as he blotted up the coffee and tried to save what papers he could.

"What is with you?" I said.

"She makes me nervous."

"I'm sure you have the same effect on her."

He looked up. "Really?"

I smiled. "Absolutely not. Ready? Or did you want to tear a hole in your pants first?"

Danny looked down to check, just in case, and then the two of us made our way upstairs.

I PUSHED OPEN THE DOOR WITH THE FRIEDLANDER & SKALD nameplate to find Christian and Cyn in their conference room. Christian was once again wearing an impeccably tailored suit with a shirt that appeared mortally afraid of wrinkling while Cyn was wearing a dark suit with a white silk shirt that somehow made her hair an even deeper red. The conference room table was covered with piles of papers and a whiteboard was filled with names and tasks. It was the familiar, organized chaos of beginning to prepare a case for trial.

Cyn looked up. "Good morning, Nathan. Daniel."

Danny stammered so I gave her the exceedingly eloquent greeting of, "Morning."

Christian nodded without looking up.

"Just checking in," I said. "Need anything?"

"Thank you, Nathan," Christian said. "I think we have everything under control right now."

I looked at the papers. "Need any help with briefing?

Christian moved a paper from one pile to another. "I have three associates back at the home office in Minneapolis typing their fingers to the nub as we speak."

"How about researching Ohio law?"

"Computer database works just as well for Ohio as it does for Minnesota."

"What about Ohio quirks?"

Christian finally looked up. "As I mentioned to the judge on Friday, I've tried murder cases in Ohio before. I have a good bank of briefs to draw from and what I don't have, my firm has the resources to create."

I can't explain how but Christian gave the distinct impression that he was looking around at our rental office space as he said "resources" even though his eyes never moved.

"The home office will prepare briefs for your signature and mine. When they're done, you can look at them and," he wiggled his fingers, "Ohio them up."

I sat down in front of his desk. Christian raised an eyebrow and straightened. Danny shifted his weight from foot to foot as he remained standing. "Maybe it's a good idea if we have a conversation about what you'd like us to do," I said. "I'll play whatever role you want. I just don't want to have you relying on me to do something and not know that you wanted it done."

Christian set down his paper and glanced at Cyn, who nodded. "That's actually a very good idea, Nathan. I will be lead trial counsel. I'm going to give the opening, question all the witnesses, and give the close. I'll manage our firm's resources and direct where I want research done and create a defense strategy. I may consult you about how a certain argument will play with the local jury or the judge, but we'll be researching that too so I might not. You've tried enough cases to know that there's no way to know when things will come up so I will want you available at all times in case there's an emergency and we need feet on the ground here in Ohio. You'll be at trial every day as the local man, sitting with me at the counsel table. I want Daniel there in the courtroom but not at the table because I don't want it to seem like Mr. Braggi has too many resources. Although I'm deciding strategy, I want you conversant with the file so that I can ask you questions if I need to." He looked at Cyn. "Did I miss anything?"

Cyn leveled her green eyes at me, which was fortunate because I didn't much feel like cleaning Danny-jello off the floor. "Our firm has a well-known reputation, Nathan. Every court we appear before, every one, knows we can be trusted."

I met Cyn's gaze. "If I tell you something, Cyn, it's true."

"That's how we operate. That's one of the reasons we retained you."

I nodded.

"We also try to keep a low profile in these matters, as much as we can. A certain amount of publicity is to be expected, especially when a musician is involved, but we'll try to keep a lid on it unless we're controlling it."

I nodded again. "So are you guys behind the Silver Fox thing?"

Cyn's eyes became intent. "What are you talking about?"

"#SilverFox? Trending all weekend?"

In response to blank looks, I pulled out my phone, pulled up Twitter, and searched for #SilverFox, then handed it to Cyn and said, "Scroll through."

Cyn did. After a moment of swiping, I saw her type something in and start swiping again. "How could this have so many views?"

"Who knows how the masses work? All I know is that I have a teenage niece who was all over the murder, the singer, and the Silver Fox."

Christian held out a hand, scrolled, handed it back. "That's more views than I would expect. Let's put the home office on a response."

Cyn nodded. "I'll let the PR department know. They're going to want to shape this. Right away." She handed my phone back to me. "Thanks."

I pocketed the phone. "No problem. One of the benefits of teenage nieces."

Cyn looked at Christian. "You're under the gun on prep. Why don't we send Nathan out on witness interviews?"

"We have investigators," said Christian.

"True," said Cyn. "But it wouldn't hurt to have a trial lawyer's view on some of them."

"Whatever you want," I said. "Who are the main witnesses?"

Christian began ticking off on his fingers. "Lizzy Saint, Jared Smoke the lead guitarist, the coroner, and the victim's two friends, Blake Purcell and Aaron Whitsel." Christian tapped the top of his pen on the desk. "Do you have friends in local law enforcement?"

"A few."

"Why don't you have them check background on Purcell and

Whitsel?" said Christian. "If we can tie them in to local drug traffic, Mr. Braggi's story will be more compelling."

I felt a twist in my gut at the thought of diving into local drug
traffic but I kept it off my face. "Sure."

"Let's start with that then," said Christian.

"Sounds good." I stood.

"What about ..." Danny's voice trailed off

Cyn stared at him. It wasn't a glare or a stare or even the
slightest bit harsh; it was just a look that was totally present and
attentive and it just about made Danny crumple. He sputtered
once before I said, "You can help me."

The corner of Cyn's mouth ticked up. "That's a good idea."

We went into the temporary offices on the third floor that
Cyn had made up for us. "Pull everything we have on these two.
We'll read it then head over to see Warren this afternoon."

Danny nodded and got to it, clearly glad to have something
to do.

My stomach twisting didn't improve at all as I thought about
calling Warren Dushane, the local sheriff and head of the Tri-
State Drug Task Force. I forced it down and got to work.

WARREN DUSHANE WAS A BURLY CEMENT BLOCK OF A MAN. IN HIS
late fifties, his hair was still dark brown with no sign of gray. He
was average height with thick shoulders, popping forearms, and
the thickening waist of a man approaching the end of his career.
I'd known him most of my life—he'd coached our peewee football team with my dad and he had always looked just as
comfortable with a whistle around his neck as he did with a gun
around his waist.

Warren was the sheriff of Ash County, Michigan, so his jurisdiction included the Michigan section of Carrefour and the area

twenty-five miles north of that. He'd been elected twenty years running, in no small part because he'd coached half of the male voters in the county. Five years ago, Warren had taken on a lead role in coordinating the cooperation between counties and states to stop drug trafficking in general and heroin in particular. Because so many spokes of transportation—train, highway, and air—ran through Carrefour, he'd become a natural choice to lead the effort. More than one bust had been made when a sheriff from a neighboring county or a state trooper had let Warren know that a packed mule was on its way. That's why I'd come to see him.

When Warren opened the door to his office, his face broke into a grin. "Shep! It's not time for preseason practice yet, is it?"

I coached with Warren and my older brother Tom sometimes. "No, no."

"Come in then, come in." Warren pointed me to a seat. The office was the small, messily functional room you'd expect of a lifelong county official. "I wasn't going to put together the preseason workouts for a while yet but you can take a look if you'd like."

"Not necessary, Warren, although I'm looking forward to seeing what new torture devices you found this offseason."

Warren grinned. "Ropes. Fifty pound, twelve foot long, awkward ropes."

I laughed. "Even worse than I thought. No, Warren, I'm here on business."

Warren's grin faded and he looked away, uncomfortable, which wasn't a natural state for him. "Shep, I'm sorry. I really don't have any other leads yet. I've had the boys working on it but—"

I realized Warren thought I was here on my own personal case. "No, Warren, not for me. Sorry, I should've said that right away."

Warren looked distinctly relieved and I realized I got that look a lot.

"Oh," he said. "I assumed…"

"No, it's for a new case. I wanted to see if you know if someone has any associations I should be aware of."

Warren leaned back in his chair. "With drug trafficking?"

"With heroin trafficking. It's for a new case in south Carrefour."

"Ohio side?"

I nodded.

"You should be talking to an Ohio officer then. Pearson probably."

I shrugged. "Maybe. But I thought with all the cooperating you've been doing, you'd be a good place to start."

"Sounds like you ought to get me up to speed then. Coffee?"

I nodded and, as he poured us a couple of cups of coffee, told him about Hank Braggi's killing of Dillon Chase.

"You're on that? You don't do criminal cases."

"Local counsel only on this one. Just doing a little research for the guy running the show. Ever hear of the victim?"

"Chase? Doesn't ring a bell but that doesn't mean anything. There are a lot of scumbags I haven't run into."

"He was with three other witnesses that night—Jared Smoke, Blake Purcell, and Aaron Whitsel. I don't expect you to have anything on Smoke but if the other two have a connection to dealers, I want to know what I'm getting into."

Warren sipped his coffee. "That's easy enough. Part of what the task force does is share info with each other on known traffickers and dealers. Doesn't hurt to check for connections. I have a county commissioners' meeting right now but I can let you know after."

"Perfect. I appreciate it."

"No problem." He tapped his pen on his coffee mug. "How have you been?"

"Fine."

"Yeah?"

"Yeah."

He shifted his weight. "We're still working it."

I didn't have to ask what he meant. "That's what you said."

"I mean it."

"I know."

"I'll let you know if anything turns up. On either."

"Sounds good." I stood and shook his hand. "I'll let you get to that commissioners' meeting."

"Aren't you a prince. Hey, why don't you stop by for dinner this week? Diane would love to see you."

I also got a lot of those kind of dinner invitations, although they'd slowed down some. "This case is going to keep me hopping a while. After though."

"All right. She'll be disappointed, but she has been married to me for thirty-two years so that's a state she's gotten used to."

"I imagine so." I smiled, shook his hand, said goodbye, and left.

I decided it was time to see Blake Purcell.

**8**

THERE HAD BEEN THREE OUTSIDERS IN LIZZY SAINT'S SUITE ON THE night of the killing, three men who weren't part of the tour, weren't part of the record label, and weren't part of the band's management or families: the victim, Dillon Chase, and his friends, Blake Purcell and Aaron Whitsel. According to the police report, the three had found their way backstage and then managed to get invited to the main star's suite. After which, Dillon Chase had wound up dead.

Blake Purcell's address was listed in the police report and it took me to the Ohio side of Carrefour, south of the University, to a row of upper-end brick townhomes. I checked the report again and saw that Purcell's occupation was listed as "student" but this didn't look like student housing to me. The townhomes were expensive, the kind you find young professional couples in, and the cars in the spaces were far too new and undented to be driven by undergrads. I checked the report for the number, went up to the second floor, and knocked. A young man with overly-moussed hair answered.

"Blake?" I said.

"No. I'm his roommate."

"He in?"

"No."

"Will he be back soon?"

Mousse Guy gave me a droopy-eyed look that was more cautious than sleepy. "Don't know."

Fortunately, the complex numbered its parking spaces. Both spaces for 219 were full. "Tell him I'll be waiting by his car. Is he the Wrangler or the Mercedes?"

"I've already talked to you guys three times," came a voice from inside the apartment. "This is harassment."

I raised an eyebrow but Mousse Guy didn't even twitch. "I won't take much of your time," I called back.

"I've got it, Teddy," said the voice and a young man took Mousse Guy's place. Blake's hair had even more product in it than his buddy's and that was saying something. Blake Purcell was on the lean side, a little taller than average, and wore tight tan pants and a tighter green shirt that probably rose to the level of formalwear when attending a college class. He stepped outside the townhouse and closed the door.

I smiled. The police had indeed been here three times and the kid had learned—never let the police in your house.

"I don't have anything else to say." His annoyance was clear. "I've talked to that detective three times already."

"Which detective?"

He rolled his eyes. "Peterson? Paulson? Don't you guys know each other?"

"Pearson? Mitch Pearson?"

"That's the one. Tall, arrogant fuck. Must be a treat to work with."

"I don't work with him."

"Well, I gave him all my info already. Talk to him."

"I'm not with the police."

Blake's eyes narrowed. "No comment."

The kid was sharp despite the crusty hair. "I'm not the press either."

"Then who the fuck are you?"

"I'm a lawyer and I'd like to ask you about what happened the night that Dillon was killed."

"I already told the prosecutor I'd testify. He's supposed to give me a date."

"I represent Hank Braggi. I'd like to know what happened."

Blake turned and opened the door. "I have nothing to say to you."

"I'd like to hear what you saw."

"You'll hear it in court."

"I just want to know the truth of what happened. That's all."

"I'll tell you what happened. Your client is fucking crazy is what happened."

He made to shut the door. I stopped it, leaving it open a crack. Blake pushed back but it didn't move as I said, "What do you mean? The beating?"

"You're his lawyer. Did you see the pictures?"

I nodded.

"Then you know your client is fucking nuts." He pushed on the door again. "I have to get to class. Don't be waiting by my car."

I let off the pressure and Blake shut the door, leaving me staring at the black 219 for inspiration.

Blake Purcell might have a point. Our best defense might be that Hank was crazy.

WHEN I GOT BACK TO THE OFFICE, I DUMPED MY THINGS ON MY second-floor desk and went up to the room on the third floor that I was beginning to think of as the war room.

Danny was gone, but I could hear Christian's voice coming from the conference room. "Yes, we have time to put it all together," he said. A pause. "Last week. Yes. He seemed fine. No, he agrees. He ordered me to do the same thing."

I peeked in and saw Christian sitting at the table, straight and unwrinkled as always. Cyn was next to him, leafing through a folder. She saw me and nodded.

"Three weeks now," Christian continued. "No, I think we have everything we need. I'll email you a progress report at the end of the week. Sure. Hang on a second."

I watched as Christian handed the phone to Cyn. I didn't like the sound of that conversation at all. Conversations between an attorney and client stay confidential. Reporting to someone else, though, that can be a problem.

"Yes?" she said and paused, listening. "Everything is progressing as it should. Of course. That's always my priority."

I had no idea what she was talking about. But I was coming to learn that Cyn projected an air of competence that made one absolutely believe that everything was in fact progressing as it should.

"Right," she said. "Goodbye."

Cyn hung up the phone and the two of them looked at me. "Good evening, Nathan," said Christian. "You're working late."

"I could say the same. Who was that?"

"Home office," said Christian. "The partners like to keep tabs on what's going on."

That made me feel better. Conversations within the firm would stay privileged. I nodded. "I was worried there for a moment."

Cyn gave me a look that questioned my competence because I would question her competence.

"Right," I said. "Silly."

Christian smiled. "We have done this before, Nathan." He glanced at Cyn. "Many times."

I smiled and nodded and the two of them moved to go back to work, Cyn placing a manila folder in front of Christian.

"I saw Blake Purcell today," I said.

The two of them looked up. Christian set the manila folder down on the desk and said, "I thought you were going to do background with law enforcement?"

I shrugged. "I did but I had time and thought we ought to know what he's going to say."

Cyn crossed her arms. "And what is he going to say?"

"That Hank is crazy."

Cyn arched an elegant red eyebrow. "And why would he say that?"

"Besides the fact that he saw Hank beat his friend to death?"

"Yes, besides that."

"No reason I guess."

"Hardly enough to say he's crazy then."

"We could though," I said.

"We could what, Nathan?" said Cyn.

"Say it's enough. Say that Hank's crazy."

"Insanity is not an option, Nathan," said Cyn.

"I don't think people think of it as an option. It's something that is."

She shook her head. "Mr. Braggi is not insane."

Christian waved a hand. "It doesn't matter. Not guilty by reason of insanity isn't an option in this case."

"It's always an option if the person actually is insane."

"He's not."

"You know he's up on aggravated murder, right?"

Christian's eyes grew hard for the first time since I'd met him. "I'm very aware of the legal issues in this case, Nathan."

"And you know that he's facing the death penalty?"

"Yes." There was winter in that clipped affirmation.

"And that not guilty by reason of insanity does not carry the death penalty?"

"Yes, but it carries a lifetime of institutional care, doesn't it?"

"Yes."

"That is not something that our client is interested in."

"He'd rather die?"

"He'd rather that we win."

"I don't think his 'rathers' are going to carry much weight with the jury."

"Then we'll have to convince them."

"Listen, I know I'm just local guy but—"

"Yes, Nathan. You're just the local guy." Christian's eyes were still, blue ice. "We've discussed this with our firm and with our client. If the strategy changes, we'll let you know. But right now your job is to help us implement it."

His gaze softened and he went back to being a polite, charming lawyer from a movie. "Still, Purcell's comments are good to know." His gaze softened further. "Thank you, Nathan. I didn't mean to seem harsh, but our client's directive is very, very clear so we'll be doing everything we can to execute it."

"No, I'm sorry. It's your case. Execution is just what I was trying to avoid."

"Touché." Christian smiled and waved a hand at the manila folders. "This is the prosecutor's file. Let me get through the rest of it tonight and we'll talk about what else you can do in the morning."

"Sounds good. I'll see you then."

The two of them made no move to resume working. Instead they looked at me, obviously waiting for me, and it wasn't until I was walking out the door that they resumed talking, in lower voices this time.

I still wasn't crazy about the strategy. Hank was facing an

aggravated murder charge so to me the priority was to eliminate the risk of execution. That meant arguing that he was insane, trying to eliminate the aggravating factor of attempted murder on Whitsel, or taking the plea deal. The strategy of simply winning seemed the least likely at this point. Still, my orders seemed pretty clear—help Christian implement the strategy they'd decided upon.

Meanwhile, I decided to implement my own strategy of going home. I got in the Jeep and left.

## 9

W<small>E WERE THREE WEEKS OUT FROM TRIAL, IN THAT TIME WHERE</small> you're not preparing for the trial exactly but you're preparing to prepare. I spent my time digging out from under emails, answering pleadings and motions that would be due in the next few weeks, and otherwise clearing the decks to make sure nothing fell through the cracks while we were in Hank Braggi's trial.

Most of a lawyer's life is boring like that. I'm not the first one to call it legal whack-a-mole but that's exactly what it is most of the time. You manage one crisis so that you have time to deal with the next one, which inevitably pops its furry little head up as soon as you think everything is managed.

That also meant that I spent very little time on the Braggi case that week. That didn't worry me either. Since I was just the local guy, Christian was going to be doing all the heavy lifting and it appeared that Cyn had the details more than managed. I fielded the odd question about how many copies the Court wanted, whether we should send things to the judge directly or just give an extra copy to the clerk, and other little local customs that vary from court to court. I read Hank's file, I was conversant with it, and I had a general understanding of what was going on, but I really wasn't involved in the day-to-day management of the case. So when my phone buzzed at 8:30 a.m. one morning and the caller ID showed that it was from the Carrefour courthouse, I didn't have any expectation of who it was when I answered. "Nate Shepherd."

"Nate, it's Anne Gallon."

I straightened. "Good morning, Judge. Did we have a pretrial today?"

"No."

"Well, I'm on a different floor from Christian so let me see if he's in and I'll connect you."

"No, Nate, I'm calling for you. You're going to hang up this phone and get on your computer. You're going to go to Channel 9's website and look up the Addiction Specialist Network, and then you're going to get yourself and your out-of-town co-counsel down to my chambers by 9:15."

I looked at the clock. "This morning?"

"This morning. And don't you dare be late." She hung up.

It was close to 8:40 when I found the Channel 9 report online. After a lead-in by a young reporter, I saw a woman whom the graphic identified as Tammy Sheehan, chairwoman of the Addiction Specialists Network. She was addressing a group of about twenty-five people, half of whom appeared to be reporters. She adjusted the microphone behind a small lectern and said, "We are pleased to announce that our local office of the Addiction Specialist Network has received a grant from the Skald Foundation to help us fight addiction right here in the city of Carrefour."

She looked from camera to camera. "Overdoses, violence, and theft have become common in our community, threatening to overrun our medical system and our court system with heroin and opioid-related problems. The Skald Foundation has generously set up an endowment which will help us continue our mission to attack addiction at its roots. I would like to thank the Foundation for its generous support and introduce you to its representative, Christian Dane, who will now say a few words."

Oh shit.

I'd seen Christian almost every day and it turned out that he was one of those rare people that looked even better on TV than in person. He stepped to the lectern, all white hair and silk suit, solemnly looked into the camera, and said, "Heroin is a scourge. It creeps into communities and destroys them from within, undermining the bonds that hold us together. It is no respecter of persons and it is no longer the drug of the derelict or the criminal. This menace comes for our friends, for our partners, and for our children."

"The heroin scourge and the opioid epidemic are invading our communities. They're overwhelming our healthcare system, they're overwhelming our courts, they're overwhelming our schools. In this Carrefour is not alone. Communities all over the country, just like Carrefour, are fighting the same battle. The Skald Foundation wants to fight that war in the vanguard. We wish to lead the fight against heroin wherever it's found. We want to eradicate opioid addiction where it starts. We want to support the people who make a difference. That's why the Foundation was created and it's through these grants that we bring families and neighbors together to beat back this menace."

Christian paused and I swear to God it was like he was delivering the speech from Independence Day.

"You can't be in Carrefour long without learning about the good work that the Addiction Specialist Network does. They are out there every day, ministering to our neighbors, to our families, to our children, fighting the battle against addiction. That's not enough though. It's too late if we only fight after these dreaded drugs have sunk their talons into our families. At the

Skald Foundation, we believe in attacking a problem at its roots, and that's why, for every dollar we donate to rehabilitation organizations like Addiction Specialist Network, we donate another dollar to prevention, to campaigns in our schools and churches, to local law enforcement, to anyone who can root out the distribution network of heroin before it takes hold in the community. The people who bring this scourge into our community are not our neighbors. They are vipers lying in wait for our friends, they are carrion crows waiting to sweep down on our children, they are the worst kind of evil that bends all that is good to their purpose."

"I have not been here long, but I know that Carrefour has fought this battle boldly. It is the deep privilege of the Skald Foundation to help. Thank you to the Addiction Specialist Network for fighting this battle without thought of credit, and thank you for allowing the Skald Foundation to join you."

Holy shit balls.

The video cut back to the reporter, who said that the size of the donation was not known but that Tammy Sheehan had said that it was the largest one her organization had ever received.

I knew why the Judge wanted to see us.

I went upstairs and gathered Christian and then the two of us went to see Judge Gallon.

JEFF HANSON WAS ALREADY THERE WHEN WE ARRIVED. HE WAS sitting next to the bailiff's desk, both hands resting on his large belly. Stacy Cannon served as Judge Gallon's bailiff, as she had for the two judges before her. She had pure white hair, a soft smile, and just about as sweet a disposition as you would find in the Carrefour courthouse. She was also quietly efficient and eminently proper so that the moment we walked in, she stood and said, "Mr. Shepherd, Mr. Dane, I'll let the Judge know you're here. Please sit."

Jeff hummed and made a point of looking pleasantly at the ceiling. "Somebody's in trouble."

"What did you do, Jeff?" I said.

He shook his head. "A gag order is a gag order, Nate. And Judge Gallon is pretty particular about them."

I glanced at Christian who seemed entirely unconcerned by Jeff's comments and Judge Gallon's impending anger. Stacy returned and said, "Come in, gentlemen."

The three of us rose and went through the little swinging gate to Judge Gallon's office. I went first and as we entered said, "Good morning, Your—"

"Sit," Judge Gallon said.

Christian picked the chair right in the center, directly in front of the judge. I took the chair on the right and Jeff sat last, descending heavily so that the chair strained and rocked just a little.

Judge Gallon didn't wait. "Mr. Dane, Mr. Shepherd, the reason I called you over for a pretrial instead of putting you directly in jail is because you've both just come onto the case and so may not have read all of the pleadings. I'm giving you the benefit of the doubt that you haven't read the gag order I issued in this case right after the indictment came down."

"I've read it, Your Honor," said Christian.

Jesus Christ. The judge had given us an out and Christian hadn't taken it.

Judge Gallon's eyes narrowed over her sharp cheekbones. "Then what was that little stunt yesterday?"

"What stunt are you referring to, Your Honor?"

The judge's eyes narrowed further. "There better not have been more than one, Mr. Dane."

"I don't recall any stunts, Your Honor."

I'd seen Anne lose her cool twice in the time we practiced together. I saw the signs of a third time coming and so said, "Are you talking about the press conference, Judge?"

"Of course I'm talking about the press conference, Mr. Shepherd!"

Christian sat there in calm innocence. "Oh, Your Honor means the Skald Foundation event?"

"This is not something to joke about, Mr. Dane. I specifically directed all of you not to talk to the press."

"You directed us not to talk to the press about this case, Your Honor. I did no such thing."

"You spoke for fifteen minutes about heroin."

"I most certainly did, Your Honor."

"Heroin is involved in this case."

Christian raised an eyebrow. "Is it? Has the prosecutor added a drug charge?"

"Mr. Dane, you are barreling right into a contempt charge."

"Am I, Your Honor? I'm sorry, perhaps we should discuss the scope of your order so that I don't run afoul of it then. You said we shouldn't talk about the case to the press. I did not. I did make an announcement that the Skald Foundation is donating funds to this community to help fight heroin addiction and the opioid epidemic. I didn't think that was related to the case, but if you are taking a broad view, I will, of course, abide by it."

"How considerate of you."

"I assume you will be directing the prosecutor's office to do the same?"

"There's no need to admonish us, Your Honor," said Jeff. He dropped his hands from his belly and sat straighter. "We've been in compliance."

"Oh?" said Christian. "Because it seems to me that since the charges were filed, I saw you on Entertainment Buzz, Hollywood Z, all of the national networks, Rock City—"

Jeff waved a hand. "That was a wire story that was picked up nationally because Ms. Saint was involved."

Judge Gallon stared at Christian over her glasses. "And the reason I issued the gag order in the first place."

"Fair enough, Your Honor." Christian sat there, legs crossed and utterly unconcerned. "But since you issued the gag order, Mr. Hanson has appeared on three local news stories for the DARE campaign, encouraging junior high students not to use drugs. He's been interviewed by one local station and the Carrefour Courier about Carrefour's fifteen percent drop in drug-related crimes since his boss, Victoria Lance, was elected. He's appeared with Police Chief LaBeau on Channel 3's Sunday Community Roundtable talking about how his office is taking the lead in getting first-time drug offenders into rehab and diversion instead of jail."

Jeff shifted in his chair. "That's not the same."

Christian ignored him. "And it's not just Mr. Hanson, Your Honor. The chief prosecutor, Victoria Lance, has appeared on the local news for four events involving Well Center Rehab, which she's apparently a board member of. Another prosecutor, Ben Wilson, won the Run for Rehab 10k in some sort of record time and appeared in the paper and on the news. His paralegal, Melanie Szorchek, ran a Go Fund Me page to pay the NICU bills for a local newborn who was born addicted to opioids. All of that has happened since you issued your gag order, Your Honor."

Judge Gallon looked at Jeff.

"None of that is about the case, Your Honor."

"Neither is the Skald Foundation's donation," said Christian.

Jeff glanced at him. "That's different."

"Why? Because I'm not from here? Heroin is destroying communities all over the country and the Skald Foundation helps fight it wherever it can. I'm here and saw a need. The

Skald Foundation wants to help. I did not say one word about the case."

Judge Gallon removed her glasses and looked stern. All of us took the hint and kept our mouths shut. She stared at me for a long moment before she turned to Christian and said, "I assume part of your defense is going to be that Mr. Braggi acted in reaction to seeing Dillon Chase injecting Ms. Saint with heroin?"

Christian didn't so much as twitch under Judge Gallon's scrutiny. "I haven't decided yet, Your Honor."

Judge Gallon pressed her lips together as she replaced her glasses. "Let's just assume for a moment that you're a good trial lawyer and that it is part of your defense. I don't want you to be appearing on traditional or electronic media from now until the trial is over for any damn thing. Not so much as a like or a retweet. Am I understood?"

Christian didn't blink. "Does that apply to everyone, Your Honor?"

She looked at Jeff. "It does."

"His entire office?"

"Everyone working on the case."

"What if someone else from his office comments?"

"You're part of a big firm, aren't you, Mr. Dane?"

"I am."

"Do you want me to gag all of Friedlander & Skald?

"I don't, Your Honor."

"Then I'll expect all of you to use your heads. You too, Nate."

I smiled. "I'll keep Danny on lockdown."

"Fine. Trial starts in three weeks so this shouldn't be a hardship. Inquiries are inevitable. I expect all of you to say that the judge has prohibited comment on this matter until after trial. See you then."

Jeff and I stood at the implied dismissal but Christian remained seated. Judge Gallon raised an eyebrow.

"May I assume that I will not be sanctioned for violating the gag order."

Judge Gallon stared at him. "The Court finds that you did not. This will be listed on the docket as a status pretrial."

Christian rose smoothly. "Thank you, Your Honor. And thank you for seeing us this morning."

"Good-bye," said Judge Gallon and went back to her papers.

As we walked out of the courtroom, Jeff said, "Have you considered our offer, Christian? Second degree is still on the table."

"We have, Mr. Hanson, thank you. We will not be accepting it."

"We're not going any lower."

"I didn't ask you to."

Jeff stared at Christian. "Your client went beyond the pale, Christian. Way beyond. No way a jury's letting him off."

Christian shrugged. "We'll see." He made a point of turning to the ornate stairs that led down to the first floor.

Jeff raised his chin and there was a hard flash in his eyes that lasted for just a second and was gone. "See you, Nate," he said and walked to the elevator.

I joined Christian on the stairs. "The heroin angle is part of our defense, right?" I said.

"Absolutely."

"Then that was very well done."

"Thank you. Let's pick up lunch for Cyn and Danny on the way back."

"Sounds good."

As we walked to my car, I thought about what I'd just seen. That was about as subtle, competent, and complete a takedown as I'd ever witnessed. He didn't defy the judge, he didn't defy her order, and he'd neutralized the prosecutor's non-stop soft public relations campaign. Then I realized something else.

"You can't be *that* subtle," I said.

"How's that, Nathan?" I swear to God he buckled his seatbelt without creating an errant line in his suit.

"The judge has prohibited us from appearing on camera 'til the trial's over."

"Yes."

"But she can't prevent a station from running the footage they already have."

"No, she cannot."

"And if the only footage they have is of the lead defense attorney speaking out against the evils of heroin, they'll just have to keep running it every time they need a picture or sound."

"Goodness." Christian smiled a little. "That would be subtle indeed, Nathan."

"Holy shit."

"I certainly wouldn't want you to give me credit for that idea." He glanced at me. "Not in front of the judge anyway."

"Jesus Christ."

"Yes. Credit him. How about Subway?"

I was still swearing when we pulled in.

---

## 10

DANNY HAD POLISHED OFF A FOOT-LONG CLUB WHILE CYN HAD made excellent progress on a six-inch chicken bacon ranch deluxe when I crumpled my wrapper and said, "So how are you going to spin the facts on this?"

Christian precisely brushed the shredded lettuce that had fallen on the table into his wrapper, folded it, and placed it in the trashcan before he said, "I don't spin facts, Nathan. I present them."

"Which facts are you going to present then?"

"All of them."

I sighed. "Which facts are you going to emphasize? Highlight? Blow up?"

Christian looked at Cyn, who glanced at me before she said, "Broad strokes can't hurt."

"Broad strokes are still all I have," said Christian. "I don't know how you work, Nathan, but some of the theme comes together when I'm preparing my questioning."

"Sure."

"But, broad strokes. Hank is worried because he doesn't like the feel of the new guys and goes up to the room. Door is open so he walks in. That part's important because we can't have him breaking in."

"Why is that?" said Danny.

"Because if he breaks in, he's breaking and entering and that's an aggravating factor that could support the death penalty," I said.

"Exactly," said Christian. "So Hank walks in, sees Lizzy on the edge of drunken consciousness, and sees this scumbag Dillon Chase in the act of injecting her full of heroin. Now Hank knows that Lizzy doesn't use so he immediately jumps to her defense and beats the guy down."

"That part's easy," I said. "How do we explain the extent of what Hank did? That he went berserk when he saw what was happening?"

"Berserk is not a word we want to use."

"So how else do we describe what he did to Dillon's face?"

"Hopefully someone can establish that Dillon fought back."

"He would have to be fighting pretty hard to justify that beating."

"True."

"What does Hank say?"

"Hank hasn't confirmed that yet for me. But since I don't intend to put him on the stand, we have to establish it another way."

"Who else witnessed it?"

"According to the police, Jared Smoke saw the end of the encounter."

I smiled at the word "encounter." Lawyers. "What about Lizzy?"

Christian smiled. "To date, her recollection has been hazy. We'll have to interview her and see what we can get."

I picked up one of the pictures and looked at the way the left side of Chase's head was caved in like a rotten pumpkin. "We're going to have a hard time convincing the jury that this was a measured response."

Christian nodded. "That's where the heroin comes in. We need the evil of pushing heroin to offset the violence of Hank's response."

That was going to be a thin line indeed. "What can Danny and I do?"

"You're checking with your contacts on Dillon Chase's connections to local heroin traffic?"

"Already started that."

"Saint and Smoke aren't in town right now so those interviews will have to wait." He thought for a moment. "You already saw Blake Purcell. Want to see if you can run down Aaron Whitsel? Compare the two?"

"Do we have an address?"

"The address on the police report isn't valid anymore. Think you can track him down? If not, I can send it to my people in Minnesota."

"No, I have someone here who can take a quick look."

"Can he move quickly?"

"She. And faster than all four of us."

"Good. Give her a call and let us know what she finds out."

"Will do."

Cyn turned to Danny. "Daniel, can you help me with the evidence inventory? I need to match each piece to the exhibit list and make sure we have access to what we need at trial."

Danny stuttered once, then again, under Cyn's frank gaze before he nodded.

Christian rapped the table once and we all scattered. As I went back downstairs to my office, I called Olivia Brickson. "Hey, Liv."

"Shep! Am I going to see you down here today?"

"Yep. That's not why I called though."

"What's up?"

"I need a name run down."

"Witness or perp?"

"Witness."

"What do you have?"

"A name, an address that isn't any good anymore, and two known associates."

"That's something."

"One of those associates is dead."

"Ah. That what he witnessed?"

"Yep."

"What's your interest?"

"My client killed him."

I heard her smile. "Allegedly?"

"Nope. Deader than shit."

"I'm no lawyer, Shep, but..."

"Yeah. I'm just local counsel on it but, yes, it's a little dicey."

"Okay. Timeframe?"

"Easy stuff this afternoon, deep dive next week?"

"Done. Text me the info. Any constraints?"

"Keep it legal."

"I always keep it legal. I meant what's my budget."

"Unlimited."

"Really?"

"The client engaged a heavy-hitting firm out of Minneapolis. Knock yourself out."

"Excellent. Send it to me now and I'll do a preliminary search this afternoon. You can pick it up at the gym on the way home."

"Five-thirty?"

"Perfect."

"Talk to you then." After I hung up, I sent Olivia the information we had on Aaron Whitsel and included information on

Dillon Chase and Blake Purcell for good measure. Then I spent the rest of the afternoon putting out other legal fires. Before I knew it, it was five o'clock and I left the office to go to the Brickhouse.

MY FAVORITE PART OF CARREFOUR IS ON THE NORTH SIDE, A FEW miles up into Michigan where the hills start to roll and the Cache River makes its way through a still wooded area before it turns south down to Ohio. There's an abandoned spur of railtrack that's nestled next to the river that houses a water tower that they used to refill steam engines back in the day and a couple of old buildings, including an old brick warehouse they'd used to store goods.

The building to the left of the water tower was the Railcar, a bar and restaurant that served the best barbeque around. As I stepped out of my car, the sharp smell of the hickory smoke drifting up from its firepit made my mouth water and subtly suggested that I change my plans. I ignored it, pulled my gym bag out of the Jeep, and headed to the warehouse instead.

The warehouse was made of used brick, a mottled orange brick with blunt edges that had built countless warehouses all over the Midwest. A white sign with sharp black letters over the door announced that this was "the Brickhouse."

I entered the gym owned by Olivia Brickson and her brother Cade, the bail bondsman. Half of the gym was set up with traditional free weights and the other half had racks of cross-training equipment and all the related torture devices you could think of from ropes to kettlebells to chin-up bars to an honest-to-goodness salmon ladder, and if you don't know what that is, I'd have to say you're better off for it. The softest thing in the gym was a wrestling mat in the back and I'm pretty sure that the only reason Olivia installed it was because her insurer wouldn't let her train by throwing people onto concrete.

The gym was busy and Olivia stood behind the front desk beneath a sign that said "Brickhouse" and there wasn't the slightest irony in that picture. Her shock of short, bleached white hair stood up on top and swooped down over her left eye, barely covering the semi-reflective glasses she always wore. She wore tights and a tank top that left her arms bare so that I could see the tattoo that spiraled out around her left shoulder until it connected to a sleeve of dark green and black ink that covered her left arm from elbow to wrist. I can only tell you that, unlike many people who sport ink, this totally fit.

Olivia was checking in two guys and a woman when she saw me and smiled. "Shep!" She handed the others their cards back. "'Bout time you hauled your soft ass back in here."

I handed her my card to scan. "Been catching it at home."

"That's not the same and you know it. You joining us for a class?"

"I'm not man enough for that. You want to talk to me about Whitsel now or later?"

"Later. Hour?"

"Perfect. Thanks." She waved, jogged over to her class and clapped. "Alright, if you shirk you shrink. Let's get going!"

There was a small box with knit stocking caps and gloves where she'd been standing. Above it was a sign: "If you want to run, the road's outside." If you ever stop by on your way through Carrefour, you won't find any treadmills in Olivia's gym.

I smiled and went back to the locker room to change.

AN HOUR AND TEN MINUTES LATER, I HAD FINISHED MY LIFT AND the wreckage of Olivia's class was lying strewn about the gym, sweating, gasping, and, for one poor newbie hunched in a corner, heaving. Olivia, who'd led by example through the whole thing, wiped some sweat from her forehead with a small towel and, in an even, ungasping voice, said, "Shep!" and pointed to her office.

It seemed like a good idea to follow.

In Olivia's office, a battered desk sat in front of a wall plastered with pictures of her students and trainees competing at different events. There were only two pictures of her—one with Arnold at the Arnold Classic in Columbus and another with Royce Gracie from the time when she had spent I don't know how much to bring him in for a ju-jitsu clinic. It was altogether what you'd expect in a gym office except for the ceiling-high bookshelf on one side and the row of three computer monitors on the other.

She offered me a water, took one herself, then sat down at the desk and hit the keyboard until the monitors blinked on. She cracked her own bottle and said, "Why didn't you tell me this was about the Lizzy Saint case?"

"Does it matter?"

"Hell yes, it matters. Well, it doesn't matter for my research but it sure as hell matters for you."

"Why?"

"Are you shitting me, Shep? Do you really think you should be involved in that case?"

"I'm just local counsel, Liv."

"So? Even as local counsel you're going to be chin-deep in this shit for weeks. You really want to do that?"

I shrugged. "They're paying the bills."

I had a pretty good poker face but Olivia had known me a long time. She glared at me, shaking her head slightly. When the silence stretched on though, she eventually said, "All right. But if we end up sparring five nights a week again, I'm charging you this time."

"Fair enough. So what did you find out?"

"Aaron Whitsel hasn't lived at the address he gave the police for about a year. We found him at some off-campus housing near the University where it's a mix of grad students and people in their first jobs. Blake Purcell lives in a nicer complex a mile away."

"Are they in school?"

"Whitsel's in the second year of his MBA program. Purcell looks like he dropped out of undergrad after three. No obvious source of income for Purcell to support the townhouse. Whitsel's place is less expensive and he has a good-sized student loan balance to explain it."

I thought. "Shoot me the address, will you? I'll check in on Whitsel and see if he'll talk to me. And I need you to do a little deeper dive for me."

"On all three of them?"

"You got it. I need you to run arrests and convictions. And I need you to find out if they have any connections with anyone who deals heroin."

Olivia went still. "You know that makes me more visible, Shep. To the dealers and the feds. They're all watching whoever is watching them."

"Don't go too far then. We know Dillon is connected some-how. Purcell's lack of employment or school is suspicious, especially with the car and the townhouse." I remembered how he'd looked when we'd spoken. "And the clothes and the watch. I want to know who his connections are. And let's make sure Whitsel is the struggling student he appears to be and just had the bad luck to be there."

Olivia clicked out some notes. "How does this matter for your case?"

"Doesn't heroin make you angry, Liv?"

"Of course."

"My client too. The more connections we can show, the better."

"Okay. Give me a couple of days then I'll update you."

There was one last pause before she said, "I'm really not crazy about this, Shep."

"Noted, Liv."

Most people pushed their hair back when they were sweating but Olivia teased her hair down around her glasses before she nodded and looked over my shoulder at the gym. "I have another class yet but do you want to join Cade and me for dinner after?"

"Can't tonight. Thanks, though."

She stared at me. "Eat something good. Get some sleep."

"I will."

"Finish that book yet?"

"*That Obstacle's in My Way*? Still working on it."

"*The Obstacle is the Way*, you asshole, and you haven't cracked it, have you?"

I grinned. "Working on it."

She shook her head and waved at the shelf. "Let me know when you're done and we'll load you up again."

"Got it, Coach. Thanks." I stood.

"Shep?"

I waited.

"I mean it. Take the time to make something good and then eat it."

"Sure thing, boss."

"Talk to you tomorrow."

I waved, gathered my things, and left.

It didn't take me long to get home and when I did, I was true to my promise and ate some chicken and some green, leafy shit. Then I neutralized it all with beer, which hadn't been part of our negotiation. After, I moved to the couch and turned on Sports-

Center. *That Obstacle's in My Way* stayed on the end table. I fell asleep during Bad Beats.

Some days, you can only go so far, you know?

## 11

THE NEXT DAY, I WENT UP TO THE THIRD-FLOOR OFFICE TO SEE Christian and found that he wasn't there. Instead, Cyn was in the main conference room, a tablet on one side and a stack of photos on the other.

It was a little hard to describe Cyn's presence except to say that, even as she sat there in front of the computer, she projected a certain unyielding hardness and competence. She'd taken off her jacket and her eyes were focused on the screen as her long fingers flew across the keyboard. "Mr. Skald called," she said without looking up. "He expects an update from you this morning."

"Do you have his number for me?" I said.

Cyn started and I found that I enjoyed that unusual crack in her competence. She smiled. "Sorry, Nathan. I thought you were Christian."

"He in yet?"

A look of irritation flashed across her face and was gone. "No. But we worked late last night."

"Doesn't hurt to sleep once in a while. Trials are a marathon, not a sprint."

She raised a red eyebrow. "Until you get to the sprint part."

"True enough. We're not quite there yet though."

She stared at me and I found that I was glad her green-eyed ire wasn't directed at me. "Not quite. But soon."

I nodded and decided that was one argument neither Chrisitian nor I were going to win. "Is Skald one of the principal partners?"

"His name's on the door."

"Is he the original Skald?"

Cyn smiled like I'd said something amusing. "They go back a ways."

"Does the home office always keep close tabs on a case like this?"

"Not always. Just ones that have the attention of important clients."

"Like Hank's father?"

Her focus turned completely on me. I decided my earlier estimate was correct. "Why do you say that?"

"Hank. When we met with him, he gave me the impression that his family's important. And rich. Anything else I should know?"

"Does it matter?"

"If it affects our representation of Hank, it does."

Cyn pulled her hands back from the keyboard and thought, sitting straight as a fishing spear. She appeared to pick her words carefully as she said, "Mr. Braggi's father wants us to give his son the best representation possible."

"A man with means doesn't usually want the best representation possible. He wants to win. Which may or may not be possible."

Cyn nodded. "Mr. Braggi's father understands the parameters of our circumstances." She focused back on me. "You didn't come up here for a genealogy lesson."

"No. I put the investigator on Aaron Whitsel."

"And?"

"She found his address. So I put her on Chase and Purcell too and told her to look for connections to the local heroin distributors."

Cyn's face grew serious. "We have plenty of resources for an investigation like that."

"I'm sure, but my local person has gone down this road before. She won't be starting from scratch so it'll probably be more efficient."

"Do you have a history with this investigator?"

"I do."

"Is she reliable?"

"She's a pro. And yes."

"Give me her billings and I'll see that they're paid directly."

"Thanks. I'd prefer to wait a couple of days to see if she finds anything on the heroin before I go see Whitsel."

"Good. I'll tell Christian."

I looked at the hyper-organized files. "If you remember?"

Cyn smiled then, which was exceedingly more pleasant than her focused stare. "I'll let him know what you found, suggest that you investigate further, and he'll agree that that is an excellent idea."

She went back to typing and did so for almost a minute before she looked back up at me. "Was there something else?"

"I don't think Hanson will leave the deal on the table forever."

"We don't expect him to."

"A deal could get Hank out in his lifetime."

"I'm sure it would. But he's not interested in spending decades in a cell."

"Nobody is. That's not the point."

"Our client's wishes are very clear, Nathan. No deal. Fight to win."

"Our client's wishes or his father's?"

Cyn's eyes grew very hard at the implication of what I'd said. "In this case, they are of one mind."

I stood and shrugged. "Had to be said. As local counsel, I have to tell you that Judge Gallon and a Carrefour jury won't hesitate to do it."

"We've done our homework, Nathan. But," she held up one finger, "as long as you're so intent on acting in your local counsel role, do you know the coroner?"

"I do."

Cyn rolled her chair down the table, reached into the middle of a stack of manila folders, and rolled back with a folder labeled "Autopsy." "We know the prosecutor's going to call him to testify about the body."

"Want me to talk to him?"

Cyn nodded. "We want to get a sense of his reaction to the findings, to know if he's going to add any flavor to the cause of death."

"I'll see him today."

"No appointment?"

"His patients can usually wait."

Cyn did not appear to be amused by my joke. She nodded and went back to typing. I decided to claim that as a victory and left.

It was time to talk to the coroner, Ray Gerchuk.

## 12

——————

You don't run into many guys named Ray anymore and you certainly don't run into coroners like Ray Gerchuk. Ray was about as sunny a guy as you would ever meet, which I knew because he was an old fishing buddy of my dad's. Going against every stereotype of his position, Ray was tall and fit for a man who was almost sixty years old. He still had all of his blonde hair, although there were some lighter spots around the edges that were either white hair or a reflection of the light. He had a hint of tan on his skin that let you know he spent time outside in addition to time behind the microscope and, if you talked to him for any length of time, you would learn that an inordinate amount of that time outside involved the pursuit of largemouth bass. Hence his friendship with my father.

"Nate!" Ray said as he came out to the reception area of his office. "How's your pops?"

"On the water as we speak, I expect."

"Lucky bastard."

"To say he's enjoying retirement would be an under-statement."

"Don't rub it in. Three more years for me." He grabbed my

shoulder. "How have you been? Haven't seen you on the boat in a while."

"Been churning to keep afloat, just not on the water."

"Ain't that the truth. Your dad said you've been pretty busy."

"That's why I'm here. Wanted to talk to you about a case."

"Sure, Nate. Which one?"

"The Hank Braggi case. The Dillon Chase exam."

"Ooooph." He shook his head. "You're on that one?"

That was definitely not the reaction I was hoping for. I kept my face straight and said, "Local counsel. Just checking on your findings."

"You know the deal. I'll tell both sides my findings. Don't tell me anything confidential about your case because I'm not on anyone's side."

"Ray. I *am* a lawyer."

Ray smiled. "I know, Nate. But you'd be surprised how many lawyers forget it." He waved a hand. "Come on, let's go back to my office and I'll pull the file."

We went down the hall, passed four examination rooms that were fortunately closed, and went into Ray's office. As Ray pulled up the file at his computer, I gazed absently at his degree from the University of Michigan that was displayed on the wall next to a picture of the football stadium with the moderately annoying title of "The Big House." I liked him anyway.

"Here it is," he said. "Ask away."

It's always tricky in an interview like this. You need to know what the coroner knows, but you don't want to suggest adjectives or terms to describe the body that he will turn around and use against you at trial. You need to stay general. "Do you need the file to remember this case?"

Ray smiled a little. "No."

"What do you remember?"

"I remember thinking the guy got hit by a truck."

"Really?"

"I'm not exaggerating, Nate. These are the kinds of injuries I see after a semi has hit someone."

This seemed bad. "How so?"

"In most fatal fights, you have one skull fracture, maybe two. Not seventeen."

I'd read it but it sounded worse when he said it. "He wasn't struck seventeen times was he?"

"I won't be able to say how many times he was struck."

"Will you say a range?"

Ray nodded. "I can't say an upper range because it's conceivable Braggi hit him without breaking anything. Conceivable but not likely. From the location of the fractures, I can say he was struck no less than six times. Of course, that's just the blows to the skull. There were more fractures to the ribs and arms."

"Two each?"

"Two each."

"Method of injury?"

"Blows to the arms. Blunt force trauma—a table, a knee, or something like it—for the ribs."

It just kept getting better. "Any opinion on cause of death?"

"You don't need a medical degree to know he was beaten to death, Nate."

"No, I meant which blows killed him."

"The first blows to the head most likely. The body blows are a close second, but it would've taken longer."

"Did you do toxicology?"

"I did. Clean."

That surprised me. "No alcohol?"

"No."

"No heroin?"

"No heroin."

I thought. "Any other health conditions that would have made him susceptible to dying?"

Ray fiddled with his mouse and then said, "Nate, I know you're just doing your job and that everyone deserves representation, but I've never seen anything like this. Not in a fight. To do this, you'd have to be insane."

I thought for another adjective. "Furious?"

"Furiously insane maybe."

"That what you going to say at trial?"

Ray shrugged. "If asked. I don't know that I'll volunteer it."

I had everything I needed and so stood. "Thanks, Ray, I appreciate you seeing me on such short notice."

"I think your dad and me were going to go fishing the week of the trial. Should we postpone or do you think it'll plead?"

"I'm just the local guy, Ray. Not my call."

"Guess I'll see you in a few weeks then." Ray stood and shook my hand. "Let me walk you out."

"I've taken up enough of your time, Ray, thanks. I know my way."

"Okay." He smiled and went back to his computer as I left his office. As I walked down the hall, I thought about the good-looking, personable coroner from the University of Michigan taking the stand at trial.

He was going to destroy us.

Ray's physical findings didn't support a theme of a white knight charging in to rescue a semi-conscious damsel. No, what he'd found was the wreckage of uncontained, animal rage. Seventeen. Seventeen fractures in the skull made by at least six blows, blows that kept coming after Chase was dead, or worse, pulverized him while he was still alive. Hanson was going to keep pounding on that physical evidence almost as often as Hank had pounded Chase, and Ray was going to do it in a smiling, competent way that would eviscerate us.

I was so deep in thought that I didn't see the exam room door open as I passed. Its hard metal edge hit my shoulder and I caught it with one hand to catch my balance. It stopped the people on the other side too so I grabbed it, opened it the rest of the way, and stepped aside.

A man had his arm around a woman whose head was buried in his shoulder. She was sobbing.

"I'm sorry," I said. "Excuse me."

The man flicked a glance at me, nodded, and led the woman away. I held the door for them and, out of reflex, looked into the room.

A medical examiner in blue scrubs was standing on the far side of a stainless steel table, pulling a sheet over the body on it. I had a quick impression of a young woman with pale skin and brown hair pulled back in a ponytail before the sheet settled, leaving only the silhouette of the form under the cover.

I felt a flash that started in my chest and pulsed out to my hands and feet. I pushed the door shut as the hall tilted to the side. I took a few steps before I had to stop and put a hand on the wall. My head was light but staying here was not an option so I staggered forward a few steps, then let the momentum carry me down the hall, through the lobby, and out into the warm sunlight. I climbed into the Jeep and even though the afternoon sun had heated the car like a furnace, I sat there, letting the heavy heat burn away the smell of ammonia and the smooth coolness of stainless steel.

I didn't sit there long, I don't think, but I did start to sweat before I started the car and blasted the air. It was five o'clock. Ish. I sat there, deciding whether I was going to the Brickhouse or the Railcar. Then I chose and drove.

~

IT WAS CLOSE TO SEVEN THAT NIGHT WHEN I CAME HOME AND
tossed my gym bag onto the couch. I went over to the fridge,
grabbed a water, and drank it in two goes. I stared at the fridge
and then I stared at the empty kitchen table and decided I really
didn't have it in me to sit in there now. Not on a beautiful
summer night.

Michigan summers being what they were, it was still sunny
out and I figured I probably had another good two and a half,
three hours of daylight. I grabbed another water, drank half of it,
and went to the garage. It was a bit of a mess really, with bags
and tools strewn about on shelves and, as I opened the garage
door, the Jeep and the Accord sat side-by-side in the driveway as
mute evidence of my failure as a garage cleaner. I finished the
water, tossed the bottle in the garbage, and went to the far wall
to get my bike. We'd installed those hooks into the ceiling that
let you hang your bike by its wheels and I ducked my head
under the purple bike and removed the black one from the
hook. The wheels still seemed plenty springy so I hopped on
and set to pedaling down the road.

I'm not a big biker, but like I said, this really was too nice a
night to sit inside. I did a few laps around the neighborhood and
found I was getting dizzy from going in circles so I headed out
onto the county road. We were far enough north that there
wasn't much traffic and I found that I could really uncork on the
long, straight, traffic-light-free, mile-long sections of roads.

Like any good workout, my mind went elsewhere and soon I
realized I'd done a couple of four-mile blocks. Or maybe three.
The sun was getting close to the treetops and I figured I better
get back before it was fully dusk. I coasted up the driveway and
into the garage. When I dismounted, I had that wobbly feeling
that the earth was moving that you get when you stand again
after riding for a while. Straightening my legs seemed like an
effort and I decided that I didn't really want to wrestle the bike

back up onto its hooks next to its partner. Instead, I rolled it over to the other side of the garage and leaned it against the wall.

I pulled a beer out of the garage fridge and went out back to the pool. I stripped off my shirt and shoes and dove into the water wearing my shorts. We'd had a few cool nights so the water was a little cold, but it felt great after the ride. There are people that want the heater on all the time but that kind of defeats the purpose for me. As it became fully dark, I swam back and forth one more time then climbed out and sat in a deck chair. I hadn't brought a towel so I sat there and let the air dry my skin and the beer wet my lips.

I was dry after a while and I went inside to change. I made a quick meal of eggs and rice and plopped down in front of SportsCenter.

I didn't remember falling asleep.

WHAT I REMEMBERED WAS MY PHONE BUZZING. I REACHED OVER TO the ottoman without looking and declined it.

It rang again. I had no reason to answer a call in the middle of the night. Not anymore. I declined.

It rang a third time. I tilted the phone my way. It said 5:23 a.m. and "Cyn." My legs felt stiff and my head felt like mush as I answered. "Don't you two ever sleep?"

"I'm sorry, Nathan, but I need you at the office."

"Alright." I rubbed my eye. "I'll be in about 8:00."

"No, Nathan. I need you now."

I turned the TV down. "I'm just the local guy, remember, Cyn? Have Christian handle it until I get in."

"I can't, Nathan. Christian is dead."

My stomach sank. The words bounced around on top of my head for a few moments before I absorbed them. I sat up.

"Nathan?"

"I'll be right there, Cyn."

"Thanks." She hung up.

I stumbled to the shower, didn't bother to shave, and dressed before I made my way, head swimming, to the Jeep and drove back to the office to find out how Christian Dane had died.

# DISCOVERY

## 13

I BARRELED INTO THE THIRD-FLOOR OFFICE, SWEATING FROM running up the stairs. It wasn't the scene I expected.

Cyn sat at the main conference desk, phone to her ear, as she lifted a hand for me to wait. "Yes, Mr. Skald," she said. "I'll notify the courts in the McKenzie, Reynolds, and Porter cases as soon as they open. I have six other substitutions to file by end of business. Yes, I'll send you the roster of who's been substituted." She paused. "We don't know yet." Another pause. "I expect by Monday. Yes, sir. I'll update you tomorrow. Thank you."

As Cyn ended the call, she put her phone on the table and went back to her keyboard, fingers flying. "Just one moment, Nathan. Mr. Skald wants this right away."

I watched her as she typed. Her features were sharp, her eyes were clear, and her face showed no sign that she had been roused in the middle of the night or that she might be in mourning. Instead, she was focused completely on whatever message she was typing. I waited about thirty seconds until she hit return and turned her chair towards me. "Sorry, Nathan. That really did have to go."

I waved it off. "Cyn, what happened?"

She folded her hands. "Christian's dead."

"I know that. What happened?"

"He didn't show yesterday, which isn't unusual since he works in his room sometimes when he wants to think. I had emails from him though throughout the day. But then he didn't return my calls last night and he didn't answer my wake-up call this morning either."

"You make a wake-up call?"

Her gaze was cool. "It helped him plan his day. So I went to his room at the hotel and checked on him."

I didn't comment on the fact that she had a key.

"He was sitting at the hotel desk, slumped over with his face on the wood. There was what was left of a room service hamburger on a plate so I assume he died last night."

"Do we know how?"

There really wasn't any emotion at all showing on Cyn's face as she said, "They're investigating, of course, and I imagine they're going to do an autopsy, but according to the rescue squad, the working diagnosis is heart attack."

"Just sitting there?"

Nothing changed on her face. "I've been doing this a long time with a lot of attorneys, Nathan. Christian would not be the first one to die at his desk."

That was true as far as it went. I had known three myself. "Okay. What do we need to do about arrangements?"

"Nothing. It's been handled."

"Already? It's 6:15 in the morning."

"We're a big firm. We've already put several people on it. As soon as the medical inquiry is done, we'll get him back to Minnesota to his family."

"Let me know if you need any assistance with the local examiners."

"Of course," Cyn said and it was obvious that she highly doubted that any such assistance would be necessary.

I thought about the arrangements and the sorrow of a family I didn't know and the logistics of handling the cases of a lawyer who'd suddenly died. Which brought me to, "So not to be callous about this but when is your firm sending someone else out?"

"We're not."

I cocked my head. "So you're withdrawing from the case? You're going to need the Court's permission for that this late in the game."

"We're not withdrawing, Nathan. We're going to continue to appear and give you all the assistance you require."

I blinked, but only once. "What the fuck are you talking about?"

"At least that's what we hope. Friedlander & Skald would like you to continue to represent Mr. Braggi and we will assist you in any way necessary."

"You just got done saying you're a big firm. You can assist me by getting on the phone and getting another one of your master litigators out here to handle this shit."

Cyn shook her head, eyes cool. "You heard me just now. I'm managing coverage of all of the other cases Christian was on. That's taking up all the other lawyers. None of them will be able to get here and up to speed in two weeks."

"The judge will give us more time."

"She might. But that's not what Mr. Braggi wants. Or the partnership."

"What?"

"Like the judge, neither Mr. Braggi nor my firm wants any delays."

"This isn't a delay. It's a tragedy."

"Even so."

"What if I don't want to do it?"

"You accepted our engagement as local counsel to serve in any role we'd like. This is the role we'd like."

"The role you'd like is stupid and it's going to get your client killed."

"Our client."

"Our client will be a dead man."

"Nathan, Friedlander & Skald would not have hired you if you weren't the most capable attorney for the job."

"I'll withdraw."

"On what grounds? You're being paid, Mr. Braggi wants you, and you've not been asked to do anything the least bit unethical."

I thought. She was right. Still, "I'm talking to Braggi. It's his decision. If he says I'm off, I'm off."

"Then I suggest you go to see him right away. We have a lot of work to do."

"Maybe."

Cyn was back to typing before I passed through the door.

As I was walking to my car, Danny pulled in. "Cyn told me," he said as he got out of his car. "You hear anything else?"

I shook my head. "Sheriff Dushane will be investigating. See if you can find out anything else."

"I think their hotel was on the Ohio side of town."

I cursed our infernal city boundaries. A death on the Ohio side meant that we'd be dealing with the Carrefour City Police instead of the Ash County Sheriff. The Carrefour City Police meant Detective Mitch Pearson and Detective Mitch Pearson meant a pain in my ass.

"Call Pearson then. See if there's any other info he has on Christian's death."

Danny nodded. "What are we going to do?"

"She wants us to take over the case."

The look on Danny's face indicated that he really couldn't guarantee the state of his pants as he said, "Can we do a murder case?"

"Can we isn't the same as will we."

"So what are we going to do?" Danny's eyes were wide.

"You're going to call Pearson. I'm going to visit Braggi."

"And then?"

I thought. "Put together a motion to withdraw this morning and a motion for a continuance. Just in case."

"What's the basis?"

"Strategic differences." I climbed into the Jeep. "I'll be back in a couple of hours."

When I pulled away, Danny was still staring at the back of the Jeep, a little like my childhood dog. Unfair but true.

I drove off to tell Hank Braggi that his lawyer was dead.

"So Fancy Pants bought it, eh?" Hank's eyes were ice blue and unmoved. "Can't say as I'm surprised. You hungry?"

Hank was standing in the doorway to Cade's kitchen in a khaki green Lizzy Saint concert shirt and faded jeans. He was just as big, his hair and beard were just as uniformly wild, and his eyes as glitteringly amused as I remembered even though it was barely seven in the morning. While it wasn't exactly the response I'd been expecting, I also realized I'd been up for a while and that I was starving. "Actually, I am."

"C'mon." He waved and headed back into the kitchen. "Eggs it is. Cade left a bunch."

"Why would you say that?"

He pulled a bowl out of a cupboard. "Offer you eggs?"

"Say you're not surprised. About Christian."

He shrugged and grabbed the eggs out of the fridge. "Sitting hunched in a room and only coming out to argue doesn't seem like the healthiest way to live. Now if you actually came out and fought each other, that would be a different story. But making clever little arguments like a gnome isn't much of a life. Amazing he lasted as long as he did."

I had not expected to be told I was living the gnome-life today. Excellent.

Hank started rhythmically cracking the eggs into the bowl and throwing the shells into the sink. "So, with Fancy Pants gone, you're going to handle the trial?"

"That's what I came to talk to you about. I think you should get a new attorney."

"Why would I do that?"

"Because I don't have the experience that Christian had." I smiled. "Or the suits."

"Pffft." He flipped a shell backhanded into the sink. "Armor doesn't make the warrior."

"No, but a warrior shouldn't go buck naked into battle either."

"Unless your camp's attacked at night. Then you fight as you are."

Great. Now I was in a renaissance fair. "Fortunately, we haven't been attacked at night, Hank. We're being attacked with plenty of notice. So we have time to get you a different lawyer.

"Hmpf." Hank stared at me. "I took you for more of a scrapper, with the ear and all." He turned to me, his eyes intent. "Wrestling?"

"The ear?"

He nodded.

I shrugged. "No. I mean yes I wrestled but no that's not how I got it."

"So?" He pulled out a knife, a pepper, and a cutting board.

"Hank, we have serious shit to discuss here."

His eyes grew serious. "Nothing's more serious than war stories, Nate."

I sighed. "Then the representation?"

"Then the representation."

"You know Cade?"

"My jailer?" The knife danced over the cutting board, turning a whole pepper into delicious squares. "Of course."

"I spent some time training with him."

Hank lined up a neat pile of red pepper squares with the knife and lit a fire under the pan. "People don't get cauliflower ear lifting weights."

"Not lifting. Fighting."

"With him?"

"Sometimes."

Hank smiled. "My jailer is a large individual."

"I'm not small."

"No. But still."

I shrugged. "The world has no weight classes."

"Truth." Hank dumped the eggs into the pan. There was a sizzle and the smell of cooking egg drifted over. "So what happened?"

"We were sparring. He landed a right hook. My ear filled up with blood."

"Did it knock you out?"

"No."

"Did you keep fighting?"

"Sparring. And yes."

Hank was smiling now. "When was this?"

I wasn't going to answer that.

"Hank, we're not talking about fighting. We're talking about a trial."

"Don't see much of a difference."

"There is."

Hank jiggled the spatula under the eggs and flipped over the now solid egg-circle. As he sprinkled the peppers along one half and folded the egg-circle in half, he said, "Have you tried cases?"

"Yes."

"Have you won?"

"And lost."

"Anyone who fights takes a beating now and then."

"Hank, this is for murder. If we lose, you'll die."

"Which is what will happen at the end of my life, isn't it?"

I took a deep breath. "But that end could come much sooner. With a different attorney, you have a better chance of going free."

Hank brought those ice blue eyes back into focus on me. "Will getting a new attorney delay the trial?"

"Only for a little while."

"But it will delay it?"

"Yes."

"I want a scrapper, Counselor."

He flipped the folded eggs to the other side. "And I'm not going to stay cooped up any longer than I have to."

I changed tack. "I wasn't supposed to be the lead, Hank. I need more time to prepare. You might as well get a new attorney in the meantime."

Hank raised his eyebrows. "You need more than two weeks? To argue?"

"It's not that simple."

"It is that simple."

"Hank, it's not. There are things that have to be prepared for the trial."

"Maybe in other cases. Not in this one."

I waited for his explanation.

Hank smiled. "There's no question I beat that cowardly shit-bird to death. You just have to explain the reason why."

He had a point.

Hank slid the omelet onto a plate and handed it to me along with a fork. "Is Cyn still involved?"

I raised an eyebrow. "You know her?"

"Old friend of the family. So is she?"

"Yes."

Hank waved before dropping more beaten eggs into the pan. "Then you'll be fine. She'll give you all the help you need and I can certainly work you into my busy schedule whenever you want to meet."

I studied Hank. His face matched his words—he seemed utterly unconcerned at the prospect of me handling his murder trial or the fact that he was facing death. The purpose of this visit was accomplished—I knew where Hank stood. And he wasn't going to give me the easy way out.

"I'll need to talk to the Judge," I said. "We'll see what she says."

"You have to tell her the truth, right?"

"Always."

"Then you be sure to tell her that I want you, that I don't want a delay, and that I won't cooperate with anyone else."

Great. "I'll talk to you as soon as I talk to the Judge."

Hank pointed the spatula. "Eat. Don't waste the heat."

I did. It was delicious. I was five bites in when Hank said, "Have drug dealers become so precious?" said Hank.

"How so?"

"That we mourn their death?"

I took another bite. "It's not his death that's the problem, Hank. It's your enthusiasm."

Hank's eyes glittered. "I do get carried away. But that's rock and roll now, isn't it?"

With that, Hank let me finish my omelet as I tried to figure out how I was going to get new counsel on the case when my client didn't want them. A short time later, Hank joined me.

And yes, it was delicious.

CYN WAS STILL AT THE TABLE TYPING AWAY WHEN I GOT BACK. "DID you get to him first?" I said.

She didn't look up. "What are you talking about, Nathan?"

"Did you tell Hank to keep me on?"

"Mr. Braggi is perfectly capable of making decisions for himself. And no."

Danny stuck his head out of his office. "Judge Gallon's bailiff called."

I gave Cyn a glare, which she was totally oblivious to because she never took her eyes off her work. Then I said, "What did she want?"

"A telephone pretrial."

"When?"

"Five minutes. I emailed you the call-in number."

"Thanks. This isn't finished," I said to Cyn.

"We'll find out in five minutes," she said without pausing.

I went to my temporary office, turned on my tablet, and loaded the Braggi file just in time to call-in. When Stacy had Jeff and me on the line, she connected us to the judge.

"Judge Gallon here. Do I have Mr. Shepherd?"

"Yes, Your Honor."

"And Mr. Hanson?"

"Yes, Judge."

"Nate, I understand that Mr. Dane has passed away."

"He has, Your Honor."

"My condolences."

"I hadn't heard, Nate," said Jeff. "Mine too."

"Thank you both."

"Will you be participating in arrangements?"

"No, Your Honor. He's being taken back to Minnesota and his family is handling things there."

"The reason I called the pretrial is that I assume you're going to be asking for a continuance while you sort this out," said Judge Gallon. "Since we're only about two weeks away, I wanted to bring this to a head now."

"We might not be, Your Honor."

"Might not what?"

"Be asking for a continuance."

There was silence on the line for a few beats before Judge Gallon said, "And how could that be?"

"Because I could be handling the case."

"As lead attorney?"

"We're still working that out, Your Honor, but that's what my client wants."

"I see. I assume you would still need a continuance?"

"My client doesn't want one, Your Honor."

"That's not what I asked, Mr. Shepherd."

Sometimes the truth is the most disarming, effective weapon you have. "Judge, we found out that Christian died today. Can we have until Monday to decide?"

"Of course," said Judge Gallon. "But I'll want a decision then. Any objection, Mr. Hanson?"

"Of course not, Your Honor."

"And Nate, just so you know how the Court's leaning, I know you're a skilled attorney and that you're technically qualified to represent a client as lead counsel on a capital murder case."

"It sounds like there's a 'but' there, Your Honor."

"But if you're going to keep the trial date, you don't have time for a refresher course. I strongly suggest that you bring in co-

counsel who's been in that arena more recently to do it with you."

"Lindsey Cooper is already up to speed, Your Honor," said Jeff.

I chuckled with mirth I didn't feel. "Aiding the defense now, Jeff?"

"I don't want to hand Braggi an ineffective assistance of counsel appeal when he gets the death penalty, Nate."

"So polite. So mean."

Judge Gallon shifted to her clipped, authoritative tone. "Alright. Email Jeff and the bailiff Monday with your decision, Nate, and we'll go from there. Anything else?"

"No, Your Honor," Jeff and I said.

"Then have a good weekend," she said, and hung up.

"Still there, Nate?" Jeff said.

"Yes."

"We'll keep the second-degree deal open until Monday. Can't say if we will after."

"Got it. Thanks."

"See ya."

I hung up, made a call and found out that Lindsey Cooper was in, then left the office to go see if I could get her to come back onto Hank Braggi's defense.

## 14

Lindsey Cooper's office was in the Barrister Building, an old brick structure dating back to the early 1900s that a variety of attorneys shared office space in. Located right next to the courthouse, it was once the pride of Carrefour and the office of legendary judge William Flintlock. Those glory days were long past now though and using the elevator meant risking a one in ten chance of being stuck in it for half an hour. I couldn't, so I took the stairs to the fourth floor. Three solo offices were set up there and I went to the middle door which said, "Lindsey Cooper, Attorney at Law."

Carrefour wasn't big enough to have a public defender's office so what it had instead was a list of practitioners who would take individual appointments from the Court. Lindsey was a couple of years ahead of me in law school and had built her solo practice on those appointments. That's how I had first run into her, when I was a prosecutor fresh out of law school. Since then, Lindsey had developed a thriving family law practice; Carrefour was big enough to manufacture a steady stream of divorces, custody disputes, and child support arrearages. She continued to take appointments on criminal cases though, both from a sense of obligation to what got her started and to keep her trial skills sharp.

With the advent of telephone answering programs, most solo practitioners didn't have a secretarial staff and Lindsey was no exception. When I opened the door and knocked, Lindsey called, "Back here, Nate," and I let myself in.

She was on her cell phone when I walked into her office. She raised her hand to me then said, "Oh, go to hell, Spencer. If you had a witness, you would have produced him by now. And you know you don't have any prints so there's no way you can put my guy at the scene." She rolled her eyes. "Well, of course he resisted, the cops detained him without cause! Last time I checked, you're allowed to be at a Taco Bell at three in the morning. Shit, it's their whole business plan. Fine, talk to Victoria and then get back to me with an offer that doesn't include time. Sure, see you at volleyball Tuesday."

Lindsey had straight, shoulder-length brown hair and an appealing face that engendered a belief that she was telling the truth. I'm almost certain that she knew it. She was a little taller than average and was always busy so she always looked a little bit tired. She hung up the phone, waved at the chair, and said, "What's going on, Nate? I'm pretty sure I sent you all of the file materials."

I looked around at an office strewn with the wreckage of dozens of files, a state that was not at all uncommon for a trial lawyer. "Sure?"

"All this way to insult my housekeeping? I have missed you."

Probably not the best opening to enlist someone's assistance. "No, it wasn't the documents. My lead counsel is dead."

"Shit, really?"

"Really."

"I'm sorry. Out of town guy right?"

"Minnesota."

"So what do you need—wait a minute, you're not looking to boomerang this thing back around on me, are you?"

"No."

"Good."

"Not exactly."

She stared, silent.

"I'm not letting go of the boomerang. But I do need your help."

"My schedule is remarkably free of murderers, Nate. I enjoy that."

"I'd still be the lead."

"Thinking of taking some 'me' time."

"We've still got the backing of the Minnesota firm."

"Maybe get my hair done."

"Danny would do all the research."

"Run a 10K."

"I'll do most of it—open, close, most of the witnesses."

"I've been meaning to write a book."

"Or all of the witnesses."

"In fact, I might not do anything at all. That's kind of the point of not having a murder trial on your calendar."

"Judge Gallon might not let me stay on unless you join me as co-counsel."

The smile left Lindsey's face and she looked at me in the same way she had when I had watched her eviscerate a cop who had planted a gram of cocaine in a car during a traffic stop gone bad. "Has anyone had the balls to ask you if you're emotionally equipped to handle this case?"

I didn't drop my eyes. "Some people have danced around the edges. No one has asked me directly."

"Well?"

"Well what?"

"Can you handle this case without losing your shit?"

"Is that the technical term?"

"Yes."

"I can."

"This seems awfully close to home, Nate."

"It is."

"You know I'm sorry about Sarah."

I knew she was. She'd come to the funeral. I nodded.

"But a murder trial is no place to work through it."

"I'm fine."

"I don't know how that's possible."

"I'm not the first person to lose their wife, Lindsey."

"I didn't say you were. But this seems like dancing right up to the edge."

"We don't make the facts, Lindsey. We just present them."

She stared at me. "You'd really be taking the lead?"

I nodded. "You just keep me honest and guide me around the traps."

"I suppose it's at the public defender rate?"

"What kind of friend do you take me for? It's at the Friedlander & Skald rate."

"Which is?"

I told her.

"Jesus Christ, Nate, why didn't you say that in the first fucking place. I'm in." She leaned back. "Is Jeff's deal still on the table?"

I nodded. "Hank made his views on that pretty clear to me."

Lindsey shook her head. "Me too. Doesn't make any sense."

"No, it doesn't. Any objection to getting started right now?"

"And leave all this?" Lindsey stood and snapped her tablet shut. "You're lead counsel. Lead away."

We left for my office, driving separately. It was on the way that the realization really hit me.

I was neck deep in it. I would be defending Hank Braggi at his murder trial.

## 15

"ALL RIGHT," I SAID. "WE HAVE TWO WEEKS UNTIL THE TRIAL. We're going to organize today so that we get a jump on the weekend."

The trial team was sitting around the conference table in our third-floor temporary office. I was at one end, Cyn was at the other, and Lindsey and Danny were on either side.

"We know he did it," said Lindsey. She had this trick where she could make a pen spin in a circle between her thumb and forefinger and she did it now as she spoke. "So what's the strategy?"

"Self-defense," I said. "Well, you know what I mean, defense of another but essentially self-defense. Our theme is that Dillon Chase was a scumbag who was shooting up an unconscious woman who wasn't a user and that Hank Braggi did what any one of us would do when confronted by the same situation."

Lindsey's pen spun faster. "That would've been fine if Braggi had tackled him. How are we going to explain bone-breaking?"

"I'm thinking a combo of outrage at seeing an unconscious woman assaulted combined with righteous anger at the heroin epidemic."

"Do you think Judge Gallon will let you get away with that?"

"To a point."

"Enough of a point?"

"I guess we'll see."

The pen slowed. "We'll need to talk to Gerchuk, see how he's going to describe the cause of death."

"I did. The description's not good."

The pen stopped.

"He said it looked more like a truck accident than a fight."

The pen started again. "I was afraid of that."

"He was very convincing."

"I was afraid of that too. So that's our whole strategy, huh? Righteous indignation?"

"So far. We're going to see if we can get any dirt on Dillon Chase and either of the other boys to muddy the water some more."

"I like the story," said Lindsey. "But the autopsy's going to undermine all of it."

"We're going to have to paint a picture of Hank as a protective uncle who was enraged by what he saw."

Lindsey's pen paused. "Uncle?"

"Do you know of anything more?"

We both looked at Cyn. She shook her head. "Not that I know of. But I wouldn't put it past him. You'll want to ask."

I made a note. "There's a second layer to this. If we don't win the case, we have to at least beat the aggravating circumstances."

"What do you mean?" said Danny.

I kept forgetting that he had no experience with this kind of thing. "Just killing someone isn't enough to warrant the death penalty. The prosecutor has to show something more, either that the killing was part of a premeditated plot or that it happened in the course of some other crime like burglary or robbery. Here, they're charging him with attempted murder against Whitsel too. If we beat the attempted murder charge, we eliminate the death penalty."

"And what's the defense there?" said Danny.

"Hurting Whitsel was an accident. Hank was trying to get to Chase. He had no intention of harming Whitsel so no attempted murder."

Cyn tapped a single red nail against the table. "Mr. Braggi isn't interested in life in prison."

"I doubt he's interested in death row either," said Lindsey.

Her pen kept spinning. "Have we thought about an insanity plea?"

"Mr. Braggi is not insane," said Cyn.

"Dillon Chase's body says otherwise," said Lindsey. "Listen, I had a psychiatrist on board before I was canned the first time. Let's send her the written file, just in case. Then if we decide to call her in, she can hit the ground running."

"Mr. Braggi will not consent to that," said Cyn.

"An insane person wouldn't," said Lindsey.

Lindsey's pen was spinning while Cyn's red nail was tapping. It was riveting. Then I realized they were both looking at me. "Send her the materials," I said. "But hold off on the review. It's just in case."

Cyn's lips pressed together slightly but didn't say anything.

I raised a hand. "Like I said, it's a precaution. We may not use it. Let's focus now on showing that Chase was a scumbag. I have Olivia Brickson investigating his background. I should have something over the weekend. Danny, get to work on the jury instructions."

"Got it," said Danny.

"Lindsey, you spend the weekend getting familiar with the file."

"I've read it."

"I'm sure, but Cyn has organized it and I need you to know

where everything is. I'd also like you to put your prosecutor's hat on and think about how they're going to present the murder case."

"I bet it starts with a five-foot-tall picture of what was left of Dillon's face."

"Then pick the worst ones and think about how you would present that without turning off the jury."

"Got it." She pretended to write a note. "Prepare the easiest case ever."

"Probably. Cyn, I assume they're going to call the police officers that investigated the scene and arrested Hank. I want you to find statistics about the number of heroin arrests and convictions in Carrefour in the last ten years. Then I want you to make a couple of graphs."

"Of the arrests and convictions?"

I nodded. "I'm certain they've skyrocketed. We're going to want to convey to the jury the scope of the heroin problem. I think most people have a sense that this is going on, but I want them to see it in black and white."

Cyn's fingernails rattled across her keyboard. "Should I do the same thing for deaths and overdoses?"

Danny's eyes darted towards me while Lindsey stared at the table.

"Absolutely," I said. "Let's make it so they can see that the risk was real when Hank entered that room. We're going to have to build the feeling that any one of them would've done the same thing and that all we're talking about is the method."

"Done."

"We need to take another shot at interviewing Purcell and talking to Whitsel but that can wait until Olivia gets us more information on them. I'd love to talk to Lizzy Saint and Jared Smoke, but they're not going to be back in town until trial."

"Do you want to speak with them?" said Cyn.

"I want to do a lot of things."

The nails rattled on the keyboard again. "They're in Raleigh, North Carolina tomorrow, Wilmington the day after that, and then Charlotte on Tuesday."

I gave her a bobbling head shake. "Okay."

"You want me to book your flight?"

I blinked. "That's an option?"

Her eyes were cool but I swear I saw a little amusement in there. "I told you, Nathan. All of the resources of our firm are at your disposal for this one."

"Then yes. Can we get a hold of her?"

She nodded. "Hank gave us her contact information. We can reach her."

"I better get down there right away then. Do we know how she feels about all this?"

"We know she was on good terms with Hank before this. She's distanced herself from the situation now."

"I can't imagine she's thrilled about the whole heroin angle," said Lindsey.

"She was the victim on that," I said.

Lindsey shrugged. "Still."

"All right. I'll leave tomorrow."

"So basically," said Lindsey, "we'll all start working on the case and you'll fly off to talk to a rock star?"

I pointed. "Exactly."

"Just making sure."

I looked around. "Anything else?"

"Sure you don't need to check in on Taylor Swift to see if she has any information?"

"I'll catch her on the way back." I looked around and no one else had anything so I said, "All right, that's it."

"Mind if I take the file home?" said Lindsey. "What with you going to rock concerts and all."

Cyn turned her chair, grabbed a tablet off a side table, and handed it to Lindsey. "It's all on there."

Lindsey looked at me.

I smiled. "Told you."

We broke up. Danny went to his office to start on the jury instructions and Lindsey took her tablet and left. As I started to leave, Cyn said, "I take it I can tell Mr. Skald that you're in?"

"You can."

"Good."

Cyn was hard to get a handle on. It's not that she was distant —she engaged in small talk and she was always considerate, but I just never really felt like I knew what was going on in her head. Just now, she could just as well have been discussing the weather as planning strategy for a murder trial. "Do they get it?" I said.

"Get what, Nathan?"

"That Hank is in big fucking trouble."

"The language I used was different. The connotation was the same. And yes, they understand."

"I'm not sure Hank does."

"That's not true, Nathan." Cyn's eyes were like green stones. "Mr. Braggi understands exactly what's at stake. That's why he's acting the way he is."

"That doesn't make a lot of sense."

"It does to him."

"You're going to have to explain that to me."

"Maybe he will at some point. In the meantime, let's get you to Raleigh."

## 16

I WAS WALKING THROUGH THE RALEIGH-DURHAM AIRPORT THE following afternoon when my cell buzzed. Olivia Brickson. "Hi, Liv," I said.

"I have some info for you on Chase, Purcell, and Whitsel."

"Great. Shoot."

"Whitsel seems to be exactly what he looks like."

"Which is?"

"A slightly douchey MBA student living on internships and student loans."

"Got it. And Purcell?"

"Murkier. Dropped out of school a couple of years ago but still hangs around it. No discernible source of income but could be living off indulgent parents or under the table work. Nicer car and house than you'd expect for the unemployed."

"Consistent with what I saw. Keep checking. And our victim?"

"Dillon Chase was a professional facilitator."

"A what?"

"From what I can see, Chase floated around the music tour

scene, glomming on to different acts and acquiring what they needed as they moved from place to place."

"Rock groups?"

"All sorts—hip-hop, country, rock. Usually one rung below the biggest thing—a hot group on the way up, an old group on the way down, or a successful journeyman who was making a big living."

"Or journeywoman."

"Bingo."

"Any common denominator?"

"Not that I can see yet."

"Can you tell what he provides?"

"He doesn't provide. He facilitates. And literally anything— the usual drugs and booze, but also companionship, venues, and exotics."

"Exotics?"

" I'm pretty sure he got a certain popstar in touch with an elephant trainer."

"You're shitting me. For that Music Awards stunt?"

"You got it."

"We're in the wrong line of work, Liv."

"Sure seems that way—it's a bitch getting your own elephants all the time. Want to stop by and pick up the file?"

"I'm in Carolina right now. Why don't you email it to me?"

Olivia paused. "I'd rather not, Nate. I'm leaving enough footprints as it is."

"Okay. I'll pick it up at the gym when I get back."

"Perfect. What's in Carolina?"

"A rock star witness."

"Will she see you?"

"I hope so."

"You don't know?"

"Cyn's working on it."

"Good luck. And get a workout in when you're down there."

"Yes, Boss. And thanks."

I had just hung up when the phone buzzed again. Cyn. "Hey."

"I got your tickets to the show at the North Carolina campus but you're not going to be able to see her until after."

"No hello? No how was your flight?"

"Hello, Nathan. How was your flight?"

"Well hello, Cyn. A little bumpy over the Appalachians, but I can't complain."

"And yet. Can we go back to why you flew to North Carolina now?"

"If you'd ever stop with the small talk we could. It's only three o'clock. I really can't talk to her before the show?"

"It took all the connections we had for you to see her at all. Apparently, Ms. Saint has a pre-concert routine that will brook no disturbance."

"All right. When's the show?"

"Opening act is at seven, Saint at nine, and you should be able to talk to her sometime after midnight."

"Jesus."

"Rock stars being what they are, I imagine that qualifies as an early morning meeting."

"I imagine it does. Flight home?"

"Ten a.m. I booked you at the Chapel Hill Marriott. I'm texting you the information."

"I'm not sure what I did before you, Cyn."

"Floundered. Make sure you're on that flight."

I noticed I was taking a lot of orders at the end of these conversations. Apparently, I needed direction. "Got it. Do they know why I want to see her?"

"They do. They're fine with it."

"All right. I'll let you know what I find out."

"Excellent. I truly hope that you enjoy your accommodations, Nathan, and that your flight home is pleasant and utterly without incident."

"That's just mean-spirited."

"One can never go wrong with concern for one's coworkers."

"Goodbye, Cyn."

"And not even the slightest inquiry about my well-being or weekend evening? Fine, Nathan. Goodbye."

"Wait, Cyn. What about your—"

The call disconnected. I had the score as Cyn 1, Nate 0.

I caught an Uber to the hotel, which wasn't too far from the Dean Smith Center on the UNC campus where the concert was going to be. I had just checked in and found my way to the room when my phone buzzed with a number I didn't recognize but was from my home area code. "Nate Shepherd," I said.

"Nate, it's Lindsey."

"Oh, I guess I have to add you to my contacts."

"I'm hurt."

"My apologies. Why aren't you out on a Saturday night?"

"What am I going to do, go to a rock concert? I have a trial to prepare for."

"Good point. Only an asshole would do that."

"Exactly. Hey, have you really studied this autopsy?"

"I thought so. What's up?"

"It takes a while to break this many bones and then smear the guy all over the hotel room."

"What do you mean?"

"I mean punching him in the head and breaking his arms and smashing his ribs and then bouncing him off every wall in the room takes some time. I'm telling you right now that the prosecutor is going to reenact it or at least measure out the pace of it and it's gonna seem awfully goddamn long."

"Alright."

"So when you talk to Saint or to Smoke, try to nail down what, if anything, they saw. My thought is that if we can confirm that no one saw it, then maybe we can keep the prosecutor's presentation about how long it took out of evidence."

"Good point. From the reports, Lizzy was unconscious or on the verge of it and Smoke was out of the room for a time."

"Exactly."

"Thanks, Lindsey. That's helpful."

"Thanks. Sound surprised again and I'll whip your ass."

"A lot of that going around today. Doing anything tonight?"

"On my personal time?"

"Yes."

"Personal things."

"Excellent. See you Sunday."

"Right. Enjoy your concert."

I hung up. I had about three hours until the concert started and to tell you the truth, I really didn't have much of an appetite for Five-Fold Death Cake or whoever it was that was opening for Lizzy Saint. I decided to take Olivia's advice and worked out, then cleaned up and got some dinner before heading over to the concert at about eight.

The fact that I called all this work is basically why my dad says I don't have a real job. And tonight, I couldn't really argue with him.

MY EARS WERE STILL RINGING WHEN I LEANED IN TOWARD THE security guard and showed him the credential around my neck. "Nate Shepherd to see Lizzy Saint."

The man looked at me, looked at the plastic card, and looked at the tablet in his hand. His lips moved, but I couldn't hear him.

"I'm sorry?" Even though I'd been up in a luxury box (honestly, Cyn is amazing), two and a half hours of spine-grinding music blasting out a thirty-foot-high wall of amps takes a little while to get over. Although, to be fair, I think it was the cannons at the end that were giving me trouble.

The security guard leaned closer. "Ms. Saint said to show you to her road manager and he'll take it from there."

"Thanks. Where do I go?"

The security guard waved to another man who guided me down the hall behind the stage. The Dean Smith Center was where the Tar Heels played their basketball games so he led me down to the home team locker room, which sounds dreary until you see just what a modern-day basketball locker room of a top-five basketball team looks like. Staffers were scurrying around everywhere, along with roadies and community members and about fifty other people who had credentials just like mine. The security guard passed me off to a runner who pointed me to an intern who introduced me to the assistant to Lizzy Saint's road manager, a harried-looking man in his mid-twenties with a look that I assume he hoped would work in the presence of both corporate sponsors and rock stars. "Who are you?" he said, looking over my shoulder.

"Nate Shepherd. Appointment to see Lizzy Saint."

"You and everybody else here."

I looked around and revised my estimate up to more than a hundred people crammed into the locker room. "All of them?"

"Every single one. Make-A-Wish, United Way, WRCK, and fifty meet and greet tickets. So, which group are you?"

"Hank Braggi's lawyer."

That got the assistant to the road manager's attention and he looked at me directly for the first time. "How is Hank?"

"Good as can be expected."

"Is he going to fry?"

"That's what I'm trying to prevent."

"That why you're here to see Lizzy?"

I nodded. "We cleared it."

He looked at his tablet. "I see that. But you're not gonna get jack-squat done here." He pulled a black leather wristband out of his pocket and motioned. I held my arm out and he attached the wristband to me. "It's going to be a zoo here. Go to the Regency. There's an after-party in the main suite. This'll get you in."

"When?"

"The party's started now. Lizzy will be there after she works her way through this."

"Thanks," I said and I meant it.

"Hank helped me a lot, man."

"Yeah? How?"

"Helped me get with my girl. Man knows how to lay it down."

A look must've flashed across my face. The assistant to the road manager laughed and said, "Words. The wrap. He told me exactly what to say. In ways I never would've thought to say it. I owe him."

I nodded and extended my hand. "I'll tell him."

"Do that." And then the assistant to the road manager was consumed with a flood of coeds who demanded better lighting to take their selfies in when they met Lizzy Saint.

I decided it was time to head to the Regency.

MY OSTENTATIOUS, TRYING TOO HARD, BLACK LEATHER WRISTBAND gave me entrance to the magical world at the top of the Regency where a full-blown party was going on in a series of adjacent suites. The chip hidden in the band got me past an outer circle of security and functionaries to the next circle of beer, liquor, and seafood before depositing me in a suite with blaring music filled with metal rock's version of the beautiful people—long hair, dark eyeliner, and clothes combinations that seemed more selected for what they revealed than any discernible color pattern.

You know, the type of party Michigan lawyers go to all the time.

Jeans, collared shirt, and boots weren't a Tom Hanks tuxedo at a Christmas party but it didn't exactly blend in either. I grabbed a water (after getting over my shock that there was water available), drifted to a corner, and watched.

It didn't take long to figure out the crowd: crew, friends, family, and a local radio guy who called himself "the Mad Man" and expounded on the size of his syndicated audience to anyone who would listen, which, judging from his volume, he presumed was all of us. I had apparently made it to Dante's fifth circle of hell, the section of the afterparty reserved for DJs and lawyers.

"You must be management," said a voice.

A woman in her thirties whose hair actually seemed to be real blond stood next to me and I was surprised I hadn't noticed. "I'm not," came my witty reply.

She took a sip from a bottle of beer then pointed one finger over it at me. "PR?"

"No." Which I think I had just proved.

"Hmm." She took my wrist, turned over my hand and ran a finger over my fingertips. "Not a musician either, though that would have surprised me." She let go, a little more slowly than I'd expect. "You're big, but not rockstar bodyguard big, though that fucked-up ear gives you some juice."

"Thanks?"

She took another sip before she said, "So?"

"So what?"

"So what brings you to Lizzy Saint's party?"

Somehow saying I wanted to interview a witness to a murder didn't seem like the below the radar appearance I was looking for. I shrugged. "I enjoy music."

"Lots of people enjoy music." She snapped my wristband. "That doesn't get them to the after-party."

"We know some of the same people."

She nodded in that way people have when it's a little loud, looked away, and leaned in. "From where?"

"A while back."

She smiled. "That's when, not where."

"Up north."

"The north is a big place."

"It is. But I wouldn't make too big a deal of that in North Carolina."

"You, Nate?" said a voice. A man in a black t-shirt sporting onyx stud earrings and a crow's head tattoo on one arm came up to us. He was a little taller than me and a lot more jacked.

"I am."

"Come with me."

I turned to say good-bye to the woman and found that she was gone. As I followed the security guard, I realized that she hadn't said her name and that she hadn't been wearing a wristband.

I followed the guard through the party and two more adjoining doors. When I came to the second one, two more men waited and my guide had me put my arms out.

"Really?" I said.

"Really," said the man.

They patted me down in a way that convinced me that they'd have found something if I'd been carrying it. Satisfied, the man said, "Go ahead."

So I went in to see Lizzy Saint.

I ENTERED A ROOM THAT WAS JUST AS BIG BUT NOTICEABLY QUIETER than the others. There was food and there were drinks and there were probably about two dozen people milling around. The guard pointed me in the direction of a corner where a man and a woman stood sipping on beers. The man was dressed entirely in black, of course, and he looked a little pale, a little soft, and had the high, uniform hairline of someone who was fighting mother nature. He looked to be closing in on forty and, when he saw me cross the room towards them, his lips twisted like he'd bit into a lemon.

The woman was entirely different. She had reddish hair cut in a way that was constantly messed so that she always looked like she'd just finished a concert or climbed out of bed. She wore black leather pants, high black boots, and a sleeveless shirt that was open most of the way to her waist and was held in place by a dark belt with a big silver buckle. She had dark theater makeup on her eyes that made them look incredibly almond-shaped and she smiled as I approached. "Nate Shepherd?"

"I am. Lizzy?"

The man snorted and scowled. "Did this clown even see the show?"

It's nice when people confirm your initial impression. Makes you feel less bad for assuming they're an asshole. "I did, Mr. Smoke. Just trying to be polite."

Jared Smoke took a long drag of a cigarette and blew the smoke up into the air in a way that I'm sure he thought was both cool and intimidating rather than reeking of stink-filled insecurity. "What's this clown here for, Lizzy?" Another drag. "You have some columns that need adding?"

Lizzy had a towel draped over one shoulder and she used one end to dab at the back of her neck. "No, baby. He's a lawyer."

Smoke snorted and smoked. "Guess the party can start now."

Another time, another place. But it wasn't, so I said, "Thanks for seeing me, Ms. Saint."

"Jesus Christ, it's Lizzy. And anything for Hank."

Smoke's eyes hooded. "This is about Braggi?"

I didn't respond. Lizzy did. "He just has a couple of questions about what happened. I told him I would help."

"It's all in the police report, Chaser," Smoke said.

I raised an eyebrow.

Smoke took a swig of beer, took a drag off his cigarette, and puffed up his chest. "That's what you do, right? Chase ambulances? Leach off stars?"

"Yes, Mr. Smoke, I leach a living off someone far more talented than me. It's hell, isn't it?"

Lizzy reached out and grabbed Smoke's arm in mid-puff. "He's helping Hank, baby."

Smoke pulled a little bit against Lizzy's hand in the way of someone who wants to be held back. I stood there and waited while he decided which way this was going to go. He wasn't going to be a problem, but there were things I'd rather do than get thrashed by a bunch of security guards.

Finally, he deflated by a peacock feather or two, and said, "Anything for the band family." Lizzy patted his arm, took a drink of beer, and put her almond eyes on me.

I nodded. "I'd like to talk to you a little, Lizzy, but I can't do it in front of another witness."

Smoke waved for me to go ahead and speak. Lizzy tugged his arm and said, "That means you, baby."

It took Smoke about five seconds to realize he'd just been dismissed. "I'd like to catch you next if you don't mind, Mr. Smoke. For the band family."

"Sure," Smoke said in a voice that meant the opposite and

took his beer, his smoke, and his ruffled peacock feathers to the other side of the room.

"Beer?" said Lizzy.

"Water is fine."

"You just evicted my drinking companion, Nate, and I'm not drinking alone after a concert." She held a bottle out.

Lizzy's voice was difficult to describe. Just speaking, it had a rasp to it, a growl and a depth that was compelling even when it wasn't echoing three octaves higher from a wall of amps set to eleven. I found that I wanted to hear more of it, regardless of the information I was seeking.

"Fair enough," I said and took the beer, finding its coolness a relief in the Carolina night.

"So how is Hank?" said Lizzy. "Is he holding up okay?"

"Pretty well. A little stir crazy."

"I bet. He couldn't stand the tour bus or the plane. Sitting in a cell all day…" Her eyes grew dark. "Well, that would be hard for him."

There didn't seem much point in telling her that aversion could kill him. "He's managing."

She took another drink. "So you're representing him?"

"I am."

"Thought he had some old, fancy pants guy."

I laughed.

"What?"

"That's what Hank called him."

Lizzy smiled in a way that would reach the back row. "We do talk the same way sometimes."

"He's dead. The fancy pants guy."

Her eyes darkened again. "Oh. Sorry."

"It happens. I'm taking over. I know you might have talked to him."

She shook her head. "I didn't."

"So I just wanted to find out what you saw, so that I know what's going to be said at trial."

She looked at me, grabbed two more beers, and handed one to me, gazing significantly at the half-full one in my hand. I drank it and took the new one.

She laughed and I was beginning to understand why Hank and Smoke would do whatever she said. "I don't remember much," she said.

"That's fine."

"I'm not sure what I do remember is helpful."

"That's fine too. I just don't want to be surprised, Ms. Saint."

"Call me Ms. Saint again and I'll know I can't trust you."

I tipped my bottle and she clinked it. "How do you know Hank, Lizzy?"

"Met him five, maybe six years ago."

"Back in Chicago?"

Lizzy nodded. "I was part of a different band then." She smiled and took a sip. "Fatal Echoes, if you can believe that. Last remnants of my high school band. "

"No one ever likes their first band's name." You know, because I talk to rock stars all the time.

"True that. So we were opening at some dive bar, the Gjallarhorn I think, and we took a break and this big, wild-looking guy comes up and tells us that our amplifiers are out of balance, that we need to jack up the vocals and the bass, and dial back the lead guitar. Three of the four of us agreed—"

"Everyone but the lead guitarist?"

"You got it. And I'll be goddamned if we don't blow the doors right off the fucking place and destroy. So it was Hank, of course, and he becomes our roadie and sound guy and pretty soon we're blasting the shit out of every bar on the north side of Chicago."

"Is that this band?"

Lizzy shook her head, raised one hand, and two more beers

appeared out of nowhere. I finished mine off, set it down, and took the one she offered. "Like I said, we were the last remnants of our high school band. Two of them finished college and went off to real jobs and our drummer decided that ski bum in Colorado had more potential than drummer in north Chicago. So it was pretty grim there for a little bit, just a lead singer and a sound man with no fucking band."

"What did you do?"

"Well, I have no fucking band so that's when I pick up the guitar and start to learn. Hank doesn't really play a lot, but he shows me the chords and shows me some exercises and pretty soon I can at least crank out some rhythms. Then as long as I'm doing rhythms, it seems like I should put some words with it and Hank starts building lyrics with me. After a month of that, it occurs to me that I should get a fucking notebook and put some of this shit down and I do and so for the next three months, I'm learning chords and writing songs."

Lizzy shook her head and her eyes went distant. "I didn't have a fucking dime and I don't think I ate anything other than Ramen noodles, but at the end of that summer, I could hold my own on a rhythm guitar and I had a notebook full of songs. And Hank tells me, 'Fuck it, you don't need a band. Why don't you just book a gig on your own.' So I do, at a bar that used to let Fatal Echoes play regular, and I knock it out, and three weeks later I have a record deal and a studio band."

"Was that the *Ripper* album?"

Lizzy smiled. "Well, you were nice enough to do your homework anyway. Yes. Followed it with another one a year later, all with songs out of that fucking notebook. Most productive summer of my life."

"Was Hank with you the whole time?"

Lizzy nodded. "Every step. Always stayed in the background, except on *Ripper* when one of the label's engineers was doing his best to fuck up our sound and Hank had to step in and show him how it was meant to be blasted. After that album went platinum, the label didn't fuck with us anymore."

"You two pretty close?"

Her almond eyes glanced sidelong at me. "We weren't fucking if that's what you're asking." She took a long drink. "I would've, especially at the beginning. But he never tried and the couple of times I was drunk enough to give it a whirl, he kept working on the music and then tucked me in when I passed out." She gestured at her body with both hands. "Can you believe that?"

Frankly, I could not. I smiled, gave a neutral shake of the head, and shrugged.

"And the motherfucker's not gay either. Had women in and out of his room all the time. Just not me." She looked at me. "What was the fucking question?"

I smiled. "How do you know Hank?"

She smiled back. "Me and Hank go way back. All the way to the fucking beginning."

So tight friends but not romantic. Jeff was going to build up their connection so that anything she said that supported the prosecution's case would be even more damning coming from her.

"Did you bring your wife to the concert?"

Lizzy's words jolted me out of my thoughts. "What?"

I was holding my beer in my left hand. She clinked the top of her bottle on my wedding ring. "Did you bring her along?"

I struggled to keep my thoughts off my face. "This was more of a work trip."

"Hmm. She like rock?"

I thought for a moment. "We're not together anymore."

She nodded and put the bottle to her lips for a moment. She drank then said, "Transition's a bitch."

I nodded.

"You seem like a good guy." She smiled. "For a lawyer."

"Rock stars are a piss poor judge of character."

Lizzy's smile deepened. "She's a fool for leaving you."

She didn't mean to.

Lizzy offered the clink again and I took it before I said, "What did you see?"

"That night?"

I nodded.

"Not much. We weren't playing the next day and we didn't have to travel so we all pretty much blew it out."

"Hank too?"

"Always Hank. The man can put it away. And he's always in the center of the party."

"Were you partying with him that night?"

A look I couldn't read flashed across her face. "Not that night. We were—"

"Lizzy." The security guard with the onyx stud earrings appeared before us.

"Hey, Rick."

"Phil needs to see you."

"Tell him I'll be there in a minute."

"He's got Grant with him."

Lizzy swore. "I'm sorry, Nate. President of the label. I can't put him off anymore. Can you hang around for a little bit yet?"

Other than charming back story, I hadn't learned anything about the night Dillon Chase was killed. "Sure," I said.

She grabbed two more beers and pushed one into my hand. "Hang for a little bit. I'll be back." Then she was gone.

The second Lizzy left, Jared Smoke came right over to me. He was drinking Jack Daniels straight out of the bottle now, just like they taught in Poser 101. As he lowered the bottle and took another drag from his cigarette, I upped my age estimate of him to over forty instead of under. "What do you want with Lizzy?" he said.

"Same as I want with you. Just wonder what you saw."

Smoke took another draw, squinted, and smiled in a way that I didn't particularly care for. "I saw Hank murder that mother-fucker is what I saw."

"Did you?"

Smoke nodded. "The old man went ballistic."

I didn't think that Hank looked older than Smoke but who knew. "Did you know Dillon Chase?"

Smoke took a drag on his cigarette and exhaled straight up into the air, thoughtful. "No. Not really."

He didn't ask me who Dillon Chase was. "No?" I said. "Or not really?"

"You examining me, Chaser?"

I shook my head.

Smoke shrugged. "Guys like that are always around a rock band. Are you a good lawyer? Seems like Hank might need one."

"Guys like what?"

"Guys that want to say they hung out with rock stars."

I was tempted to ask if there was more than one rock star there that night, but I needed him to be as neutral as possible so I needed to stay that way too. "Was that the first time you'd met him?"

"I couldn't tell you," said Smoke. "I'm not even sure if we'd come through that town before."

"So was Chase local?"

Smoke smirked. "He is now."

"How'd he get into the suite?"

Smoke shrugged and waved a hand at the fairly crowded room we were standing in. "How did any of these motherfuckers get here?" He pointed the whiskey bottle at me. "Damn near anyone can find their way in."

Fair enough. "So you said you saw Hank kill him?"

Jared put his cigarette into a Solo cup and lit another one. "Beat the living shit out of him."

"Lizzy was pretty drunk?"

"Her name is Lizzy Saint, not Saint Lizzy."

"So if you saw Hank kill him, you must've seen him shooting Lizzy up."

Smoke froze for a moment before he put his lighter back in his pocket. "What the fuck are you talking about?"

"Hank went after the guy because Lizzy was unconscious and Chase was shooting her up. If you saw Hank kill the guy, then you must've seen Chase shooting Lizzy up."

"Don't much care for your tone, Chaser."

I shrugged. "You either saw Dillon Chase shooting up Lizzy and didn't do anything about it or you didn't see how this whole thing started. Which is it?"

There are certain times as a lawyer that you wish you were on the record, where you waste a good examination that no one was ever going to see. This was one of those. I'd let my irritation get the better of me and caught Jared in a lie when it didn't matter. Now, by the time Smoke got to trial, he'd have his story straight and he would sandpaper all the rough edges off of it. For the momentary pleasure of being clever, I'd just made Hank's case a little harder, goddammit.

I could see Smoke's wheels turning for a moment before his face lightened and the sandpapered story came out. "Lizzy and I went back to the suite with those guys. More people were on the way. Two of the guys were going to get more beer, I went to the bathroom, and everything was fine. When I came back, Braggi was stomping on that poor bastard's face."

"Was Hank with you and Lizzy earlier in the night?"

Smoke's face pinched. "Braggi was always hanging around."

"That a problem?

Smoke smirked. "It was for Chase."

"Do he and Lizzy still write together?"

"Not from prison."

"Before that."

Smoke looked away and dragged damn near a third of his cigarette down. "Braggi's time had passed. Lizzy and I wrote the last album. We were going up to work on it some more the night Braggi went nuts."

"When you were that fucked up?"

"You've obviously never worked with rock stars." Smoke tapped out the butt of his cigarette in the same cup. "Much as I like being cross-examined after a three-hour concert, I think I'll go have someone give me paper cuts instead." He took a drink out of the whiskey bottle and saluted me with it like he was shooting a 90's music video.

I tipped my beer bottle back. "I'll tell Hank you said 'hi.'"

"You do that." Smoke wandered across the suite, mingling from group to group before he went out the door.

Smoke was not going to be Hank's friend at trial. The prosecutor was going to get some good testimony from him about Hank's brutality and now that I'd warned him, like a fucking moron, about the inconsistency in his story, he'd make sure he got the details just right. I'd need to get more information from Lizzy to salvage this trip.

Unfortunately, she still hadn't come back.

## 17

I NURSED MY BEER AND CHECKED THE TIME AND WONDERED HOW long it takes to meet with a record label executive. I suspected that rock time was very different from lawyer time but that record label executive time might be a little closer to mine.

The room got a little more crowded and the party grew a lot louder, and the occasional guest, usually a woman, came over and started a conversation. Two of them even brought me a beer. Once they learned I wasn't with the band and couldn't introduce them to the guitarist/bassist/drummer/road manager, the conversation usually ended. One woman went a little farther and pressed to see if I was a part of the label and gave me a thumb drive of what I was told were three songs that would blow Lizzy Saint out of the water. I nodded and smiled and pocketed the drive and wondered when Lizzy would return. There were at least thirty people in the room now and I wondered if this was typical after a concert. If it was, then it made the small gathering the night of the killing even more unusual.

I knew this was probably a once-in-a-lifetime opportunity and I should be enjoying it more, but all I could think about was that I had to get back to Carrefour and get to work. So much of preparing for trial is just sitting down and slogging through everything you need to know. It's time-intensive and there's no shortcut. This interview was necessary, but partying with a rock band was not the best use of my time.

The ebb and flow of the party was interrupted by a man who cut straight across the room. He wore a well-tailored blue-gray suit with no tie and a bright white shirt and a matching pocket square. He came right up to and extended his hand. "Nate Shepherd?"

I shook it. "Yes."

"Max Simpson. Lawyer for Grindhouse music. And Ms. Saint."

Ah. "Lizzy's not coming back, is she?"

"Unfortunately, Ms. Saint was pulled away by other responsibilities."

"She told me to wait."

Max nodded. "She did. She said to tell you that she's very sorry."

"Can I set up a call with her?"

"That won't be possible."

"Is she going to testify at trial?"

"Ms. Saint will comply with any legal process that summons her to court."

"Has she spoken with the prosecutor?"

"She gave a statement to the arresting officers. I assume you saw that?"

"I did. My question was whether she's talked to the prosecutor about what happened that night."

"I believe she might have before I became involved."

"I'd like the same opportunity."

"I understand that. But your interest is in defending Mr.

Braggi. My interest is in protecting Ms. Saint. And her reputation."

"Hank was trying to protect more than that."

Max nodded. "I'm sure Mr. Braggi sees it that way."

"Has she spoken with you?"

"Of course."

"Did she know Dillon Chase?"

"She tells me that she had not met him before that night."

"Does she know who introduced them?"

"She does not recall."

"How does a stranger get to her room?"

"She doesn't remember that. She was very drunk that night."

"So I've been told."

"Drunk enough that she doesn't remember most of that night."

"Hank tells me that Lizzy doesn't use heroin."

"I've been told the same."

I thought. I cursed myself again for spending time on small talk and finding common ground with Lizzy instead of cutting straight to what I needed to know. Now I was going to have to go through Max the Guard Dog to get any information. "So Max, what I need to know is, will Lizzy testify that she has any recollection at all of the physical encounter between Hank Braggi and Dillon Chase?"

"You mean the killing?"

"Yes."

"She does not. She remembers drinking with the band an hour or so before and, later, coming to in the hotel room with the paramedics."

"She remembers drinking with the band. Hank too?"

Max stared at me for a moment before he nodded. "Hank too."

"No other memory at all in that window?"

"None."

"Do you anticipate her recovering any of that memory?"

Max looked at the ceiling in a way that one does when choosing one's words carefully. "I don't think that effort, during the middle of a corporately-sponsored, headlining tour, is the best use of Ms. Saint's time."

That was as good as I was going to get. "Thanks, Max," I said and extended my hand. He shook it. "I imagine the label would like me to head back to my hotel room so they can wrap this party up."

Max smiled and nodded. "That would be most helpful."

"Do you have a card?"

"Of course." He produced one. I noted the New York area code. "Mind if I call if questions come up?"

"I don't mind at all. In fact, we would insist that any communications come through me."

"You got it. Thanks again."

"Certainly." Max made a beeline back the way he'd come.

I set down my beer and started to make my way out of the room, turning this way and that with the random jostling of a crowded party. I was halfway there when a shoulder rammed into my chest and the contents of a red Solo cup sloshed onto my shirt.

"What the fuck, man?" said a man with big arms and blood-shot eyes.

"Sorry," I said automatically, and kept moving past.

The man jabbed at my chest with this free hand. "You spilled my fucking drink!"

I stopped. The man was wearing the gear of a Lizzy Saint roadie—boots, worn jeans, and black crew t-shirt. He was big and he was drunk and, by the look on his face, he was angry.

I started to apologize again. Then I saw Smoke on the other side of the room with two other roadies, looking at me, laughing.

"You fucking idiot," the Roadie said, and pushed at my chest again.

I caught his wrist with both hands, bent his hand in, twisted his arm out, and took it straight to the ground. The rest of him followed, flat to his back. The Roadie's eyes were wide as he hit the ground and they grew wider when I punched him, hard, right in the solar plexus. His mouth opened and his lips puckered like a fish but no sound came out.

I stood and kept walking. Judging from the reaction of the crowd, which was none, falling down at an after-party is not an unusual experience.

I glanced over. Smoke wasn't laughing. I waved and left.

Rick, the black-earringed giant, was waiting for me by the door. "I was just leaving," I said.

"I thought I'd walk with you," said Rick.

"Any problem?"

The black-earringed giant gave a small smile that quickly vanished. "You seem to have taken care of it."

We made our way through the hallway and down the elevator to the lobby.

"We've arranged an Uber for you, Mr. Shepherd," Rick said when we arrived.

"Very considerate. Thanks."

Rick walked me all the way to the car and opened the door. "Tell Hank to hang tough."

"I will."

"Have a good night," he said and shut the door behind me.

As we drove away, I was pissed that I hadn't gotten more information from Lizzy. But, if what her attorney said was true, it was helpful to know that she wasn't going to offer any testimony one way or the other about the encounter. Sometimes eliminating the negative was just as important as picking up something positive. If she really didn't have any memory of what happened, then she couldn't be another source of the brutality of Hank's killing. That would have to do.

And of course, I'd gotten a good sense of Jared Smoke. Now that I knew he was going to be a problem, I could prepare for him. That was something anyway.

Now I had to go put together the rest.

## 18

THE WATER ON GLASS LAKE WAS AS SMOOTH AS ITS NAME AS I paddled out to see my dad. It was Sunday afternoon and I had flown back from North Carolina that morning. I was tired, but I knew that this was going to be the last Sunday afternoon barbeque I was going to be able to go to for a while and, to be fair, my dad's barbequed chicken wasn't something I liked to miss. It was a perfect Michigan summer afternoon—mid-80s, slight breeze, intense sunshine—and my dad was exactly where you'd expect him to be: on his boat in the middle of the lake, fishing with two of his seven grandkids. It took me a little while to get the paddle board out there, but I didn't mind at all. I'd been cooped up all week and I was about to be cooped up again so standing in the sun while paddling on the water was about as good as it could get.

As I closed on the boat, I saw three lines in the water. My dad was out there with my brother Tom's middle two daughters, Taylor and Page. "Uncle Nate!" they yelled and waved.

I waved back as I paddled around the far side of the boat.

"Look what you've caught, girls," said my dad. "That's about as ugly a carp as I've ever seen."

The girls giggled.

My dad reached out a hand to help me into the boat then paused and turned to the girls. "Should I throw it back?"

"Yes," screamed Taylor and giggled.

"No," screamed Page and did the same.

"Bah, it's so ugly it will scare all the other fish away. I think we'll have to keep it in the boat." He smiled and pulled me in.

My father was a weathered hickory plank of a man. He was lean and he was strong and, it being summer, he was deeply tan, making his thick white hair even more shocking. His iron grip pulled me in and he gave me a quick hug around the shoulder. He pointed to his rod and its holder on the side of the boat and said, "Now Taylor, you watch my line and if that whale comes back and tugs on it, I want you to reel it in."

"There aren't any whales in here, Pops," said Taylor.

"Only small ones. Your dad caught all the big ones."

My dad tossed me a rope, which I used to tie-off the paddle board, then tossed me a beer. "Want a line?" he said.

"Haven't picked up my license yet." I cracked the beer and sat.

My dad's smile crinkled the sides of his eyes. "You need to get your priorities straight, Mr. Lawyer. What good's all that knowledge if you can't walk outside and drop a line?"

"Not much."

He smiled and sat in his chair. "How'd the trip go?"

"Good."

"Your mom was worried about the flight this morning."

"No problems."

"What was in North Carolina?"

"A witness. They biting today?"

My dad smiled, a white flash on a brown face. "They were earlier." He raised his voice. "A certain two princesses didn't want to go out until after lunch though. You know, when the fish are napping."

"Pops!" said Taylor. "We didn't get here until after lunch!"

"That's no excuse."

"Uncle Nate got here after lunch!" said Page.

"Uncle Nate's not fishing. He's just out here scaring the fish with his ugly face."

The girls giggled. "See, it's your fault, Uncle Nate!" said Page.

"Well then, let's wake those fish up!" I leapt across the boat, grabbed Page under the arms, and whirled around to throw her into the water. "Cannonball!"

Page screamed and I didn't let go and Taylor laughed as I put her little sister back on her seat.

I grabbed them both a water out of the cooler and sat back down as the two of them debated whether Page's screams or my ugly face were scaring the most fish.

My dad leaned back in his chair and smiled. Without looking away from his granddaughters, he said, "Your mom said you're going to trial again?"

I nodded. "Couple of weeks. Won't be able to come up for a few weekends."

"Figured." He looked out over the water. "That murder case?"

"Yeah. You know about it?"

He shrugged. "Your mom keeps me up to speed." He leaned forward and fiddled with the depth of his line. "Didn't think you did that kind of work."

"Unusual situation. One-time thing."

He glanced at his granddaughters before reeling in a little more line. "Sure it's a good idea?"

My dad and I usually talked about football and fishing and my nieces and nephews. For him to know one of my cases in particular was unusual. For him to comment in any way was unprecedented.

"I'll be fine, Dad."

He nodded. "You know best." He stood and reeled his line all the way in. "Bring 'em in, girls."

The girls screamed "Nooo!" in uniform protest.

"We're not stopping. We're just seeing if there's a fish party in the shade on the west shore over there."

I stood. "I think I'll head in."

"Tell your mom we'll be back in an hour or so."

"Can I go with you, Uncle Nate?" said Page.

"I thought you were going to the fish party?"

"I want to ride the paddle board!"

I frowned down at her. "No free-loading trolls allowed."

"I'll paddle!"

"I don't know."

"Pleaaaaaase?"

"Hmmph," I said.

She made a paddling motion with her hands.

"I guess." I untied the board, lined it up alongside the boat, and hopped on. I held it steady as my dad lifted Page over the side and deposited her squarely on the front of the board, where she immediately sat cross-legged.

"Don't let the whales get you," my dad said.

"There are no whales, Pops!"

My dad waved a hand. "I fed them yesterday. You should be fine."

I pushed the board away from the boat with my paddle and started back, me standing in the middle, my niece sitting in the front. We saw five ducks, a loon, and a turtle on the way back.

But no whales.

WHEN WE GROUNDED OUR BOARD ON THE SHORE BACK AT MY parents' place, my brothers, my sisters-in-law, and my nephews had a circus of yard games going on that looked like it included bocce and cornhole. My oldest niece Reed, though, was standing in the water up to her knees, waiting for us. "Uncle Nate! You're famous!"

No lawyer wants to hear that unexpectedly. Well, maybe a couple do but they're assholes.

"Because you're my niece?"

"No. You're all over Entertainment Buzz!"

I scowled. "What are you talking about, Troll?"

She didn't even let me get out of the water as she walked in to meet me, phone extended. Reed, Page, and I huddled around it as I shaded the screen with one hand against the sun until I could see the headline: "Mystery Man meets with Rock Star about Murder." There was a picture of me at the after-party last night, leaning in close to Lizzy Saint so I could hear her. It looked cozier than I'd like.

"Did you really meet her, Uncle Nate?" said Reed.

"I really did."

"Here." Reed hit the button and a fifteen-second loop of video played with me leaning in, nodding and smiling, as Lizzy spoke. Below was the text:

> *Rising star Lizzy Saint was seen with the new lawyer who will be defending her former sound engineer, Hank Braggi, in his upcoming murder trial. Mr. Braggi is accused of killing Dillon Chase in Ms. Saint's hotel suite last spring.*
>
> *EB has learned that the mysterious new attorney is Nate Shepherd of Carrefour, Michigan. After lead attorney Christian Dane died last week, Mr. Shepherd stepped in to take over Mr. Braggi's defense. He appar-*

*ently lost no time in snuggling up to one of the prosecution's chief witnesses and purported source of the fatal dispute, Lizzy Saint. This reporter watched Mr. Shepherd operate at close quarters to Ms. Saint in the late evening hours after a concert this weekend in North Carolina. Ms. Saint certainly did not seem to mind.*

*When asked for comment on Ms. Saint's involvement in the upcoming murder trial, record label attorney Max Simpson stated that Ms. Saint cannot comment on the pending trial but that she will cooperate with authorities at every stage of the process, as she has all along.*

*Mr. Shepherd is a relatively new player in all of this but described himself as knowing some of the same people as Ms. Saint. That's a circle we'd all like to run in! We'll update you with everything we find out about this mysterious charmer.*

The byline at the bottom said the story was filed by Maggie White, Entertainment Buzz Reporter. I expanded her picture with my thumb and forefinger.

It was the blond woman from the after-party. She'd talked to me, run with my evasive quote, then taken video during my meeting with Lizzy. "Shit."

"That's ten, Uncle Nate!" said Page, clapping.

Their dad was a football coach. His discipline methods were predictable. I got out of the water and started my ten push-ups. "When did that post, Reed?"

"This morning," said Reed.

"7, 8, 9, 10," said Page. She clapped.

"Did you go to her concert too?" said Reed.

I stood and brushed the sand from my hands. "I did."

Reed's eyes got big. "How was it?"

"Loud."

Reed giggled. "You're so old, Uncle Nate."

"But pretty great. The woman can sing."

"Did she sing 'Rainbow Bridge?'"

"It was the encore."

"With the *a cappella* part?"

"You got it."

Reed couldn't take her eyes off her phone. "What was she like?"

I thought for a minute. "Strong. Charming. A little wild."

"Was she nice though?" said Page.

"She was. To me anyway."

"Why would anyone want to hurt her?"

"What do you mean?"

"Isn't that why the man you represent killed that person? Because he was trying to hurt her?"

I hope the jury saw things like my youngest niece. "Yes."

"Why would somebody do that?"

"Sometimes we're wrong about people. We think they're our friends but really they're doing something that hurts us."

"Like with Aunt Sarah?" said Page.

"Page!" said Reed. Her eyes were big as she looked up at me. "I'm so sorry, Uncle Nate."

"Don't be, honey." I crouched down and took Page's hand. "Especially like Aunt Sarah. And if you're ever not sure if someone is your friend or if you're not sure if something's going to hurt you, you come to me or your mom or your dad or to Pops or to Grandma. Okay? We'll help you figure it out."

Page's eyes were welling up. "I'm sorry, Uncle Nate. Mom told us not to talk about it with you. I forgot."

"Don't worry, Page. Aunt Sarah would want you to ask me questions. And I do too. Come here." I gave them both a quick hug and a kiss on top of the head. "Now go tell Grandma that

Pops will be back in an hour and I'll put away this paddle board."

Reed and Page hesitated for just a second before they ran through the yard games up to the cottage to find Grandma. Tom tossed a bocce ball in the air and said, "C'mon, Nate. Izzy and Kate are getting cocky."

"Is it cocky if you win every time?" said Izzy to Kate.

"I just think it's truthful," said Kate.

"Coming," I said and turned away. I grabbed the paddle board but it slipped and I dropped it, splashing lake water up onto my face.

Which was just as well because I had realized that I hadn't said my wife's name out loud in a very long time.

## 19

I was on my way to the office Monday morning when my phone buzzed. Olivia. "Hey, Liv."

"I've got some hints, Nate, but still no answers.

"Shoot."

"Aaron Whitsel's records still check out. He's a full-time grad MBA student at the University, he's a decent student, and he's spent his last two summers interning at major finance companies in Chicago and Detroit. Where he lives and what he drives matches up with what he made in the summers. Wardrobe and car are a little pricey, but he was working at pretty big companies and his student loan balance makes up the difference."

"Loan balance high?"

"Of course, but everyone's is now. Nothing unusual there."

"Okay. Any more on Purcell?"

"Blake Purcell is murkier."

"How so?"

"Remember how I told you that he dropped out of school after a couple of years but has been living the same life on his own near the University?"

"You did. We guessed that maybe his parents were still footing the bill."

"Right. They're not. He was always on scholarship, part academic, part soccer. His parents live in Indiana and his dad works at an ethanol plant whose production keeps fluctuating. Mom's in and out of part-time work. Doing okay but sure doesn't seem like enough left over to keep a separate residence going for a kid."

"Does he work?"

"Not that I can see."

"Expenditures?"

"High priced car and condo. No student loans to fund it and no job. Nothing flashy but the expenditures seem higher than what's coming in."

"Turn up any dealing indicators?"

"Nothing major. If he is receiving a lot of money, he's being smart right now about doling it out slowly; nothing to attract attention unless you really had a reason to dig in."

"Which we do. And?"

"I have a theory."

"Which is?"

"Blake was the supplier and Dillon provided the access."

"I thought Dillon was the supplier?"

"I did too, at first. But think about it—Dillon travels all over the country with these tours. He doesn't bring everything the stars need with him and he's certainly not going to risk carrying something like heroin with him everywhere. What makes more sense is that he has contacts in different cities for whatever the tour needs and uses each one when he needs them. His phone is his trade. So the star says what he wants, Dillon makes a call, and Purcell appears."

"Hmm. Good thought. Keep digging. If Blake takes the stand, I'm going to need all the ammo I can get."

"Nate, this isn't the kind of ammo you can just walk into court and shoot."

"Got it, Liv. But I need to be ready just in case."

"The people Blake's dealing with aren't gonna want the publicity."

"Isn't that more dangerous for Blake than me?"

"It should be. But..."

"I'll only use what's necessary. Great work. Send me a bill for what you've done so far."

"It's more fun to have you owe me."

"I've got deep pockets right now. Take advantage of it."

"True. I'll have the rest of these reports ready when you come to the gym."

"Great. Thanks."

"Sure. I'll talk to you...Oh, I almost forgot. Heard any good songs lately?"

"Go to hell, Brickson."

"I've been listening to 'Give Me the Whole Thing.'"

"All the way to hell."

"Although I do like 'Roll Me One as You Roll on Out.'"

"I don't think you'll need a navigation system to find it."

"Personally, I like to get close to the speakers when I listen."

"Just follow the path you're on."

"Really close. But then again, I'm not a mysterious lawyer."

"Fuck off, Liv."

"Rock on, Nate."

We both hung up. It wasn't a lot but it was something. Hopefully, by the time we went to trial, I'd have something we could use.

∾

Cyn was already at work in the conference room when I arrived. She glanced up at me and went back to typing. "Why would you talk to a reporter?"

"Good morning, Cyn. My flight was fine, thanks. Thanks for making the arrangements." I picked up a mug and went to the coffee machine.

Cyn stopped typing, looked at me, and folded her hands on the table.

I poured. "I didn't know she was a reporter."

She went back to typing. "Enjoy the party?"

"That's where Lizzy wanted to meet."

"Lizzy is it?"

"That's what she preferred."

"So you got close?"

"No."

"That's not what it looked like in the picture."

"It was hard to hear."

Cyn sighed. "There's a certain amount of attention that goes with a case like this. Try not to make it worse."

"Will do. And I accept your apology too."

Cyn raised one dangerous eyebrow.

"For sending me to North Carolina and putting me in such a terrible position. I know you didn't mean it."

Cyn ignored me.

I walked around the conference table to the ever-present stacks of papers and files. "Anything important happen over the weekend?"

She glanced significantly at the picture from Entertainment Buzz that was conveniently loaded on her tablet.

"Besides that," I said.

"Daniel prepared the preliminary jury instructions. He emailed you a set to review. I sent you a follow-up with notes on which ones need attention."

It was my turn to raise an eyebrow at her.

"Based on what Christian used in our last two murder trials. Olivia wants to talk to you about the results of her investigation into Mr. Purcell and Mr. Whitsel."

"She caught me on the way in."

"Good. And Lindsey worked on categorizing the physical findings."

"Such as?"

"She's putting together a diagram of the broken bones. She figures we're going to see one at trial."

I nodded. "That's what I would do if I were them."

"Finally, the prosecutor is filing a motion today to sanction you for tampering with a witness."

My stomach did a little flip at the word sanction before I thought it through. "He talked to Lizzy Saint too."

"Exactly. So I took the liberty of having Daniel draft a memo opposing the prosecutor's motion and filing a cross-motion to sanction him for the same conduct."

"Oppose it by mucking it up?"

"I don't see the pursuit of equal and proportionate justice as mucking it up, Nathan."

"Of course not. Anything else need my attention?"

"Not before noon."

"Good. Let me catch up and we'll all meet here in the conference room then. You want to order everyone some lunch?"

Cyn stared at me.

"I meant to say do you like deli sandwiches or pizza?"

"Sandwiches."

"Excellent." I nodded, went to my office, and set to work digging out from under the electronic shit that had piled up in my absence.

CYN, LINDSEY, AND DANNY WERE ALL WAITING WHEN I ARRIVED
with the sandwiches.

"Which one's the egg salad?" said Danny.

"No one that I'm associated with would order such an abom-
ination."

Danny grinned. "Don't worry, I'll 'Roll on Out' as soon as I'm
done."

Lindsey shook her head and took a turkey club. "If you do,
make sure you 'Roll Him One First.'"

Cyn sat straight in her chair, unfolding her sandwich
wrapper with precise motions. "I'm sure he'll 'Give You the
Whole Business,' Daniel."

Lindsey snorted. "The Whole Thing, Cyn," she said before
taking a huge bite.

Cyn folded her wrapper into a placemat. "Yes, of course.
He'll 'Give You the Whole Thing.'"

I opened my own sandwich. "If you three fail as attorneys,
I'm sure it won't take you long to fail as comedians."

Lindsey pointed at Danny over her sandwich. "See, Danny,
don't forget where you came from. You start staying out all night
with rock stars and spending all your energy on being mysterious, and pretty soon you get cranky and tired and can't even
interact unless you have the adrenaline rush of the paparazzi."

"You done?" I said.

"I don't know," said Lindsey. "Has Entertainment Buzz
posted anything else yet today, Danny?"

Danny made a show of scrolling through his phone. "No. But
it's not rock 'n roll o'clock yet, is it?"

"That was a real *Ripper*, Daniel," said Cyn.

"Is that his name?" I said. "I'd forgotten, Sandy, thank you."

There were a couple of more comments about bosses jetting
to all-night parties while real lawyers worked before I said,
"Okay, Cyn, where are we?"

"Since your weekend cost the most, why don't you fill us in on what you found out first."

I told the group about how Lizzy claimed she didn't remember anything and about Jared Smoke's general antagonism. I also let them know that Max Simpson had cut off any further contact with Lizzy but that he confirmed that she wouldn't testify to anything that wasn't in the report.

"Honestly, I think we are better off with that," said Lindsey.

"Why?

"I spent the weekend making an illustration of all of Dillon Chase's broken bones."

"Cyn mentioned that."

"The last thing we want is a witness who saw it happen."

"Yeah?"

"Yeah. We're going to get it stuck up our ass with diagrams and photos. We're going to hear about what a painful way this would be to die. If we have a witness give us the individual blow-by-blow of screams and cracks and pops too, we're screwed."

"Dying from heroin addiction isn't too pleasant either."

"No, but we aren't going to be able to prove that would have happened."

"I think we might."

"How?"

"I've got an idea about a toxicologist. I'll let you know if it pans out."

"So I put together the injury chart."

"And?"

"This is one of the most brutal killings I've ever seen."

I sighed. "I'm hearing that a lot."

"I mean it, Nate. I think a traditional self-defense argument gets him fried."

"Ohio doesn't fry people anymore, Lindsey."

"Fried, injection, what's the difference?"

"I imagine a pretty significant one."

"Nate, no jury is going to excuse what he did."

"We're not looking for an excuse, we're looking for a justi-fication."

"Is there a difference?"

I sighed again. "Not a significant one."

"Invaders crest the final hill, and drop their lance on me, I rise and fight, the last to stand, futile though it be."

We all stared at Danny.

He shook his head, and looked down, embarrassed to be the center of attention.

"What was that?" I said.

He half-smiled and didn't meet our eyes. "It's from *Ripper*. 'Last Stand.' It seemed appropriate."

I thought. "I don't remember that from the concert."

"What about 'stand and fight, stand and fight, stand and fight and bleed?'"

"That I remember," I said. "That's one of Hank's songs then?"

Danny nodded. "Third hit off the album, I think."

"Getting back to the *murder* trial?" said Lindsey. "I was saying it's going to be hard to explain these injuries?"

"Right," I said. "Danny, I want you to work on a motion *in limine*. There's no basis for the prosecution to say that Lizzy remembers anything from that night and they should be excluded from speculating or citing hearsay reports unless she appears at trial. And no conjecture about what she might have witnessed when she was half-conscious."

"Got it."

"I'll be back in a couple of hours."

"Where are you going?" said Lindsey.

"To talk to Hank. You're coming with me. We're going to talk to him about Lizzy and Smoke. And about breaking a man to pieces."

## 20

---

Cade Brickson answered the door and I swear that every time I saw him, I was surprised again at just how big he was. He waved us in and said, "He's out back."

"Outside the house?" said Lindsey.

"He's allowed in the yard. You going to talk about the case?"

I nodded.

"I'll stay in here then." Cade sat down at a table and started tapping on a laptop.

We made our way through the common room and out the back door to Cade's deck where we came upon Hank in the act of spitting a chicken. Two chickens, actually, which looked to be in the final stages of being trussed and mounted. Hank's hair was a little wilder and his skin a little tanner, as if he'd been spending a good part of his days outside. His blue eyes gleamed when he saw us. "I don't suppose you snuck some beer in for me in that file folder of yours."

"Sorry, Hank," I said. "That would violate the terms of your release."

"*If* they learned about it."

"And put you back in a cell," said Lindsey.

Hank sighed and stared at the sun for a moment. "Can't have that I guess."

I pointed. "Expecting company?"

Hank blinked. "What do you mean?"

"The chickens."

He cocked his head. "Dinner. One for me, one for Cade."

"Of course."

"Here, let me just get this on." Hank finished tying off the legs of the last bird then set the spit on Cade's gas grill that had been adapted to cook rotisserie style. "There we go, not as good as an oak flame but not bad."

Hank took a seat at Cade's patio table and motioned for us to join him. As we sat, I said, "How've you been?"

"Counting the days until this is over, Counselor. How many days 'til trial?"

"Fourteen."

"The trial will take a week?"

"More or less."

"So only three more weeks." He drummed his fingers. "I suppose I can handle that."

Lindsey shook her head. "Mr. Braggi, you could be looking at considerably longer than three weeks."

"See, that's the thing," said Hank. "You offset those long legs of yours with a downright somber disposition. It's unbecoming."

"I'm not worried about me being becoming. I'm worried about where you're going."

"It's always work with you two." Hank's eyes glittered. "Fine. What's happening with the defense?"

"I saw Lizzy last weekend," I said.

Hank leaned forward. "Did you go to the concert?"

"I did."

"How did she sound?"

"Loud."

"And?"

"Fantastic."

Hank nodded. "She always does. Did she sing any of that new trash?"

"Off the latest album? Most of it."

Hank shook his head.

"You don't like it?" Lindsey said.

"Doesn't take advantage of her range. And the lyrics are for shit."

I shrugged. "I didn't go to see her sing, Hank."

"Then you're a fool, Counselor."

"I talked to her about what she saw. After."

Hank shook his head. "She didn't see anything."

"That's what she told me."

"She was unconscious at the time."

"That's what she told me too. And they whisked her away before I could ask how she met Dillon Chase that night."

Hank looked at me blankly.

"The man you killed."

Hank's eyes lit in recognition and then he shook his head. "I didn't see them meet either but that's not unusual. There's a whole team of people introducing her to folks after a concert."

"But how could they have gotten into her suite?"

"An invite from her, or management, or one of the band."

"You?"

Hank smiled. "I'm just the sound guy."

"And the lyricist."

He twitched his hands modestly. "Not anymore."

"I saw Smoke this weekend too."

"Sorry about your luck."

"You two get along?"

"As much as a man and an overaged, talentless shit-bird can get along."

"But how do you really feel?" said Lindsey.

Hank shrugged.

I nodded. "Smoke said he saw you kill Chase that night."

Hank snorted. "That shit-bird had left Lizzy alone with a drug-pushing cowardly motherfucker. He didn't see anything."

"So he wasn't in the room when you came in?"

"Nope."

"What about later?" said Lindsey.

Hank shrugged again. "He came in at some point."

"Do you know what you were doing when Smoke came back?"

"Beating the piss out of this Chase guy, I imagine."

"But do you remember *what* you were doing?"

Hank stared at her, blankly.

"Were you breaking his arms? His ribs?"

A blank look.

"Were you fracturing his skull the fourth, fifth, or sixth time?"

Hank smiled now as he looked at me. "So is that how you two divided the case up? You do the talking and she does the counting? Very efficient."

"It does seem like you were enraged, Hank," I said.

"I was certainly a good bit pissed."

"Furious?"

Hank gave a flowery gesture with one hand. "I ride on a storm of fury."

"Angry?"

He gestured with the other. "I roll on a tide of anger."

"Mad?"

An interesting thing happened then. Hank lowered his arms and went totally cold and the look he gave me now was calm and present and full of precise calculation. "I know what battle madness is, Counselor. But I'm not some sort of berserker and my mind wasn't clouded, at all, when I killed that shit-bird."

"What were you doing then?" said Lindsey.

"I was sending a message."

"To?"

"Anyone else who wants to mess with Lizzy."

"Don't you think it was excessive?"

"Have you seen anyone else try?"

"No," said Lindsey. "But she has more security now."

Hank smiled. "I'm sure that's the reason."

His comment about battle madness clicked for me. "Did you serve in the military, Hank?" I said.

Hank eyed me skeptically. "I don't see how that would matter."

"This could be helpful," I said. "When did you serve? What branch of the military were you in? Were you sent to the Middle East? We can use this to create an argument that you had post-traumatic stress or a flashback or you were reacting to some stimulus that goes back to—"

Hank raised a hand. " I knew exactly what I was doing and I did it to protect Lizzy."

It was hard to think of the cheerful man sitting across the table from me as the same person who'd broken Dillon Chase to bits. But he was. And the prosecutor had dozens of pictures to prove it.

I leaned forward. "Hank, saying you just wanted to protect her isn't going to be enough. You're only allowed to use as much force to protect another person as that person could use to protect themselves. And no one is going to believe that it was necessary to break every bone in Dillon Chase's body to stop him from 'messing with Lizzy.'"

"That's not all, Mr. Braggi," said Lindsey, tapping her finger on the table with each sentence. "The jury has to believe they would have done the same thing if they had been in your shoes and no one, not a single one, is going to believe that they would've done what you did. They're not going to believe that they're even *capable* of doing it. They're going to be repulsed and sickened, no matter what Chase tried to do to Lizzy, because there are pictures of what you did to Chase and there are only your words to describe what Chase was doing to Lizzy."

"So what're you saying?" Hank said to Lindsey.

"I'm saying you need to think about taking the prosecutor's plea deal."

Hank sat back, his eyes still glittering in amusement. "Well, I'm not."

"Then you might die."

"I might. And I might win."

We all sat there, staring at each other—Hank amused, Lindsey angry, and me trying to figure out how to get Hank out of this.

Hank drummed his fingers. "Tell you what, how about you two work on winning my case and I'll go back to occupying myself with writing lyrics and cooking chickens. Unless you want to stay and eat?"

"We need to get back." I extended a hand and Hank grinned and squeezed. His hand was calloused and rough and surprisingly strong. "We'll prepare with you this weekend."

"Will do, Counselor."

We showed ourselves out, waving good-bye to Cade on the way. As we walked down the driveway, I thought, then said, "Those lyrics Danny quoted earlier and Hank's comments on battle madness...I wonder if we have a PTSD angle? That what he saw with Lizzy set him off."

Lindsey cocked her head. "But post-traumatic stress from what?"

"It seemed like our client was a little hesitant when I asked him about military service. I wonder if there's something there."

Lindsey looked unconvinced. "That sounds like a long shot."

"Do you have another angle right now?"

Lindsey thought. "Tell Olivia I said 'hi.'"

I CALLED OLIVIA ON THE WAY BACK TO THE OFFICE AND PUT HER ON researching Hank's background. Then, when we returned, we went straight to the conference room where Cyn was still banging away on the computer. "Will your firm pay for a clinical evaluation?"

Cyn stopped, folded her long fingers, "For what?"

"PTSD."

The side of Cyn's mouth twitched. "From what?"

"I'm working on it. My question is, would your firm pay for an evaluation if I think it's necessary."

"It's a little late in the game for that, isn't it?"

"Will you pay for it?" I said to Cyn.

"I won't pay for anything," said Cyn.

I sighed. "Will your firm pay for it?"

"No change of strategy without running it past the home office."

"We're the feet on the ground, Cyn."

"The feet don't always have the best view, Nathan."

"I'm managing the defense."

"I understand that. We just want you to take input."

I thought and nodded. "I have no problem with input."

"Fine. The firm will pay for the exam."

"Don't you have to check?"

"No." She had the decency not to smirk.

I left her then and we all went back to our offices. I was

starting to work on witness examinations and that afternoon was dedicated to coroner Ray Gerchuck. As I dove into the autopsy findings and outlined my cross-examination, I couldn't find a way to avoid the brutality of the killing.

I hoped Olivia could find something to help us explain it.

## 21

THE NEXT MORNING I STEELED MYSELF TO DO SOMETHING I HAD been avoiding—it was time to go see Mitch Pearson.

Mitch Pearson was the Chief Detective of the Serious Crimes Division for the Carrefour, Ohio Police and yes, his card had all of those things capitalized. Carrefour was a good-sized city, but it really wasn't big enough to have a homicide division and a robbery division and a sexual assault division. Instead, it was divided into serious crimes, the general division, and computer crimes. Serious crimes were homicide, rape and sexual assault, and armed robbery. There were enough of those that one man could supervise the investigations and Pearson was that guy.

Pearson was a contemporary of mine. He'd worked his way up from beat cop to general detective to serious crimes to head of serious crimes in just over ten years. He was a serious cop, seriously talented, and a serious asshole.

Mitch Pearson had been an all-state quarterback at Carrefour South High School and I had been an all-county outside linebacker at Carrefour North. Our relationship really didn't require any more of an explanation than that. He had enjoyed lighting up our defense and I had enjoyed making him loopy from the blindside. Our senior year, he had his team up by two touchdowns in the fourth quarter when I knocked him unconscious and stripped the football away. Zach Stephenson had scooped it up and run it in for a touchdown to put us within seven. Mitch returned to the game—that was in the days before concussion protocols—but he wasn't right and I'm certain he doesn't even remember it. I hit him again, our free safety picked him off, and our offense made the two-point conversion to win the game. He had never forgiven me and I had never much cared.

Pearson had gone on to attend the University of Michigan and I had gone to Michigan State. That really didn't improve things. In the end, both of us had returned to Carrefour, him to start a career in law enforcement and me to start practicing law. We'd worked together for a time when I was in the prosecutor's office and things had actually settled down for a little while until we'd had a professional disagreement about one of his arrests. Shortly after, I'd gone on to a big firm, we didn't have much more contact with each other.

Until a year and a half ago. He'd been the chief investigator on an incident involving my family and I hadn't much cared for the way he had handled it. Fortunately, I guess, he had declined to press charges.

Since Chase had been killed on the Ohio side, Pearson was in charge of the investigation in Hank's case. By talking to him today, I didn't expect to learn anything more about the killing itself but I was hopeful that he might have found out more details about Chase or Purcell or Whitsel. He didn't have to talk to me but I thought he would, if only to lord it over me that he had information I wanted. So I drove the twenty-five minutes from Carrefour, Michigan over the imaginary line to the police headquarters of Carrefour, Ohio where I walked in to the office of Chief Detective in Charge of Serious Crimes, Mitch Pearson.

It had been all of eighteen months since I'd seen him and he really didn't look much different. He still looked like a quarterback—tall, square-jawed, and a little too pretty to really respect. He was never muscular, but he was still lean as a whip and looked like he could run a marathon and bike a hundred miles, which really wasn't a coincidence if the Iron Man medal hanging prominently on his wall was to be believed. He smiled when I entered, stood up from his desk, and acted like he was glad to see me. "Shepherd, heard you were on the Braggi case. Wondered if you would be man enough to see me."

"No one's that big a man, Pearson." He squeezed my hand. It was stupid. "How've you been?"

"Never better," he said. "Crime's down and I've actually had time to coach my kids' baseball teams. Actually two baseball teams and one T-ball team. Seems like I'm at a game every damn night, but Julia keeps it all organized for me. We're running all over every damn place but she lets me know where to go and I just show up and coach. Did you know you actually have to bring treats now every time you have a practice?"

"I did not."

"Juice or oranges or rice crispy treats or some damn thing every damn practice. Don't think I'd even be able to coach if it weren't for Julia. I'd be too busy shopping all the damn time for these kids."

"True enough."

"How about you? You have kids?"

He knew the answer but I told him anyway. "No."

"You're lucky, believe me. Never a moment of quiet from six in the morning to eleven at night. Have to come in to the office on Saturday morning sometimes just to hear myself think. If there are no games of course." He sighed. Loud. "Still, I wouldn't trade it for anything." He pointed to a picture on the desk which was facing outward so that a visitor could see it as opposed to facing him where he could. "That's them there."

I leaned forward a little bit and took a quick glance at one of those overly posed pictures on a beach. You know the type—all of them were in matching shirts, barefoot in the sand with the ocean behind them. Tall, square-jawed police officer, tall blonde wife, and three towheaded kids with their hair neatly combed for maximum beatification. I nodded. "Good looking kids."

"All Julia," he said in a voice that almost meant it. "She has a sister down in the Outer Banks so we try to get down there every summer." He gave me a stare and a grin. "Usually have a big family reunion there at that beach house, right on the ocean. Kids love it."

"I bet."

"That's what I say! Gotta get these kids out of the house, away from those video game consoles and into the outside air! Am I right?"

"You are."

"So," he said with a smile that didn't reach his eyes. "How about you? No kids, so what fills your time?"

"Work mostly," I said.

"Work, right, I assume that's why you're here. Still, you have to make sure you make time for family." He stared at me. "If you don't have that, you don't have anything."

I knew how he meant it but that didn't mean it wasn't true. "True. Mind if I ask you a couple of things about the Dillon Chase case?"

"Sure. I won't necessarily be able to answer but..." He waved one large hand to proceed.

"Were you with the first responders the night of the killing?"

Pearson nodded. "Came in with the ambulance." He shook his head. "We didn't need an ambulance. We needed a cleanup crew."

"Turns out you did need the ambulance though, didn't you?"

Pearson gave me a gritted-teeth grin. "Nobody was reviving Chase after the beating your man put on him."

"No, not for Chase. For Lizzy Saint."

"Oh, yeah, right. For her. Sure."

"Was she conscious when you got there?"

"In and out." Pearson had a look of distaste on his face. "She was pretty drunk." He shook his head. "Such a waste."

"How so?"

"All that talent. Pissing it away on booze and drugs." He stared at me as he said it.

I kept my face neutral and said, "Did you find any drugs?"

He nodded. "I did."

"Heroin?"

Pearson nodded again. "A bag, paraphernalia, the works."

"Did you find a needle?"

"Yep."

"Was it full or empty?"

Pearson thought for a moment. "I don't remember."

Liar. I nodded and said, "You did an inventory of the scene contents, though?"

"Always."

I'd find the information I wanted there then. Pearson just wasn't going to gift-wrap it for me. "Did you find my client there?" I asked.

"Sure did. Covered in Dillon Chase's brains and blood."

"How was he acting?"

"Like a stone-cold killer."

"How so?"

"The woman's boyfriend, Smoke, was sitting on the bed with Ms. Saint. The paramedics were working on her and on the scraps of the victim. And your man was just sitting in a chair, hands on knees, staring at the woman as calm as you please."

Pearson shook his head in disgust that may or may not have been real. "He was covered in blood, you know."

"You mentioned that."

"Yeah. It was impossible not to be. It was spattered everywhere. His hands, his forearms, his face. Blood on everything. It was as bad a beating death as I've ever seen. Looked like he'd used a couple of sledgehammers. But it was his fists."

"Did my client try to flee the scene?"

"What?" The question looked like it surprised him.

"Was my client there when you arrived?"

"Yes."

"Any indication that he had tried to leave?"

"He wasn't leaving once we got there. We cuffed him right away."

"I understand. But before you got there—any evidence he tried to leave?"

Pearson shrugged. "I don't know what he did before I got there. All I know is that the killer was in the room when I arrived."

"And he didn't resist?"

"Not me. I understand he hassled the paramedics until they started treating Ms. Saint first. Didn't want them treating the victim. Although in fairness, he probably knew that Chase was already deader than shit."

"So Braggi was there and Smoke and Saint?"

"Yes."

"What about Purcell and Whitsel?"

"What about them?"

"Were they there when you arrived?"

"No."

"So they fled?"

"I don't know that."

"They didn't stay to talk to you?"

Pearson's eyes hardened and his grin broadened. "I imagine they fled a brutal killing. Probably thought they were next."

"How did you find the two boys then?"

"Detective work."

I stared at him.

He shrugged. "We got their names from the road manager who'd given them passes. It didn't take much to track them down."

"That night?"

"Next day."

"Have you done any background on them?"

Pearson shook his head. "I solve crimes, Shepherd. This one took about five seconds."

"Did you take statements?"

Pearson nodded. "You should read the file."

"I have. I mean, did you take them personally?"

"If I signed it, I took it."

"Were they charged with anything?"

Pearson laughed. "Like what? Unlawful blood tracking? First-degree pants-shitting?"

"Drug possession."

Pearson's eyes narrowed. "Why would they be charged with that?"

"They had drugs there, didn't they?"

"I don't know who had drugs there."

"But you found drugs there. It was in the inventory?"

"If it was in the inventory, then there were drugs there."

"So whose were they?"

Pearson's grin disappeared and he leaned forward. "I had a dead body, Shepherd. I didn't give a shit whose drugs they were."

"And if Chase was giving drugs to Lizzy Saint against her will, that would be a crime, right?"

"I'm not like you, Shepherd. I don't travel in rock 'n' roll circles. And I don't give a shit if some rock star is getting drunk and shooting up in her hotel room. What I give a shit about is a man getting beaten into a broken heap of bones."

"But if Chase was injecting her—"

"If Chase was injecting her, it was just one more junkie getting a fix. And who gives a shit about that?"

Pearson extended that lantern jaw of his as he said it, and, unlike the last time, I sat there and took it. Then, I stood. "How do you think the Lions will be this year?" I said.

The jaw stayed out. "I'm more of a Browns fan."

"Of course you are." I extended my hand. "Thanks for the time."

He shook it again and tried that stupid squeeze. I smiled and let him try. "Did you see that new CTE study?" I said.

He raised an eyebrow. "No."

"It said concussions can cause dementia and all sorts of shit. Interesting read. See you."

"Looking forward to it," said Pearson.

I was sure he was. Mitch Pearson, Chief Detective in Charge of Serious Crimes was going to do everything he could to bury me at trial.

## 22

---

When I arrived at the office, they were all standing there —Danny, Cyn, and Lindsey—lined up in a neat row, staring at me. "What's this, the tardy police?" I said.

"Where have you been?" said Cyn.

"Checking with Pearson to see if the police had investigated Purcell and Whitsel. This'll shock you: they didn't. Didn't charge anyone with drug possession either. On the bright side, he confirmed that, in his expert opinion, our client is a stone-cold killer who committed murder. So yes, I had a productive morning, thank you. And you?"

"Something's come up," said Cyn. Cyn never had a bubbly personality but even she seemed subdued as she surveyed me carefully. Lindsey and Danny were giving off a completely different vibe, like they were nervous. And they couldn't take their eyes off me.

"Jesus, guys," I felt around on my forehead. "Did I grow a third eye or something?"

"Have you been online yet today?" said Lindsey.

"No, and that doesn't make me feel any better about it."

"Come here," said Cyn and led me into the conference room. She indicated the chair. I raised an eyebrow. She slid her tablet over to the empty seat. I came around the table and looked.

The top of the screen had the Entertainment Buzz logo. Right below that was a huge headline:

*Mystery Lawyer's Tragic Heroin Connection*

I sat down.

The byline showed me that the story had been written by Maggie White, the blonde reporter who I'd met at Lizzy Saint's party. I read:

 *Nate Shepherd is the little-known local defense lawyer who's been thrust into the national spotlight in the Hank Braggi murder trial involving Lizzy Saint. Although the trial is still a week away, police reports indicate that Hank Braggi will claim that the killing was justified because the victim, Dillon Chase, was attempting to inject Lizzy Saint with heroin when Hank Braggi fatally stopped him.*

*Mr. Shepherd has his own tragic connection to heroin.*

I felt three sets of eyes on me. I kept my face straight and read on.

 *Eighteen months ago, Mr. Shepherd lost his wife Sarah to an accidental heroin overdose. She was one of five people who died in a single night in the city of Carrefour, a tragedy which local news called "Black Tuesday." According to local police reports, a batch of*

*heroin was distributed that day which was cut with fentanyl, causing the mass overdose which cost Mrs. Shepherd her life.*

*As we've reported, the Hank Braggi/Lizzy Saint murder case is tied to heroin since Mr. Braggi is claiming that he was defending Ms. Saint from receiving a dose while she was unconscious. Although his own story is not directly relevant to the defense, it certainly casts Mr. Shepherd's role as Mr. Braggi's new attorney in a different light. Our legal expert will analyze whether Mr. Shepherd can be objective enough to represent Mr. Braggi effectively. Our psychological expert will analyze whether Mr. Shepherd harbors anger toward Ms. Saint that is a projection of his own anger towards his wife. And we'll delve into the thing on everyone's mind – how did this courtroom-heart-throb ever wind up marrying a junkie?*

*We'll bring you the answers to all these questions and more. Stay tuned for Entertainment Buzz coverage of the Saint murder trial which is set to start next week.*

I took a quick glance at the story links below the article and saw that there was nothing other than the original article putting me at Lizzy Saint's party and another one about Christian Dane's death.

I looked up. "Okay. What's the problem?"

Danny and Lindsey's expressions changed from nervousness to confusion while Cyn transitioned from caution to cool assessment. Danny spoke first, which wasn't a surprise since he had been with me through all of it. "Nate, it's just that they mentioned..." He trailed off.

"Sarah, I know. I wish they hadn't."

"What are we going to do about it?"

"Nothing. It's all true. I suppose the part about me projecting is conjecture but no judge is going to prevent them from doing that." I stood up. "Was that it?"

Lindsey stared. "That's it."

"I'm going to need to call Sarah's parents. I'll probably be downstairs the rest of the morning and then I'll come up and we'll talk about the cross of the prosecution's case."

Danny looked confused. Lindsey stared. Cyn nodded and went back to work.

I went down to my office on the second floor and closed the door because I didn't want any of them to see me right then. And I don't want you to either.

EVENTUALLY, I CALLED SARAH'S PARENTS. "JAN? IT'S NATE."

"Nathan? Why are you calling in the middle of the day? Is everything okay?"

Jan's voice had always had a tremble to it. There was more now than there used to be.

"No, I'm fine. Nothing is wrong. Well, sort of. Something's come up in one of my cases that I wanted to warn you about."

"What is it?"

I told her about the report. And I told her that they were bringing up Sarah.

Silence at the other end of the line. And then, "I see. Is there anything that can be done about it?"

"Not really. I'm sorry, Jan, but I'm afraid there are going to be more."

"What do you mean?"

"I mean if this story generates interest, there are going to be more of them." There was no point in explaining clicks.

"And I'm afraid that with the type of case it is, there will be."

Silence again. "Kevin's not doing well, you know."

"No?"

"He won't eat. He's working all the time, taking doubles whenever he can."

"I'm sorry."

"It's going to be in the headlines again, isn't it? All about Sarah and heroin."

"Maybe." That was a lie. "Probably."

"Nothing about her volleyball. Nothing about the triathlons. Nothing about what a sweet girl she was. Just heroin."

It was cruel, just like the drug. "Yes. I'm sorry, Jan."

The warm tone when she'd answered the phone went cool. "I'll keep Kevin away from the computer for a while which shouldn't be too hard. Thanks for telling me."

I started to say goodbye when she said, "Is this ever going to end, Nate?"

"The trial should be over in a couple of weeks, Jan."

"That's not what I meant."

I feared she was right so I didn't say anything.

"All right. Thanks for calling, Nate. Good-bye."

I had just hung up when my phone buzzed again. It was my sister-in-law, Izzy.

I declined the call.

A text popped up immediately. *Pick up the phone asshole.*

I texted back. *Sorry. Working.*

*We need to talk.*

*I saw it.*

*You okay?*

*Yes. Just can't talk now.*

*Fucking assholes.*

*Yes. Thanks.*

Izzy's texts were interrupted by a call from my older brother Tom. I declined it. I knew he wouldn't text since he'd never been able to get his sausage thumbs to do it. As soon as I turfed his call, the phone buzzed again. My mom. I swore. She'd be worried. I had to take it.

"Hi, Mom."

"Nate, are you okay?"

Moms.

"I'm fine, Mom. Don't worry."

"How can they print such a thing? Can you sue them?"

"No, Mom. It's mostly true."

"But they make it sound so awful."

That's because it was awful. Just not in the way they described. "I know, Mom."

"Jan must be beside herself."

"I called her and warned her but there's not much else that can be done."

"But it's just so—"

"Mom, I'm sorry, but I have to go. I have a meeting."

"Oh, of course, I'm sorry. It just makes me so mad!"

"Me too."

"Will you be coming Sunday?"

"Sorry, not until the trial's over."

"Make sure you get enough sleep."

"I will."

"And make sure you eat something besides eggs."

"Don't worry, Mom."

"And don't let them ruin your thoughts about Sarah."

"They can't. I love you, Mom. I'll talk to you later."

"Good-bye, honey."

We hung up and I immediately texted Izzy. *Will you do me a favor and run interference with fam? I saw the article, they're all assholes, and I'm fine.*

I got a smiley face and a *Done* in response, followed a moment later by *and kick some ass while you're at it.*

*Will do. Thanks.*

I got a gif of Jack Nicholson blowing me a kiss in response.

I went to go back upstairs when my phone buzzed again. "Jesus Christ!" I said as I checked the number. Olivia Brickson. This one I was happy to take.

"Liv," I said. "What do you have for me?"

"A heavy bag, a jump rope, and a brother who's willing to spar with you until you drop."

I smiled. "I'm fine, Liv."

"Bullshit. Nobody's fine with a story like that."

"I'm not fine with the story. I can handle it being published."

There was silence on the other end of the line for a moment before she said, "Don't you go deep-ending on me. Get your ass down here if you need to."

"I'm too busy with this trial for anything else. I'll be pissed later."

"Promise?"

"Promise. Now, what do you have for me on Hank?"

"You know you could have saved me a shit-ton of time?"

"What? How?"

"Why didn't you tell me your client was Norwegian?"

There was a simple answer for that. "Because I didn't know."

"Do you talk to your clients?"

"Not about the right things apparently. How'd you find out?"

"I spent hours mucking around in the usual places looking for social security numbers and birth certificates before I found the records from when he became a U.S. citizen three years ago."

"So he's from Norway?" I asked.

"By way of Minnesota. Any guesses what firm handled his naturalization application?"

"Friedlander & Skald, right?"

"Right. Looks like he entered the country from Norway about six years ago, got a work permit, and eventually started working for Lizzy Saint and earning a shit-ton of money off song royalties."

"A lot?"

"Mountains."

I reconciled rich mogul with the rough, merry guy spitting chickens on Cade Brickson's grill. "Huh."

"Eloquent summary."

"So, Norwegian and lyricist. Doesn't seem like a recipe for PTSD."

"It's not," said Olivia. "But the Home Guard might be."

"What's the Home Guard?"

"I'm not sure. I found it right before I called. It's some sort of quasi-military unit in Norway. There was an article about it training in Minnesota. My guess is that's how Braggi found his way over here."

"Can you research it for me?"

"I could, but I have a faster way."

"What's that?"

"Get off your ass and ask your client."

Some comments, although rude, are totally fair. "Right. Anything else?"

"Nothing new. Still checking on Chase, Purcell, and Whitsel."

"Keep digging. We need anything you can find."

"I know and I will." There was a pause on the other end. "You're really okay? With the story?"

"The worst has already happened, Liv. The rest is just a reminder."

"I'm not kidding, Nate. Call me if you need to."

"I know, Liv. And thanks. And thank Cade for the offer too."

"No reason to thank him. He enjoys kicking your ass."

"Talk to you soon." We hung up. I felt bad about not knowing that Hank was from Norway but, when I thought about it, there was no reason I would. The Home Guard though, the Home Guard at least sounded like it might get me where I wanted to go with Hank's defense so I followed Olivia's advice.

I went back to see Hank.

## 23

"Two days in a row, Counselor?" said Hank. "I feel so loved."

Cade had shown me to the back deck where Hank was once again sitting in the sun. This time, he was shucking a dozen ears of corn.

"You having company tonight?"

Hank raised an eyebrow. "Just me and Cade."

"A dozen?"

"We didn't have this growing up. Not sweet like this anyway." He closed his eyes and sniffed. "Gotta enjoy it when you can."

"Why didn't you tell me you were from Norway, Hank?"

Hank raised an eyebrow. "It's no secret. Cyn knows, I assumed you did too."

I filed that one away.

"Does it matter?" he said.

"It might. Tell me about the Home Guard."

If you've ever played poker, you know what I mean when I say that Hank's face became studiedly casual, as if the ear of corn in front of him occupied all of his attention and the conversation I was having with him was a distraction from the all-important act of shucking. "What about it?" he said.

"Did you serve in it?"

"I did."

"What is it?"

Hank looked at me. "Do you really not know? Or are you testing me again?"

"I really don't know."

Hank shrugged and kept shucking. He appeared to think, then said, "Norway and Russia share a northern border. The Home Guard is Norway's first line of defense."

"So, you're like border guards?"

Hank looked at me then and I got a glimpse, just a small one, of what Dillon Chase might have seen. "No," he said.

I raised a hand. "I'm sorry. Tell me."

He shucked an ear clean before he continued. "Russia has men and arms and factories stacked along our border. We could never hope to match the Soviet military machine before or the Russian industrial complex now. So, instead of sinking all of our money into weapons that wouldn't be enough to repel the invasion, we have the Home Guard." He looked at me. "You really don't know this?"

I shook my head.

"The Home Guard is a force of forty thousand. Our job, if the Russians ever attacked, was to fight a guerrilla war. We were supposed to vanish into the woods and mountains then use our knowledge of the land to harass and slow and sabotage the Russians until the regular army, and NATO, could respond. Destroy bridges and roads, night raids, that sort of thing."

I thought. "Is that where you're from? The northern border with Russia?"

Hank nodded. "A small town near the Pasvik Valley. I spent my life in those woods and rivers."

"Even in winter?"

He smiled. "Especially in winter."

"How did you end up here?"

Hank raised an eyebrow, pointed at his ankle monitor, and smiled.

"I mean in the U.S.?" I said.

He brushed the last of the hair off an ear of corn and set it on top of a growing pyramid. "There are a bunch of Norwegians in Minnesota so the Home Guard trains with the Minnesota National Guard; every year they send a group of their National Guard to Norway to train with us and we send a group of the Home Guard to Minnesota to train with them. Been doing it since the '70s."

"I'm surprised I've never heard of this."

Hank shrugged. "If you're not Norwegian or a Minnesotan, there's no reason you would. Anyway, I was sent to Minnesota to train some years ago. One night at the end of our stint, we went out in Minneapolis and the bands we heard blew me away. You wouldn't even know who any of them were and they were just killing it. And I knew I had to get back here."

He stripped the last husk off the last ear and topped his corn on the cob pyramid. He smacked his hands together to rid himself of the last of the corn silk, then slapped his legs. "I finished my stint with the Guard, immigrated to Minneapolis, and started my life in music. And six years later, here I am."

I realized something. "You don't have an accent."

He chuckled. "You've heard *Ripper*?"

"I have."

"I have a gift with words."

I decided to leave that for now and said, "Did you see any actual combat with the Home Guard?"

Hank smiled. "Have you heard of any armed conflict between Norway and Russia?"

"No."

"Then I guess you have your answer."

"What if there was an incursion I hadn't heard about?"

"I would guess, Counselor, that there would be a very good reason why you hadn't."

I decided to lay it out there. "Hank, if I can show that you have been in combat and that you had a PTSD reaction to what happened with Chase, it might help your defense."

"I don't have PTSD, Counselor. And the only reaction I had was anger at seeing what Chase was doing."

"And a desire to protect Lizzy."

"Of course."

I sighed. "You're not making this easy, Hank."

Hank smiled. "No fight ever is."

"I'd like to have you tested, just in case."

Hank's smiled. "Test away. But you're going to find that I'm surprisingly well-adjusted."

When I stared at him, silent, Hank leaned forward, elbows on knees. "It's pretty simple, Nate. What I did was right or it was wrong. Show them I was right."

"But if the jury thinks it was wrong?"

"We'll burn that bridge when we come to it." He sat up and waved at the pyramid of corn. "Wanna stay for dinner? Cade can pick up another dozen."

"I better get back to the office."

Hank grinned. "I feel more innocent already."

"I'll be back this weekend to prepare you."

"I'll be waiting."

I said good-bye to Hank, waved to Cade, and drove back to the office. As I went, I felt some optimism that Hank had actually been in the service but concern that it wasn't going to do me any good. Testing was going to have to be my next priority to see if we could find anything useful.

I was halfway back to the office when I remembered what Hank had said about who else knew about his past. When I returned to my office, I opened my tablet and found an email from Olivia with Hank's U.S. citizenship paperwork attached, including the application he'd filed after he'd arrived from Norway.

I took a look at the firm that had filed the paperwork for him and can't say that I was at all surprised. Then I went upstairs to confront Cyn.

# 24

---

LINDSEY WAS SITTING AT THE TABLE WITH CYN IN THE CONFERENCE room when I entered. Both looked up. "Could you excuse us for a moment, Lindsey?' I said.

Lindsey pursed her lips but didn't object. "Just make sure you check on the status of the autopsy blowups, okay?" she said to Cyn.

"Of course." Cyn flipped her red hair back from her brow as I followed Lindsey to the door and shut it behind her. Both of Cyn's eyebrows were raised as I took the seat across from her. She waited for me to speak. It was one of her most effective and most annoying traits.

"Just visited Hank."

"Good. And?"

"Why didn't you tell me he was from Norway?"

Cyn shrugged. "I thought you knew. And it doesn't impact whether he killed Dillon Chase."

"True. Your firm represented him in the naturalization process."

Cyn sighed. "Have you been to Minnesota, Nathan?"

"No."

"You can't swing a dead *katt* without hitting an immigrating Norwegian."

"Very funny. So you know how he first came here, to the U.S.?"

Not a twitch. "I don't do immigration work."

"No. But you know."

She was still before she said, "Yes."

"You know he was with the Home Guard."

"Yes."

"You know I've been looking for sources of PTSD with him."

Cyn shook her head. "I don't believe he wound up seeing combat."

"I'm not so sure."

"I'm sure if there had been a Russian incursion we'd have heard about it."

"Interesting. That's exactly what he said."

"So there you go."

I decided on another tack. "You've mentioned Hank's family a few times. Have you met them?"

Cyn sighed. "You know we have a trial coming up?"

"That doesn't answer my question."

"I'd love to work on it."

"Have you ever met Hank's father?"

"I don't see how that's relevant."

Again, that wasn't an answer. "I want to ask him if Hank ever saw combat."

"Hank already told you."

"Cyn. Answer my question."

Her eyes were still calm. "I don't appreciate being talked to like that."

"I don't appreciate it when people don't tell me the truth."

I got the first legitimate reaction I'd gotten out of Cyn that day. She straightened and her eyes burned. "I don't lie."

"I didn't say you did. I said you didn't tell me the truth. Have you met Hank's father?"

"Mr. Skald has for sure. I'm not sure about Mr. Friedlander."

"Cyn."

"I'm just a paralegal."

"And that also doesn't answer my question."

Cyn stared at me.

"Cyn, your firm helped him come to this country. You handled his citizenship. You're apparently in touch with his family. If all that's true, then you know what his problems are."

"Hank's problem is that he's accused of murder."

"So help me solve it."

"PTSD is not a solution they're interested in."

"They?"

"Hank. The firm."

"His family?"

Cyn didn't answer me. Instead, she said, "Have you thought about the cost of that victory?"

"What do you mean?"

"I mean PTSD, an insanity defense, the one where he's locked up with insane people until he dies."

"You mean the one where he doesn't die?"

Cyn shook her head. "Death lies at the end of the road either way. Hank should be able to choose the path."

"If he's competent."

"Is there really any doubt about that?"

"PTSD does funny things to people. Are you going to tell me about him or his family so I can check for myself?"

Cyn stared at me.

"Then I'm going to have him examined," I said.

"That's not what he wants."

"It doesn't matter what an incompetent person wants any more than it matters what a three-year-old wants. If his competency is interfering with his decisions, it's my job to act in his interests."

"He told you what his interests are."

"That's what he thinks his interests are. That doesn't mean it's true. I'm having him tested."

"And if he comes back normal?"

"We don't say 'normal' anymore. But if he does, I'll have to do what he says."

"Then get it done so we can stop wasting time."

I stood to leave but stopped. "You still haven't answered my question."

Cyn's eyes were green ice. "I've met his father. I know his stepmother better. They come back and forth from Norway all the time."

"Rich?"

"Very."

"Which is how Hank ended up with the best firm in Minneapolis?"

Cyn shrugged in a way that indicated my statement was narrow in geographic scope.

"Where are they now?" I said.

"Across the ocean. I doubt you can reach them. Better to focus the time you have on preparing the case."

I nodded and left.

LINDSEY WAS WAITING FOR ME IN THE GENERAL CONFERENCE AREA. "What's going on?" she said.

"Get your psychiatric evaluator over to Hank for testing," I said. "Today if you can. Tell her we need the results right away."

"Want to tell me what we're looking for?"

"Anything that would make him generally incompetent of

course but I think what we're really looking for are any signs of PTSD that could trigger a violent reaction."

"He change his mind on a plea?"

"No. But he's so close to it, he might not even realize he's reacting to the trauma."

Lindsey stared at me. "That's true."

"Let me know what you find out."

She nodded and we went to our respective desks. It was a small office so I heard her call and make the arrangements. Meanwhile, I stayed out of Cyn's way or she stayed out of mine and we worked the rest of the afternoon.

Later, Danny came into my office with a handful of papers. I looked up. "What have you got?"

"Do you have a copy of the autopsy?" he said.

I shuffled through the piles of paper on my desk that were organized by how recently I'd needed them—the longer it had been, the farther they got pushed away by the new piles. A revolutionary and authentic system. "Here you go. What's the issue?"

"I think I might be missing a couple of lines. It looks like the text got cut off when they copied it."

"What section?"

"External description of the face and head."

Danny held up two papers and looked back and forth. "It's the same on yours too."

"Compare it to the original from Lindsey's file. If it has the same issue, re-request it from the coroner's office."

"Okay. Look at the jury instructions yet?"

"Not yet. Will soon. Working on Smoke's cross-examination right now."

Danny hung in the doorway. That was always one of his issues, never being sure when a conversation was over. It was endearing when we weren't getting ready for trial. "I think that covers it, Danny."

My mind was back on Smoke's cross-examination before he left.

I WAS PRETTY TIRED WHEN I GOT HOME LATE THAT NIGHT. MY mind was preoccupied by Smoke's cross-examination as I went into the kitchen to scrounge up something to eat and came face-to-face with the hole in the wall.

The hole was the size of a fist. Its edges were ragged, with white drywall showing beneath the beige paint. A few cracks radiated out from the hole, traveling farther into the wall itself. By pure luck, the hole was between the studs with no wiring or piping behind it. Just pure empty space, a gap in the wood supports that opened like a mouth in the otherwise elegantly-designed kitchen. A mouth that screamed accusations of self-involvement and accidental ignorance and neglect.

Most times, I didn't see it. I hadn't had much company since it appeared so I hadn't felt self-conscious about it and, in my daily life, I'd stopped seeing it months ago. But tonight I saw that ragged mouth and I heard it screaming the headline from this morning.

*Mystery Lawyer's Tragic Heroin Connection.*

I had buried the story with thoughts of PTSD and the Home Guard and Smoke's cross-examination but now the story came rushing back. I didn't care about the headline. I cared about what people who didn't know Sarah were going to think of her.

I didn't feel very hungry then. I went into the living room, plopped down on the couch, and turned on the end of the Tigers game. As soon as I sat, my phone buzzed. A 323 area code. LA?

I thought then answered. "Hello?"

"Nate Shepherd?"

"Yes."

"It's Maggie White."

I felt a surge of anger then pulled it back. "No comment."

"I haven't asked you for one."

"Can't take chances, Ms. White. Small talk with you has a way of ending up in a story."

"It's Maggie and you can't possibly be mad that I quoted our conversation. It was harmless."

"We do things a little differently here in the Midwest, Ms. White. You know, simple courtesies like introducing ourselves and letting people know why we're talking to them. We're rubes that way."

"That's why I'm calling, Nate. To offer you a simple courtesy."

"And what's that?"

"A chance to comment on my story."

"We're under a gag order. Judge Gallon's very strict about it."

"Not about the trial. About your wife."

I squeezed the phone. "May I make a comment off the record?"

"I'd rather it was on the record."

"Then I have no comment."

A pause. "Go ahead."

"Leave my wife alone. She doesn't deserve it."

"Her story deserves to be told."

"My wife's story doesn't deserve to be clickbait."

"All the clicks mean is that people are interested."

"And that's all you care about. Not my wife. Not her story. Your clicks."

"Her story can help a lot of people."

"Yes, that's exactly what an entertainment reporter from Los

Angeles who hangs around at after-parties and writes salacious stories about attorney's wives is looking to do. Help people."

There was silence for a moment. "I did not deserve that."

"Was there something inaccurate about what I said?"

"No. And there was nothing inaccurate in what I wrote."

"And yet we would both feel better if neither had happened."

"Let me know if you change your mind."

"Leave my wife alone."

"We probably won't release it for a few days. You can reach me at this number anytime."

I did the math. "To coincide with the trial? So you can help the most people?"

"Good luck with your trial. The man your client killed was a scumbag."

I didn't say anything and, after a few moments, Maggie White hung up.

I immediately texted Izzy and told her to warn the family that a reporter was nosing around. I thought that they wouldn't want to comment either, but they weren't as used to dealing with reporters as I was. I gave her a few different ways to say no comment and told her that if worse came to worst and they had to say something, just say that we love Sarah and miss her.

Sometimes the simplest truths are the most effective.

I went back to the kitchen and decided on an omelet. I usually made my late-night omelets with red peppers, jalapeno, and cheese, but tonight I made it with ham because it was her favorite and I'd always enjoyed the smell of the ham cooking when I made hers first. I let the eggs sizzle in the hot pan and I let the hole in the wall scream that I'd failed Sarah when she'd needed me most.

After a few minutes, the omelet was done. The hole wasn't. I turned off the fire, slid my eggs onto a plate, and smothered them in the welcome heat of Frank's Red Hot sauce. I took them to the family room and ate at the coffee table just as Scott Van Pelt came on for the evening. I couldn't see the hole from the couch but tonight I heard it; tonight it offered more than just accusations of neglect and inattention, it also lamented the wrong conclusions people were going to draw about Sarah and about her life.

Not too long after, I fell asleep.

I agree. That kind of compartmentalization is despicable.

THREE DAYS LATER, THE RESULTS OF HANK'S PSYCHOLOGICAL evaluation came back. He passed with flying colors. He was more sane and well-adjusted than ninety-three percent of the population if the off-the-record comments of the psychiatrist were to be believed. According to her, Hank was charming and he was funny and he was smart and there was absolutely no basis to believe that he was psychotic, sociopathic, delusional, schizophrenic, bipolar, or even rude to strangers.

Except for the fact that he'd beaten a man beyond recognition until he was dead.

She also found that Hank did not have the faintest trace of PTSD. In fact, from what she could see, Hank had never been remotely traumatized by anything in his life.

To her credit, Cyn didn't gloat. Instead, we all got ready for trial.

# TRIAL

## 25

On the first day of trial, it took most of the morning to pick the jury. There had been a couple of obvious exclusions—a police dispatcher, a man who had been convicted of shoplifting as a teen and felt the justice system was a mass of conspiracies and pricks, and the woman who was caring for a sick mother and three kids under five. Other than that, Jeff Hanson and I had pretty much agreed on the rest of the jurors.

Which terrified me.

In the end, we were left with a panel of twelve jurors and two alternates. I won't tell you their names because you won't remember them so I'll list the quick facts for you the way we had them on our seating chart.

Number one – Pepsi Driver: woman, mid-50s, married, three kids, two grandkids, drove a Pepsi delivery truck.

Number two – Principal: man, late 30s, married, young kids, middle school principal.

Number three – Hipster: young man, single, no kids, beard and flannels, manager of a microbrewery.

Number four – Single Mom: 20s, single mom of two, between jobs, grandmother watching the kids.

Number five – Nurse: woman, married, two kids, obstetrical nurse.

Number six – Artist: man, early 30s, single, painter and new media artist.

Number seven – Guardswoman: woman, mid-30s, National Guard reservist, air refueling crew.

Number eight – Retired Math Teacher: woman, mid-60s, widow, three kids, eight grandkids, taught math at Carrefour South High School for thirty years before she retired just in time to have her husband die.

Number nine - Insurance Agent: man, early 30s, single, just starting out and worried about missing work.

Number ten - Delivery Man, late 20s, between gigs, takes care of Mom, smiled a lot.

Number eleven - Church Music Director, woman, mid-40s, married, three kids, the last a surprise, fine with serving as long as we're out on time on Wednesday.

Number twelve - Carry Out Clerk, woman, early 50s, on a disability leave so glad to be out of the house.

Alternate One: Maintenance Man: man, early 40s, 2$^{nd}$ shift maintenance supervisor at a Ford Tier Two supplier.

Alternate Two: Admissions Officer: man, mid-40s, married, one kid, admissions officer at the University.

It had taken the morning, asking them questions and exploring whether they had any preconceived notions about the case. Jurors usually skewed older so it was no surprise that we'd had to eliminate the bulk of the jurors in their 20s; they were so online and knew so much about the Saint case that many of them had already made up their minds. Surprisingly, the same was also true of many of our older jurors. Turns out that retired folks were on Facebook entirely too much. Most of them had seen pictures of Lizzy and pictures of Hank and one said she'd even seen pictures of me. That wouldn't normally be enough to disqualify them, but in this case, those pictures were often accompanied by all sorts of fan conspiracy theories. Since this was a capital murder case, if Judge Gallon heard even the slightest hint of potential prejudice, she dismissed the juror for cause. In the end, we were left with a jury of people who worked too hard or were too preoccupied with surviving day-to-day to follow celebrity gossip.

As Judge Gallon charged the jury, I took a last look at the courtroom set-up. There were two tables for counsel; we sat at the one farthest from the jury and Hank sat at the far end of the table. Cyn had bought him an expensive blue suit that somehow fit his huge frame perfectly and his long hair and beard had been trimmed so that any wildness looked like a fashion choice rather than a state of mind. I sat on the inside of the table, closest to the jury and to Jeff Hanson, while Lindsey sat in the middle between Hank and me. Cyn was seated behind us on our side of the barrier from the gallery where she would manage our digital presentation.

I looked behind her and saw a few people in the gallery, but not as many as I had expected. There were two reporters, one for the Carrefour Courier and one for the local NBC affiliate, but no cameras as Judge Gallon had kept them out. There were a couple of more people I didn't recognize, but there were no family members for Dillon Chase and there certainly weren't any for Hank.

Judge Gallon finished the introductory jury charge and said, "Counsel, will you approach please?"

Lindsey and I went up on one side while Jeff came up on the other. Jeff was wearing a gray-brown suit with a yellow shirt that was, I swear, purposely ill-fitting. Jeff was trying the case by himself, with no help from the prosecutor's office, which stood in sharp contrast to all of the well-dressed people scurrying around our table. Jeff was giving exactly the impression he wanted to give: he was just a humble prosecutor doing his job with limited resources while a high-priced defense team rustled around in their fancy suits setting up digital projectors. Bastard.

"It's 11:15, counsel," said Judge Gallon. She peered down at us over her prop glasses. "How long are you going to be with your openings?"

"No more than twenty minutes for me, Your Honor," said Jeff.

"Less," I said.

"Good. We'll open and then break for lunch."

"Thanks, Your Honor," Jeff and I both said and we went back to our tables.

"Counsel for the State," Judge Gallon said. "You may proceed with opening statement."

"Thank you, Your Honor." Jeff stood, tucked a corner of his yellow shirt back into his pants, and shrugged his jacket straight on his shoulders. He picked up a plain yellow legal pad from the table and wandered over to the lectern as if he'd half-forgotten why he was there. He fidgeted as he set the legal pad down, then sighed a bit, tucked in his shirt a little more, and flipped the top page of his legal pad over.

He had the jury's complete attention.

He raised his head and smiled then, appearing as calm and as cool and as comfortable as a man who had tried hundreds of cases. Which he had.

"Members of the jury," he said. "This is normally when I tell you what this case is about. When I tell you that this is a case of murder, where a defendant purposefully and brutally killed a man and attempted to kill another. It's normally the time when I tell you that the victim was beaten severely, with a brutality seldom seen outside of truck accidents and falls from thirty-story buildings. It's when I would normally tell you about a life cut tragically short without remorse and without honor."

Jeff hadn't looked at his notes a single time.

"But I'm not doing this in the usual order because this is not the usual case. Instead, what I'm going to do is tell you first what this case is not about. This case is not about self-defense. It is not about the defense of another. It is not about heroin and its effect on lives or our community." Jeff paused to look at each of the jurors. "Mr. Shepherd is going to tell you about those things. He's going to try to tell you that that's what matters in this case. But it doesn't. It doesn't matter at all." Jeff circled around to the other side of the podium.

"What matters is that on a Saturday night after Lizzy Saint and her band played at the University Arena, defendant Hank Braggi went up to Lizzy Saint's hotel room without an invitation. That night, Mr. Braggi opened the door and went into a room that wasn't his and found Lizzy Saint and Dillon Chase. He found them doing heroin."

Jeff came out from behind the podium and walked a little closer to the jury.

"There are many reactions Hank Braggi could've had to that scene. He could've called the police. He could've gotten Lizzy's manager or the hotel manager or some crewmembers. Or, God forbid, he could have simply told them to stop." Jeff put his hands in pockets and looked up in the air as if he was thinking. Then he waved his hand and said, "He could've pushed Dillon Chase to the side, knocked him down even. Mr. Braggi is a big man. Bigger than me and that's saying something."

A slight chuckle from three of the jurors.

"He could have picked Mr. Chase up by the scruff like a puppy and set him down on a chair in the next room." Jeff shook his head. "But that's not what Mr. Braggi did. That's not what he did at all."

Jeff had a set of 3 x 5 blowups in a big, zippered case. He

turned his back to the jury as he unzipped the case, pulled one out, and flipped it onto an easel.

The ruptured face of Dillon Chase looked back. I knew what was coming and I still had to work to keep an expression off my face. Instead though, I nodded, agreeing that's what Hank had done.

Jeff tapped the picture once. "No, Mr. Braggi rushed Dillon Chase and punched him in the back of the head. We know because two of Mr. Chase's friends, Blake Purcell and Aaron Whitsel, interrupted the attack. Mr. Whitsel tried to defend his friend but Mr. Braggi punched Mr. Whitsel in the head and knocked him aside, breaking his arm. Mr. Purcell and Mr. Whitsel will tell you about that attack and tell you that they were afraid for their lives and ran away."

"There's a gap then where we don't have any witnesses. There won't be anyone who will sit in that witness chair and tell us what happened."

Jeff straightened the picture on the easel. "But Mr. Chase's autopsy will tell us what happened. It will tell us that Mr. Chase's skull was fractured seventeen times by at least six blows. It will tell us that Mr. Chase's right arm was broken above the elbow and the left arm below. It will tell us that Mr. Chase had eight fractured ribs and a cracked sternum. It will tell us that those injuries killed him."

"We'll hear from Jared Smoke, the lead guitarist in Lizzy Saint's band. Mr. Smoke returned to the room just as Mr. Braggi was finishing the job on Dillon Chase. He'll testify to the damage, to the blood, and to Mr. Braggi throwing Dillon Chase's limp body around the room."

Jeff took down the picture of Dillon Chase's face and replaced it with a diagram of all the fractures in Dillon Chase's body, just like Lindsey said he would. It was a good move to keep the jury from getting used to the carnage. "We'll bring in the coroner," said Jeff. "He'll testify all about the fractures so that you know exactly how it was that Mr. Chase died and the agony he suffered. The evidence will show that the police talked to Lizzy Saint that night, and to Jared Smoke, and even to Hank Braggi, and you'll hear from Carrefour's own Chief Detective for Serious Crimes, Mitch Pearson, about the results of his investigation. And you'll hear from Lizzy Saint and Blake Purcell and Aaron Whitsel and Jared Smoke about what happened that night before Hank Braggi charged in."

"Mr. Shepherd might present evidence to you suggesting that Mr. Braggi was protecting Lizzy Saint." Jeff shook his head. "But protecting Lizzy Saint would have involved saving her, getting her out of the room, calling the police, getting her help. Instead, what happened was that Hank Braggi brutally killed one man, Dillon Chase, and attempted to kill another, Aaron Whitsel."

Jeff turned the diagram around now so that all that faced the jury was the blank white back of the poster board, hiding the injuries on the other side. "At the end of the case, when you've heard from all of these people, we're going to ask you to convict Hank Braggi of the murder of Dillon Chase. We're going to ask you to convict Hank Braggi of the attempted murder of Aaron Whitsel. And because of the brutal nature of this killing and the attempt on another man's life, if we obtain those convictions, we will ask you to impose the death penalty."

Jeff paused and looked at them all again. "I appreciate your time and the sacrifice you're making to be here. Dillon Chase deserves it."

Jeff picked up the yellow notepad that he'd never looked at, flipped back the pages that he'd never read, and coolly ambled back to his seat. The man was a silky-smooth, portly assassin.

When he had taken his place, Judge Gallon said, "Mr. Shepherd?"

"Thank you, Your Honor."

I circled around Hank's side so that I could put a hand on his shoulder as I went to the podium. The Nurse, the Hipster and the National Guardswoman all looked at me expectantly. The Pepsi Driver, the Single Mom, and the Artist all scowled and looked sick while the Retired Math Teacher's face was so sour that I thought she might actually hold her nose when I came up to speak.

I put my trial notebook on the lectern and stood to the side. I paused for a moment, then said, "Lizzy Saint is a rock star so she's surrounded by people all the time. At her concerts, she's surrounded by fifteen thousand people, all watching her, all listening to her. Her band surrounds her when she's on stage. When the show's over, she has fans that wait in line to be near her for just a few seconds and when she's done with that, she's surrounded by record executives and acquaintances and friends of friends who all wonder if she can spare just a minute."

"It seems incredible, doesn't it? Singing and playing a guitar for a living. Having thousands of people screaming and cheering every day when you do your job. Having parties after every show where you're surrounded by throngs of people who say that you're great and that they love you and that they can't wait to see what you're going to do next."

The jury was listening. A couple nodded. Only the Retired Math Teacher was stuck, staring at the back of the bloody photo that Jeff had turned around.

"And yet, after Lizzy performed here in Carrefour, she wound up isolated and alone. Somehow, this rock star who's always surrounded by fans or friends or management, was alone in her suite with Dillon Chase. The evidence is going to show that Lizzy had never met him before that night. The evidence is going to show that Mr. Chase knew her boyfriend, Jared Smoke, and that Mr. Smoke got him into the party that night with the band. The evidence is going to show that the band partied more than usual that night because they knew they didn't have to perform the next day and that Lizzy Saint got after it just as much as the rest of them. The evidence is going to show that Lizzy drank a lot that night and that by 3:45 a.m., she was so drunk that she was barely conscious."

Drunk rock stars are interesting. The jury was paying closer attention now.

"The evidence is going to show that as the party wound down, there came a time when none of Lizzy's friends or Lizzy's fans or Lizzy's management or even Lizzy's boyfriend were with her anymore. It was just Lizzy and this man she'd never met before that night. Alone. In her suite."

I moved to the other side of the lectern. "My client, Hank Braggi, is one of Lizzy's oldest friends on the tour. He knew her before she was famous, had worked with her when she was struggling, and co-wrote songs with her when she was on her way up. The evidence is going to show that Hank was worried when he saw Lizzy leave the party with Smoke and three strangers. The evidence is going to show that, after a few minutes, Hank went up to her suite to check on her. Hank knocked, and when there was no answer, went in."

I paused.

"The evidence is going to show that when Hank entered the room, Lizzy was barely conscious. She was sitting in a chair, head rolled back, mouth slightly open, eyes half-closed. Her boyfriend, Jared Smoke, wasn't there. No one was there except Lizzy and Dillon Chase."

I shook my head.

"The evidence is going to show that when Hank entered the room, Dillon Chase was on one knee holding Lizzy's arm in one hand while he was jamming a syringe into her vein with the other. This woman, this star who was always surrounded and never alone, was passed out in her hotel room with a stranger injecting something into her arm."

I paused. "Hank stopped him."

I spoke faster now. "You're going to hear from a toxicologist who's going to tell you that what was in that syringe was heroin. You're going to hear from multiple witnesses that Lizzy Saint is not a drug addict and doesn't use heroin. You're going to hear that there was no one in the room to stop it until Hank arrived."

"The evidence will show that Hank charged into that room to protect his unconscious, helpless friend. The evidence will show that Blake Purcell and Aaron Whitsel returned from getting beer and tried to stop Hank and that Hank punched Aaron Whitsel right in the chest, driving him back. The evidence will show that Hank knocked Dillon Chase aside and got the needle out of Lizzy's arm but that, before he could check on her further, Chase punched Hank. Hank made him stop that too."

"The prosecutor is going to present you with a bunch of evidence about the nature of Mr. Chase's injuries. In fact, that's probably what Mr. Hanson is going to spend the most time on, the injuries. " I shrugged. "It's all true. And it was justified. Hank Braggi protected Lizzy Saint in the same way that Lizzy was allowed to protect herself, if she'd been able. Hank protected Lizzy when no one else—no one who listens to her or manages her or makes their living off of her—was there. She was all alone and Hank was the only one there to protect her. So he did."

"For that reason, at the end of this case, we'll be asking you to return a verdict of not guilty on all counts. Thank you."

I wasn't registering the jurors individually just then. I knew I got some nods and I got some stony stares but at that moment I was treating the jury as a group, as an entity that was feeling things collectively. If I started focusing too soon on one juror, I risked ignoring someone else, someone who might be the key vote. So I nodded back generally to all of them and went back to the table.

Hank nodded and I believe he gave me a low growl. Lindsey didn't look at me but instead kept her eyes focused on the jury, taking notes. Just because I couldn't watch the individual reactions didn't mean somebody shouldn't.

"Members of the jury," said Judge Gallon. "We have a strict legal tradition when an opening statement ends at this hour."

The jurors looked at Judge Gallon expectantly.

"It's called lunch."

The jury chuckled.

Judge Gallon glanced at the clock. "It's 12:05. We'll go back into session at 1:05." The judge then instructed the jury not to talk to each other about the case and not to be offended if the lawyers didn't talk to them. She hesitated for a moment then, and said, "This is an unusual case. Normally, I would admonish you not to look things up, not to investigate or do independent research about things like property lines or people's histories. This case is a little different. I have to ask you not to check your feeds or hashtags for things that might be related to this case. Some of the people involved are famous and have followings. It is vital that you do not review those items. The only thing you may consider in reaching your verdict is the evidence that is presented right here in this courtroom. Much of what you read on social media is false. It needs to come through the filter of the courtroom for you to consider it. Any questions?"

The jurors looked around, looked at each other and collectively shook their heads.

"Good. You're dismissed until 1:05."

We stood as the jury filed out of the room and, once they were gone, I waved to Danny, who was sitting in the first row of the gallery. "Take Hank to get something to eat would you?" I said.

"Sure. Where?"

"Anywhere you can get him back by ten till."

"What about me?" said Lindsey.

"Do you have the injury diagram?"

"All loaded."

I look to Cyn, who'd been running the presentation software. "Any problems?"

She shook her head. "All set."

"You two are free to get something to eat too then."

"What about you?" said Lindsey.

"I'm going to go over my cross one more time."

"Need anything?"

I shook my head. "Brought my own. Thanks though."

Danny, Hank, Lindsey, and Cyn went to get something to eat. I took my bag lunch and my trial notebook and went to find a quiet place to finish getting ready for the cross-examination of Carrefour's Chief Detective of Serious Crimes, Mitch Pearson.

The man who was going to try to bury my client. And me.

## 26

"WELCOME BACK, MEMBERS OF THE JURY," SAID JUDGE GALLON. As severe as she could be when scolding a defendant or an out-of-line lawyer, Judge Gallon was charming when she met with voters and jurors, and she was now. "Thank you for coming back on time. The prosecution will now begin its case. Mr. Hanson?"

"Your Honor, the prosecution calls Detective Mitch Pearson."

Pearson stood from his seat in the back of the courtroom and made his way to the front. There was no question that Pearson had picked his seat in the back so that all eyes would be on him for a longer time as he walked to the witness box. Pearson made a slow turn at the witness chair, straightened his suit, and sat down. He unbuttoned his suit coat so that the gun in his shoulder holster and the badge at his belt were clearly visible, then folded his large hands in front of him.

Jeff shambled up to the podium with his usual self-deprecating nonchalance and gave a casual wave toward the jury. "Sir, could you please introduce yourself to the jury?"

"Detective Mitch Pearson."

Jeff smiled. "It seems to me that you're being modest, Detective Pearson. Please tell the jury your full title."

Pearson shrugged and smiled in a humble way that I'd never seen from him in real life. "Chief Detective for Serious Crimes, Carrefour Ohio Police Department."

"Thank you, Chief Detective Pearson. You are employed then by the Carrefour Police Department?"

"I am."

"And what is your job?"

"I'm in charge of investigating any serious crime that occurs in Carrefour, Ohio."

"And what falls into the category of serious crimes?"

"Arson, robbery, rape, burglary, murder."

"I thought I was going to have to ask you specifically there but you said it. You are in fact in charge of murder investigations in Carrefour?"

"The Ohio side, yes, sir."

"Were you involved in the investigation of the death of Dillon Chase?"

"I was."

"What was your role in that investigation?"

"Lead investigator."

"And when did you become involved as the lead investigator?"

"On the night of the murder."

I stood. "Objection, Your Honor."

"Sustained," said Judge Gallon. "The detective will refrain from making legal conclusions."

"Of course," said Pearson. "My apologies, Your Honor."

Judge Gallon looked over her glasses at Pearson. "You don't need to apologize to me, Detective. Just don't do it."

"Yes, Your Honor."

"How did you become involved that night?" said Jeff.

"On the night Dillon Chase was *killed*, I received a call to go to the University Marriott. Once there, I was directed to the penthouse suite."

Jeff smiled. "We have a penthouse in Carrefour?"

The jury chuckled.

Pearson smiled. "Apparently. I took the elevator and entered the suite. Once there, I found Mr. Braggi and the body of the man I would learn was Dillon Chase."

"Was Mr. Chase alive?"

"He was not."

"Would you describe the scene for me please, Detective?"

"Sure. The body of the victim was lying in the middle of the suite floor. His arms were twisted and his face was unrecognizable."

"Why is that, Detective?"

"Because his face was smashed and broken and covered in blood. We learned who he was at the scene from his driver's license. The victim was covered in blood and blood was covering many of the surfaces in the room."

"And was Mr. Braggi there?"

"He was. We found Mr. Braggi sitting in one of the chairs."

"And what did Mr. Braggi look like?"

"He was covered in blood too."

"Was he injured?"

"Not that I could see."

"Could you describe his appearance a bit more please?"

"Sure." Pearson looked at the jury now. "His hands were covered almost completely with blood. He was wearing a short-sleeve shirt and the blood extended up his forearms to his elbows. It was so solid that it looked like he'd dipped his arms in red paint. It was on his clothes too. The front of his shirt had numerous blood spatters on it with one broad swipe which we believe was from when he lifted the victim up."

Jeff nodded solemnly. "Anything else?"

"His face and beard were covered in blood as well."

"His mouth?"

"Yes, there was blood around his mouth."

"His boots?"

"Yes, there was blood on his boots, both on the toes and the heels."

"Was that in spatters?"

"No. It was solid, consistent with kicking and stomping."

"Did you investigate who killed Mr. Chase?"

"I did. It took less than a minute."

"How so?"

"Officers on the scene had already Mirandized and cuffed the defendant. I read him his rights again and asked him what had happened." Pearson paused. "Mr. Braggi said to me, 'I killed the little piss-ant.'"

Jeff paused, nodded, and looked at the jury. "Did you find any evidence that that was the case?"

Pearson cocked his head. "Besides him telling me that he did it?"

"Yes."

"Mr. Braggi was covered in blood. His hands were slick with it. His knuckles were scraped. His elbows and boot toes and boot heels all had markings of blood that were consistent with delivering blows. Do you want me to list more?"

"Not just now. Did you take Mr. Braggi into custody?"

"I didn't personally. I had a patrolman take Mr. Braggi to the station for processing while I stayed and completed the investigation at the scene."

"I see. Did you take photos?"

"I supervised the taking of photos."

"Good. I'm handing you what's been marked as State's Exhibits 22-38. Would you identify them for the jury, please?"

He leafed through the pictures. "These are the photos of the hotel suite that were taken that night."

"Let's go through them then. Let's start with Exhibit 22. Please tell the jury what that is."

"That is the corner of a dresser."

"And what is the significance of that?"

"The corner is covered in blood. And that spot right there? That's a wad of hair."

As Pearson picked up each photo, Jeff put a blowup of the photo on the easel right in front of the jury.

"And Exhibit 23?"

"That's the TV set. The screen is broken."

"Is there anything significant about the broken screen besides the damage to the hotel room?"

"Yes. That's blood and hair on the shards of glass."

"And Exhibit 24?"

"That's the wall next to the bathroom."

"And is that a dent in the wall?"

"Yes. We determined that it was head-shaped."

It went on like this for one photo after the next, sixteen in all. I listened, and I kept my face straight, and then nodded at times as if confirming that's exactly what I would expect the photos to show. I watched the jury. They were all paying attention. I didn't see a significant reaction from them until Pearson got to Exhibit 33. It was a photo of the tile entryway to the suite. There was a pool of blood, complete with a swirl of footprints and a scattering of teeth —one whole, three fragments. The Retired Math Teacher winced.

"Did you determine whose teeth those were?" said Jeff.

"I didn't but—"

I stood. "Objection, Your Honor."

Judge Gallon nodded. "The witness may only testify as to what he knew or did."

Pearson's eyes hooded a little bit. "I did not hear that the tooth came from the victim at that time."

"Detective Pearson." Judge Gallon's voice cracked like a whip. "Do that again and you're going to get reacquainted with some people you've put away recently."

Pearson ducked his head. "My apologies, Your Honor." With his head bowed, Judge Gallon couldn't see the small smile.

"Now, I understand that you took more photos than these sixteen," said Jeff.

"We did."

"What is significant about these sixteen?"

"They are representative of the damage in and around the suite."

"How so?"

"These sixteen pictures show that every wall and every piece of furniture in the main room had blood, hair, or bone on it."

"Detective Pearson, you investigate crime scenes as part of your occupation?"

"I do."

"How many crime scenes have you investigated over the course of your career?"

"It's in the thousands."

"You have experience in determining what happens from the evidence that's left behind?"

"I do."

"Based on your examination of the hotel suite, did you reach a conclusion regarding how Mr. Chase was killed?"

"I did."

"And what is that conclusion?"

"That the person who killed Mr. Chase banged his body and his head into every piece of furniture, every wall, and every hard surface in that room."

"And were you able to reach a conclusion about the force used to create that damage in the hotel suite?"

"I am."

"And what is that conclusion?"

I stood. "Objection, Your Honor. Foundation."

Judge Gallon looked at me for a moment before she said, "Overruled. Go ahead, Detective Pearson."

"That the force was enough to shatter glass, dent drywall, and break wood."

"And you found sixteen instances of this? Of these blows into the walls and furniture?"

"No," said Pearson.

Jeff turned back to him. "No?"

"There were more."

Jeff nodded his head as if he hadn't known what Pearson was going to say and walked slowly around the lectern to the far side of the jury, being sure to cross in front of the picture of the pool of blood and the fragments of teeth.

"So you said that at this point that Mr. Braggi had been taken into custody?"

"Yes."

"Was anyone else still in the room?"

"Yes. Ms. Saint and Mr. Smoke."

"Were you able to talk to either of them?"

"I took a statement from Mr. Smoke. Ms. Saint was not interested in talking at that moment. She was quite upset."

"Was Mr. Smoke able to tell you what happened?"

I would normally object to Pearson saying what other witnesses had told him. But I needed to get some of this information in and I couldn't put Hank on the stand to do it so I let him roll.

Pearson nodded. "He told us that he had gone to the bathroom and when he came back, Mr. Braggi was in the room, covered in blood and yelling."

"Did he report anything else?"

"He said that he saw Mr. Braggi throw Mr. Chase to the ground, kick him, pick him up again, and smash him over his knee."

"Anything else?"

"He said it continued until he screamed at Mr. Braggi to stop, that Ms. Saint was okay."

"And what happened then?"

"He said Mr. Braggi was holding Mr. Chase out in front of him when he screamed. As soon as he did, Mr. Braggi froze momentarily and then flung Mr. Chase to the ground. Then he just went over and sat in a chair."

Jeff nodded. "Did you interview any other witnesses that night?"

"Not that night."

"Later?"

Pearson nodded. "I interviewed Blake Purcell and Aaron Whitsel who had also been in the room."

"Why hadn't they stayed? Like Jared Smoke did?"

Pearson was talking directly to the jury again. "They said they were scared. Mr. Whitsel in particular said that Mr. Braggi had tried to kill him."

"Did you see any evidence that that was true?"

"I did."

"And what was that?"

"When I interviewed him, Mr. Whitsel's arm was broken and he had a black eye."

"Did he say who did it?"

Pearson nodded. "Hank Braggi."

"Now, Detective Pearson, last thing. I understand that the paramedics came as well?"

"They did."

"Were you there when they entered?"

"I was."

"Did they work on Mr. Chase?"

"If by work on you mean did they pack up his body, yes. If you mean did they try to revive him, the answer is no. He was dead by the time we got there." Pearson looked solemnly at the jury as he said it.

"Did you conduct any further investigation at the scene?"

"No."

"Why not?"

"Because I had the body, I had witnesses, I had a confession, and I had the murder weapon. There was nothing else that needed to be done."

Jeff turned back to Pearson in surprise. "You had the murder weapon?"

"I did," said Pearson. "In custody. That man's fists and elbows and boots."

"For the record, you are indicating the defendant, Hank Braggi?"

"I am."

"No further questions, Your Honor."

As Jeff ambled back to his seat, Judge Gallon said, "Mr. Shepherd?"

"Thank you, Your Honor." I stood and went over to the lectern and moved it closer to Pearson, so I was centered right in the middle of the jury. I also pulled down the bloody pictures that Jeff had left up on the easel. "Do you mind, Mr. Hanson?"

"Oh, no, I'm sorry. Go ahead, Mr. Shepherd." A bout of charming, absent-minded forgetfulness.

When I had stacked them and turned them so that their white backs were facing the jury, I said, "I'd introduce myself but we know each other, don't we, Mr. Pearson?"

"We do, *Mr.* Shepherd. Have for some time."

"Mr. Pearson, you said you talked to my client when you arrived at the room, correct?"

"Yes."

"And he told you that he killed Mr. Chase, didn't he?"

"He did."

"And you interviewed him later at the police station, didn't you?"

"I did."

"And he told you there that he killed Mr. Chase, didn't he?"

"He did."

"In fact, every time you spoke to Mr. Braggi, he told you that he had killed Mr. Chase, right?"

"That's true."

"You didn't have to investigate whether Mr. Braggi killed Mr. Chase because he told you upfront that he had, right?"

Pearson looked smug and certain. "That's what I said earlier, Mr. Shepherd."

"You certainly did. Now, Mr. Braggi also told you why he attacked Mr. Chase, didn't he?

Hanson stood. "Objection, Your Honor. Hearsay."

"Your Honor, the prosecution has solicited testimony that my client stated that he killed Mr. Chase. I should be permitted to enter the entire statement."

"Overruled," said Judge Gallons. "Continue, Mr. Shepherd."

"Do you remember the question, Mr. Pearson?"

Pearson's eyes lit at that. "I remember it just fine, Mr. Shepherd. He did."

"Mr. Braggi told you that Mr. Chase was injecting Ms. Saint while she was unconscious, didn't he?"

"That's hardly a justification for killing someone."

"Your opinion is very interesting, Mr. Pearson, but that's not the question I asked you. The question was Mr. Braggi told you that Mr. Chase was injecting Lizzy Saint while she was unconscious, didn't he?"

"That's still not a reason—"

I stepped back and held out my hands. "Tell you what, Mr. Pearson. I'll take this slower. Mr. Braggi talked to you when you arrived in the room, didn't he?"

Pearson glowered but he said, "Yes."

"And he told you that he killed Mr. Chase, didn't he?"

"Yes."

"And he said that Mr. Chase was injecting Ms. Saint with a syringe, didn't he?"

A pause. "Yes."

"And Mr. Braggi said that Ms. Saint was unconscious, didn't he."

"We don't know—"

"I didn't ask you what you know, Mr. Pearson. I asked you if that's what Mr. Braggi said to you."

Pearson ground his lantern jaw. "It is."

I nodded and stepped back a little further. "Now Mr. Pearson as the Chief Detective in charge of Serious Crimes in Carrefour, Ohio, you investigated the scene in the hotel room, right?"

"I did."

"And you were thorough?"

"Yes."

"You supervised the taking of the pictures that you just showed the jury?"

"I did."

"And you also collected evidence at the scene, didn't you?"

"I did."

"Now Mr. Pearson, you were told at the scene by Mr. Braggi that Mr. Chase was injecting Lizzy Saint with heroin, weren't you?"

"We just covered that, Mr. Shepherd. *Remember*?"

"So the answer is 'yes?'"

"Yes."

"And you found a syringe at the scene, didn't you?"

"I believe someone did."

I went back to the evidence table and picked up a plastic bag with a syringe in it and held it up so the jury could see. "Mr. Pearson, I'm going to hand you what's been marked as State's Exhibit 48. Can you identify that for the jury, please?"

Pearson took the plastic bag from me. "It's a syringe."

"And that's the syringe that was recovered at the scene, true?"

"It was."

"And since it was recovered at the scene, that syringe has been under the care and custody of the Carrefour police department, right?"

"Right."

"Detective Pearson, that syringe is empty now, true?"

"It is."

"It was not when you found it, was it?"

"I don't recall."

I handed him a photo which Cyn also put up on the big screen. "Detective Pearson, I'm handing you a photo that's been marked as State's Exhibit 49. That's a picture of this syringe, isn't it?"

"It appears to be."

"The syringe collected and kept by your department, true?"

"It appears so."

"Detective Pearson, I want you to look closely at the photo."

Pearson glanced at it then looked at me.

"Detective Pearson, that syringe is full, isn't it?"

"I don't know that I could say."

"You can't say whether that syringe is full?"

Pearson made a show of studying it. "No, I don't think I could."

I gestured and Cyn blew up the photo even larger on the screen. I went over to it, talking now to the jury more than Pearson as I said, "Detective Pearson, that syringe has markings that go up to 10 milliliters, right?" I circled the "10 ml" with a laser pointer.

Pearson was looking down at the photo as he said, "I don't know that."

"Detective Pearson, could you please look at the photo you are holding in your hand and determine if the highest number listed on the syringe is 10 ml's."

Pearson stared at it but didn't say anything.

"It's the number right above 9," I said.

"Yes," said Pearson.

"You see the number 10?"

"Yes."

"Is there a number 11 on there?"

"No."

"So there is no number higher than 10 on that syringe, is there?"

"No." Pearson looked up at me, realized the photo was blown up for the jury, and glared. If he was anything other than a quarterback I might've been concerned.

"Detective Pearson, in the photo that your department took, there is still liquid in the syringe, isn't there?"

"There is."

"The liquid in the vial goes up to 10 mL, doesn't it, Detective Pearson?"

"It does."

"So the syringe is full, isn't it?"

"It looks like there's still some air at the top," said Pearson.

"But there are no more numbers where the air is, are there?"

"No."

"Detective Pearson, your detectives could be trusted to maintain the chain of custody of the syringe, right?"

"Absolutely."

"Once you take a piece of evidence from the scene, you maintain it in a pristine condition, don't you?"

"We do."

"You do not alter any evidence that you take from a crime scene in any way, do you?"

"We do not. And I don't like what you're implying."

"I'm not implying anything, Detective Pearson. My point is that since this picture was taken at the scene and since the picture shows that the syringe is full, the jury can assume that this syringe was full when your officer found it, correct?"

"That's correct."

"In other words, the jury can assume that because this syringe was full —"

"It's not full."

"I stand corrected, Detective Pearson. Let me say it another way. Because this picture shows that there are 10 milliliters of liquid in this 10-milliliter syringe, the jury can assume that the syringe had 10 milliliters of liquid in it when your officer found it, true?"

"True," said Detective Pearson. "But I don't see why that matters."

I smiled. "That's okay." I stepped back a little bit and said, "Detective Pearson, you found heroin in the room that night, didn't you?"

"We did."

"And you also mentioned that you interviewed both Blake Purcell and Aaron Whitsel the next day after the incident, didn't you?"

"On the day after the mur—the killing. Yes, I did."

"Did you charge either of those men with drug possession?"

"I did not."

"Why not?"

"I didn't know whose heroin it was."

"Both Lizzy Saint and Jared Smoke told you that it wasn't theirs, right?"

Pearson sat straighter and his eyes hooded. "All of the people in the room that night denied that it was theirs."

"Really? Everyone in the room denied it was theirs?"

"Yes."

"Detective Pearson, you didn't ask Blake Purcell if the heroin was his, did you?"

A pause. "I don't recall."

"And you didn't ask Aaron Whitsel if the heroin was his either, did you?"

"I don't recall."

"Well, if either Blake Purcell or Aaron Whitsel had admitted that the drugs were theirs, you would've written it in your report, wouldn't you?"

"Yes."

"And you didn't, did you?"

"I don't recall."

"Well, let's check." I went to the evidence table and picked up a small stack of stapled papers. "Detective Pearson, I'm handing you what's been marked as State's Exhibit 56. That's a copy of your report of your investigation, isn't it?"

Pearson scanned the paper. "It is."

"Detective Pearson, please read to the jury the section of your report where you state that you asked Aaron Whitsel whether the heroin was his."

Pearson scanned it for a moment but it was just for show. "It's not in there."

"It's not? Is that because you were sloppy in your reporting or because you didn't ask him?"

Pearson set the report down. "I didn't ask him."

"I see. Well, as long as we have it out, why don't you read to the jury the section where you asked Blake Purcell if the drugs were his?"

Pearson glared. "I didn't ask him."

"All right. So you didn't ask them if the heroin belonged to them but what did the fingerprints reveal?"

Pearson blinked. "What?

I picked up the plastic bag with the syringe and held it up for to the jury to see. "The fingerprints on the syringe. You finger-printed the syringe, didn't you?"

Pearson's eyes refocused. With heat. "We did not."

"Now that's interesting." I stood in front of the jury, my back half-turned to him and flipped the bag with the syringe around in my hand. "Because I would think that you could get good prints of the forefinger and middle finger on the two tabs here and it sure seems like you could get a perfectly square thumbprint right here on the plunger." I faced the plunger toward the jury. "I mean that would tell you, wouldn't it? Who was using the syringe?"

Pearson straightened. "That wasn't part of my investigation."

"It wasn't?"

"It wasn't."

"Chief Detective Pearson, I understood from your earlier testimony that you're in charge of investigating all serious crimes in Carrefour, Ohio."

"I am."

"In fact, I thought I heard you say to the jury that you *personally* oversee the investigation of any serious crime in Carrefour."

"I do."

"So the possession of heroin isn't a serious crime in Carrefour?"

"Of course it is."

"And the trafficking of heroin isn't a serious crime in Carrefour?"

"It is."

"So why didn't you investigate it?"

Jeff stood and held his hands out to the side. "Your Honor..."

Silence filled the courtroom for three beats. "Yes, Mr. Hanson," said Judge Gallon.

Silence again.

Judge Gallon peered over her glasses. "Was there an objection in there, Mr. Hanson?"

"Yes," said Jeff.

"And it is?"

Jeff stared for a moment. "Argumentative."

"Overruled."

"Do you remember the question, Detective Pearson?" I said.

"I do."

"And your answer?"

"The murder investigation was more important."

"I believe you told Mr. Hanson just a moment ago that your murder investigation took about a minute. Was that a true statement you made to the jury?"

He lifted his chin. "Yes."

"Great. Detective Pearson, you also testified that paramedics rendered aid to Ms. Saint that night, didn't you?"

"I did."

"Was she conscious?"

"She was when I saw her."

"Was she able to speak to you?"

"She was."

"She was drunk, wasn't she?"

"Apparently."

"She wasn't high though, was she?"

"I don't have any idea."

"She wasn't nodding, was she?"

"Only when I asked her questions."

"She wasn't nodding off into unconsciousness, was she?"

"She was able to talk to me."

"She was slurring her words a little, right?"

"A little."

"But she showed no signs of opioid intoxication, did she?"

Jeff stood. "Objection, Your Honor. Officer Pearson is not a doctor."

"Sustained."

I nodded. "Officer Pearson, look at your report again."

"What part?"

"Paragraph two, third line. Cyn, blow it up for the jury, would you please." Cyn blew it up three feet tall on the screen and highlighted it in yellow. "Do you see that text, Detective Pearson?"

Pearson looked from the paper to the screen. "I do."

"Read it to the jury, please."

"Objection, Your Honor," said Jeff.

"I'm only asking what he wrote in his contemporaneous report, Your Honor. I'm not asking if it's true."

"Overruled," said Judge Gallon. "Please read the line of your report, Detective Pearson."

The muscles in Pearson's jaw twitched, then he said, "Although intoxicated, Ms. Saint shows no sign of opioid intoxication."

"That's your signature at the bottom of the report, isn't it Detective Pearson?"

Cyn blew it up three feet tall without my asking.

"It is."

"And by that signature you are attesting that what you wrote in your report is true, correct?"

"To the best of my knowledge."

"That's all anyone can ask, Detective Pearson. For the breadth of your knowledge as the Chief Detective in charge of investigating all Serious Crimes in Carrefour, Ohio. In your role investigating serious crimes, you have seen people who are intoxicated on opioids, Detective Pearson, haven't you."

His eyes lit up now. "I sure have. I've seen people who have overdosed too."

I let it go. "They act differently than people who are intoxicated on alcohol, don't they?"

"They do."

"And Ms. Saint displayed signs of alcohol intoxication, right?"

"She did."

"But not opioid intoxication."

He paused. "Not that I saw."

"Thank you, Detective Pearson. That's all."

Judge Gallon looked at Jeff. "Redirect, Mr. Hanson?"

"Just a few, Your Honor. Hank Braggi told you that Dillon Chase was injecting Ms. Saint?"

Pearson nodded. "He did."

"Did any other witness report this to you?"

"No."

"Not Blake Purcell?"

"No."

"Not Aaron Whitsel?"

"No."

"Not Jared Smoke?"

"No."

"Not Ms. Saint herself?"

"No."

"So no one but Mr. Braggi reported seeing Dillon Chase trying to inject Ms. Saint?"

"That's correct."

"That's all I have, Your Honor. Thank you."

Judge Gallon looked at me. "Mr. Shepherd?"

"Thank you, Your Honor. Detective Pearson, Hank Braggi told you that he killed Dillon Chase, didn't he?"

"He did."

"Blake Purcell didn't see it, did he?"

"Blake Purcell saw a part of the attack."

"And then he fled right?"

"Right."

"So he didn't report actually seeing Hank Braggi kill Dillon Chase, did he?"

Pearson clenched his jaw. "He did not."

"And Aaron Whitsel didn't report seeing Hank Braggi kill Dillon Chase, did he?"

"Aaron Whitsel's arm was broken."

"His arm was broken. He wasn't blind. He did not report seeing Hank Braggi kill Dillon Chase, did he?"

"He fled with Mr. Purcell."

"I understand. So I'll ask you for a third time—Aaron Whitsel did not report seeing Hank Braggi kill Dillon Chase, did he?"

"No."

"Jared Smoke did not report seeing Hank Braggi kill Dillon Chase, did he?"

"He saw him slam him to the ground."

"Detective Pearson, Jared Smoke never told you that he saw Hank Braggi kill Dillon Chase, did he?"

"Members of the same organization often don't want to accuse one another."

"Three times seems to be a common theme with us, doesn't it, Detective Pearson. Let me ask it again—Jared Smoke never said he saw Hank Braggi kill Dillon Chase, did he?"

He hesitated and glared at me. It was a look we had shared since high school. "No."

"Lizzy Saint didn't report seeing Hank Braggi kill Dillon Chase, did she?"

"She did not."

"So Hank Braggi is also the only one who told you that he'd actually killed Dillon Chase, right?"

"Yes."

I turned away.

"But you can't go around killing every person who injects a junkie."

I froze then forced myself to turn back with a straight face. "You don't think much of junkies, do you, Detective Pearson?"

Jeff was on his feet. "Objection, Your Honor. That's beyond the scope of the trial."

Judge Gallon looked at me. I shrugged. "He opened the door, Your Honor. I was done. I'm just following up now."

"He did open the door, Mr. Hanson. I will allow a limited examination." That look over the glasses was now directed at me. "Very limited, Mr. Shepherd."

"I understand, Your Honor." I turned to Pearson. "You don't think much of junkies, do you Detective Pearson?"

"If they don't care for themselves, I don't see why I should."

I nodded. "You think they get what's coming to them, don't you?"

Pearson shrugged, his eyes glittering. "Whatever happens to them, they did to themselves."

"And because they did it to themselves, there's no reason to investigate further, is there?"

Jeff stood. "Your Honor, it seems that we're getting beyond those limits."

"Almost," said Judge Gallon. "Mr. Shepherd?"

"There is no reason to say, take thirty seconds to fingerprint a syringe, right?"

"Fingerprints on a syringe don't solve a murder."

"No, but it's evidence of another crime, one you're not interested in investigating. Because it's not serious."

"Objection. Your Honor."

"Withdrawn. I have no further questions for the Chief Detective in charge of Serious Crimes for Carrefour, Ohio, Your Honor."

"Detective Pearson, you may step down." Mitch Pearson left the witness stand and gave me one last haughty look as he left. He walked out on the far side of the courtroom, though, away from me.

Quarterbacks.

Judge Gallon looked at the clock. "Ladies and gentlemen, that concludes our testimony for the day. Please be here at 8:30 tomorrow morning. And again, I must admonish you, please do not speak to anyone or to each other about what you've heard today. You must wait until all of the evidence is in to begin your deliberations. Also, again, because of the unusual nature of the case, I ask that you please do not research or go on social media to investigate or read about this case. Now I understand that's like asking you not to think about a polar bear twirling a pink umbrella, but it's necessary."

The jury chuckled as each one of them thought about a polar bear twirling the pink umbrella.

Judge Gallon smiled. "It's difficult but it's important that you do it. It will only be about a week. You are excused."

We all stood as the jury filed out.

Lindsey ducked her head near mine. "You okay?"

I stared at her. "Why wouldn't I be?"

She stared back. "No reason. Good."

"What did you think?"

"He made a lot of headway with the blood. You got a little bit back with the heroin."

"Enough?"

"Not quite. But a start."

"I agree."

"It's going to be worse tomorrow."

I knew she was right. Tomorrow, Coroner Ray Gerchuk was going to testify.

## 27

LINDSEY AND CYN AND DANNY AND I WERE ALL SITTING AROUND the conference table back at the third-floor office munching on the Subway we'd picked up on the way home. Court was typically over around five. My practice was to grab something for us on the way back to the office, eat while we talked briefly about what needs to be done for the next day, and then get to work.

There's always something to get ready for and there's never enough time to do it. Those TV shows that have lawyers running around all over town at night during a trial are good fun, but if a lawyer was out kicking ass at night, he'd be getting his ass kicked in court the next day and I was doing a pretty good job of getting my ass kicked without the running around town part. Just then though, I think I'd have welcomed the chance to go out and get in a real fight. It's cleaner, more satisfying, and more fun.

Jesus. I was spending too much time with Hank.

"So tomorrow we have Ray Gerchuk and Blake Purcell for sure," I said. "Maybe Aaron Whitsel if we have time."

Lindsey nodded. "You saw my outline for where I think they're going with Gerchuk?"

"I did. Any other suggestions for cross?"

Lindsey shook her head. "Honestly Nate, you need to get him off the stand as quickly as possible. The more time that jury spends looking at that body, the less likely it is we're going to win."

"Jeff's going to put those pictures up every chance he gets."

"I know. And his main chance is when Gerchuk is on the stand. You need to get him out of the courtroom."

I looked at Cyn. "You agree?"

She nodded. "I do. You'll be able to explain a few of the breaks. That would still leave about twenty."

"Got it. Danny, did you talk to Olivia today?"

Danny started when I said his name. "I did."

"Any more on Purcell?"

He checked a legal pad. "Still no source of income. Still living in the same apartment he was in before he dropped out of school."

"What's the rent on that?"

He told me. It was about the same as the mortgage on our first house. "That's a lot for somebody with no income. He has to be the local connection, doesn't he?"

"Sure seems like it."

"We don't know that," said Cyn.

"No, but we do know that our client beat a man to death and our only chance is talking about the local heroin connection."

"I understand that. I'm saying be careful."

"Got it. All right, Lindsey get in touch with Sheriff Dushane, tell him we're looking at Thursday for his testimony."

"Done."

"And the same goes for our toxicologist."

"Thursday?"

"Yes. Cyn, I'll email you the outline of my topics for tomorrow so that you can load any exhibits into the software."

"They're already loaded."

"Right. I mean so that you can get to them quickly."

She smiled. "I will get to them quickly."

A good lawyer knows when to concede the point. "Danny, make sure you add the jury instruction that a witness can't speculate. We want their testimony limited to what they've seen."

Danny cocked his head. "Does it matter?"

"It might on appeal. I'll be working on my cross-examination. Let me know if you need anything."

As one, we crumpled our Subway wrappers and scattered to our offices.

IT WAS JUST PAST ELEVEN O'CLOCK THAT NIGHT WHEN I WALKED into my house. Just enough time for a quick snack and sleep before I had to be up at five and back into the office to prepare for day two. My phone buzzed. A text from my sister-in-law, Izzy.

*Fucking bitch wrote another article about Sarah.*

I sighed and put my tablet case on the kitchen table. *What now?* I texted.

*It's all about how that flaming asshole Pearson was the officer who investigated her death. Some of his comments from back then on how there are just certain risks for drug addicts that the police department can't protect against.*

I felt a familiar flash of rage and quashed it. *Didn't see it. Can't do anything about it right now. Trial prep. Thanks for letting me know.*

*Sorry to bother you. Thought you should know.*

A pause of three dots and then, *Fuck Pearson.*

I smiled. I could hear Izzy's raspy voice as she typed it. *Fuck Pearson,* I replied.

I set my phone down, grabbed a bowl, and poured some

cereal. Raisin Bran in case you were wondering. I sat at the table and munched, staring at my phone.

I couldn't look at the article. I couldn't afford to take the journey it would send me on, not when I had to be back at work in five hours. So I finished my cereal and I put the bowl in the sink and I went to the family room, set my phone alarm, and went to sleep.

Eventually.

THE NEXT MORNING WE WERE IN THE COURTROOM ORGANIZING things for the day's testimony when Judge Gallon came out of her office. "I want counsel in my chambers," she said without preamble. "Now."

Jeff and I looked at each other and both of us shook our heads and shrugged, not knowing what was happening. Lindsey joined us as we went into Judge Gallon's chambers with the exact same feeling as when you'd been called to the principal's office with no idea what you'd done but with a clear impression that it was bad.

When we entered, Judge Gallon had her computer monitor facing us. The Entertainment Buzz logo was at the top of her screen and underneath it a big, red headline:

### DOUBLE JEOPARDY

*Defense attorney cross-examines officer
who investigated wife's death*

I expected the headline, or something like it, thanks to Izzy's text last night. I did not expect the picture of my wife smiling back at me. I covered by looking away and sitting down in one of the chairs.

Jeff plopped his bulk into a chair too. As Lindsey took a seat on the other side of me, we all knew enough to keep our mouths shut until Judge Gallon spoke.

She let us stew in it for about thirty seconds. I didn't look at the screen. Couldn't was probably a better description but close enough. Instead, I stared at Judge Gallon, waiting.

She took off her glasses. Many people who wear glasses all the time seem lost when they're off, as if the focus of their face has changed. Judge Gallon was the opposite— when she took off her glasses, it was like unhooding a hawk. She glared at all three of us before she said, "I think my gag order was pretty clear. No press. No talking about the case."

I nodded. Jeff and Lindsey did too.

"This is a capital murder case," Judge Gallon said. "It's not a soap opera."

I looked at Lindsey, who shook her head and shrugged. "Your Honor," I said. "I haven't read the article but I haven't spoken to any press and neither has Lindsey."

Jeff shook his head. "I haven't either, Your Honor. Your order was very clear."

"Well, I've read it and while none of you are quoted, your family is," she pointed at me, "and your officer is," she pointed at Jeff. "And that's going to stop."

That surprised me. "My family?"

"Yes." She turned the monitor back towards her. "One Isabella Shepherd. She's your sister-in-law, isn't she?"

Shit, Izzy. "She is. What did she say?"

"That the police haven't done enough to find out who poisoned her sister-in-law. And the object of her particular scorn is one Chief Detective in Charge of Serious Crimes, Mitchell Pearson who, when asked for his comments, said that we'd all be better off if junkies stopped blaming others for what they do to themselves."

Hate is a strong word. I felt a surge of it toward Pearson.

"Your Honor, I—" said Jeff.

Judge Gallon raised a hand. "Oh, there's more—quotes from the sister-in-law about the failure to stop the flood of heroin into Carrefour and from the detective about individual responsibility and hard choices and self-determination. Do I need to go on?"

Three voices said, "No, Your Honor."

"One man's life has been taken and another's is at stake. I will not have it played out in a Hollywood tabloid, do you understand me?"

"Yes, Your Honor."

Judge Gallon pointed at me again. "You will button up your family until this trial is over."

She turned to Jeff. "And you will button up all law enforcement witnesses. I know you don't have control over laypeople, but if you call a witness, I expect you to direct them not to comment until after the trial is over and to make sure that it happens." We nodded.

Finally, she turned and pointed at Lindsey. "As far as I can see, you're the only one I'm not mad at. Don't make me start."

"Understood, Your Honor," said Lindsey.

"All right," Judge Gallon said. She put her glasses back on and waved a hand. "We've delayed the jury long enough with this nonsense. Are you ready to go, Mr. Hanson?"

"I am."

"Who do we have next?"

"Ray Gerchuk, Your Honor."

"Nothing like an autopsy first thing in the morning. I hope they ate."

I cocked my head.

"Usually doesn't sit well on a coffee stomach," she said.

I nodded and we went out into the courtroom to take the testimony of the Carrefour coroner, Ray Gerchuk.

RAY GERCHUK'S TESTIMONY WAS EVEN WORSE THAN I EXPECTED. He was taller and he was tanner than he had seemed in his office and his blonde-white hair had a distinguished surfer look to it that made him seem accessible and smart. He was congenial and charming and it made no sense that he was a coroner until he started talking about his qualifications—about how he went to undergrad at the University of Michigan and got his medical degree from Penn and served a tour in Afghanistan as a physician before coming back and diving into his true love of pathology and investigation—and then you got a clear sense of his intellectual curiosity and of his love of figuring out how things had happened to people. Ray was immensely talented— he'd investigated hundreds of cases that were unclear, had put together subtle physical evidence from victims' bodies that led to arrests where the police were stymied, had solved mysteries where the police hadn't even realized that there had been an intentional killing.

This was not one of those cases.

Ray Gerchuck, with a devastating mix of charm and respectful seriousness, took the jury through each and every one of Dillon Chase's fractures. He showed them how he knew that the skull had been fractured in seventeen places. After showing them a raw picture, he worked from a diagram that showed each crack and indentation in Dillon Chase's head. He gave an elegantly simple explanation of what those fractures would do to a person's brain and why any one of them alone would likely be severe enough to kill a person. He described his eminently reasonable basis for thinking that the seventeen fractures were caused by six blows, linking five of them to Hank's fist or furniture, and candidly admitting that the last one might have been linked to the impact of Chase's head smacking the tile floor but that he wasn't certain.

He showed the jury how both of Chase's arms had been broken, the right one at the humerus above the elbow and the ulna below, and the left one across both bones in the forearm. He opined that these were typical defensive injuries that happened when a person raised their hands to protect their head but the blows continued.

He led the jury through the eight rib fractures, explaining that it wasn't clear whether this was done by a fist or an elbow or a boot but acknowledging that it was certainly possible that half of them had come, if an upcoming witness's testimony was to be believed, when the body of Dillon Chase had been lifted and slammed over Hank Braggi's knee. He showed the internal damage the slam had caused, how two of the ribs had punctured a lung, how the liver had been lacerated, and how Dillon Chase's spleen had exploded in a way that you only saw when someone ran into a semi-truck at sixty miles an hour.

After leading the jury through all of these injuries, Ray Gerchuck opined that the internal chest injuries probably happened after Dillon Chase was dead. He was able to tell this from the way the blood pooled and they didn't hemorrhage the way they should have if Dillon Chase had still been alive. And when he was done with the scientific explanation, he stopped using animated diagrams and switched to the external photos. He testified that the pictures of the bent and twisted arms were indeed accurate, that the solid wall of bruise on the ribs was consistent with what he had found, and that, even though the face was an unrecognizable pulp which made visual identification impossible, he had identified Dillon Chase from his dental records and fingerprints.

It took all morning. When he was done, the jury looked nauseated. And angry.

As Jeff sat down, Judge Gallon looked at the clock and then looked at me. "Mr. Shepherd, how long are you going to be?"

It was 11:45.

Lindsey leaned into me. "You *cannot* let this go into the afternoon."

"I don't have much, Your Honor," I said. "I can finish with Dr. Gerchuk before lunch and let him get back to work."

I knew Ray well enough to know that he would typically crack a joke about his patients dying to see him or cooling their heels in the waiting room but, since it was a capital murder trial, he kept a straight face and simply nodded when Judge Gallon said, "Proceed then, Mr. Shepherd."

"Thank you, Your Honor. Dr. Gerchuk, you testified a little bit ago that Mr. Chase's broken arms were defensive injuries, correct?"

"I did, Mr. Shepherd."

"The forearm injuries could have been offensive injuries as well, couldn't they?"

Dr. Gerchuk thought for a moment. "They could have been. Defensive is more likely though."

"You examined Mr. Chase's hands and knuckles as well, didn't you?"

"I did."

"His knuckles were scraped and torn, weren't they?"

"They were."

"That's consistent with an injury from striking someone, isn't it?"

"It is."

"You would agree with me that although there are other possible causes of the abrasions on his knuckles, striking someone is the most likely explanation, true?"

"That's true."

I pointed at the back of the prosecutions' blow-ups. "Dr. Gerchuck, you and Mr. Hanson spent several hours going over the detail of Mr. Chase's injuries this morning."

Ray nodded. "We did."

"Is it fair to assume that the skull fractures are the cause of death?"

"It is."

"Could one of them alone have done it?"

"Yes. But to kill him as quickly as it did, it was probably more than one."

"How many was enough? Three, four?"

I wouldn't normally ask an open-ended question like this of an opposing expert but I knew Ray would give the jury an objective opinion. He thought, then said, "Judging from my examination, I'd say any three of the fractures would have hemorrhaged his brain, causing his death."

"Three punches are all it would have taken?"

"Or two," said Dr. Gerchuck. "If one of the punches also caused Mr. Chase to hit his head on the floor or the wall."

"Let's say three. Bam, Bam, Bam." I hit my fist into my palm each time. It took about two seconds. "You're saying that's all it took?"

"Most likely."

I nodded and moved to the next topic. "Dr. Gerchuk, when you're performing an examination, you can fingerprint the body, can't you?"

"I can. Usually, I do it in association with someone from the police department since they fingerprint more than I do."

"Sometimes it's done for identification purposes, right?"

"It is."

"That fingerprinting was done in this case, wasn't it?"

"It was."

"Was that done for identification purposes here?"

"We had his ID and other witness testimony about who he was so it wasn't strictly necessary for identification. I assumed the police wanted it as part of their investigation."

Jeff stood. "Objection, Your Honor."

Judge Gallon nodded. "Please limit your thoughts to what you knew, Dr. Gerchuk."

"Sure, Your Honor," said Dr. Gerchuck. "At the request of the police department, I assisted in taking Chase's fingerprints."

"And you delivered those fingerprints to the police department, didn't you?"

"I did."

"Immediately? Before your examination was complete?"

Dr. Gerchuck nodded. "Yes, I gave them fingerprints before I had completed my report in case they needed them."

"And you were able to get good clear prints, weren't you?"

"I was."

"Sufficient to use for identification, correct?"

"Assuming you had an accurate sample to match, yes."

"Now Doctor, as part of your examination you performed a toxicology study on Mr. Chase, didn't you?"

"I did."

"And Doctor, so that the jury understands what we're talking about, by toxicology we mean that you analyzed the level of certain drugs and alcohol in Mr. Chase's system, true?"

"That's true."

"You tested for opiates?"

"I did."

"You tested for marijuana?"

"Yes."

"Amphetamines?"

"Yes."

"Heroin?"

"Yes."

"And you tested for alcohol too, didn't you?"

"I did."

"Doctor, I'm handing you what's been marked as State's Exhibit 52. That's a copy of your autopsy, correct?"

Dr. Gerchuk flipped through the pages. "It is."

"And on page twelve, that's a copy of your toxicology report, isn't it?"

"It is."

"Cyn, could you blow that up for the jury please." The toxicology page of the autopsy went up on the big screen. "Doctor, you didn't have any significant findings on toxicology, did you?"

"I did not."

"That means Mr. Chase didn't have any marijuana in his system, did he?"

"He did not."

"He didn't have any alcohol in his system, did he?"

"He did not."

"He did not have any heroin in his system, did he?"

"He did not."

"He did not have any amphetamines or fentanyl or any other drug in his system that you were able to find, correct?"

"That's true."

"In other words, he was sober in the hours leading up to his death, wasn't he?"

"He was."

"He was not under the influence of any drugs, medications, or alcohol which would have inhibited his judgment in any way, was he?"

"He was not."

"So he would have known exactly what he was doing, wouldn't he?"

Jeff stood. "Objection, Your Honor."

"Sustained."

"Let me put it another way, Dr. Gerchuk," I said. "I want you to assume that people in the hotel suite that night were drinking alcohol or using drugs. Mr. Chase was not one of them, was he?"

"Based on my testing, Mr. Chase did not drink alcohol or use drugs in the hours before his death."

"Thank you, Dr. Gerchuck. That's all I have, Your Honor."

"Redirect, Mr. Hanson?"

"Yes, Your Honor."

Jeff stood and made his slow way to the podium and seemed to think for a moment. "Dr. Gerchuk, you mentioned that both of Mr. Chase's arms were broken, didn't you?"

"I did."

"And you indicated that those were most likely defensive injuries?"

"Most likely."

"And those injuries occur when a person raises their hands to block blows coming in, right?"

"That's true."

"So the blows that he was blocking would've been powerful enough to break bones, right?"

"These were, Mr. Hanson, yes."

"Now Mr. Shepherd asked you about some scrapes on Mr. Chase's knuckles. Do you remember that?"

"Yes."

"That's what they were, scrapes on his knuckles?"

"Yes."

"Is it possible for a person to scrape his knuckles when he's blocking blows that break his bones?"

I stood. "Objection, Your Honor."

"Withdrawn, Your Honor. Now, Mr. Shepherd also asked you about the fingerprints you took of Mr. Chase. Do you recall that?"

"I do."

"You received the personal possessions of Mr. Chase along with the body, didn't you?"

"I did."

"And did that include a driver's license and photo ID?"

"It did."

"So you had Mr. Chase's driver's license?"

"I did."

"Then why did you have to take his fingerprints to help identify him?"

Ray Gerchuk didn't blink. "Because his face was unrecognizable."

"What do you mean his face was unrecognizable, Dr. Gerchuk?"

"I mean it wasn't possible to match his face to the picture on his driver's license."

"Are you telling the jury that Mr. Chase's face was so broken and misshapen and bloody that it wasn't possible to determine who he was?"

Sometimes you have to pass on an objection, even though it might be sustained, because the objection will just emphasize the point. If I objected here, I would be emphasizing that Chase's face was so broken, misshapen, and bloody that it was impossible to identify him, which the jury had already seen in photos six feet high. I stayed seated.

"That's true," said Dr. Gerchuk. "His features were distorted from the blows."

"Now Dr. Gerchuk, I understand that Mr. Chase's features were distorted. Were some of them also missing?"

I glanced at Lindsey, quickly so the jury wouldn't notice. She shook her head slightly.

"They were. Or one was, I should say."

"One identifying feature was missing?"

"Yes."

"And what was that?"

"The victim's nose."

The court grew silent. All eyes were on Dr. Gerchuk, and when no questions were forthcoming, they shifted to Jeff, who stood there slowly shaking his head. "Dr. Gerchuk." He drew it out. "Are you saying Dillon Chase's nose was gone?"

"Yes."

Jeff rummaged around in his pile of blow-ups, taking his time, until he found the one he wanted. I looked at it. I looked at the jury. All of their eyes were on the picture.

"Could you show me what you mean?" said Jeff.

Ray Gerchuk took a laser pointer and circled an area in the center of Dillon Chase's misshapen head. It might just as well have been the laser sight of a rifle pointed right at Hank Braggi's head.

"Do you see this area here?" Dr. Gerchuck circled the laser pointer around a bloody hole.

"I do," said Jeff.

"That's where the nose would normally be."

I had stared at that picture a hundred times. I had seen the caved-in skull and the misshapen mass and the broken teeth, but the head was caved-in in such a way and the damage was so catastrophic that it just hadn't occurred to me to emphasize that the nose was gone. Not once.

"Can you tell the jury what happened to it?"

"I don't know exactly. My understanding is that the tissue was never found at the scene."

"Do you have a theory?"

I stood. "Objection, Your Honor. Dr. Gerchuk can only testify as to what's probable."

"Sustained," said Judge Gallon, but she clearly wanted to hear as much as everyone else what Dr. Gerchuck thought.

"Fair enough," said Jeff. "Dr. Gerchuk, does the physical evidence indicate to you that Mr. Chase's nose was removed?"

"It does.

"How?"

"The nose should be here." Ray circled the gaping hole with the laser pointer again. "Do you see this jutting bone?"

"I do." Jeff looked at the jury to make sure they saw it too.

"That's the base of the nose and the skull. Now, do you see this torn tissue?" He traced a ragged line of flesh in a triangle up and down the bone ridge. Now that the coroner was pointing it out to me with the laser pointer, I saw it clearly.

"I do."

"That's the skin where the nose used to be connected. The cartilage, though, is all gone."

"Can you tell how it was removed?"

"I've seen this before and it's consistent with one of two things."

I stood. "Objection, Your Honor. If he can't testify to a probability as to which one it is, then the evidence doesn't come in."

"Your Honor, I believe Dr. Gerchuk is going to testify, to a certainty it was one of two things."

Judge Gallon looked at him. "Is that true, Dr. Gerchuk?"

Ray Gerchuk nodded in a solemn, charming, defense-killing kind of way. "It is."

"Overruled. You may answer the question, Dr. Gerchuk."

Dr. Gerchuck used the infernal laser pointer. "Do you see how the skin is jagged here on the right and then becomes smooth and tails away on the left?"

Jeff shook his head in a disingenuous, questioning way. "I'm sorry, Dr. Gerchuk, I don't. Can you show me?"

Dr. Gerchuk ran the laser pointer over the jagged line on the right side of the hole. "See how it's jagged here"—he traced the line—"and then it becomes a smooth tear that tails up toward the eye?"

"I do now, thank you. What does that tell us?"

"It tells us that the skin was grabbed here on the right and then lifted and torn to the left."

"And what does that tell us about the mechanism of injury?"

"See these squared off indentations here, on the right?" He circled with the laser pointer again.

"I do."

"In this situation, I would say that this is consistent with one of two things."

"And what are those?"

"It is either the front tread of a work boot or teeth."

Jeff looks surprised. "Teeth? Are you saying Dillon Chase's nose was *bitten* off?"

"Or kicked off. I'm not sure which. But it was one of the two."

"Goodness," said Jeff and slowly made his way back toward his table. When he got there, he turned and tapped the table three times with one of his thick fingers. "Dr. Gerchuk, were you ever provided with Mr. Chase's nose?"

Ray shook his head. "As I mentioned, I was not."

"Would you expect it to be given to you if it was found at the scene?"

"Usually I'm given anything related to the body so I can examine it."

"But no nose here?"

"No."

"No further questions. Your Honor."

Judge Gallon turned to me. "Re-cross, Mr. Shepherd?" Her look made it clear she thought that would be an awful idea.

"Just one, Your Honor. Dr. Gerchuk, the injury to Mr. Chase's nose didn't cause his death, did it?"

Ray Gerchuck appeared to actually think about it. "No, Mr. Shepherd, it didn't."

"No further questions, Your Honor."

Judge Gallon nodded. "You may be excused, Dr. Gerchuk." As Ray Gerchuck walked down the aisle out of the court, Judge Gallon looked at the clock and said, "It's now 12:10. It was a long morning. Let's take a little extra time for lunch. Members of the jury, please return at 1:30 and we will continue with testimony. Thank you."

The jury filed out. A few looked at the picture still on the easel. None of them looked at me or Hank. Jeff kept his head down, straightening papers that had no need of straightening, careful to keep his face neutral as the jury filed past.

Lindsey leaned in so that her mouth was right next to my ear. "If there's still a deal out there, we need to take it."

I looked at her. Her eyes were cold steel as she mouthed, "We're fucked."

## 28

We were all huddled tightly in the hallway—me, Lindsey, Cyn, and Hank. "Did you bite his nose off?" I said. I kept my face neutral for any passers-by but my teeth were clenched.

Hank shrugged. "I couldn't say."

"What?"

"I was pissed."

"You mean that *could* have happened?"

"It's a fight, Counselor. Anything can happen." He tapped his ear, then pointed at me. "You know that."

Hank's ice-blue eyes were open and without guile and he seemed utterly unaware of the disaster that had just occurred. Cyn touched my arm. "Why don't I take Hank to get some lunch?"

I nodded and the two of them went to get a sandwich from the deli stand.

"I'm sorry, Nate," said Lindsey. "I totally missed the nose."

"Not your fault, Lindsey. I've looked at that picture dozens of times and I was so caught up in the overall damage that I missed the implication."

"But I was in charge of figuring out what they would do with the autopsy."

"And I'm in charge of the case. My fault." Lindsey looked unconvinced but it didn't matter, we had to get ready for the next witness. "Jeff's calling Purcell next."

"Did you get anything on him?"

"Nothing solid. But it doesn't matter. We have to go with it."

Lindsey looked over my shoulder at the courtroom doors. "Is it too late to take the deal?"

"It's not on the table anymore. And Hank wouldn't take it if it was."

She ground her teeth. "We're not letting him get executed."

"No, we're not. Go get something to eat."

She nodded. "Want anything?"

I raised my paper bag and bottle of water. "Got a movable feast right here."

She touched my shoulder and then went to join Cyn and Hank. I went to the other end of the hall to where Cade Brickson sat, unobtrusively keeping an eye on his two million dollar investment in Hank's continued presence. He wore a suit that didn't fit right since the only way to make a suit fit over those massive shoulders was to pay a tailor ten thousand dollars but he still looked impressive.

"Was it as bad as it looked?" I said.

"Every bit."

I nodded. "Have you seen a blonde reporter in the gallery?"

"Investigations are my sister's thing."

"Let me know if you see her questioning any of our folk, will you?"

"You want me to let you know if she's nosing around?"

"If you could."

"Make sure she's keeping her nose clean?"

"Just keep your eyes open is all."

"Then follow my nose if I see something?" Cade's face was expressionless.

I sighed. "Will you?"

He nodded in a way that made no promise.

"Thanks."

I took my sandwich and my water and my trial notebook and found a corner on the third floor to eat and review my cross-examination of Blake Purcell.

∾

"COULD YOU STATE YOUR NAME FOR THE RECORD PLEASE?" SAID Jeff.

"Blake Purcell." He was wearing a fine blue suit with an open collar shirt and seemed as at home as if he were sitting in his living room in front of the TV or, more likely, at a bar filled with coeds. His hair had an extra layer of product and the suit looked a little nicer than an out-of-work former college student would wear.

"And what do you do, Blake?"

"I'm a student at the University."

"Were you at the Lizzy Saint concert the night Dillon Chase was killed?"

"I was."

"Were you a friend of Dillon Chase?"

"I met Dillon that night, at the concert. Aaron knew a girl who knew him and he promised to get us backstage passes."

"That's Aaron Whitsel?"

"Yes."

"Why would Dillon get you backstage passes?"

Blake shrugged. "I'm not sure," he said. "I think he liked Aaron's friend."

"And he just invited you to go backstage with him?"

Blake smiled. "A concert's a concert, sir. Things happen."

"Did you watch the concert?"

Blake smiled again. "You don't watch a Lizzy Saint concert. You experience it."

It was Jeff's turn to smile now. "You'll have to forgive an old, fat lawyer. Did you experience the Lizzy Saint concert that night?"

"Sure did. And you're never too old to 'Rip It.'"

"I don't think my daughter would agree with you."

Blake smiled and the jury chuckled.

Shit.

"So after you experienced the Lizzy Saint concert, what happened next?"

"Me and Aaron, we found Dillon and he gave us a couple of passes to get us back."

"What about the woman?"

"It's a concert. People...drift."

"So what did you do then?"

"We hung out and we drank some beer and we talked. It seemed like a lot of the people in the room were VIPs or people who had bought the special experience or crew members. It was a good crowd. Fun."

"And then?"

"And then after a little bit, we noticed that people were funneling off one or two at a time through a doorway in the back. So Dillon just tells us to wait for a little bit and disappears, and sure enough, about half an hour later, he comes back and leads us right through."

"Right through to where?"

"To the next level of the party. Now we see people that look like management and other artists and the opening act and the quality of booze—" Blake put his hand over his head and made a quick "pffft" noise, "Next level. So we hang out there for, I don't know, two or three beers worth and then Dillon says, 'Time to pass the next gate, boys.'"

"What did he mean?"

"Hell if I knew—"

"Mr. Purcell," said Judge Gallon

"I'm sorry, Judge." He didn't look sorry at all. "I didn't know what he meant at the time but he said just to stay close to him and we'd get to the real party."

"Was Aaron with you still?"

"He was. He was real nervous. Felt like we were crashing even though Dillon had IDs for all three of us because we didn't really know anybody but Dillon said he had it handled so not to worry about it."

"And did he? Have it handled?"

Blake shrugged. "They passed us through sure as sh—shooting, we were through to the next level."

"Which was what?"

"The main party. We were back there with Lizzy Saint and Jared Smoke and David Bender and the whole damn band. It was amazing."

Judge Gallon started speaking and Jeff raised his hand. "Blake. This is court. We need to be careful with our language."

"Right, right. Sorry."

"Thank you. Now Blake what was Aaron doing during this time?"

"When we actually saw Lizzy, he was kind of freaking out. Dillon pulled him aside and told him not to worry, that we were allowed to be there, and we were allowed to have a great time. That calmed him down and once he started talking to David Bender about the baselines he used in *Ripper*, well, that was pretty much it. We couldn't believe our luck and we couldn't believe how much fun we were having."

"And were you there for a while?"

"We were."

"Do you know how long?"

"Not really. Four or five beers maybe?"

"Now Blake, I have to ask you, were you drinking that night?"

"Sure."

"A lot?"

He shrugged. "It was a Lizzy Saint concert."

"So that's a 'yes?'"

He smiled. "It's an 'of course.'"

"Did you use anything else?"

For the first time, Blake shifted in his seat and looked around. "Uhm, can't I say the Fifth Amendment or something?"

"You could. To the extent it matters though, recreational use of marijuana became legal in this state a year ago."

"Oh, well, in that case, I did smoke a little."

"So you smoked and you drank, yes?"

"I did."

"Did you lose any memories from that night?"

"No. The opposite."

"By the opposite, what do you mean?"

"Well, it was the scariest night of my life so I remember it pretty clearly."

"What do you mean?"

"What do you mean, what do I mean? That lunatic killed Dillon and almost killed Aaron."

"Objection, Your Honor." I stood and said it and immediately realized I shouldn't have.

"Basis?"

"Characterization and speculation."

Jeff smiled. "I'll withdraw and rephrase, Your Honor. Was it scary because Hank Braggi killed Dillon and almost killed your friend Aaron?"

"Exactly."

Nice going, Shepherd.

"So what happened next?"

"So we were having a great time. Aaron was talking to David Bender, Dillon and I were talking to Jared Smoke, and Lizzy was drifting in and out of our conversations."

"Was Hank Braggi there?"

"He was. He mostly was talking to Lizzy but he was also talking to a lot of other people."

"Did you talk to him?"

"I did not. Seemed like a decent enough guy at the time."

"Nothing unusual about his behavior."

"Not yet."

"So what happened next?"

"So the party was winding down a little but, you know, after a concert, two in the morning is like two in the afternoon to the band, and Dillon and Aaron and I were so jacked up from being with them that we were wide awake too. So after the suits left and the crew started to scatter, Jared gets riled up and says, 'We don't have to travel tomorrow, so there's no goddam way we're crashing early.' Sorry, Your Honor, that's what he said."

"The Court understands," said Judge Gallon with a slight smile.

"So Jared invites us all up to the suite to keep the party rolling."

"By 'us all' you mean Dillon Chase and Aaron Whitsel and you?"

"Yep. So we fill a bucket with beers and head up to the suite."

"Was Hank Braggi with the group going upstairs?"

Blake shook his head. "No. I didn't see him until later."

"So what happened next?"

"We went up to this suite—I got the impression it was Lizzy and Jared's and that they were some kind of thing—and hung out."

"Hung out. What do you mean?"

"I mean Aaron and I were talking and we were drinking and we couldn't believe how lucky we were. I mean, we were partying with Lizzy Saint. It was nuts."

"Were you talking to Lizzy?"

"We had been but not right then though. Her and Dillon were talking."

"Now this is important, Mr. Purcell. Was Ms. Saint unconscious?"

"Not up until then."

"You said you had smoked?"

He glanced at the judge and looked down with the right amount of concern and said, " A little."

"Did you smoke then?"

"No. I had had enough."

"Did you take anything else while you were in that room?"

"Like what?"

"Like heroin?"

"No. No, sir."

"Did Aaron use any heroin?"

Blake laughed. "Have you met Aaron?"

"I have."

"Then you know the answer to that is no way."

"How about Lizzy Saint and Dillon Chase? While you were in that room that night after the concert, the night that Dillon Chase died, did you see either of them use heroin?"

"I did not."

"Not Lizzy Saint?"

"No."

"And not Dillon Chase?"

"No."

"So what happened next?"

"So Lizzy was drifting a little bit, seemed as tired as she was drunk, and we asked Jared if we should go and he said, 'Hell no, that's what she looks like right before she rallies.' Then he told us to go back downstairs and get another bucket of beers and a bottle of Jack and to bring it back and we'd keep things rolling. So we did."

"How long were you gone?"

Blake shrugged. "A little while. It took us a little bit to find the bartender."

"What happened next?"

"We went back upstairs to the suite and as we turn the corner, we see Braggi going into the room. Then we heard screaming and a crash and we ran down the hall."

"What happened next?"

"Well, we get there just behind him and we see Braggi flying across the room at Dillon."

"How do you know he was running at Dillon?"

"Because he knocked him clean off his feet; put his shoulder down and tackled him, just like an NFL linebacker. Only madder."

"Where was Ms. Saint when this happened?"

"She was sitting in one of the chairs."

"Did she react in any way?"

"I didn't really notice. I was too worried about what was happening."

"And what was happening?"

"Like I said, Braggi here knocks Dillon to the floor and goes down on one knee and just starts whaling on him, big swings with those huge hands of his right down on Dillon's head. So Aaron gets there first and he runs over and tries to knock Braggi down like Braggi had done to Chase, but Braggi just takes it and catches his balance and comes to his feet and whirls around and pops Aaron."

"Mr. Braggi attacked Aaron?"

"You bet your a—you bet he did. He'd sort of been on a knee and he stands up and launches one right at Aaron's head."

"What do you mean 'launches one at his head?'"

"I mean, he throws a punch at Aaron's head and fortunately Aaron ducks and the punch hits him in the shoulder, but then Braggi hits him again on the top of the head and then throws an elbow that opens up one of his eyes and then he drops."

"Aaron does?"

"Right. So now I'm running over and Braggi doesn't even look at me. He turns back to Chase, who was on his feet punching at Braggi, and takes another swing at him."

"Did you see what happened to Mr. Chase next?"

"I didn't, but I wasn't looking. I run over and I see Aaron on the ground and his eye's bleeding and his head is sort of lolling around and I pull him to his feet thinking this crazy man is going to kill me."

"What did you do next?"

"We got the hell out of there."

"You left Mr. Chase?"

Blake shrugged. "We had just met him. We didn't know what beef he had with Braggi. And my friend was bleeding all over the place and couldn't move his right arm. So yeah. I got him out of there."

"Where did you go?"

"We went to my place first. We got the bleeding stopped over his eye, but then the more we sat there and the more the booze wore off, he realized he couldn't move his arm so eventually I took him to the hospital."

"You went with him?"

"I did. He was in a lot of pain. No way he could drive."

"Did you call the police?"

"We did not."

"Why not?"

"We were busy going to the hospital."

"But you had seen an attack."

Blake shrugged. "Getting medical care from the attack seemed more important."

"But this was serious."

"So was Aaron's pain. And, at the time, we didn't know how serious it was."

"What do you mean by that?"

"We didn't know that Dillon was dead."

"Were you surprised when you learned that Dillon was dead?"

"No. Braggi's attack was vicious. Aaron is lucky that he wasn't killed too."

"Did it seem to you like Hank was trying to kill Aaron?"

"Objection, Your Honor," I said.

"Sustained."

"Did Hank attack Aaron with the same fury that he attacked Dillon with?"

"Objection, Your Honor," I said again.

Judge Gallon paused. "I'll allow it. Overruled."

"Enough fury to break his arm and cut his face. He's lucky I got him out of there."

"Eventually the police found you, is that right?"

"They did."

"I'm going to hand you what's been marked as State's Exhibit 53. Can you identify that for the jury, please?"

Blake examined a piece of paper before saying, "That's a copy of the witness statement I gave the police."

"And did you give the police that statement the day after the killing?"

"I did."

"And is it accurate?"

"It is."

"Thank you, Mr. Purcell. That's all I have, Your Honor."

Judge Gallon looked at me. "Mr. Shepherd?"

Jeff had made a lot of points there. I had to undo what I could. "Mr. Purcell, you did not see Hank Braggi kill Dillon Chase, did you?"

Purcell cocked his head. "What?"

"When you ran out of the room, Dillon Chase was still alive, wasn't he?"

"He was getting the crap beat out of him."

"But he was alive, true?"

"He was."

"Because if you thought he was being killed, you would have called the police, right?"

"Yes."

"Unless you had some other reason not to call the police, right?"

"Like getting my friend medical help, yes."

"You mentioned that you saw Mr. Braggi open the door and then walk into the room, true?"

"I think I said run into the room. But yes."

"And you arrived just behind him?"

"I did."

"And you saw Mr. Braggi tackle Dillon Chase, true?"

"I did."

"That's because Dillon Chase was injecting Lizzy Saint with heroin, wasn't he?"

"Objection, Your Honor," said Jeff. "He can't say why Braggi did anything."

"I'll rephrase, Your Honor. When you saw Hank Braggi run across the room, Dillon Chase was injecting Lizzy Saint with heroin, wasn't he?"

"No."

"He wasn't injecting Lizzy Saint with heroin or you didn't see him injecting Lizzy Saint with heroin?"

Purcell shook his head. "I didn't see him inject her with anything. And I think that I would've because it wasn't that big a room."

I went to the exhibit table, picked up the plastic bag with the syringe, and held it up. "This syringe was found in the suite that night. You're saying you did not see this in Dillon Chase's hand?"

"I did not."

"You're claiming that you did not see anyone using in the suite that night?"

"I'm not claiming it. I didn't."

"But somebody was, weren't they?"

"I don't know that."

"And somebody brought the heroin into the suite that day, didn't they?"

"I don't know that."

"Really? Do you see legs on this syringe, Mr. Purcell?"

"Objection, Your Honor."

"Withdrawn. Did you say anything to Mr. Braggi when he entered the room?"

"No. I was surprised by the suddenness of it. And then there was the scream and we got there and before I knew it, he was on Dillon. I yelled at him then to stop."

"Did he respond to you?"

Purcell shook his head. "No, he was yelling. Bellowing more like."

"You said Hank knocked Aaron down, right?"

"He did."

"And that Dillon Chase was able to get to his feet while Mr. Braggi was hitting Aaron, true?"

"True."

"And that Mr. Chase struck Mr. Braggi when Aaron was knocked down, right?"

Blake paused a long moment before he said, "Yes."

"So the jury understands, you saw Mr. Chase strike Mr. Braggi."

"After Braggi attacked him, yes."

"You saw Chase strike Braggi three times, didn't you?"

"I don't recall that," said Purcell.

"Mr. Purcell you still have your statement in front of you, do you see it?"

"I do."

"And at the bottom, you certified that everything in your statement was true and accurate, didn't you?"

He looked at the statement. "I guess."

"Is that your signature at the bottom?"

"Yes."

"Mr. Purcell, if you go to the second paragraph of your statement on the third line it says that 'Dillon Chase got to his feet and punched Braggi three or four times while I pulled Aaron away.' Did I read that accurately?"

A pause. "You did."

"So you saw Dillon Chase punch Mr. Braggi three or four times, didn't you?"

"I guess so."

"That's not a guess. That's what you said in the statement you gave the next day, right?"

"Yes."

"Mr. Purcell, Dillon Chase wasn't drinking that night, was he?"

Blake cocked his head to the right and stared at me. "I thought he was. It seemed like he was having a good time."

"Did you actually see him take a drink at any point during the night?"

"He had to have. Everyone was."

"Dr. Ray Gerchuk testified earlier this morning that Mr. Chase's blood was free of alcohol. You don't disagree, do you?"

Purcell shrugged. "I guess not."

"So Mr. Chase was in control of his decision-making that night, wasn't he?"

"I wouldn't know," Purcell said before Jeff could object.

"You didn't see anything that would indicate that Mr. Chase was incapacitated, did you?"

"No."

"Ms. Saint was pretty drunk that night though, wasn't she?"

Purcell shifted in his seat. "Not at first."

"But by the end of the night she was, wasn't she?"

"I suppose."

"Did you see her eyes fluttering shut?"

"I might've."

"You saw her stagger, didn't you?"

"I don't remember that."

"We can look at your statement again if you like."

"I guess maybe once or twice."

"She was drinking whiskey, wasn't she?"

"She was."

"And you had at least three shots with her, didn't you?"

"You have to do a shot with Lizzy Saint if you have the chance."

"And you saw other people do shots with her that night too, didn't you?"

Purcell shrugged. "She's a rock star, man."

"There were security guards there that night, right?"

"There were people checking IDs as we went to each level of the party."

"Did you see a guy named Rick?"

"I don't know any of their names."

"Big guy. Black earrings. Tattoo of a crow's head on his arm?"

"Oh, yeah. I remember the tattoo."

"He was outside of the room that led to the suite, right?"

"I believe so."

That was all of the basic information I knew for sure. There was one other area though, an area I needed to win. I didn't have the background information to confirm it, but I was pretty sure I was right, so the next question I asked was, "Mr. Purcell, you live in the College West apartment complex, don't you?"

"I do."

"And you've lived there for five years?"

"I have."

"That's predominantly college housing, isn't it?"

"Mostly. There're others like me that used to go to the University."

"You went to the University for three years, right?"

"I did."

"Stopped going two years ago?"

"That's right."

"My understanding is that you didn't fail out but that you stopped going, correct?"

"That's true."

"Why did you stop?"

Blake shrugged. "I wanted to pursue other opportunities."

"Oh? Where do you work?"

Jeff stood. "Your Honor, this area of inquiry doesn't seem relevant to what Mr. Purcell witnessed on the night Dillon Chase was killed."

Judge Gallon looked at me in a way that said she agreed. "Mr. Shepherd?"

"If you give me a little bit of leeway, Your Honor, I believe this ties into why Mr. Purcell was there on the night Dillon Chase died."

"A very little bit of leeway, Mr. Shepherd. Let's try and get to the point."

"Your apartment is a three-bedroom, isn't it, Mr. Purcell?"

"It is."

"But you live there alone, right?"

"I do."

"The rent runs about two thousand a month?"

"More or less."

"You drove your Wrangler here today, right?"

Blake gritted his teeth. "Does that matter?"

"Pretty simple question, Mr. Purcell."

"I drove here."

"In the Wrangler?"

"Yes."

"But you don't have a job, do you?"

"I'm more of an independent contractor."

"Doing what?"

"This and that."

"Do you sell things?"

"Your Honor," said Jeff.

"You're out of leeway, Mr. Shepherd," said Judge Gallon. "No more questions on this topic unless you have something directly relevant to ask the witness."

"Did you bring heroin with you that night to the concert, Mr. Purcell?"

Blake smirked. "No."

"Did you give it to someone else to bring?"

"No."

"Did you sell heroin to anyone that night?"

"I did not."

I held the syringe up. "And it's your testimony to this jury that you never saw this syringe full of heroin in the suite."

"That's right."

"And you're telling us that you haven't seen this syringe until today in this courtroom."

"That's right."

"Or this rubber tubing."

"Correct."

"Or this baggie."

"None of it."

"No further questions, Your Honor."

"Mr. Hanson?"

"Just a couple, Your Honor. Mr. Purcell, do you have a source of income?"

Blake looked away and shrugged. "I get by."

"Now, Mr. Shepherd was just implying that there might be something suspicious about your income."

I stood. "Objection, Your Honor. I said no such thing."

"That's what implied means, Your Honor," said Jeff.

"Counsel will direct their arguments to me," Judge Gallon snapped. "Overruled. This door was opened by Mr. Shepherd. Go ahead, Mr. Hanson. Briefly."

Jeff nodded. "I know you don't like to talk about it, Blake, but you are here in court under oath and it's important. Do you have a source of income that explains your car and your apartment and your lifestyle?"

Purcell looked away and for the first time on the stand, he looked uncomfortable. He shrugged and said, "I guess."

"And what is that source of income?"

"My grandpa was pretty well off. He left a trust that gives me a monthly payment."

"And when did your grandfather pass away, Blake?"

"About two years ago."

"About the same time you quit college?"

Purcell looked down and nodded his head.

"I'm sorry, Blake, but you have to answer out loud."

"Yes."

"Is that what you've been living on?"

"Yes."

I pretended to write a note on my pad but I was really just working to keep a straight face. I'd mistaken a trust fund baby for a drug dealer.

Shit.

AFTER PURCELL WAS FINISHED, JUDGE GALLON DISMISSED THE jury for the day and then dismissed us. As people filed out, Cade came up to collect Hank and take him home. I glanced at the back of the courtroom but didn't see Maggie White, the reporter. "Anything?" I said.

"Not that I saw," said Cade.

Hank slapped Cade on his massive shoulder. "What's for dinner, Tiny?"

I wasn't in the mood for banter. "I'll see you guys tomorrow," I said and told the rest of the team we'd meet back at the office in forty-five minutes.

I drove back by myself. The day had been a disaster. Ray Gerchuk had been just as effective as I'd thought he would be describing every broken bone in Dillon Chase's body. That had been bad enough, but the extra evidence of either beating or biting the nose right off Chase's face probably destroyed any argument that Hank had used reasonable force to defend Lizzy. I'd established some evidence that Dillon Chase was sober so that if he was injecting an unconscious woman, he was a knowing scumbag, and I'd established that he and Hank had fought, but I didn't see any way that an Artist or a Pepsi Driver or a Retired Math Teacher would think that they'd do what Hank had done in the same situation.

And then there was the red herring I'd chased with Blake. I'd been certain with his high-priced expenses and no source of support that he had been the connection to the drugs, that he had been selling to Dillon and that that was why he had been there. Instead, I'd looked like a jackass when it turned out his money had come from his dear departed grandpa.

Sweet Jesus. If I were Jeff, I'd be tempted to end the trial right there. It had been that bad.

It wasn't until I was all the way back to the office that I realized the other thing Blake's testimony meant.

Aaron Whitsel was the drug dealer.

## 29

"Well, that was a disaster," said Lindsey. The four of us were sitting around the conference table munching on Potbelly sandwiches.

"How could we have missed the nose?" said Danny. He was taking that particularly hard because he'd been studying the autopsy right along with Lindsey.

I shook my head and took a bite, chewing on hot peppers and shame. "You haven't read that many autopsies, Danny," I said. "My fault."

Lindsey shook her head. "That one's on me."

"Things happen at trial, guys. We learn and move on."

"But I—"

Cyn cut Danny off. "Nathan's right, Daniel. We have to figure out how to address it, not worry about whose fault it was. We have to make the jury believe that what Hank did was necessary to stop Chase."

Danny stared at his sandwich. "The jury was having trouble keeping their lunch down."

"We'll keep playing the drug angle," I said. "Of course, I did accuse the wrong guy of being a drug dealer today. So there's that."

Cyn nodded coolly. "That was a setback, but you just have to hit Whitsel with it when he's on the stand and then beat this heroin drum until the jury is just as sick from it as it is with Hank."

"Agreed." I turned to Lindsey. "Your thoughts?"

"We're in deep shit." She wiped a little olive oil from the corner of her mouth with a napkin and crumpled it into her sandwich wrapper. "I think the jury heard more than enough today to have the state push the plunger on Hank. I think we need to take Jeff's deal."

I glanced at Cyn and said, "The deal is a non-starter."

"Well, you better fucking start it because our client's about to get the death penalty."

"Would it even still be on the table?" said Danny.

"We need to find out," said Lindsey.

"No way he's offering us less than life," I said.

"That's better than death."

I thought for a moment and then tapped the table. "I'll talk to Hank tonight and see where his head's at."

"If it's on his shoulders, he should take a deal," said Lindsey. "So what do we have tomorrow?"

I smiled. "Tomorrow the circus comes to town. Saint in the morning, Smoke in the afternoon."

"You need to call Hanson tonight," said Lindsey.

"I can't call Hanson the day he kicked our ass, Lindsey, you know that." I said. "If I call today, there's no way we get less than life without parole. We'll see if we can make some headway tomorrow with Saint and Smoke and then bring it up."

"It doesn't matter," said Cyn, folding her hands. "Hank won't go for it."

I raised a hand. "We need to make some ground back tomorrow. We need to make our case to people like the parents of Lizzy Saint who would be grateful that someone prevented an amoral sycophant from pumping their daughter full of poison."

I checked the time. "I'll go see Hank now. Lindsey, call Warren Dushane and make sure he's ready to talk about his drug tag task force on Thursday."

She nodded.

"Danny, make sure the toxicologist is ready to go the same day."

"What time?"

"Morning."

"Okay."

"Cyn, you better come with me."

"You know what my position is on this."

"I know. I want all my 'no's' in the same place when I talk to them."

"Fine." She stood, somehow still as neat and unwrinkled and sharp as she had been at seven o'clock that morning.

We left and went to see Hank.

USUALLY, WHEN A LAWYER AND HIS TEAM IS MEETING WITH THE client, the lawyer and the paralegal sit on one side and the client sits on the other. It's unconscious and it doesn't matter, it's just the way that people will tend to sit. Tonight, though, I was on one side of the table and Hank and Cyn were on the other. Cade had left us each a cup of coffee then gone into his family room and turned on the Detroit Tigers game.

Although it had only been three days since his haircut, Hank's curls already seemed to be getting as unruly as his glittering blue eyes. Cyn was all sharp angles and neat lines but her green eyes seemed just as bright and just as hard. They didn't look anything alike, but at that moment, their gaze was exactly the same.

I didn't give a shit.

"You know today didn't go very well, Hank."

Hank shrugged. "Every battle line has its surge and retreat."

Hank and his goddamn battle metaphors. Well, if that's what it took. "They've got us fighting a rearguard action right now, Hank. They're beating us back pretty good."

"But we haven't had our turn to attack yet, right? When we get to put on our own case?"

"True. But today dug us a pretty deep hole."

Hank cocked his head. "How so?"

"The autopsy was pretty bad. The jury was having a hard time looking at it."

"But I was defending Lizzy."

"True. But the way you did it was so brutal that I think the jury is going to have a hard time getting past that."

"So, let me get this straight, Counselor. I'm allowed to use force to defend Lizzy?"

"You are."

"As much force as she would be allowed to use, right?"

"Right."

"So if she would be allowed to use deadly force, I would be allowed to use deadly force."

"Exactly."

"Well, bolts and balls, Counselor, that's exactly what happened. Dillon Chase was about to inject Lizzy in a way that could have killed her. So I stopped him just like she would have if she'd been able."

I shook my head. "You didn't stop him like she would have, Hank. That jury isn't going to believe that Lizzy Saint would've broken Chase's skull in seventeen places, they're not going to believe that Lizzy would've broken his ribs and his arms, and they're certainly not going to believe that she would have knocked his nose right off his face. They might believe that she was justified in defending herself, but they will never believe that she would've done all that."

Hank laughed then and it was a clear sound that was surprisingly joyful. He laughed and he laughed and he kept laughing until even Cyn started to smile, which was a fairly amazing sight. As his laughter trailed away, he shook his head and said, "So you're telling me that the jury might believe I was allowed to use deadly force, but that I used too much deadly force?"

"Yes. You would've been better off shooting him. The beating served no purpose, especially after he was dead. What it showed was that you're brutal and dangerous."

Hank chuckled again. "Well, both of those are certainly true. So. There you go."

I thought. Cyn was being no help but I knew she wouldn't be. "Hank, it's my job to tell you what the risks are. And I'm telling you that after what happened today, there's a good chance the jury's going to convict you and there's a good chance that they're going to impose the death penalty when they're done."

"I understand what you're saying, Counselor. What I'm saying is that I still want you to fight."

"I will, Hank. But if we lose, you're going to die."

Hank smiled then and it seemed to me that he was looking at me with glittering happiness. "That's how you know you're in a real fight."

I stared at the two of them, my crazy client and his ice-cold enabler. "That's insane, Hank."

Hank smiled. "Your fancy-ass tests say otherwise."

"Let me call the prosecutor and see if we can get you a deal.

Let me see if I can avoid the death penalty for you. I think a plea is the best chance you have."

"No."

Finally, all I could say was, "Hank, why?"

Hank seemed amused but he listened and, it was clear, he thought. After a moment, he said, "I grew up near a long valley that Norway and Russia share. There are woods and there are rivers and lakes and it's about as beautiful a place as you'll ever see. I spent all my time out in it, wandering, fishing, bird-hunting." He smiled. "Do you know the sun doesn't set for two months in the summer there?"

"No."

"It doesn't. When I was sixteen, me and three friends camped out until the sun set. Two months." He smiled. "The Midnight Sun camp out."

The smile faded. "Nikel, Russia is just four miles from the border. You can see the smoke and filth of the smelter from Norway, a plume of ugly brown that's always there. From our town of Kirkenes, we could see the migrating waterfowl of the Pasvik Nature Reserve and the clouds of sulphurous smoke rolling out of Russian smelts in the same sky. On any day, if the wind was right, Russia would send acid raining down on our town from the sky."

Hank's normally cheerful gaze was icy-serious. "The job of the Home Guard was to fight if Russia ever sent troops over that border along with the smoke. I told you before, if Russia invaded, the Home Guard was to vanish into our woods and then do everything we could to harass and fight and hamper the Russian forces."

"You mentioned it. Fight a guerilla war, right?"

Hank nodded. "Exactly. Our job was to fight, Nate. Against an overwhelming force. Even if it meant destroying our own bridges, our own roads, our own towns. We were to fight that Red Army until help arrived or until we were dead."

Hank stared at me then, with blue eyes that carried the weight of centuries of Viking fury in them. "Our job was not to negotiate terms for Norway's surrender."

"I understand, Hank," I said. "But we're not talking about a country's survival here. We're talking about yours."

Hank smiled then, and it was like the midnight sun in winter. He gestured with both hands. "I'm more songwriter than soldier, Counselor. You know that. It's why I took advantage of the Guard training program to come to Minnesota, see the States, and eventually immigrate here. But I'm still both things. We're going to fight. We're going to meet fury with more. We're going to win or we're going to lose. And we're going to write a song about it after. A proper one for Lizzy to sing, with a voice as pure as a nightingale and as rasping as a deathblow."

The passion in Hank's voice almost made me believe it was true. I looked to Cyn for help and found none. Finally, I said, "Okay, Hank. I won't call Hanson about it. But you know this is probably our last chance, right?"

"Our last chance for a deal," said Hank. "Not our last chance to win."

"Fair enough." I stood. "Sorry Hank, but I had to bring the idea to you."

"Every commander has unpleasant tasks to manage. You're just handling yours." He turned to Cyn. "Love to my stepmother?"

"Of course," said Cyn smoothing her already smooth skirt. "Anything for your father?"

Hank grinned. "Hell no. Just tell him we're still fighting. He'll like that part."

"He will." Cyn put a hand on his shoulder and made to leave.

I extended my hand and he shook it with those big powerful sledgehammers that felt like they could grind bone.

Which, of course, they could.

"Goodnight, Hank," I said and we left.

CYN AND I WERE DRIVING BACK TO THE OFFICE IN MY JEEP. "Thanks for nothing," I said.

"My company is not nothing."

Very true. "You could at least try to convince his family to talk to him."

"I already told you, I have and they agree with Hank."

"Is that the truth?"

A passing set of headlights revealed a flash of green eyes as she glared at me in the dark. "The truth is the only thing I deal in."

"Then the truth is that Hank is fucked. Excuse me, I mean screwed."

"No, he's fucked. Unless you can get the jury to see the truth of what he did. Of what was at stake."

I shook my head. "It's a good thing you're so talented at trial."

"Why is that?"

"Because you're no help otherwise."

We didn't talk the rest of the way back to the office.

It didn't seem to bother Cyn at all.

## 30

WHEN WE PULLED INTO THE COURT PARKING LOT THE NEXT DAY, SIX news trucks had beaten me there. There were the three local affiliates and some unmarked satellite trucks that I assumed were local stringers that had been hired by national outfits to broadcast. There were people lined up on the courthouse lawn, four and five deep on either side of the walk. The police department had erected some temporary rope and positioned a few officers along the path to keep it clear. One of them nodded and waved me over. "Come with me, Mr. Shepherd. We'll take you straight up."

Lindsey and Cyn seemed to take it all in stride but I thought Danny's eyes were going to pop out of his head. There was a little bit of shouting, but not much, and instead a sea of phones went up into the air as we passed and there were shouts of "Over here!" and "Nate! Nate! This way!" It was a circus and a far cry from what you normally saw at the Carrefour courthouse.

Lizzy Saint had come to town.

∾

Rick Reynolds, the big security guard with the black earrings and the crow's head tattoo, was the first one to testify. He seemed even bigger in the confined space of the courtroom than he did mingling with rock stars and crowds. Jeff put him on the stand, led him through the basics of where he worked and what he did and how long he had worked with the tour before he asked, "Mr. Reynolds, were you working the night Mr. Chase was killed?"

"I was."

"Where were you?"

"I was working the door to the main party." He looked at Hank. "Our security was a little different then."

"So you didn't follow Ms. Saint around?"

"No. I just made sure people had a credential to enter the banquet room."

"Did you see Ms. Saint and Mr. Chase that evening?"

"I saw just about everybody that evening."

Jeff nodded as if he meant to elicit that response even though we both know he hadn't. "I understand. Did you see Ms. Saint leave the main banquet room that night?"

"I did."

"How did she seem to you?"

"She seemed fine."

"Did she leave under her own power?"

"How else would she leave?"

"Good point. By that I mean did she walk on her own?"

"Yes."

"Was anyone helping her?"

"Not that I saw."

"Did she leave by herself or with a group?"

"With a group. That's why I wasn't concerned about it. She was with Jared, like she usually is, and there were a couple of other people with them."

"By Jared, you mean Jared Smoke?"

"Yes."

"Can you identify any of the other people who were with her?"

"I couldn't at the time. Now I know that one of them was Dillon Chase."

"How do you know that?"

"By seeing his picture on TV."

"You recognize him from his picture?"

"I do."

"Do you recognize any of the others she left with that night?"

"I don't."

"So you saw them leave?"

"I did."

"Mr. Chase didn't have his hands on Ms. Saint?"

"No."

"He didn't appear to be pulling her away or coercing her?"

"No."

"And is Jared Smoke Ms. Saint's boyfriend?"

Reynolds smiled. "I don't know if that's exactly how they'd describe it."

Jeff smiled. "Fair enough. They're together?"

"You'd have to ask them that."

Jeff looked at the ceiling for a moment as if he was a father trying to figure out just who his teenager was dating. "You have observed Jared Smoke and Lizzy Saint spending a lot of time together?"

"I have. Same as the rest of the band."

"It's not unusual for them to leave together though?"

"No."

"It was common enough that, as a security guard, that didn't bother you, right?"

"That's true."

"As a security guard for Lizzy Saint's tour, you also know Hank Braggi?"

The guard looked at Hank and nodded. "I do."

"Do you get along?"

"We did."

"Don't you now?"

Reynolds shrugged. "We don't see each other much now."

"Of course. Did you see Hank Braggi the night that Dillon Chase was killed?"

"I did."

"When?"

"All night. It was a concert night and Hank was the sound man."

"Of course, I'm sorry. Let's keep it to the after-party. Did you see Hank at the party after the concert?"

"I did."

"Was he drinking?"

"I don't recall. Probably."

"Why would you say probably?"

"Because most people were."

"Did you see Hank before Ms. Saint left the party?"

"I'm sure I did, but I don't remember that."

"Did you see him after Ms. Saint left the party?"

"I did."

"What did you see?"

"A little bit after Lizzy left, Hank asked if I had seen her. I told him that she had left with Jared and some other guys. He said 'Who?' I said, 'I don't know, some guys I hadn't seen before.' He asked if they were with the tour. I told him I didn't think so. He said, 'Which way?' I told him, and he left."

"Did he seem agitated?"

I stood. "Objection, Your Honor."

"I'll rephrase. How did Hank act when he left?"

"Like he was in a hurry."

"And did he leave in the same direction that Ms. Saint had?"

"Yes."

"Did you see Mr. Braggi again that night?"

"I did."

"When?"

"There was a report of a problem in Lizzy's suite. I ran up there, found Lizzy and Hank and the body, and called the police."

"Jared Smoke was there too?"

"Yes."

"Did Hank tell you he'd killed Mr. Chase?"

"He did."

"What happened next?"

"There were two officers in the hotel already so they were there right away and took over things."

"Did you see Mr. Braggi again that night?"

"As the police were leading him out."

"After he'd killed Dillon Chase?"

"Yes."

"And how was Hank acting then?"

"Well, he was in handcuffs so he wasn't doing cartwheels."

"Was he shouting?"

"No."

"Yelling?"

"No."

"Crying?"

The guard laughed a little. "No."

"Was he calm?"

"I guess."

"And was he covered in blood?"

"Yes."

"No further questions, Your Honor."

"Mr. Shepherd?" said Judge Gallon.

"Thank you, Your Honor. Mr. Reynolds, you had never seen Mr. Chase before?"

"No, I hadn't."

"You don't know who Blake Purcell is, do you?"

"No."

"You don't know who Aaron Whitsel is, do you?"

"No."

"Have you seen their pictures on TV since the incident?"

"Yes."

"Having seen their pictures, you can identify them as being at the party that night, right?"

"Yes."

"You saw them run out of the hotel, didn't you?"

"Yes."

"Were you able to catch them?"

"I didn't chase them."

"What did you do?"

"I went to Lizzy's suite."

"Were you the one who called the police?"

"I was."

"Did Hank Braggi seek to stop you in any way?"

"No."

"He told you what happened in the suite?"

"Yes."

"He told you that he killed Dillon Chase, didn't he?"

"He did."

"He told you, that night, that Dillon Chase had tried to inject Lizzy with heroin while she was unconscious, didn't he?"

Reynolds nodded. "He did."

"He told you to call the police, didn't he?"

"I already had."

"But he didn't know that and he told you to call them, didn't he?"

"He did."

"What was Jared Smoke doing then?"

"Jared was holding Lizzy."

"Was Lizzy conscious?"

Reynolds paused. "She was in and out."

"Earlier, when Mr. Hanson was questioning you, you said that Jared and Lizzy left with Dillon and men that you didn't know, correct?"

"Yes."

"So Jared was there to protect Lizzy if anything went wrong, right?"

The guard smiled at that. "I guess so."

"You smiled. Why?"

"Jared's not much of a fighter."

"Musicians usually aren't, are they?"

Reynolds smiled even broader. "Plenty of musicians are fighters. I toured with Kid Rock once."

Michigan was Kid Rock country so the jury and everyone else there chuckled at that. "I stand corrected," I said.

"Fighting's just not Jared's thing. He's protective though."

"Oh? How so?"

"He's just one of those guys that's always close by, always checking on what she was doing."

"I see. Was Jared talking to these other men as he left with Ms. Saint?"

"Yes."

"It wasn't like Dillon Chase and the others were sneaking along behind them?"

"No. They appeared to be partying together."

"You talked to Jared after this happened?"

"I did."

"What did you say to him?"

"I asked him where he was."

"Where he was when?"

"When this guy was injecting Lizzy."

"And what did Jared say?"

"He said he was in the bathroom."

"So, according to Jared, he wasn't there when Lizzy was being injected?"

Reynolds shrugged. "That's what he said at the time."

"But Hank was."

"That's what he said at the time."

"That's all, Mr. Reynolds. Thanks."

People think cross-examination is a bunch of gotchas. It's not. It's laying a series of blocks, some of which seem insignificant, that you can build your closing argument upon. Though we hadn't gotten much from Reynolds, we got in blocks to show that Hank was calm, that Hank was acting in Lizzy's best interests, and that he was the only one there to do it. Sometimes that's as good as you can do.

"Mr. Hanson?" said Judge Gallon.

"Yes, Your Honor. No more questions for Mr. Reynolds. The State calls Lizzy Saint."

The room buzzed.

Lizzy surprised me when she walked into the courtroom. She was dressed in a conservative black suit with a black silk shirt and heels that were high for a lawyer and short for a rock star. Her auburn hair, which was wild and wet the last time I'd seen her, was pulled loosely back with a broad black clip at the base of her neck and not one was out of place. Her makeup was conservative with the slightest black upturn at the corners of her eyelashes. She had an edge to her, sure, but she could've just as easily been a corporate executive for a pro sports team as a rock star.

She walked up the aisle with easy confidence, fully aware that everyone was watching her. In her wake, Max Simpson, the attorney I'd met in North Carolina, slipped into the front row. Judging from what I'd seen of him before, he was here to make sure Hanson lived up to whatever agreement he'd made to bring her in to testify.

I snuck a glance at Hank. He was beaming. As Lizzy walked past the jury and took the witness stand, she glanced at Hank, smiled, and gave him a little wave. Hank's smile broadened.

Score one for us.

Jeff let things settle down a little bit until the jury was practically leaning forward to hear. "Could you state your name, please?"

"Lizzy Saint."

"And is that your legal name Ms. Saint?"

"It is."

"What was your name before you changed it?"

"Lizzy Saint was my name at the time of the incident, Mr. Hanson. I don't see how my name when I was born is relevant to what I saw."

Jeff blinked. Lizzy stared.

Jeff recovered and smiled. "Fair enough. And what do you do for a living Ms. Saint?"

"I produce music."

"Rock 'n' roll?"

"Categories are made by labels who try to box us in, Mr. Hanson. I produce music."

"And do you tour?"

"I do."

"And is that why you were in Carrefour last spring?"

"It is."

"Do you remember the concert you played here?"

"I do." She smiled. "The crowd in Carrefour was great. Three encores, I think."

"And do you remember the night after the concert here?"

"I do not."

A murmur went up through the courtroom.

"No memory at all?"

"None."

"Why is that?"

Lizzy Saint shrugged. "My band and I had a little bit to drink before the show. We had a little bit to drink during the show. We had a lot to drink after the show. I don't remember anything after the show."

"Ms. Saint, I'm going to hand you what's been marked as State's Exhibit 56 and tell you that this is a copy of the report made by Chief Detective Pearson. In it, he states that he talked to you about what happened. Are you saying you have no recollection of that conversation?"

"That's exactly what I'm saying."

"And that's because you were drunk?"

"Very. I woke up the next morning in a hotel room and didn't remember any of it. Jared had quite a story to tell me."

"Detective Pearson wrote that you said that Hank Braggi beat Dillon Chase to death."

"I don't recall that. But I understand that Hank told the officer that."

Jeff regrouped as he came around the other side of the podium. "Ms. Saint, would you describe Hank as protective?"

"No more than normal."

"At a show in Tulsa last year, did Hank throw a fan off the stage?"

"He did. The man had gotten past security and he—"

"Thank you, Ms. Saint. And at a show in Phoenix, did Mr. Braggi break a fan's foot?"

"He accidentally stepped on a fan's foot when the crowd was pressing around our car and he was trying to clear a way for me. For us."

"So the answer is 'yes?'"

"Yes."

"Mr. Braggi once threw a photographer from the *Daily Turn* into a swimming pool?"

Lizzy chuckled. "He did. Are you going to let me explain why?"

"I don't think that's relevant."

"Then you should know that he threw his camera equipment into the water after him."

There was a deep rumbling chuckle from next to me. Hank.

"So Hank has a history of violent interactions with your fans?"

"No, he doesn't."

"Ms. Saint, you used to write with Mr. Braggi, didn't you?"

"I did. Two albums." She smiled. "He helped me break through."

"I see. The first one was the *Ripper* album?"

"Yes."

"You haven't written with Mr. Braggi for more than a year, have you?"

"About two, I think."

"So Mr. Braggi is no longer your writing partner?"

"I don't know that we ever had anything as formal as that but the sitting down and writing of an album? No, we don't do that now."

"Who do you write with now?"

"The last two have been with Jared. Some on my own."

"But Mr. Braggi is still part of the tour?"

"He's the best sound engineer we've ever had." Hank smiled and nodded his head.

"That could create ill feelings, couldn't it?"

"Being a good sound engineer? I don't think so."

"No, Ms. Saint, I mean being one of your original writers and then being shut out."

Lizzy smiled. "Hank wasn't shut out. He's just giving me the space to write on my own."

"You mean with Mr. Smoke."

Lizzy shrugged. "Sure."

"Do you still socialize with Mr. Braggi?"

"Of course. We're on tour two hundred and fifty days a year. We're a tight family."

"That night, the night that he killed Dillon Chase, Hank wasn't invited up to the suite with you, was he?"

I'd let a lot go because it didn't matter. Now, I stood and said, "Objection, Your Honor. Leading."

"I'll rephrase, Your Honor. The night Mr. Braggi killed Dillon Chase, who was invited up to your suite?"

"I thought I was pretty clear on that, Mr. Hanson. I don't remember."

"So if another witness said that Mr. Braggi was not invited, you wouldn't disagree with him?

"Hank is always invited."

"But Ms. Saint, you don't have any memory of that night. So you can't say whether anyone invited him to join you or not, can you?"

"Hank is always invited."

"Ms. Saint, I appreciate that this can be difficult and I understand what your usual practice is. But you've already told the jury that you have no memory of that night, true?"

"True."

"So you can't look at the jury and tell them that you invited Hank to join your party in the suite that night, can you?"

"I cannot."

"And if someone else testifies that Hank specifically was not invited, you can't disagree with that person based on your memory of that night, can you?"

"I cannot. Although I'd like to know the asshole who didn't invite him."

Jeff smiled, looked at the Judge, and said, "No further questions, Your Honor."

"Mr. Shepherd?"

"Thank you, Your Honor. Ms. Saint, do you use heroin?"

"Objection," said a voice.

I looked over at Jeff and saw that he was still sitting in his seat, surprised. A well-dressed man in the first row was standing behind him and continued, "That goes against the terms of the agreement for Ms. Saint to testify here today."

Max Simpson, the Grindhouse lawyer I had met in North Carolina. I chuckled.

"Counsel will approach the bench," said Judge Gallon. Jeff and Lindsey and I made our way forward. Max started to walk through the gate to our side of the barrier when Judge Gallon snapped, "You will sit down, sir."

Max paused at the gate, then sat down.

When Jeff and Lindsey and I had reached the bench, Judge Gallon said, "All right, Mr. Hanson, who is that man and what is he talking about?"

"That's Mr. Simpson, Lizzy Saint's personal counsel."

"What's this agreement he's talking about?"

"In exchange for appearing voluntarily, we agreed that we would only ask questions in certain areas and avoid others."

Judge Gallon looked at me over her glasses. "Are you a party to this agreement?"

"This is the first I've heard of it, Your Honor."

Judge Gallon nodded and looked back at Jeff. "Is this gentleman licensed to practice law in the state of Ohio?"

"I don't know your honor," Jeff said. I smiled. We all had a guess.

"Very well. Return to your tables."

I went back to the lectern but, before I could resume my questions, Judge Gallon raised a hand to wait and said, "Sir, will you please stand up."

Max did.

"What is your name?"

"Max Simpson, Your Honor."

"Mr. Simpson, are you an attorney?"

"I am, Your Honor."

"Mr. Simpson, are you licensed to practice law in the state of Ohio?"

I watched the wave of nausea pass over Max's face. "No, Your Honor."

"Mr. Simpson, what jurisdictions are you licensed in?"

"New York, Pennsylvania, and Delaware, Your Honor."

"Mr. Simpson, I'm going to assume that you were just over-whelmed with excitement and accidentally and totally forgot yourself. If you speak again or so much as twitch during the rest of this trial, I will be contacting the bars of New York, Pennsylvania, and Delaware to inform them that you attempted to practice law in a capital murder case in a state in which you are not licensed. Do you understand me?"

"I do, Your Honor. My apologies."

"Sit." Judge Gallon turned to the jury. "The jury will disregard the statement from this unlicensed gentleman. Because he is not a lawyer in this state, he has no right to speak in these proceedings and should not have done so. Further, Mr. Braggi's counsel has the right to cross-examine any witness who testifies against Mr. Braggi, regardless of any arrangements which the prosecutor entered into in order to procure that witness's attendance. Mr. Shepherd, you may proceed with your cross-examination."

"Thank you, Your Honor. Ms. Saint, do you use heroin?"

"No."

"Have you ever used heroin?"

"No."

"Do you drink?"

"I do."

"Do you smoke marijuana?"

"On occasion. Not often. It's bad for my voice."

"Have you ever used anything stronger than alcohol or marijuana?"

Lizzy thought for a moment before she said, "There was a period about four years ago when I was having trouble sleeping and the doctor prescribed me Ambien. The second time I woke up halfway through eating a pizza with no memory of ordering it, though, I quit. Nothing since."

"Ms. Saint, do you have any desire to try heroin?"

"I do not."

"Why is that?"

"I've had exposure to people who use in my line of work. They either quit or die from it."

"Ms. Saint, if someone held you down and tried to inject you with heroin, would you try to fight them off?"

Jeff stood. "Objection, Your Honor."

"Overruled."

"Yes, I would," said Lizzy.

"Would you do everything in your power to stop them?" I asked.

"Yes, I would."

"If you were unable to stop them, would you want someone else to?"

"Objection, Your Honor," said Jeff.

"Overruled," said Judge Gallon.

Lizzy nodded. "Yes, I would."

I paused for a moment and looked down at my notebook. I knew exactly where I was, but I wanted to let that answer sit there for a moment before I went on to a new area. Eventually, I flipped the page and said, "Ms. Saint, Hank Braggi cowrote your first album with you, didn't he?"

"Yes, he did."

"That album was *Ripper?*"

"It was."

"That album went platinum?"

"Several times."

"It won a Grammy for best new album?"

"It did."

"Hank co-wrote your second album with you too, right?"

"He did."

"That album was *Jacked*?"

"It was."

"That album also went platinum?"

"It did. As many times as the first."

"Ms. Saint, did you fire Hank Braggi from cowriting albums with you?"

Lizzy smiled. "I did not."

"What happened?"

"I wanted him to work on the third album with me but Hank stepped back. He said I needed to find my own voice without any influence from him or others and he encouraged me to write in exactly the way I wanted."

"There were no ill feelings between you?"

"Absolutely not."

"He stayed on as your sound engineer?"

"He did."

"He did not have any conflict with your management?"

"He did not."

"A little bit ago, Mr. Hanson asked you about Hank throwing a reporter from the *Daily Turn* into a swimming pool. Do you remember those questions?"

"I do."

"Mr. Hanson didn't give you an opportunity to explain why Hank did that. Would you like to now?"

"I would." Lizzy turned to the jury with the air of someone who's used to communicating with a lot of people at once. "We were in the first floor of the hotel, right by a pool courtyard. There was a gap in my curtains and Hank caught a reporter trying to take pictures through it while I was changing. Hank picked him up and encouraged him to try from a new, wetter angle. Then he returned the man's camera to him." She smiled. "Turns out soggy memory cards don't hold up well."

"And the time he stepped on a fan's foot?" I said.

"We were trying to get into a car and people were pressing up all around it so that we couldn't even get the doors open. Hank cleared the way so that we could crack the door, get in, and leave. When he did it, he accidentally stepped on a fan's foot."

"And the time he tossed a man off the stage?"

"A fan got past security and grabbed me to say something. Turns out he had a restraining order against him from several other artists that he'd become obsessed with. Hank got rid of him without hurting him."

Time to shift gears again. "Ms. Saint, before the night of the incident, did you know Blake Purcell?"

"I did not."

"Before that night did you know Aaron Whitsel?"

"I did not."

"Before that night did you know Dillon Chase?"

"I did not."

"To your recollection, did you ever give any of these gentlemen permission to inject you with heroin?"

"Absolutely not."

"No further questions, Your Honor."

Jeff Hanson stood before I had taken my seat. "Ms. Saint, would you fracture someone's skull to keep them from giving you heroin?"

Lizzy Saint raised her chin. "I would."

"In seventeen places?"

"If I could."

"Would you break both of his arms?"

"He would deserve it."

"You would break his ribs and puncture his lungs?"

"Every time."

"You would bounce him off every piece of furniture in the hotel room?"

"Like a basketball."

"Would you bite the nose off his face?"

I stood. "Objection, Your Honor. Foundation."

"Sustained."

"Would you beat him until his nose came off?"

Lizzy Saint leaned forward, projecting a stare that could reach the upper deck of a stadium. "If he was injecting me with heroin against my will, he had it coming."

"Would you leave the person like this?"

Jeff pulled out his five-foot-tall blowup of Dillon Chase's face and showed it to Lizzy. Lizzy Saint flinched and her eyes widened. It was clear that she'd never seen a picture of what Chase looked like after Hank got through with him. She shrank backwards and it took her a moment to regain her composure before she said, "I would."

But she had flinched and she had blanched and she had

hesitated. Only for a moment but that moment was enough for everyone to see.

There's no way she would have done it.

Jeff nodded. "Thank you, Ms. Saint. That's all, Your Honor."

"Re-cross, Mr. Shepherd?"

"Ms. Saint, I understand you received medical treatment that night?"

"I did."

"I understand you were given a toxicology screen to determine whether you had been given any drugs, is that true?"

"Yes."

"Was any heroin found in your system?"

"No."

"That's all I have, Your Honor."

"Thank you, Ms. Saint," said Judge Gallon. As Max Simpson hustled Lizzy out of the courtroom, the judge looked at the clock. "We'll break for an hour for lunch. Members of the jury, please be back by 12:55."

The jury filed out. The broken face of Dillon Chase watched them go.

## 31

Jared Smoke's grand entrance into the courtroom was a stark contrast to Lizzy's. Where Lizzy had made the concession from rock singer to hard-edged corporate raider, Smoke decided to stay full on Rocker. His hair was black, of a shade that indicated he was hiding gray hair or brown. He had the drawn, weathered look of someone who'd smoked a lot and slept less but hadn't quite taken the hard turn into Keith Richards-territory yet. He wore black pants, a black shirt, and a long black coat, and if they weren't leather, they were some sort of leather-adjacent material. You know, exactly what you wear in the summertime. He took the stand with the certainty of one who knows their shit absolutely, unequivocally, does not stink. He leaned back, slouched a little bit, and rested his elbow on the handrail as he raised his hand to be sworn in.

When that was done, Jeff said, "Could you introduce yourself to the jury, please?"

"I'm Jared Smoke." He appeared to be used to pyrotechnics when that was announced.

"And Mr. Smoke, are you in Lizzy Saint's band?"

Smoke sat a little straighter. "We're in a band together."

"My apologies. And how long has that been the case?"

"About two years."

"And did you know each other before then?"

"It's a small community. We'd run into each other. Jammed a bit here and there."

"You were on the most recent tour with Ms. Saint?"

"We toured together, yes."

"So you were at the concert at the University the night Dillon Chase was killed?"

"I was."

"Had you met Mr. Chase before that night?"

"I had."

"How?"

"Chase had been around for a while. He's a big music fan and he knew bands and he knew management and venue operators."

"Was that helpful?"

"Very. If you were looking to find someone to fill in on bass for a leg of a tour, or looking to play a certain kind of club to work out some kinks, or even wanted help finding a producer at a label, Chase always knew someone, or knew someone who knew someone, to help you solve the problem."

"Did you invite Mr. Chase to the concert that night?"

Smoke smiled. "Chase didn't need me to invite him to a concert. He probably had about nine different connections that would've given him tickets."

"But you saw him afterwards?"

"I did. It was always good to see Chase. I didn't know he was coming and when I saw him at the meet and greet after, we started talking and catching up."

"I understand Mr. Chase had a couple of friends with him that night?"

"I believe so."

"Did you meet them?"

"I did."

"Do you remember their names?"

"I don't."

"Does Blake Purcell and Aaron Whitsel sound familiar?"

Smoke smirked. "Not really. Party was a little loud."

"I want you to assume that those were the names of Mr. Chase's two friends, okay?"

"If you say so."

"Had you ever met either of them before that night?"

"No. Or if I did, I don't remember."

"Was Lizzy with you when you were catching up with Mr. Chase?"

"Here and there. She had some obligations with meet and greets where you shake hands and take pictures with special fans. My guess is that she was in and out."

Jeff raised a hand. "I'm going to spare Mr. Shepherd the trouble of getting up and objecting. If you don't know something, Mr. Smoke, you need to say so. Please don't guess about whether something happened or not. It's very important that the jury understand what you know and what you don't."

Smoke looked like Jeff had just told him not to walk to Borneo. "Okay."

"So the four of you spent some time at the after-party?"

"We did."

"Did Ms. Saint eventually join you?"

"She did."

"What happened next?"

"The party was winding down so we decided to head on up to the suite and keep it going for a little bit."

"Mr. Smoke, was Ms. Saint intoxicated by this point?"

"We were all intoxicated some by this point."

"What did you do about it?"

He raised an overly dark eyebrow. "We grabbed more beers and a couple of bottles and went to the suite."

"Could Ms. Saint walk?"

"Yes."

"Did she know what she was doing?"

"Seemed to."

"Now, before you left to go to the suite, did Hank Braggi ever join your conversation?"

"No."

"Is that unusual?"

"No. Hank and I don't hang around much."

"Is there a reason for that?"

"Not from my end. Seemed like he stopped hanging around once Lizzy and I became a thing."

"I see. You and Lizzy are a thing?"

"We are."

"You'll have to excuse me, my daughters mock me most days for not knowing the right terminology anymore. Does that mean the two of you are in a relationship?"

Smoke smiled. So did the jury. "It does."

"Are you exclusive?"

"That seems pretty nosy. Did the *Daily Turn* put you up to that one?"

The jury chuckled, as did Jeff. "No, sorry about the rudeness, but it's somewhat important to the case. Are you in an exclusive relationship with Lizzy Saint?"

"I am."

"Does that mean you care for her?"

"It does."

"Does it mean you look out for her?"

"Every day."

"So you and Lizzy and Dillon, Blake, and Aaron all went up to your suite. What happened next?"

"Well, we hung for a while and talked and drank and Dillon was giving us the lowdown from some of the other tours and we were talking about our plans for the next album once this tour was over. Basically having fun. We knew we didn't have to travel the next day so we were able to cut loose a little bit."

"How was Lizzy during this time?"

"Fine. She was a little tired like you would expect after a two-and-a-half-hour concert and she was a little lit, but all in all, she was fine."

"So what happened next?"

"So Dillon and Lizzy were talking about what it would take to add a couple of northwest dates around Labor Day because she had always wanted to be in Seattle and Portland for the fall, and the other two guys had gone to get some more beer because we were running low and I had to use the head so I got up and left."

"To go to the bathroom?"

Smoke nodded his head.

"You need to answer out loud, Mr. Smoke."

"I got up and went to the bathroom." He drew out the syllables in ba-th-a-roooom.

"How long were you gone?"

"Just a couple of minutes at first. But then I got a text from our tour manager saying that the plans had changed and that we needed to leave before noon the next day and so I was texting him back telling him to fuck off because there was no way in hell we were getting up before two-thirty."

The court went silent.

"Mr. Smoke," said Judge Gallon. "You will watch your language."

"What?" He looked around and honestly didn't seem to know what had just happened.

"You can't swear, Mr. Smoke."

"Except to tell the truth, right?"

The joke fell flat and no one laughed. Smoke ducked his head and muttered, "Sorry."

"So you got a text," said Jeff, "and you answered it?"

"I did."

"How long do you think that took?"

"I don't know, maybe five or six more minutes? The bastard —the manager wouldn't let up."

"And did you return to the room?"

"I did. "

"And what did you find?"

"When I opened the door to the bathroom, I heard a crash and a scream. No, not a scream, more like a bellow, like one of those wildebeests you see on the Discovery Channel, and I hear another crash so I run down the little hall from the bathroom to the main room." Smoke paused.

"And what did you see?"

"Blood. The first impression I had was blood. On the wall. On the fridge. On the counters. Everywhere. And then a body flew by and hit the wall right next to me."

Jeff looked surprised. "A body?"

Smoke nodded. "Right through the air. Then right behind it was this crazy-eyed man, covered in blood. In his beard, on his arms, everywhere. "

"Did you recognize him?"

Smoke nodded. "It took me a second but he was so damn, so darn big, it was easy to tell. It was Hank Braggi."

"The defendant?" Jeff pointed.

"Yes."

"What happened next?"

"Well, I didn't know who the body was and I didn't see Dillon or the other two guys, so I assumed we'd been attacked by some nutjob so I looked for Lizzy right away. When I found her on the chair across the room, I ran over to her."

"Was she conscious?"

"Not exactly. Her head was lolling around a little bit and she was muttering but she wasn't really focusing on me either. I was scared that something had happened to her."

"Mr. Smoke, what was Ms. Saint wearing that night?"

Smoke looked confused. "What was she wearing?"

"Her top or shirt in particular."

Smoke's face cleared. "Oh, she was still wearing what she wore at the concert. Black leather vest, no shirt underneath. She likes to show off the guns." He smiled as he said it, but only a couple of jurors smiled with him.

"Mr. Smoke, this is important. Did you find a needle in Ms. Saint's arm?"

He shook his head. "I did not."

"Mr. Smoke, I want you to assume that when someone shoots heroin, they tie tubing or string or a belt around their arm, okay?"

Smoke smirked. "Okay."

Lindsey started jotting a note. I nodded that I understood.

"Did you find tubing or string or a belt tied around her arm?"

"I did not."

"Did you find it on the floor next to her?"

"I did not. "

"Did you find a syringe on the floor next to her?"

"I did not."

"Did anyone use heroin in the suite in your presence that night?"

"No."

"Did anyone say they wanted to use heroin in the suite that night?"

"No."

Jeff nodded and let that sink in a little bit as he walked back to the podium. He tapped it twice with his thick fingers before he said, "What happened next?"

"Well, I was worried about Lizzy and I didn't know if something had happened to her so I was checking her out and I think I was yelling for security but I'm not sure. It was kind of a blur."

"What was Hank doing?"

"Well, remember, I thought that someone had attacked us. Hank was handling it." He shook his head and paused.

"What is it, Mr. Smoke?"

He shook his head again. "I've never seen anything like it. Hank picked up the body so that he was holding it lengthwise and smashed it over his knee. Then he raised it over his head and slammed it to the ground but it hit a coffee table on the way, right in the side of the head, and there was a pop like a melon or something."

"Was the body moving?"

"No. It was flopping around like one of those blow-up balloon advertisements you see outside a car dealership. Just arms and legs everywhere."

"Then what happened?"

"Then Hank kicked it a few times and I'm yelling at Hank what the hell is going on"—he paused and looked at the judge—"that's what I said, Judge."

"That's appropriate testimony, Mr. Smoke," said Judge Gallon.

"And Hank just ignores me and he says something that sounds like gibberish and picks up the body and holds it close to his face and slams it down on the ground one more time."

"He held the head close to his face?"

Smoke nodded.

"Is that a 'yes?'"

"Yes."

"Did he hold it close to his mouth?"

"I can't say that for sure," said Smoke. "His back was to me. He might have."

"I see."

"And this time Hank stops and the body's laying there and it's a bloody mess, bent every which way and I can't tell who the he—heck it is, and then I recognize the boots."

"The boots?"

"They were these awesome vintage drifters, heavy black boots with buckles, mid-calf high. They were Dillon's. Then I knew it was him."

"What did you do next?"

"I freaked out. I start yelling at Hank and yelling for security but I can't move because I'm holding Lizzy with both hands, so I start screaming that she's okay. And Hank just goes kind of still and he stands there for a second and then he goes and sits on a chair in the corner, hands on his knees, straight up and down, as if he's not covered in blood and brains. I keep screaming at him and he ignores me and a few seconds later Reynolds runs in and says he's called the cops and he looks around and he can't believe it and the two of us agree we have to get Lizzy out of there."

"You took her out of the room?"

Jared nodded. "No way I was going to have her wake up and see that."

"You just left Mr. Braggi there?"

"He didn't seem to be going anywhere. And Reynolds was with him."

"Did you eventually talk to Detective Pearson that night?"

"Detective Pearson?"

"The police officer in charge of the investigation. He would have been wearing a suit."

"Oh yeah, big guy? Square jaw like the Tick?"

He had been trying before but that one did get a laugh from the jury. They'd seen Pearson.

"That's the guy," said Jeff. "Did you speak to him?"

"I did."

"What did you tell him?"

He shrugged. "Pretty much what I just told you."

"Your testimony is very similar to the statement he took from you that night. Is there anything else you'd like to add?"

"Not really."

"Did you continue to keep an eye on Ms. Saint?"

"I did."

"Did you see her talk to Detective Pearson?"

"I didn't but there were times when I had to talk to management or the crew to figure out where we were gonna stay and what we were gonna do. This pretty much derailed our travel for the next couple of days so we had some arrangements to make."

"That's all I have, Mr. Smoke. Thank you."

Judge Gallon nodded to me. As I walked to the podium, I said, "Your legal name is Gerald Winkson, isn't it?"

Smoke stiffened. "I go by Jared Smoke."

"I understand that Mr. Winkson but I didn't ask you what you go by. I asked what your legal name is. Your legal name is Gerald Winkson, isn't it?"

"I sign everything Jared Smoke just like Lizzy signs everything Lizzy Saint."

"Well, Ms. Saint has already testified that she's legally changed her name to Lizzy Saint so that's her name. You haven't legally changed your name to Jared Smoke, have you?"

"No."

"So, to be accurate, the record should reflect that Gerald Winkson is testifying here today, right?"

His jaw twitched. "If that makes you happy."

"Are you more comfortable with your assumed name?"

"Yes."

"Okay. Earlier, Mr. Hanson asked if you found a syringe on the floor next to Lizzy Saint. Do you remember that?"

"Yeah."

"You said you didn't find one, correct?"

"Yes."

"You didn't look for one, did you?"

"Well, I saw the floor around her."

"Mr. Smoke, I'm going to hand you what's been marked as State's Exhibit 48." I put the plastic bag marked with a "48" on the witness stand in front of Smoke. "That's a syringe, isn't it?"

"It is."

"An officer has already testified that he found this syringe in the hotel suite that night. Are you saying that's untrue?"

"I'm not."

"You just didn't see it, right?"

"I guess."

"Mr. Hanson also asked you if you saw rubber tubing or string or a belt on Ms. Saint, didn't he?"

"He did."

"You said you did not, true?"

"True."

"I'm going to hand you what's been marked as State's Exhibit 49." I put another baggie on the witness stand. "That's rubber tubing, isn't it?"

He glanced forward and slouched back. "Yes."

"An officer already testified that he found this rubber tubing on the suite floor. Do you have any reason to doubt that?"

"Not really."

"Just because you didn't see it doesn't mean it wasn't there, right?"

"I guess."

"Well, there's no reason to guess Mr. Smoke, is there? The tubing's right there on the witness stand in front of you."

"It is."

"You said you didn't see a needle in Ms. Saint's arm, correct?"

"I didn't."

"You said you didn't see rubber tubing on her arm, correct?"

"I didn't."

"Now, Mr. Smoke, at some point your group was running low on beer, true?"

Smoke nodded. "And whiskey."

"And you sent Mr. Purcell and Mr. Whitsel to get more, right?"

"I thought it was their idea."

"You told them where to get it though, right?"

He shrugged. "Maybe."

"But they definitely left to get the beer, correct?"

"Yes."

"And while Mr. Purcell and Mr. Whitsel were getting beer, there was a time when you went to the bathroom and were not with Ms. Saint, true?"

"Yes, but—"

"—but nothing, Mr. Smoke. My question was simply that there was a time when you were in the bathroom and not with Ms. Saint and Dillon Chase, right?"

Smoke gnawed on the inside of his lip for a moment. "Yes."

"Or to be more accurate, I should say that there was a time that Ms. Saint was drunk and half-conscious, and was alone with Dillon Chase, true?"

"I don't know that."

"Sure you do. When you went to the bathroom, was there anyone in the suite besides Lizzy Saint and Dillon Chase?"

A long pause. "No."

"You weren't worried about that though, were you?"

"I wasn't."

"Because you knew Dillon Chase, true?"

"That's true."

"For many years?"

"Yes."

"Going back to a time when you played with other bands."

"That's true."

"Earlier, you mentioned that Mr. Chase had a lot of connections, right?"

"He did."

"He could put you in touch with all sorts of people, right?"

"Well, some sure."

"No, Mr. Smoke, Mr. Hanson asked you what he could do and you said that he could put you in touch with all sorts of people. Do you remember that?

"Yes."

"That included musicians in other bands, label executives, venues, right?"

"That's true."

"Mr. Chase had been around long enough that he could put you in touch with just about anyone you needed, right?"

"I guess that's true."

"Mr. Smoke, you said you joined up with Lizzy Saint's band about two years ago, right?"

He bristled. "We decided to partner together about two years ago, yes."

"Before that, you were a member of the band Tower, right?"

"I was."

"And for a few years before that, you were part of the band Red Sails, true?"

"I was."

"Mr. Smoke, why did Red Sails break up?

Jeff stood. "Objection, Your Honor. While this would be great for *Behind the Music*, I'm not sure how it's relevant to this case."

"It is, Your Honor. I'll get there directly."

"See that you do, Mr. Shepherd," said Judge Gallon.

I looked back at him. "Mr. Smoke, why did Red Sails break up?"

Smoke was biting the inside of his cheek now. He glared at me and said, "Our lead singer died."

"Johnny Turn, right? That was his name?"

Smoke nodded. "It was."

"He died of a heroin overdose, didn't he?"

Jeff flew from his seat. "Your Honor!"

Judge Gallon was looking at me sternly as she said, "Up here, Counsel."

The two of us went up to the bench and bent close to the Judge so that we could talk quietly but still be heard by the court reporter. Jeff started. "Your Honor, I believe that Mr. Shepherd is about to talk about the circumstances of the death of Johnny Turn from a drug overdose and, potentially, the presence of certain people involved in this case at that incident."

Judge Gallon looked at me and the look she gave me was not pleasant. "Mr. Shepherd?"

I nodded. "Mr. Smoke was with Johnny Turn that day and they had seen Dillon Chase the day before. Close enough in time that the police interviewed Chase about it." I held up the paper.

"Is that the police report?" said Judge Gallon.

"It is."

"That case is not on trial here, Mr. Shepherd. You will not mention anything else about it. Do you understand?"

"But Your Honor the circumstances are so similar—"

"The circumstances are separated by years and miles and

victims. You will not mention it, do you understand? And you will not try to get a mistrial from using it."

"Yes, Your Honor."

"Objection sustained."

I went back to the podium, shifted gears, and said, "So Mr. Smoke, you went from Red Sails to Tower to Lizzy Saint, right?"

Smoke stared at me for a moment, then smirked when he realized the topic had changed. "I think we covered that, Counselor."

"So the answer is 'yes?'"

"Yes."

"And you started writing with Lizzy Saint right away, correct?"

"I did." He smiled. "We hit it off right away."

"Once you started with the band and writing with Lizzy, Hank Braggi no longer wrote with Lizzy, true?"

"That's true. Lizzy was branching out in new directions."

"You've written two albums with her?"

"I have."

"Those albums have done well commercially, haven't they?"

"They have."

"You're familiar with the sales numbers for those albums, aren't you?"

"Very much so."

"Those albums have only sold about a third as much as her original album, *Ripper*, right?"

Smoke's eyes grew hard. "Maybe."

"They've only sold about half as much as her second album, *Jacked*, true?"

"I don't know."

"You don't know? You're very familiar with the sales numbers of your albums but not Lizzy's prior albums?"

"I don't pay as much attention to those. Those are in the past."

"*Ripper* won the Grammy for best new album, didn't it?"

"It did."

"Neither of your albums with Lizzy Saint has won a Grammy, have they?"

"Art's not about awards."

"So is that a 'yes?'"

"Do you think that the Rolling Stones care that *Goat's Head Soup* never won a Grammy?"

"I don't know, when I have Mick Jagger on the stand, I'll ask him. Neither of your albums with Lizzy Saint won a Grammy, did they?"

"No."

"Does it bother you that your albums with Lizzy haven't been as commercially successful as Hank's collaboration?"

"No."

"Mr. Smoke, you told Mr. Hanson and the jury that nobody used heroin or talked about using heroin in the suite that night. Do you remember that?"

"I do."

"Do you use heroin, Mr. Smoke?"

Jeff stood. "Objection, Your Honor."

"Mr. Hanson is the one who brought it up, Your Honor," I said. "He elicited testimony from this witness that no one used or talked about using in the suite that night and yet we have a syringe of heroin here. I have the right to explore that with the witness."

"Overruled. Answer the question, Mr. Smoke."

I heard a stirring behind me and turned. Max Simpson had stood and waved Jeff over to him and was whispering furiously. "A moment, Your Honor?" said Jeff.

"Briefly."

Simpson's face was animated and a little red as he talked rapidly and made small gestures with his hand. Jeff listened impassively before he straightened and said, "Your Honor, I find myself in an interesting position as a prosecutor. However, I am the one who called Mr. Smoke to testify and I believe that if the Court is going to allow this line of questioning ..." He paused.

Judge Gallon stared at him. "The Court is."

"So that if the Court is going to allow this line of questioning, the witness should be advised that he has a right under the Fifth Amendment to decline to answer any question that would incriminate himself regarding the commission of the crime."

Judge Gallon appeared to think and turned to me. "Mr. Shepherd?"

"I can't control Mr. Smoke's answer, Your Honor. But the prosecution has opened the door and I believe I'm permitted to ask the question."

Judge Gallon turned to Jared Smoke. "Mr. Smoke, you have taken an oath to tell the truth and must do so in this proceeding under penalty of perjury. However, if you believe that an answer might incriminate you regarding the commission of a crime, you may decline to answer, claiming the protection of the Fifth Amendment. Do you understand?"

"I do, Judge."

I continued. "Mr. Smoke, do you use heroin?"

Smoke looked at me, a slight grin on his face. "No."

"Have you ever used heroin?"

"No."

"Have you ever helped someone obtain heroin?"

"No."

"Mr. Smoke, please roll up your shirt sleeve above the elbow."

"What?"

Jeff stood. "Your Honor, this is outrageous."

I shrugged. "Impeachment, Your Honor."

Judge Gallon thought. "I'll allow it."

Smoke glared at me as he unbuttoned the sleeve on his right arm.

"You're right-handed, aren't you, Mr. Smoke?"

"Yes."

"So roll up your left sleeve."

Smoke froze. His eyes became hooded as he buttoned his right sleeve, folded his hands, and set them on his lap. He sat there and stared at me.

"Your left sleeve please, Mr. Smoke."

Smoke stared at me, motionless.

"Your Honor, could you direct the witness to roll up his left sleeve, please."

Judge Gallon stared at him, face neutral. "Mr. Smoke?"

Smoke glared at me and then he looked over my shoulder at where Simpson was sitting. I didn't take my eyes off him. Nobody moved.

Finally, Smoke said, "I claim my Fifth Amendment right."

"Understandable," I said. "Mr. Smoke, I'm not your lawyer, but I will tell you that the Fifth Amendment allows you to refuse to answer a question but it does *not* allow you to lie in response to a question so I am going to ask you again, do you use heroin?"

"No."

"Mr. Smoke in the past have you used heroin?"

"I claim my Fifth Amendment right."

"Mr. Smoke, have you ever bought heroin?"

"I claim my Fifth Amendment right."

"Have you ever helped other people buy heroin?"

"I claim my Fifth Amendment right."

"Mr. Smoke, did you buy heroin when you were part of the band Tower?"

"I claim my Fifth Amendment right."

"Did you ever buy heroin when you were part of the band Red Sails?"

"I claim my Fifth Amendment right."

"Mr. Smoke, you knew Dillon Chase going as far back as your Red Sails days, true?"

He glared at me. "True."

"No further questions, Your Honor."

Jeff could barely be contained as he almost sprang back up to the podium. "Mr. Smoke, Mr. Shepherd talked about the commercial success of your albums and his clear implication was that you're jealous of Mr. Braggi. First of all let me ask, are you jealous of Hank Braggi?"

"Of a sound engineer? No."

"Does your professional relationship with Hank Braggi affect your perception of what happened that night in the suite?"

"No."

"Does professional jealousy of Mr. Braggi's relationship with Lizzy Saint color your perception of what you saw Mr. Braggi do to Dillon Chase?"

"Of course not. My relationship's better than his."

Jeff went to his blowups and put the five-foot-tall picture of Dillon Chase's unrecognizable face on the stand. "This is a true and accurate representation of what Dillon Chase looked like after Hank Braggi had beaten him that night?"

"It is. He was a mess."

Another picture. "This is a true and accurate representation of the angle Dillon Chase's arm was laying at when you saw him?"

"It was bent backwards like that, yes."

Another picture. "Is this a true and accurate representation of what the wall looked like in the hotel suite?"

"It is."

"Whose blood is this?"

"Dillon Chase's."

Another picture of Dillon Chase's face. "Mr. Smoke, when you saw Dillon Chase earlier that night, did he have a nose?"

"He did."

"Mr. Smoke, you mentioned that you were in a relationship with Lizzy Saint on the night of the killing?"

"Yes. Still am."

"Would you have left her in the room if you didn't think she was safe?"

"Of course not."

"You didn't see anything from Dillon Chase that you believe presented a danger to Lizzy Saint, is that right?"

"That's right."

"And when you reentered the room, you didn't see anything that presented a danger to Lizzy Saint, true?"

"True."

"What you saw was Hank Braggi killing Dillon Chase, is that right?"

"I don't know," said Smoke.

Hanson cocked his head. "What do you mean?"

"I mean I think he might've already been dead when I saw Hank throwing him around."

Jeff went through his stack of blowups and found the most gruesome picture of Dillon Chase's face that he had. It was covered in blood, the head was misshapen, and from this angle, once you knew where to look, it was clear that the nose was gone. He put it on the easel, tapped it, and put one large finger under his chin as if he were considering a question. He stood there for almost a full 30 seconds before he said, "Nothing further, Your Honor."

I stood. I went over to the easel and put the picture back in Jeff's pile, putting it blank side to the jury. Then I went over to the pile of exhibits and pulled out the baggie with the syringe and set it back on the banister in front of Smoke. "Mr. Smoke, we've established that you weren't using heroin that night, right?"

"Right."

"And Ms. Saint doesn't use heroin, does she?"

"She does not."

"Yet we know this was found in the suite that night. A syringe full of heroin. And you didn't bring it in, right?"

"I did not."

"And Lizzy didn't bring it in?"

"She did not."

"So that leaves Dillon Chase, Blake Purcell, or Aaron Whitsel, right?"

"I don't know."

"The three men you invited up?"

"I don't know."

"That's dangerous, isn't it? Carrying heroin?"

"I don't know."

"Now Purcell and Whitsel were gone when you came back, right?"

"Right."

"It was just Lizzy and Hank and Chase, right?"

"If Chase were alive, yes."

"So if Chase was a danger to Lizzy, the only one who could have protected her was Hank, right?"

Jeff stood. "Objection. Foundation, Your Honor."

"Sustained."

"No further questions, Your Honor."

Judge Gallon looked at Hanson who shook his head. "Mr. Smoke, you may step down." Judge Gallon looked at the clock. "Members of the jury, you are excused for the day. As I'm sure you noticed when you came in, there are a number of reporters and media at the courthouse today. Let me remind you that you're not to speak about this case to them or to each other. The prosecution is about done with its case and then the defense will be entitled to put on theirs and you must wait to conduct your deliberations until after you have heard all of the evidence. Do you understand?"

The jurors nodded.

"Very well, you're excused. The court will reconvene at nine o'clock tomorrow."

Judge Gallon swung the gavel.

We stood as the jury left the room. I became acutely aware as the jury filed by that I am a fairly big guy and that Hank was towering over me. He made me seem small.

Like he could pick me up and break me over his knee.

The jurors weren't looking at us as they left.

## 32

It was Cyn's turn to pick the sandwiches that night so we were munching on cheesesteaks from West of Philly back at the office. I tore a piece of melted cheese off that was stretching between my mouth and the bun, wiped my face with a napkin, and said, "Do you think the jury got it?"

"Got what?" said Danny.

"That's not encouraging," I said.

Lindsey held a finger up as she finished chewing then said, "They got that Lizzy was probably too drunk to remember what happened. They got that Jared Smoke is a prick and had a connection with someone who brought some heroin. And they got that Hank killed the shit out of Chase in the most brutal possible way."

"Do you think they got why?" I asked.

"Why what?" said Lindsey.

"Why Smoke wanted Lizzy to take heroin."

Lindsey and Danny looked surprised.

"Smoke wanted Lizzy to take heroin?" said Danny.

"Really?" said Lindsey.

I nodded. So did Cyn.

"Well, I didn't get that so I'd be surprised if the jury did," Lindsey said. "Why?"

"To control her," Cyn said. We all looked at her as she wiped the last bit of Philly steak juice from the edges of her mouth then folded her napkin and put it down squarely on the table. "Smoke's albums weren't doing as well as Hank's, who was still lurking around the edges of the tour. Doesn't take much paranoia to think Lizzy, or the label, might want a change."

"How the hell does heroin help?" said Danny.

"If Lizzy needs heroin and he controls the supply, Smoke controls her."

Danny looked back and forth between us. "I was supposed to have gotten that?"

"Bringing Chase to the room? Sending Purcell and Whitsel for beers? Leaving Chase alone with Lizzy so he wasn't involved?"

Danny looked at me blankly.

I sighed. "The judge kept the evidence about Smoke's history with the Red Sails out of evidence. If she'd let it in, I would've been able to show that when the lead singer of Red Sails died, Smoke was in the band and Dillon Chase was visiting them. It's too similar to be a coincidence."

Lindsey shook her head. "But the judge kept it out so I don't think the connection to Smoke is clear to the jury at all. Does it really matter though? Hank still has to be justified in killing Chase. The brutality is still a tough sell."

"If it's clear that there was no one except Hank to protect Lizzy, I think it would go a long way towards excusing the violence."

Lindsey thought. "Then I don't think we got there today."

I chewed before I said, "I think you're probably right. All right, I'll have to try and connect the dots with Whitsel. The prosecution's calling him tomorrow and then I'm pretty sure they'll rest. Then we'll put on Dushane and the toxicologist and that should be it."

"You're certain you're not going to put Hank on the stand?" said Cyn.

"There's no way I can, Cyn. That just lets Hanson go through every one of those photos again. And Hank's not exactly apologetic about what he did."

Lindsey shook her head. "He's practically gleeful."

Cyn nodded. "I agree. Just making sure."

My phone buzzed. It was the office line forwarding to my cell. I didn't recognize the number. As soon as I picked up, a voice said, "Mr. Shepherd?"

"Yes."

"This is Aaron Whitsel."

"Hi, Aaron." I mouthed "Whitsel" to the others, who froze. "What can I do for you?"

"The prosecutor is calling me to testify tomorrow."

"That's what I understand."

"I can't."

"I see. Why not?"

"I just can't. You need to make a deal."

"I can't right now, Aaron. There's no deal on the table."

"Listen, if your client will take a deal, I'll call the prosecutor and tell him that Braggi didn't break my arm, that it was an accident."

"Aaron, listen to me carefully. I'm not making any deals with you or with the prosecutor. I want you to get on the stand tomorrow and tell the truth, no matter what that truth is, do you understand me?"

Silence at the other end.

"You need to end this," Whitsel said.

"I would if I could. But I can't."

"It's too much. It's too much."

I didn't care a whole lot about a drug dealer's feelings. "Just tell the truth, Aaron. That's your way out."

Whitsel laughed. "It's my way out all right," he said and hung up.

Cyn was staring at me.

"What?" I said.

"That was good. Telling him to tell the truth."

I shrugged. "That's what a lawyer does."

"Not all of them."

"All of them aren't from Carrefour." I crumpled my wrapper. "Let's get to work."

We did.

I HAD TROUBLE SLEEPING THAT NIGHT. USUALLY, DURING A TRIAL, I could stay awake just long enough to eat something before I dozed off and, before I knew it, the alarm was waking me back up again. That night, though, I couldn't get the day's testimony out of my head.

Lizzy Saint was beautiful and she was talented and she had narrowly missed becoming a heroin addict or worse. Despite her success and her talent, or I guess because of it, she had people in her life who were trying to take advantage of her, trying to profit from her, who were all too happy to give it to her so that they could start her down that path and control her.

That hadn't happened though because Hank had been in her life. A man who had been attentive and looked out for her and protected her and stood ready to beat back any vultures who threatened her.

I shifted on the couch and made it all the way through Scott Van Pelt's show to see Neil Everett and Stan Verrett kick off the late SportsCenter before I fell asleep.

"Mr. Hanson," said Judge Gallon the next morning. "You may call your next witness."

Jeff stood. "Your Honor, at this time, the prosecution rests."

I stood. "Your Honor, may we approach?"

She waved us forward and we went up to the bench. "Your Honor, we understood that the state was going to call Aaron Whitsel."

Jeff shrugged. "We were Your Honor, but he went across the line into Michigan and we haven't been able to bring him in."

"In that case, Your Honor, we move for acquittal on the attempted murder charge against Hank Braggi related to Mr. Whitsel."

Jeff shook his head. "The state believes it has put on sufficient other evidence of the attempt on Mr. Whitsel and his injury for the case to go to the jury."

Judge Gallon considered for a moment. "The court finds that there is enough evidence for that charge to survive the defense motion. Motion denied."

"We were planning on his testimony as part of our defense, Your Honor," I said.

"Did you subpoena Mr. Whitsel?"

"The prosecution had, Your Honor."

Jeff shrugged again. "And now we've decided not to call him."

Lindsey stepped forward. "Your Honor, given the circumstances, while we are taking testimony, we ask that you issue a warrant and service under the Uniform Testimony Act for Mr. Whitsel's arrest so that he can be brought in to testify if he's found."

"Any objection, Mr. Hanson?"

Jeff shook his head. "If they can find him, we're happy to have him, Your Honor."

Judge Gallon looked at Lindsey. "Give the motion to the bailiff and we'll get things moving."

Lindsey and I exchanged a nod.

"Anything else?"

"No, Your Honor."

"Then let's get started."

As we went back to the table, Lindsey whispered instructions to Danny on where to find the paperwork and told him to get Olivia Brickson on finding Whitsel. He nodded and left.

Judge Gallon was kind enough to wait until we were done before she said, "Mr. Shepherd, you may call your first witness."

"Thank you, Your Honor. The defense calls Sheriff Warren Dushane."

Jeff stood immediately. "Your Honor, may we approach?"

Judge Gallon waved impatiently and I saw jurors roll their eyes and shift in their seats as we went back up to the bench. "What is it, Mr. Hanson?"

"Your Honor, Warren Dushane is a Michigan sheriff. Although he is law enforcement in Carrefour, his jurisdiction is Carrefour, Michigan. This crime occurred in Ohio, so it's my understanding that Sheriff Dushane was not involved in the investigation here."

"Mr. Shepherd?"

"Your Honor, Sheriff Dushane is part of the multi-state drug task force that works in Michigan, Ohio, Indiana, Illinois, and Wisconsin. In that capacity, he fights heroin trafficking throughout the Great Lakes in general and all of Carrefour in particular and he has knowledge of how that trafficking is affecting our individual community."

Judge Gallon scowled. "Did he investigate the crime here?"

"He did not."

"Did he interview any of the witnesses in his role as a drug enforcement officer?"

"No."

"Will he be able to identify the heroin found at the scene here? Trace where it came from?"

"No, Your Honor."

"So it's all general testimony? About heroin?"

"Yes, Your Honor. That's what this case is about."

"No, it's not Mr. Shepherd. It's about whether Hank Braggi committed murder. Unless you can show that Sheriff Dushane has specific knowledge of the events at issue in this case, he will be barred from testifying. Does he have any such knowledge?"

I paused, trying to think of a way to bend his knowledge into specifics, but I didn't have any. "No, Your Honor."

"Then Mr. Hanson's objection is sustained."

"May I make a proffer to preserve his testimony for appeal?"

"Go right ahead."

I bent down and talked quietly to the court reporter, listing the things that Sheriff Dushane would've testified to if he'd been allowed so that I could appeal it if we lost. This took some time and as I did it, I could see the jury getting antsy. They didn't know what we were saying but they saw me talking, a lot, and they didn't look too happy about it.

I finished and then said, "Thank you, Your Honor."

Judge Gallon nodded and as we walked back to our tables, she said, "Members of the jury we often have to work out details related to the trial as we go. You're not to assume anything from my rulings one way or another. In this case, Sheriff Dushane will not be testifying and you should not make any assumptions based on that ruling. Mr. Shepherd, you may call your next witness."

"Thank you, Your Honor. The defense calls Dr. Matthew Beckman."

Lindsey went and got Dr. Beckman out of the hallway and a moment later he walked in. Matthew Beckman was a stick of a man with black glasses, longish black hair combed over to the side, but in a sloppy and messy sort of way, and he wore a suit that was just the slightest bit too short at the wrists and the ankles. He stooped a little as he walked and didn't make much eye contact as he made his way quickly up to the stand. Matthew Beckman was a brilliant toxicologist but became nervous when he was with more than three people.

I smiled and said, "Could you state your name for the record, please?"

"Matthew Beckman."

"What do you do for a living, Dr. Beckman?"

"I'm a toxicologist."

"What is that?"

"I study chemicals and their presence or effect on the body."

"And are you a doctor?"

"I am."

I ran Dr. Beckman through his credentials and that seemed to get him used to speaking a little more.

"Dr. Beckman, at my request, did you analyze some chemicals in this case?"

"I did."

I picked up the plastic baggie with powder in it. "Was it the powder in this bag, State's Exhibit 50?"

Dr. Beckman squinted and lifted his glasses. "Yes."

"And what did you do, Doctor?"

"I subjected the contents to testing to determine what they were."

"And what did you find?"

"I found that the bag contained heroin. And some other compounds."

"Let's start with the heroin."

"Okay."

"Are there varying levels of purity in street heroin?"

"Yes, there are. Purity can range anywhere from three to ninety-nine percent. That's the thing that makes it so dangerous —a person never really knows the strength of the dose they're taking."

"And were you able to determine the purity of the heroin in this bag?"

"I was."

"And what did you find?"

"I found that it was fifty percent pure."

"What does that mean?"

"It means that half of the substance was heroin and half was something else."

"And were you able to determine what that something else was?"

"Yes."

"What was it?"

"I found that the other fifty percent of the substance was a drug called fentanyl."

"And what is fentanyl."

"It's another narcotic pain medication."

"What's the significance of the presence of fentanyl, Doctor?"

"Fentanyl is a narcotic that's commonly used to cut heroin. The problem is that fentanyl can be as much as one hundred times more potent than morphine."

"Does that mean fentanyl is dangerous then?"

"Very. Many of the deaths we see from heroin overdoses are because of the presence of fentanyl. We've seen one batch take out as many as half a dozen people in one night in one city."

I swallowed and cleared my throat, then I said, "Do people know that there's fentanyl in their heroin?"

Dr. Beckman shook his head. "No. Not unless they're the ones who actually cut it but those people are usually up the chain of distribution. The end-user almost never knows."

"Did you find anything else in the bag, Doctor?"

"Nothing of consequence."

"Doctor, you mentioned that part of your job as a toxicologist is to determine the effects of drugs and chemicals on the human body, right?"

"It is."

"Do you have an opinion regarding what the effect of this particular batch of heroin and fentanyl would have on the human body?"

"I do."

"And what is that opinion, doctor?"

"My opinion is that the combination of this purity of the heroin combined with this mix of fentanyl made this a lethal dosage."

"Meaning that the person who took it would overdose?"

"Yes."

"And die?"

"Yes."

"Now Doctor, in court, experts aren't allowed to offer opinions on things that are simply possible. Do you have an opinion, to a reasonable degree of medical probability, that this heroin would have caused a fatal overdose?"

"I do."

"And what is that opinion?"

"That to a reasonable degree of medical probability, this dose of heroin and fentanyl would likely kill whoever took it."

"And how can you say that, Doctor?"

"Because of its chemical composition, Mr. Shepherd. This purity of heroin combined with this amount of fentanyl is lethal."

I stepped forward. "How can you actually *know* that, Doctor?"

Dr. Beckman set down the bag, folded his hands and said, gently, "Because I've seen it before."

"Thank you, Doctor. That's all I have, Your Honor." I turned quicker than I needed to, picked up a bottle of water, and took a drink as I sat down.

Jeff Hanson stood. "Dr. Beckman, you're being paid to testify today, aren't you?"

"I am."

"$750 an hour, right?"

"That's correct."

"And you've spent what, ten hours on the case?

"Not counting today."

"And what are you being paid today?"

"$2500 per half-day of trial."

"How many cases like this a year do you review?"

"Five or six."

"And is it usually for defense attorneys?"

"No. Usually, it's in civil cases, not criminal cases."

"Now Doctor, you said that the drugs in this batch of heroin would likely cause an overdose, true?"

"I did."

"You said that to a reasonable degree of medical probability, true?"

"True."

"So that means it's possible that the drugs would not have caused an overdose, right?"

"I testified that it probably would have."

"I understand, Doctor, but that means it's possible that it would not have caused an overdose, right?"

"I suppose anything is possible, Mr. Hanson, but in this case it's not likely."

"Now Doctor, it's also possible that the person who took this could have an overdose but that the overdose would not have been fatal, right?

"Again, that is possible, but it's not likely."

"So it's possible that the person who took this dosage would not have overdosed, true?"

"Possible but not likely."

"And it's possible that a person who did overdose would not have died, right?"

"Again, possible but not likely."

"Thank you. Your Honor, that's all I have."

"Redirect, Mr. Shepherd?"

I stood. "Dr. Beckman, is it possible for anyone taking heroin to know that it contains a lethal dose?"

"I'm afraid the person doesn't know until it's too late."

"The same thing is true of a person giving heroin to another person too, right? He can't know if it will kill the person he's giving it to?"

"That is also true."

"And here the likelihood is that this dosage would have killed the user?"

"It is the overwhelming likelihood."

"That's all Your Honor. Thank you."

Jeff shook his head that he had no more questions.

Judge Gallon looked at the clock. "All right, we're going to break for lunch. Please be back at 1:15."

As the jury filed out, Hank, Lindsey, Cyn, and I leaned close together. "We don't have anyone else unless we can track down Aaron tonight. I'm going to ask the judge if she'll give us the rest of the day."

"Will she do it?" said Cyn.

"I think so. We'll see. Your Honor, a word?" Judge Gallon had stood. She sat back down and waved us forward.

"Your Honor, with the ruling on Officer Dushane, I'm out of witnesses for today."

She raised an eyebrow. "You want to close this afternoon?"

"No. If you will permit it, I'd like to adjourn for the day and see if we can find one more witness for tomorrow."

"Whitsel?"

I nodded.

She looked at Hanson. "Any problem with that, Mr. Hanson?"

"I wouldn't want to clog the Court's docket, Your Honor."

"I can manage my docket, Mr. Hanson."

"He was on the State's list as well, Your Honor," I said. "I'd think they'd want to hear from him."

She thought.

"It is a capital murder case, Your Honor."

"I'm very aware of what type of case this is, Mr. Shepherd." She turned her focus on me. "Are you calling anyone else?"

"I don't think so."

"Your client?" said Jeff. His eyes were disinterestedly hooded.

"Still deciding."

"Fine," said Judge Gallon. "We'll adjourn for the day. You have until tomorrow morning. If you find him, you can put Whitsel on in the morning and we'll have closing and jury instructions in the afternoon."

"If they don't put Braggi on?" said Jeff.

"In the unlikely event that they put Braggi on, he'll follow Whitsel. Anything else?"

We collectively shook our heads.

"Fine. See you tomorrow, counselors."

We went back to our table, gathered our things, and made arrangements to meet back at the office. I told them I'd pick up the sandwiches and be there shortly. Cade collected Hank and the two walked out with Cyn.

Lindsey made a point of hanging back. "You alright?"

"Sure. Why?"

"Just checking."

"I'm fine."

She stared at me. "Okay."

Then we left.

## 33

---

Danny was waiting for us when we got back to the office. "Did you call Olivia?" I said.

He nodded. "Got the order from the Judge's bailiff and I'll walk it through the Michigan court this afternoon. If Olivia can find him, Sheriff Dushane said he'd arrange for the arrest and transport him to court tomorrow." He cocked his head. "How is Olivia going to find him?"

"I don't plan on asking her that. Do you?"

"I guess not." He waved the papers and pointed to the sandwich. "I better take that to go."

I handed it to him. "Thanks."

"See you this afternoon. I'll tune up the jury instructions when I get back."

As he left, Hank, Cyn, Lindsey, and I sat down. Since it was still daytime, Hank was allowed to be out of his house and with us. He had two giant roast beef and hot pepper sandwiches and was working on demolishing the first. "You just can't beat flame-broiled."

I nodded.

"So what's the battle plan tomorrow? Do I get to finally explain what happened?"

"I'm not putting you on the stand, Hank," I said.

Hank paused, his eyes dangerous. "What?"

"You're not testifying."

"Why not?"

"No one puts their client on if they can help it. I'm certainly not doing it with you."

He put his sandwich down. "So we're in a fight and you're not going to let me fight?"

"I'm fighting. And I'm not going to let me lose it."

"What do you mean?"

"If I put you on, Jeff gets to go through every one of those photos again. Every single one. He's going to put them up there for the jury and he's going to ask you how you broke Chase's skull the first time, and how you broke it the third time, and how you broke it the twelfth time and why fifteen breaks weren't enough. He's going to ask if you bit off his nose or kicked it off his face—there's no good answer to that question by the way. He's going to show you the picture of the blood smear on the wall and ask if it is from Chase's nose or his ear or his mouth. He's going to show you the picture of his arm bent backwards and ask if you twisted it that way or broke it over your knee. He's going to ask if you're strong enough to lift a man and throw him the way Smoke says he saw you do it."

Hank stared.

"And that's just the physical scene. He's going to ask if you enjoyed writing with Lizzy and if you were even the tiniest bit sad to stop. He's going to ask if you love her voice, if you think she's an amazing singer and if she's the best you've ever heard and then he's going to ask for your honest opinion about Jared Smoke and his talents and his writing ability and whether he's helping Lizzy or holding her back. He's going to ask why you were monitoring what Lizzy was doing with her boyfriend that night and why you even followed them up to their own room in the first place and ask if you make a habit of lurking around like that."

"And at some point, probably for his finale, he's going to ask you if you regret killing Dillon Chase and, more importantly, if you enjoyed it and you're not going to be able to hide your reaction to either. So no, Hank, I'm not going to put you on the stand."

Hank didn't blink. He just gave me that blue-eyed stare, smiled, and said, "You don't have to get so personal about it." Then he picked up his sandwich and went back to eating.

"Do you think our defense is enough?" said Lindsey.

"I think if we can get Whitsel on it will be. Once we establish he's a dealer, I think they're going to see the predatory trap Hank broke up."

"What if they don't find him?" said Cyn.

"Then it will be close."

"The toxicologist was helpful today."

I nodded. "I thought so too. I think he established the threat. The question is whether it justified the force."

My phone buzzed. I looked down and saw that it was Jeff Hanson. I scowled. It wasn't unusual for attorneys to talk during a case. There are logistical issues that come up all the time in a trial that you need to work out with the other side. Still, this case had been fairly straightforward procedurally so Jeff and I really hadn't spoken a whole lot.

I answered. "Hi, Jeff. What's up?"

"Do you have a moment?"

"Sure." I got up and stepped out of the room, mouthing "Hanson" to Lindsey and Cyn.

"We're going to drop the attempted murder charge for the attack on Whitsel."

"Oh?"

"Yes. We think there's still enough there but since he hasn't testified, we'd rather streamline the case and will drop it."

"Okay. What about the rest of the charges?"

"We're still looking for first-degree murder for the killing of Chase. But if we drop the attempted murder on Whitsel, we no longer have aggravating circumstances so it won't be a capital case anymore."

"Got it."

"We'll still be looking for life imprisonment."

"Understood. Have your people found Whitsel?"

"No, but in fairness, once he took off, we stopped looking for him. We just don't have that kind of manpower."

"All right, Jeff. Thanks for letting me know."

"I owed you the call, Nate. I didn't want you setting up your whole closing around the death penalty."

"Thanks for the courtesy, Jeff."

"Sure, Nate. See you tomorrow." I hung up.

Son of a bitch.

I went back into the room and all three of them looked up at me. "He's dropping the attempted murder charge on Whitsel."

Lindsey's face brightened. "That means he's dropping the capital murder charge. That's great! We've beaten the death penalty!"

Cyn's face could always be impassive, but now it went absolutely stony. Hank's face darkened and then actually became red.

"What?" said Lindsey.

"He's dropping the death penalty so that he can increase his chance of getting a conviction on the first-degree murder charge."

"What's the penalty for that?" said Hank.

"Life in prison."

"No death penalty?"

"No death penalty. I think he knows that the jury is offended by the way Chase was killed but, if we're right about the heroin, probably thinks Chase deserved it. And if the jury thinks Chase deserved it, he probably thinks that a jury wouldn't sentence Hank to death no matter how over the top the killing was. But I'm sure he believes that he can convince them that a man who could do that to Chase is too dangerous to be running around free so they'll be happy to lock him up for life. It's an easier sell."

"I have to testify," said Hank.

"No, Hank, you don't."

"I can't go to prison. Not for all that time."

"If I put you on, you will."

"Hank," said Lindsey. "We got rid of the death penalty. Be glad we saved your life."

"My life?!" Hank's face reddened. "You think sitting in a 10 x 10 brick room for years and years is a life?" He waved the sandwich. "You think grilling chickens or eating sweet corn in the sun is the same as shuffling down to the cafeteria for soggy cornbread and cold beans until I'm so old I shit myself? Of course, we're forgetting that I'll be able to pop out of the cell a couple of times a day to watch yard fights and shower sodomy. Life!" he spat. "I'd rather face the death penalty."

"Mr. Braggi," snapped Cyn. "Why don't you and I go outside and cool off a little bit?"

"I'm plenty cool."

"No, you're not." Cyn stood and extended a hand. To my surprise, Hank deflated, put her hand in the crook of his massive arm, and walked outside. As they left, I heard her speak in another language, I assumed Norwegian, and his willingness to listen to her suddenly made more sense.

"What the hell was that about?" said Lindsey as they left.

"He should be doing cartwheels that he's not going to get a lethal injection."

"I don't think he sees it that way." I thought. "It was a good move on Jeff's part. Now he can straight up play the safety and danger angle. Hank doesn't deserve to be executed, but he doesn't deserve to be wandering around free of supervision either."

Lindsey smiled. "Well, you're just going to have to justify what he did."

I smiled. "Is that all?

"That's it."

"Great. Easy."

~

THAT AFTERNOON WAS THE FINAL PUSH. I POLISHED MY EXAMINATION of Aaron Whitsel, fine-tuned the direct exam of Warren Dushane in case Judge Gallon changed her mind about letting him testify, and looked at Danny's draft of the jury instructions, which I refined and emailed back to him. I thought about who Jeff might call in rebuttal, but I didn't think there was anything that we'd raised in our case that he needed to address so far, not really.

Once that was done, I worked on my closing argument, punching up the themes, incorporating testimony from the trial, and putting together slides and references to exhibits.

In the end, the case was simple. Hank had brutally killed a man who was injecting heroin into an unconscious woman. The jury would either find it acceptable or not. I had to convince them that it was the right thing to do.

Hank and Cyn came back a couple of hours later. Hank seemed to have calmed down and Cyn said he agreed that the best strategy was for him not to testify. Hank nodded, shook my hand, and said he trusted me. I thanked him and walked downstairs with him as Cade pulled up in his truck to take him home. As he opened the door, Hank turned back, looked at me, and said, "Do you like pig?"

I blinked. "I'm a fan of ribs. Not so much chops."

"No, I mean a whole pig. Cooked all night over a fire."

"Who doesn't like that?"

The mischievous delight was back in his blue eyes. "When we've won this, we're gonna have the biggest pig roast you've ever seen."

I smiled. "Sounds good, Hank."

"I mean it."

"I know."

Hank climbed into the truck and Cade drove them away.

I went back to working on my closing argument.

The sun went down and I kept working. Danny came back to the office. No word yet on Whitsel but he'd gotten the order that would let Sheriff Dushane take him into custody. He finished the jury instructions and went home. Lindsey stayed but her work was really done for now and she was a good enough lawyer to know that having people milling around is more distracting than helpful and so went home. Cyn was the last one to stick her head in before she left. Her blue suit looked as unwrinkled as it had that morning and it seemed that not one red hair was out of place.

"Do you agree?" I said.

"With the analysis or with the strategy?"

"Both."

"Yes. To both."

"How did you calm Hank down?"

"I reminded him that his way of looking at things doesn't apply here."

"He does seem to prefer handling things directly." I smiled. "Of course, that's why we're here."

Cyn didn't smile. "I also told him to trust you. That you understand why he did what he did and that you're the best one to explain it to the jury."

I stared at her then but I didn't see any extra meaning in the calm green stare I got back. "We'll see, won't we?"

"We will. You almost done?"

"Just a few more slides here on the PowerPoint. Soon."

"Rest is as important as prep at this point."

"I know."

Cyn smiled then and left. As the lights of her car left the parking lot below, my phone buzzed. Olivia.

"Tell me you found him, I said when I answered."

"I found him."

"Great work, Olivia! Did you call Dushane? Are you going to be able to get him down to the court to testify?"

"Yes, I called Dushane. No, I won't be able to get him down to court to testify."

My stomach sank. "Too far away?"

"No, it's not distance. Aaron Whitsel is dead."

## 34

"How?" I said.

"A totally random and unfortunate single-car accident," said Olivia.

"So it wasn't?"

"Of course not."

"Where did you find him?"

"State Route 127, between Jackson and Lansing. Near as we can tell, he was driving northbound, went off the road, jumped a ditch, and smashed into a tree."

"It was clear last night, wasn't it?"

"It was this afternoon. And yes. Not a cloud in the sky."

I thought. "He called me you know. Said he couldn't testify. Wanted me to take the plea deal."

"Not a surprise," said Olivia. "Drug cartels are willing to take the odd arrests and trials here and there, but testifying on a case with national attention? Not good for business."

Another connection clicked into place. "I also had a toxicologist testify this morning that the dealer was cutting their product in half."

"Also not good for business."

I sighed. "Any chance the prosecutor knows this?"

"No. It hasn't really hit the wires yet. You just hire the best."

"I do. So it was a legit offer then."

"What are you talking about?"

I told Olivia how Jeff had called earlier in the afternoon and dropped the attempted murder charge on Aaron.

"There's no way he knew then. The accident happened about three p.m."

"That's after Jeff called. I owe you, Olivia."

"Of course you do. Just make sure you get your ass in for early morning workouts after this trial nonsense is over."

"How about after work?"

"Before, my distractible friend."

I sighed. "Fine. Thanks. And thanks to Cade. You two have really helped with this thing. I appreciate it."

"We know. Peace, brother."

I hung up and thought. There was no way around it.

No more testimony was coming. I had no more evidence to give to the jury, no more exhibits or baggies or syringes.

I was going to have to argue Hank out of life in prison.

Knowing I didn't have to examine Aaron, I focused on my closing. Putting together your final argument makes you see all the flaws in your case, makes you see where the evidence doesn't support your side, and makes you see what the evidence says is true and what isn't. Hank had killed Dillon Chase. He had beaten the living shit out of him and then mangled his corpse beyond recognition. I had to convince the jury that was okay, that Lizzy Saint would've done the same thing if she'd had the strength, and the consciousness, to do it. That each one of them would do it to protect someone they loved.

And then, alone in my office in the dark of the last night of trial, I realized I'd been arguing it all wrong, that I'd accepted the battlefield that the prosecution had chosen instead of forcing them onto one of my own. I needed to be like Hank's Home Guard and fight the prosecution on different terrain.

I went back through the evidence, quickly, found what I needed, and changed the PowerPoint slides. It wasn't a change in the evidence, it was a change of focus. It was one fact that I hoped would make the jury view the whole case through a different lens.

I didn't know if it was going to be enough.

I EVENTUALLY FINISHED PREPARING MY CLOSING AND WENT HOME a little before eleven o'clock that night. I was still thinking about the change in my argument when I walked through the door.

People call lawyers sharks as an insult. It's true, but not in the way they mean it. Most lawyers are conscientious people who care about their clients and immerse themselves in the smallest details of their clients' lives so that they can help. They spend hours, that stack up into weeks and months and even years, to get their clients what they need. They're always putting things in their own lives aside to focus on their client or their deal or their trial and when that's finally done, they swim right on to the next one just like their single-minded aquatic counterpart.

As I went to the kitchen for some food, the hole in my kitchen wall hit me square in the eyes, just like the hammer they use to stun a shark before the fishermen pull it into the boat. Everything Dr. Beckman had said that day, everything that helped our case, every tiny detail about heroin and fentanyl and overdose and death, flooded over me at once.

I wobbled for a second and caught my balance on the kitchen table. Then I yelled and punched the table one, two, three times before I collapsed into a chair and wept. I wept like my heart was breaking. Which it was.

For about ten minutes. And then I started swimming again.

I got up and pulled a bottle of water out of the fridge, winced, and switched the bottle to my left hand. I made rice noodles whose primary benefits were speed of preparation and calories. Then I went to the couch and slurped up noodles and hot sauce as Scott Van Pelt told me why NBA free agency was going to be off the chain this summer.

When I finished, I fell asleep.

## 35

JUDGE GALLON HAD US IN CHAMBERS THE NEXT MORNING BEFORE the jury was brought in. "You have something to tell me, Mr. Hanson?"

"Yes, Your Honor. We'll be dropping the attempted murder charge."

"I see. You know that eliminates the aggravating factor for the death penalty?"

"We do. I informed Mr. Shepherd and both parties submitted new jury instructions last night."

"Very well. We'll go over objections before we charge the jury. Any more witnesses, Mr. Shepherd?"

"No, Your Honor. We'd planned to call Aaron Whitsel but that's no longer possible."

"Because of the dropped charge? Makes sense."

"No, Your Honor. Because he's dead."

Judge Gallon put her pen down, slowly, and folded her hands. "What are you talking about?"

I told her about the accident.

"Did you know about this?" she said to Jeff.

"I found out this morning when Nate told me, Your Honor."

"Was it under suspicious circumstances?"

"Only if you think it's suspicious that a drug dealer to a rock star died in an unwitnessed single-car accident on a sunny, clear day as he was fleeing to avoid testifying in a murder trial, Your Honor." I said.

She wasn't amused. "It could be argued that it's convenient for you too, Mr. Shepherd."

"It's not. I was putting him on the stand today. My investigator found out about it."

Judge Gallon picked up her pen and tapped it repeatedly against her desk until she said, "His death, and the circumstances of it are not in evidence here. There will be no mention of it in closing, do you both understand?"

We both nodded. "His evasion of the state's subpoena is fair game though, right?" I said.

"It is," said Judge Gallon. "And that's as far as you'll go—a subpoena was issued by the state and not complied with. Understood?"

"Yes, Your Honor."

"So are we closing this morning?"

"I have no more witnesses."

"Not putting Mr. Braggi on?" said Jeff.

I smiled. "No."

"Too bad. Seems like his story deserves to be told."

"That doesn't actually work on people, does it?"

Now Jeff smiled. "You'd be surprised."

Judge Gallon tapped her pen harder. "Gentlemen. There's another matter we won't be addressing in closing."

She turned her computer screen around in a gesture I'd come to dread. Another headline.

*ATTORNEY'S WIFE DIED IN MASS OVERDOSE.*

"Have you seen this, Mr. Shepherd?"

I kept my eyes off my wife's picture in the lower right corner. "No, Your Honor. I haven't had the time."

"Let me summarize it for you then. This Maggie Smith has drawn a comparison between the toxicologist's testimony yesterday and the way your wife died. There will be no mention of that, Mr. Shepherd."

I lifted my chin. "There hasn't been, Your Honor. And there won't be. But I have a right to talk about heroin."

"You do, Mr. Shepherd, as it relates to *this* case."

"That's what I've done."

"I know. That's why I'm telling you again now."

"I understand."

She nodded. "We'll go through the jury instructions now then."

We did. It took about half an hour. As we rose to leave, Judge Gallon said, "What did you do to your hand, Nate?"

I put my hand in my pocket. "Nothing," I said. Then we went out into the courtroom to give our closing arguments to the jury.

JEFF HANSON STOOD THERE IN FRONT OF THE JURY, SILENT FOR A good thirty seconds, adjusting the backs of his five-foot-tall photos. He was making a point of straightening them even though they were lined up perfectly. The jury had seen them enough now that they shifted in their seats, visibly uncomfortable anticipating that he was about to turn the pictures toward them again. But he was masterful and he left them blank side out, letting the anticipation of their awfulness eat away at the jury.

When he was done, he ambled over to the center of the

courtroom, right in front of them, and flicked a hand at my client.

"Hank Braggi killed Dillon Chase. Mr. Shepherd and I may disagree on some things related to this case but that isn't one of them. From the moment he did it, Hank Braggi admitted that he killed Dillon Chase. He just thinks he was justified in doing it. He was not."

Jeff began to pace a little bit. "Let's leave aside the brutal awfulness of this killing. Let's leave aside the shattered skull and the broken ribs and the pierced lungs and the smashed arms. Let's just start with the fundamental question: was Hank Braggi allowed to kill Dillon Chase? The Court is going to talk to you about self-defense and about the defense of others and I want you to listen carefully to the Court's instructions, which will tell you when someone can defend themselves with deadly force. Basically, a person can defend themselves with deadly force if they believe they are in imminent danger of death or great bodily harm, and the only reasonable means to escape that harm is through the use of deadly force. Then, and only then, a person can use deadly force to defend themselves."

"The same rule applies if a person is defending someone else. If the person being attacked could use deadly force to defend herself, a person who intervenes to defend her can use deadly force too."

Jeff pointed at me. "Hank Braggi claims that Dillon Chase was injecting Lizzy Saint with a syringe. He claims that he stopped Chase and that a fight ensued that resulted in Dillon Chase's death. I want you to ask yourself a couple of questions. Was that a deadly situation for Lizzy Saint? Would she have needed to resort to deadly force to stop Dillon Chase if that's indeed what he was doing? Or could she have just said 'no?' Could she have just smacked him in the face? Would standing up, backing away, and yelling at him to get off her have been enough? Or was killing Dillon Chase the only way that Lizzy Saint could have stopped him? Did Lizzy Saint have to break Dillon Chase's skull, break his ribs, and break his arms to make him stop?"

"I don't think so."

Jeff shook his head. "I don't think she would've had to resort to violence at all, let alone deadly force. I think, even if what Mr. Braggi said is true, she could've told Dillon Chase to stop and he would have. Now we don't know for sure of course because Dillon Chase is dead. He can't tell us what he was thinking or why he did whatever it is that he did. And the Court will tell you that Hank Braggi is allowed to be mistaken, he doesn't have to be absolutely correct about whether the situation was exactly as he perceived it to be. The question is whether a reasonable person would have thought that Dillon Chase needed to be killed in order to protect Ms. Saint. We think, members of the jury, that the answer is unequivocally no."

"And that's just the question of whether force was required. We're presented with a case where deadly force was used over and over again, where Hank Braggi kept beating Dillon Chase enough to kill him several times over. Ladies and gentlemen, that force was cruel and it was not justified at all."

Jeff went over and stood by his pictures. "It wasn't necessary to shatter Dillon Chase's skull." He put a picture of Dillon Chase's unrecognizable face on the easel. "It wasn't necessary to break his right arm." A picture. "It wasn't necessary to break his left arm." A picture. "It wasn't necessary to break his ribs." A picture. "It wasn't necessary to kick the nose right off of Dillon Chase's face." The picture of the gap where the nose used to be was the last one up. "It wasn't necessary to splash the room up and down with Dillon Chase's blood as Hank Braggi pounded his body from dresser to wall to desk to chair to floor. None of that needed to be done."

Jeff walked away from the easel shaking his head. "None of it."

"If Hank Braggi tackles Dillon Chase and he accidentally hits his head on the floor, we are not having this trial. If Hank Braggi hits Dillon Chase once with a little too much force and Dillon dies, we're not having this trial. If Hank Braggi elbows Dillon Chase out of the way, elbows him in the jaw, we are not having this trial."

"We are having this trial because Hank Braggi brutally beat Dillon Chase to death in a way that exceeded all reasonable behavior and that was utterly excessive to the situation. Hank Braggi, for whatever reason, beat Dillon Chase to death and then beat him some more. I don't know the reason. Jared Smoke testified that he'd taken Hank's place as Lizzy Saint's cowriter. So was it jealousy? Overprotectiveness? Madness? I don't know. But this act," he pointed at the picture, "this act is not a lawful one and it's not one that you should allow. Hank Braggi committed murder. He killed Dillon Chase when he didn't have to. And no reason Mr. Shepherd can offer justifies it."

Jeff shook his head. "I've heard some of Mr. Shepherd's reasons. He implied it pretty clearly in his questioning and he's talked to a lot of the witnesses about it. He's going to tell you that Dillon Chase was injecting Lizzy Saint with heroin and that the heroin might very well have been a lethal dose, although I think even Mr. Shepherd will admit that he can't tell you that with one hundred percent certainty. But ladies and gentlemen, that's not enough. Even if every word of that is true, it's not enough." He pointed at the picture. The hole where Dillon Chase's nose used to be gaped like an abyss. "Not enough to justify this."

Jeff resumed his place in the center of the jury box and stood there. He shook his head. "Hank Braggi killed Dillon Chase. It wasn't in self-defense and it wasn't the defense of another. It was murder. And that's what we're going to ask you to find, that

Hank Braggi is guilty of first-degree murder. Thank you for your time and attention this week."

He sat back down. *A lot of times the jury will look to me right away. This time, half of them were still looking at the picture.*

"I don't have a picture like this to use," I said as I walked over to the easel. "Nobody took one because at the time Dillon Chase was injecting Lizzy Saint, there were only the two of them in the room. Lizzy was unconscious so she couldn't take the picture, and Dillon Chase was preparing to inject her with a lethal dose of heroin and fentanyl, so his hands were too full." I turned the blow-up around so that its blank, white side faced the jury.

"We can picture it though, can't we? You saw Lizzy Saint. She came in here and told you she doesn't remember anything from that night. She doesn't remember because she was too drunk. Which she should be allowed to be. She's been working hard, touring the country, and finds out she has a day off the next day where she doesn't have to travel before noon. She does drink too much. Why? Because she believes she's with people she can trust. She's with her boyfriend and his friends in the privacy of their own suite. There are no fans and there's no management and there's no crowd. She can relax and be herself knowing that she can trust the people she's with."

I tapped the blank white space. "Can you see that picture? Can you see Lizzy laughing and talking and drinking and then becoming more drowsy and becoming drunk, and, not surprisingly after singing her lungs out for two and a half hours, she begins to drift off. And her boyfriend leaves her, for whatever reason, to go to the bathroom or to talk to the manager or to do whatever he says he was doing. But it doesn't matter why, what matters is that he left. He left her there with a stranger."

I pointed at the blank back of the picture. "Can you see that? Can you see that young woman drifting off, not knowing what's happening, not being able to say 'stop?' Can you see Dillon Chase pulling out a bag, boiling down the heroin, then tying a rubber tube around an unconscious woman's arm, careful not to wake her up? Can you see him pulling the drug up into the syringe and preparing to plunge it into Lizzy's arm?"

"Can you picture it? Can you picture the planning and the evil that entails? Because make no mistake." I walked over to the exhibit table and picked up the baggie with the syringe of heroin in it. "One of them brought the heroin with them. I don't know who it was and neither does the prosecutor. We've heard that Lizzy doesn't use and Smoke's claim that he doesn't use *today*. We've heard from Blake Purcell that he didn't bring it with him. We haven't heard from Dillon Chase for obvious reasons and we haven't heard from Aaron Whitsel because he avoided the government's subpoena and refused to testify in this case. Why? I don't know. So no one can nail down who brought the heroin that night."

"But you know what? The police could have figured it out if they'd wanted to. Chief Detective Pearson, the man in charge of serious crimes for all of Carrefour, Ohio, could have investigated it if he'd wanted to. But you know what is obvious? The police didn't want to know who brought it in. And how do we know that? Because they didn't bother to take the fingerprints on the syringe."

I shook the bag so that the syringe rattled against the plastic. "They had it right here. The plunger which everyone who's seen any movies knows is going to have a thumbprint right on it. And did they take one? No. Why? Because they had an easy answer. Because Hank Braggi told them the minute they walked in the door that he had killed Dillon Chase. And Chief Detective Pearson didn't want to know anything that interfered with that narrative, didn't want to know anything that might interfere with closing his case."

I picked up the bag of heroin with my other hand. "You heard from the toxicologist, Dr. Matthew Beckman. You heard what was in this bag. Fifty percent heroin and fifty percent fentanyl. A lethal concoction that would've killed Lizzy Saint."

"Now Mr. Hanson has argued that it was possible that the dosage might not have killed Lizzy, that she might not have experienced a fatal overdose. But you heard Dr. Beckman say that it would've killed her. To a reasonable degree of medical probability, this mix of heroin and fentanyl would have killed her. That means it is more likely than not that what was in this syringe was going to kill Lizzy Saint if it was injected into her veins. That means at least fifty-one percent of the time, pushing this plunger kills her."

I paused. Most of the jurors were looking at me. The Artist and the Pepsi Driver were nodding. The Retired Math Teacher, though, was just staring at the blank picture back.

"That's what Hank Braggi saw when he entered the room. That's what he told the police officers at the scene. He told them that he walked in, saw Lizzy Saint unconscious, saw her arm tied off, and saw Dillon Chase preparing to inject her veins. And he saw that there was no one else there to stop it."

I set the evidence down and pointed again at the blank, white picture back. "Can you picture it? Hank walking in to see his good friend unconscious and a stranger injecting her. Hank did what a reasonable person would do, what Lizzy would've done if she was able to. He stopped him. He stopped Dillon Chase from injecting his unconscious friend with a lethal dose of heroin."

I shook my head. "You didn't see the prosecution call a toxicologist up here. Why? Because Dr. Beckman was right. His analysis of the heroin was correct. The drug was tainted and it was lethal. That means Lizzy Saint, unconscious, was under imminent threat of dying. Of being killed. And Dillon Chase was the one who was going to kill her, in the most sneaky and despicable way possible. And if Lizzy Saint was under an imminent threat of death, she was entitled to use deadly force to defend herself. And if Lizzy Saint was allowed to use deadly force to defend herself, then Hank Braggi was allowed to use deadly force to defend her."

I pointed. "Mr. Hanson argued that Hank Braggi could have used less force. That Mr. Braggi, seeing a stranger about to kill his friend, should have been nicer, more genteel, more restrained. Is that what a reasonable person would do? Does Mr. Hanson really want you to believe that a reasonable person who sees someone about to kill his friend would just say 'stop?' Or smack the killer's face? Or just step back? Is that really true?"

I shook my head. "I don't think so. I think a reasonable person would end the threat immediately in whatever way he had to to save his friend's life."

I paused. Here we go. It was time to fight like Hank's Home Guard. On the territory of our choosing.

"The prosecution has besieged you with Dillon Chase's injuries in this case. Mr. Hanson has spent days describing them to you, over and over and over again. He's blown up five-foot-tall pictures of them, magnifying them in the smallest detail. He's had the coroner count the broken bones and he's put together diagrams listing them for you, to go along with inventories of broken furniture and damaged walls. And you know what? None of it matters."

The jury stared at me. Every one of them.

"We've told you from the outset that Hank killed Dillon Chase. Just like Hank told Detective Pearson that he killed Dillon Chase. That's not in dispute. And neither is the way Hank killed him."

I paused. Jeff looked at the ceiling, unconcerned. I continued. "Remember, when I asked Dr. Gerchuk the cause of Mr.

Chase's death? He said the skull fractures. Then I asked him how many. He said three. And then remember how many blows he said it took?"

The Pepsi Driver mouthed "two or three." Jeff scowled.

"That's right. He said two or three blows. Remember?" I smacked my fist into my palm. Bam. Bam. Bam. "Three blows, at most." Bam. Bam. Bam. "That takes a second? Two? Far less than it took the prosecution to explain it, certainly."

"Remember what else Dr. Gerchuck said? The blow to the nose didn't kill him. The internal injuries didn't kill him. The broken arms didn't kill him. It was the two to three blows to the head." Bam. Bam. Bam. "He said that many of those injuries—the ribs, the internal organs—happened after Mr. Chase was dead."

Jeff began to write on his legal pad.

"Remember what Mr. Smoke said? That when he saw Hank Braggi throwing Mr. Chase around the room, Mr. Chase wasn't moving and his arms and legs were flopping around like a blow-up balloon advertisement? That's because he was already dead."

"Mr. Hanson has said repeatedly that Mr. Braggi could have killed Mr. Chase several times over with the damage he inflicted. The State wants you to convict Hank because they think he used too much force *after* Dillon Chase was dead. But this is a *murder* trial. Any damage done to Mr. Chase's body after he was dead isn't relevant to how he killed him. I suppose all this evidence might matter if they'd charged my client with abuse of a corpse or disrespecting the dead, but they didn't so it doesn't matter at all. What matters is that Hank Braggi saw a lethal threat to Lizzy Saint and he stopped it, completely, effectively, and without a doubt."

I hit my palm again. Bam. Bam. Bam.

"Was he enraged at what he found? You can make that assumption. But it doesn't matter. Not in this murder trial."

Then I said, "And afterwards, he didn't flee, like Blake Purcell and Aaron Whitsel did. He calmly sat down in the room, made sure that Lizzy was okay, waited for the police, and told them exactly what happened."

I shook my head. "Heroin is a scourge in our community. It affects people and it affects families and it affects all of the interconnected lives that come in contact with it."

I paused. I found I had to wait a beat longer than I intended before I continued. "Lizzy Saint was fortunate. She had someone standing there, watching over her, defending her against an evil, cowardly threat. And when Hank saw that threat, he defended her and destroyed it. He didn't apologize to the police for it and I don't apologize to you for it on his behalf."

I turned the picture back around, the most gruesome ugly picture of Dillon Chase's face there was. I pointed right to the middle, right to where his nose used to be. "Dillon Chase tried to give Lizzy Saint a deadly dose of heroin, a dose that would've killed her. Hank was there to stop it. So he did. For that reason, we ask that you find Hank Braggi not guilty of murder in the first degree. Thank you."

Hank looked at me as I sat back down and I swear to God he actually gave me a low growl of approval. I put a hand on his shoulder, sat, and kept a straight face as Jeff went back up in front of the jury. He shook his head, as if in disbelief at what was hanging about in the air. "It's the state's job, my job, to prove to you beyond a reasonable doubt that Hank Braggi killed Dillon Chase and that he did it purposefully and intentionally. That's not in dispute. You haven't heard one shred of evidence that Hank Braggi didn't kill Dillon Chase or that he didn't mean to do it or that it was some sort of horrible misunderstanding. Instead, Mr. Braggi is claiming to you that it was justified, that it was reasonable, that Lizzy Saint had the right to kill Dillon

Chase to escape the harm that she was in, and that if she could, Hank Braggi could too."

He pointed at our table. "That's Hank Braggi's responsibility, his burden of proof, and it's Mr. Shepherd's job to prove to you that Hank Braggi's killing of Dillon Chase was justified. That this"—he turned and pointed to the picture—"that this was *reasonable*. That a *reasonable* person in the same situation would have made the same judgment and done the same thing. That this utter destruction of a human being, this breaking of a body, this pulverization of a man's face was reasonable, appropriate, justified, and necessary."

Jeff shook his head and stood just a little bit closer to the jury, then lowered his voice. "It is not. *It is not.* This is *not* what our system of justice allows. This is *not* what a reasonable person does. A reasonable person knocks Dillon Chase down. A reasonable person tackles him. A reasonable person holds him until the police arrive. A reasonable person does not break his body into a thousand pieces and spread his blood all over a hotel room wall."

"It was not justified. It was not a reasonable excuse. You cannot allow a person to do this. We ask that you convict Hank Braggi of murder. Because that's what he did. He murdered Dillon Chase. And it was inexcusable."

"Thank you."

Jeff sat back down.

"Thank you, Counsel," said Judge Gallon. "Members of the jury, you've heard the closing arguments of counsel. I will now instruct you with the law that will govern your decision."

Judge Gallon then read the legal instructions to the jury. The instructions are the only law the jury is allowed to consider and they are dense and they are difficult and, through no fault of the judge, it's read in a way that is almost guaranteed to make the jury drift off. The only reason they don't is because the jury is working so hard to get it right. I watched as half of the jury took notes and all of them listened with attention as the judge explained the law to them, explained the law about reasonableness, and murder, and self-defense, and circumstantial evidence, and direct evidence, and the things they were and were not allowed to consider.

There was nothing that could be done now. There was no argument I could make, no evidence to rebut, and I knew exactly what the judge was saying because I'd read the instructions a dozen times. So I watched the jury. I watched the Pepsi Driver and the Artist and the Single Mom. I watched the Nurse and the Principal and the Retired Math Teacher, just trying to figure out what they were paying attention to and which way they were leaning.

I had no idea.

To his credit, Hank sat next to me, straight as an arrow, hands folded, looking the least threatening I had seen him in our history together. He studiously listened when he should have and made notes on his notepad when it seemed appropriate. None of them were directed to me, of course. When I snuck a glance at his paper, it looked to me like he was writing song lyrics.

When the judge had finished giving instructions to the jury, she directed them to pick a foreperson and retire for their deliberations. It was about eleven o'clock so they would have time to deliberate before lunch. Since the state would be springing for the food, I figured they would at least go past one o'clock. After that, I had no idea.

We stood, and the judge dismissed the jury to deliberate, and we waited as they filed out of the room. I caught a glance from the Single Mom but that was it. Nobody else looked at me. Or at Hank.

When they were gone, Hank looked at me and said, "So now what?"

"We don't want to go too far in case the jury comes back so let's go get a sandwich. We might as well relax a little bit."

Hank smiled. "Easy for you to say. You haven't been doing anything."

"That's the truth," I said and slapped Hank's big shoulder.

"I want a sandwich with a lot of meat," said Hank.

I smiled. "I know just the place."

Twenty minutes later, we were sitting in the Black Boar Deli—Cyn and Hank and Lindsey, Danny and me. We had beaten the lunch crowd so we'd been served right away and Hank was literally licking his lips as he prepared to bite into a monstrous Cuban sandwich that was a true ode to the hog. He grinned, opened his mouth to an impossible width, and took a big bite. His eyes smiled in approval and he munched for almost thirty seconds before he said, "So what do you think, Counselor?"

I shook my head. "I don't have a good line on what this jury is thinking, Hank. These guys might have a better idea, they were able to watch them more closely."

"I think you're reaching them," said Danny. "They seemed offended by the whole heroin thing."

"Maybe," said Lindsey. "But none of them could keep their eyes on the pictures. They all turned away eventually."

"They are passing gross," said Hank, taking another bite. "Not really what you want to look at before lunch."

"I think it's too close to call," said Cyn. "I can usually tell. This time I can't. What did you do to your hand?"

I put my hand under the table. "Nothing."

"That's a lot of swollen nothing."

I shrugged.

"So what do we do now?" said Hank.

"Now we wait," I said. "The bailiff has my number. She'll call when the jury's back and we'll go hear what they have to say."

We sat there for a while and ate and I couldn't help but watch Hank do magnificent damage to the massive Cuban club in front of him. He made it through half of it in an incredibly short amount of time when he paused, looked at Lindsey, and said, "So what happens to me next?"

"What do you mean?" she said.

"Either way."

"If the jury finds you not guilty, Cade will take that anklet off you and you'll be free to go right then and there."

"After you complete some paperwork to get our bond returned," said Cyn.

Hank's eyes glittered. "Of course."

"Of course," said Lindsey. "And if they find you guilty, the county will take you into custody and you'll await sentencing."

"Right away?" said Hank.

"Right away. The time counts toward the completion of your sentence though."

"So it counts towards the completion of my life if I get life?"

Lindsey pointed at him over her Ruben. "You got it."

The pace of Hank's eating slowed considerably and soon it stopped altogether. "I'm not sure which one is crueler."

I bit. "Which one what?"

"Back in the day, the old Norse wouldn't lock you up. They would cast you out of the village, wouldn't communicate with you, wouldn't share resources, and so the convicted would have to move on and make his own way. But he was still out in the world, in the water and the wind and the earth. He was alone but not confined."

I played along. "The world's smaller now. You can't send someone out into isolation without him affecting another community."

"I get the reason," said Hank. "Like I said, I'm just not sure which one is crueler—the whole wide world and no human contact or confinement in a concrete box. I think it's the box."

My phone buzzed. It was the bailiff. I raised my hand and answered. "Hi, Stacy. It's Nate."

"We don't have a verdict yet, Nate," said Stacy. "I need you to come back though. The jury has a question."

"I'll be right there. Thanks." I hung up and said, "I need to head back. The jury has a question. You can finish up because we know it's going to take a little bit to answer the question and for them to react to it."

"What's the question?" said Danny.

"I don't know yet."

"Is that good or bad?" said Hank.

"I won't know until I hear the question. I'll text you all after we answer it."

They nodded, I left them, and hustled back to court.

JEFF AND I WERE SITTING BACK IN JUDGE GALLON'S CHAMBERS. The judge was there, and the court reporter had set up in a chair right next to her desk. The judge looked at the court reporter who nodded and the judge said, "After approximately one hour and fifteen minutes of deliberations, the jury summoned Stacy to the room and said it had a question. Stacy told them to write it down and that she would deliver it to me. They have and this is the question."

Judge Gallon looked at both of us over the glasses she didn't need then looked down at a piece of printer paper with handwriting on it. "Is one of the offenses that Hank Braggi has been charged with abuse of a corpse?"

Judge Gallon looked back at us. "My reaction is to answer that Hank Braggi has not been charged with abuse of a corpse. Comments?"

When Jeff didn't answer right away. I said, "I think you also need to say that abuse of a corpse is also not an element of any of the crimes with which Hank Braggi has been charged."

"The prosecution objects to that," said Jeff.

"Well, it's true," I said.

"What's the basis for your objection?" said Judge Gallon.

"It goes beyond the scope of the question, Your Honor," Jeff said.

I shook my head. "It doesn't, Judge. And what the prosecution objects to is the fact that it undermines half of the evidence he put on in the case."

"Watch your tone, Mr. Shepherd." Judge Gallon thought for a moment. "I'm going to include Mr. Shepherd's suggested language. The jury is clearly trying to decide where to fit that conduct within the charges before it and there aren't any. They need to know that to prevent error. I will answer that Hank Braggi has not been charged with abuse of a corpse and any action of disrespect toward Mr. Chase's body after he was dead does not form a basis of any of the crimes with which he has been charged."

"Your Honor, I object," said Jeff again.

Judge Gallon cut him off with a raised hand. "Your objection is noted for the record, Mr. Hanson. Thank you both."

As the bailiff typed up the judge's answer to give to the jury, Jeff and I left chambers. As I pulled out my phone and texted the others, Jeff said, "Well, that seems to be leaning your way."

"There's no way to tell what the jury's thinking, Jeff, you know that."

Jeff looked unconvinced and I actually agreed with him, I thought the question absolutely showed they were leaning my way and I texted that to the others too.

After about half an hour, the others joined me and I still felt good about it. When another four hours passed though, I wasn't sure at all. We spent the rest of the afternoon in the courtroom and in the coffee shop on the first floor and the more time passed, the more certain I was that we were in trouble. Hank became antsy, Danny was more jumpy than usual, and Cyn typed away on a small tablet for some other matter with her firm now that this trial was wrapping up. I sat there sipping warm coffee on a hot day and waited.

Just before five, my phone buzzed. They all heard it and looked at me. I glanced at my phone, nodded, and said, "The jury's back."

We went back up to the courtroom to receive the verdict.

WE WERE ALL THERE. I SAT AT OUR COUNSEL TABLE WITH HANK between Lindsey and me. Danny and Cyn were right behind us on our side of the barrier and Cade was in the front row of the gallery. Jeff sat alone at the prosecutor's table. When we were all there, Stacy went into the judge's office and, a moment later, Judge Gallon emerged. She sat in her chair, straightened her robe and said, "Is counsel ready?"

"Yes, Your Honor," we both said.

Judge Gallon nodded, and Stacy opened the door to the jury room. A raucous conversation went quiet. A moment later, the jury filed out.

None of them glanced over at us as they sat down and all of

them seemed to be making a point of not looking at the backs of the pictures of Dillon Chase that were on the floor next to the easel in front of the jury box. I saw the Hipster reach out and pat the Single Mom on the leg, who nodded.

I had no idea what it all meant.

When they'd all sat down, Judge Gallon said, "Members of the jury, have you reached a verdict?"

The Retired Math Teacher stood up. I felt a twinge. She'd been elected foreperson and she had not liked my case at all. "We have, Your Honor," she said.

"Stacy?" said Judge Gallon.

Stacy went over to the Retired Math Teacher and took the piece of paper from her. She delivered it to the judge who read it, checked another sheet, then nodded. Judge Gallon's face never cracked, not once, and her neutral expression didn't change as she handed the sheet of paper back to Stacy, who in turn brought it back to the Retired Math Teacher.

If this seems like an agonizing process designed to absolutely torture the parties and the lawyers, it's because it is. I smiled at Hank, who nodded.

As Stacy brought the verdict back to the foreperson, I nudged Hank and he and Lindsey and I stood up. Jeff did too.

"What say you?" said Judge Gallon.

The Retired Math Teacher took the glasses which hung on a chain around her neck and put them on. When she spoke, her voice was clear. "In the matter of State of Ohio versus Hank Braggi on the count of murder in the first degree, we the jury find defendant Hank Braggi not guilty."

Hank squeezed my arm but remained quiet. He knew there were two more to go.

"On the count of murder in the second degree, we the jury find defendant Hank Braggi not guilty."

Hank squeezed harder. Enough to break it.

"On the count of voluntary manslaughter, we the jury find defendant Hank Braggi not guilty."

There was a murmur throughout the courtroom and Hank put his hand on my shoulder and squeezed, eyes glittering. I smiled.

"Counsel, would you like to review the verdict form?"

"Please, Your Honor," we both said.

As Stacy brought it over to us so we could review the signatures, Judge Gallon began speaking to the jury. "Members of the jury, I thank you for your service. What you've done is one of the most important things that we can do in our society and I appreciate the time and attention that you spent. You are now released from your obligations to keep your deliberations confidential and you may speak to whomever you wish about this matter. Often times, I know the lawyers would like the opportunity to speak with you to find out what mattered to you during the course of the trial. You do not have to do so, but I can tell you that, if you do, it is very helpful to those involved. Again, however, you are under no obligation to do so. Thank you again for your time and attention and you are excused."

As the jury filed back into the jury room to collect their things, I walked over to Jeff and extended my hand. He immediately took it. "Congratulations, Nate. That was well done."

"You tried a good case, Jeff. I thought you had it."

He shrugged. "Maybe next time."

"With someone else, I hope," I said.

He smiled. "Me too." Then he went about gathering his things.

I turned to Danny. "Go in there with the jury and ask them what they thought."

Danny's eyes got big. "Why me?"

"Because they won't tell me the truth. If there's something I was doing that annoyed them I want to know and they won't tell me so go in and ask them what they thought about the case."

Danny looked nervously at the room. "Right now?"

"Right now."

Danny had no sooner walked by me than a bear engulfed me in a hug. Hank. Good Lord was he strong.

Strong enough to break me in half.

"Am I free?" he said.

"You are," I said. "But you'll probably want to double-check with him." I pointed to Cade who came through the gate and smiled.

"You want to do this somewhere privately?" Cade said.

Hank grinned. "Get this goddamn shackle off me right now," he said and put his massive foot up on a chair, revealing the monitor on his ankle. Cade reached down with the key, unlocked it, and pulled it off with a snap. "You're free to go, Mr. Braggi."

Cyn stepped up. "As soon as he signs the paperwork to get our money back."

Hank waved a hand. "A detail."

"Two million details," said Cyn.

Hank grinned and raised an eyebrow. "I'm good for it?"

"You most certainly are not."

"Bah, even you can't ruin my mood." He turned back to me and squeezed my shoulder again. "You kept fighting, Counselor. Good things happen when you keep fighting."

Now I raised an eyebrow at him. "Most of the time."

"Right, right, right. Most of the time."

"What are you going to do?"

His eyes clouded. "I'm not sure. I doubt the tour will have me back but I'll try anyway. If not, I may just follow the tour and listen to Lizzy from the upper deck. Either way, I can't leave for a couple of days."

"Really? Why not?"

"I have a pig roast to throw."

"Hank, you don't have to do that."

Hank raised his hand. "I know you don't like to hear my stories, but according to the legends of my country, the men in Valhalla fight every day. They go out and they spill blood and they practice killing each other and then, at the end of every day, they feast on the boar Gullinbursti to renew their spirits and their flesh. Now I know it's just an old tale but the underlying principle is true—fight hard every day. And when you're done, celebrate."

Hank grinned. "We, Counselor, are going to do some celebrating."

Cyn waited until Hank stood aside and stepped up. Her demeanor had changed a bit. Her tanned face was still flawless and her red hair was perfectly straight and her suit remained utterly unwrinkled but instead of cool precision, she now exuded a calm warmth as she extended a hand to me. "Congratulations, Nathan."

"Thank you, Cyn. You were amazing."

Cyn shrugged. "Perhaps. But the spear is only as good as its point no matter how stout the handle."

I was too relieved to puzzle that one out right then so I said, "Are you sticking around or heading straight out?"

"I need to get going. We have another case starting in two weeks."

I felt a twinge of disappointment then said, "All right, let's pack this up. Hank, if you want to go with Cade, you can finish the final paperwork and we can meet back at the office."

Cade nodded. "I'll drop him when we're done."

Hank put an arm around Cade's huge shoulders. "Come on, my little jail-keeper." And it was a testament to Hank's good humor and genuineness that Cade didn't seem to mind.

As we packed our papers and exhibits, Jeff finished collecting his and walked away with a nod. It took me a few more minutes and I had just about finished packing when the jury began to file out of the jury room. A few smiled and waved and I smiled back. The Hipster stopped at the gate and pointed. "Tell your client that his beard is outrageous."

I smiled. "Will do."

The Pepsi Driver looked like she was about to leave when all of a sudden, she darted over and gave me a hug. She wouldn't look me in the eye. Instead, she gave me a quick squeeze and then left, wiping her eyes as she did. I was taken aback and looked at Cyn who gave me a shrug and went back to packing.

The last one out, still talking to Danny, was the Retired Math Teacher. She walked straight over to me and shook my hand. "Nate Shepherd, you don't know me but I taught at Carrefour South for thirty-five years."

I nodded. "I remember that from your questionnaire, Mrs. Benson."

She smiled. "That means I was there the year you knocked Mitch Pearson out. Twice."

I laughed and looked away.

"Don't you dare look embarrassed, young man," she said. "You jumped up and down at the time if I remember correctly."

I smiled. "Well, I guess we all change, Mrs. Benson."

"You would think so but that Mitch Pearson certainly hasn't. He was the same in here as he was in my algebra class, just about as full of himself as a quarterback could be and only half-deserving. Always a bully, didn't treat anybody well, and finally got what was coming to him on the twenty-four-yard line from an outside linebacker who was sick of his bull-crap."

I actually laughed at that. I couldn't help it. But Mrs. Benson was giving me this stern look and I saw that, although she'd sounded like she was joking, she was dead serious.

"See, that's the thing, Mr. Shepherd," she said. "Mitch Pearson was a first-class little prick in high school and eventually he got what was coming to him. And you shouldn't have to apologize for being the one to deliver it."

Mrs. Benson looked at me with a hard gleam that caught me off guard. "That happens sometimes, doesn't it?" she said. "Not always, but sometimes people get what's coming to them."

She took my hand and she squeezed it. "And other times, there's no justice in the world at all."

I saw the faintest watering in the corner of her eye. "Mrs. Benson?" I said.

She squeezed my hand harder. "I had Sarah in my class too."

And that was all she said. She put her other hand on top of mine and she tried to speak but she couldn't which was good because neither could I. She nodded and I nodded back and she patted my hand and she left.

Danny was watching it all. "They had a lot to say," he said.

---

MY PHONE BUZZED. "HI, MOM," I SAID.

"Well, Nate, you have your father so flustered that he didn't go out on the boat this morning so I don't need to tell you how serious this is."

"What are you talking about?"

"All of these people swarming around the cottage and dragging their trailers across the lawn, although I suppose they didn't leave any marks on the grass. And that smoker? I've never seen one that big and it's squatting right there in the middle of my yard."

"Mom. Mom, slow down. I have no idea what you're talking about."

"You throwing a pig roast at our house without even saying anything, that's what I'm talking about!"

"Mom, I'm not throwing a pig roast at your house."

"No? Then why is there an eight-foot-tall, cast-iron smoker in the middle of my yard with a pig in it?"

"There is?"

"An enormous pig, Nate, stuffed with onions and apples."

"When was this?"

"Not an hour ago. The truck is from Newton Farms. You know the Newtons, have the place up on the north side of town where they keep pigs and cattle. Well, apparently they throw pig roasts too and you bought the deluxe package. Showed up and said they had to get it started right away if it was going to be ready by tomorrow night. Turns out a whole pig takes almost a whole day to cook."

"Who knew?"

"Everyone knows that! Anyway, your dad goes right up and asks them what they're doing in his yard although he didn't put it exactly like that, as you can imagine, and they said that our son had arranged it and he said, 'Tommy?' and the man said, 'No,' and he said, 'Mark?' and he said, 'No,' and he said, 'It can't be Nate,' and the man said, 'That's exactly who it was' and that if we didn't want to waste a whole pig that had already been paid for, we'd better let him set up and do his job and your dad steps aside for just a second and boom! There's a smoker in my yard."

I smiled. Turns out Hank Braggi could act fast when he wanted to. "I think it's a gift from a client, Mom."

"A gift?"

"We won our case today. I think the pig roast is a thank you."

"Well, why would he put it up here?"

I thought for a moment. "Because this particular client feels that families and celebrations are important."

"Well, I can't say as I disagree with him there. I think the only reason your father allowed it is because the pig will be ready on Saturday. You know how he is about doing the grilling on Sunday."

I smiled. "I do."

"So looks like you'll be eating here two nights this weekend."

"It certainly does."

"All right, Son. I'll see you tomorrow afternoon then?"

"Yes. Can Mark and Tommy's families make it?"

"They'd better. We have a whole pig to eat."

"All right, Mom. I'll see you tomorrow."

"Okay, honey. Love you."

"Love you too."

I shook my head then walked up the stairs to the third-floor temporary office. When I walked in, I saw an orderly row of boxes all packed up and ready to ship. The conference room, which had been covered in documents for weeks, was picked up, neat, and empty. Two men in uniforms of blue shirts and blue shorts were standing there as Cyn said, "Those boxes go to Minneapolis and that equipment goes to Memphis."

The tallest man nodded. "Anything else?"

She shook her head. "Everything else stays."

The man nodded again and the two began carrying boxes out the door.

"Next case in Memphis?" I said.

"It is."

"Not staying for the pig roast?"

Cyn smiled. "So Braggi made good on his promise?"

"He did."

"I'm afraid Braggi's celebrations tend to run a little long."

I smiled. "Don't worry. My dad's an early riser."

Cyn smiled again, which was more smiles in one night than I'd seen throughout the whole case. "Then maybe your dad will have more luck than Braggi's dad. I'm sorry, Nathan, I'd like to but I have to move on to the next case."

She extended her hand. "You tried a good case, Nathan. I know it was difficult but you never let it show. I respect that very much."

I shrugged. "All cases are difficult."

Cyn gave me a stare that was hard to meet. "Still," was all she said. And that was enough.

An actual ring tone came through on Cyn's phone and she

answered immediately. "Yes, Mr. Skald?" she said. She listened. "Of course, he's right here."

She handed me the phone. "Hello?"

"Nate, this is Victor Skald. Congratulations!"

"Thank you, Mr. Skald."

"Please, it's Victor. Just like you. That was very well done!"

"Thank you. I couldn't have done it without Cyn."

"That's the truth. She is a marvel, isn't she? With her on your side the battle's half won but we've all seen more than enough cases go south, haven't we?"

"Yes, sir."

"It was even odds here at the home office, just as many people thought Hank was headed for a lethal injection as thought he might be walking free. But Cyn believed that you were the perfect man for the job and it turned out we were right."

"Thank you, Mr....Victor. It was a team effort."

"Of course it was, but a spear with a blunt point is just a drumstick."

That was the second time I'd heard a spear expression that day. I shook my head. "That's very kind."

"Two things before you go celebrate," said Victor Skald. "We knew there was a very good chance that Hank was headed for execution. He's not, so we're paying you a bonus."

"That's not necessary, Victor."

"I know it's not, but we're all very happy here and Hank's parents are thrilled. They paid us a bonus and we're paying one to you."

"I can't accept that, Victor."

"Of course you can and you are. How you spend it is up to you. Make sure some of it trickles down to that young associate of yours."

"Of course. What about Cyn?"

Victor chuckled. "Cyn has the arrangement of her choosing. We give her whatever she asks for. Don't worry about her."

"Thank you, Victor."

"And you're keeping the tablets and equipment."

"That's not necessary either, Victor."

"I know it's not but you probably have files in them and sandwich stains on them so what would we do with them?"

"Thank you, Victor."

"You're welcome, Nate. And if we ever have need of counsel again in Carrefour, we certainly know who to call."

"Certainly. Thank you."

"Tell Cyn I'll wait to hear from her when she gets to Memphis. Good-bye, Nate."

"Good-bye."

I hung up and handed the phone back to Cyn. "He said he'll wait to hear from you in Memphis."

Cyn took the phone and put it in her purse.

"He's giving us a bonus."

"You deserve it."

"He said you have your own arrangement?"

"I do."

"He also said you thought I would be perfect for this case."

"You were."

"Why did you think that?"

Cyn stopped and looked up with those cool green eyes. "A former prosecutor, now independent lawyer, with a great reputation who grew up and played football in the town where the case is pending? Seems like a pretty logical choice for local counsel."

"You're the most thoroughly prepared person I've ever worked with, Cyn."

She looked away. "Thank you."

"No detail is ever too small for you."

Silence.

"Not about a case," I said. "And not about your local counsel."

Cyn shrugged her purse over her shoulder.

"Just tell me you didn't leak the story."

"I would never violate a court's gag order, Nathan."

I thought. "No, I don't think you would. But the gag order applied to the facts of the case. Not to an attorney's travel arrangements. Say to North Carolina."

Cyn held out her hand. "Like I said, Nathan, you were the perfect lawyer for this case. My firm thanks you, Hank's family thanks you, and I thank you for everything you did. And went through."

Which, of course, wasn't an answer.

I was tempted to leave her hand out there but I didn't. When I shook it, she glanced down and said, "You should get that looked at."

It was my turn to shrug.

"Hopefully next time won't be so painful," she said.

"Next time?"

"Careers are long and winding things, Nathan. You never know." She checked her phone. "I have to catch my flight. Good-bye."

"Goodbye," I said, and Cyn left. I decided that I was too charged up, too tired, and too happy to be angry about the way I'd been used. Instead, I picked up the phone and made a call. The woman answered and we arranged to meet. Then I turned off the lights to the office and left.

I WENT TO THE RAILCAR. IT WAS FRIDAY AFTER WORK SO THE place was busy, with more drinkers than eaters. I took a seat on the patio because I'd been inside too much for the last month. I found a table off to the corner, with a clear view of the river, ordered a beer, and waited for the woman.

I sat there long enough to order a second beer and it arrived at the same time as a blonde woman in a black suit. When I caught her eye and raised my bottle, Maggie White waved and made her way over. "Congratulations," she said as she sat down at the table across from me.

"Thanks. Want a drink?"

"I ordered one on my way in." She pulled her phone out of her purse and set it on the table between us. "You caught me right as I was pulling into the airport."

"Thanks for coming."

"Are you kidding? I have so many questions about the case that I'd like for you to comment on. For example why—"

"That's not what I want to talk to you about."

Maggie cocked her head. "What else would we talk about?"

"Sarah."

I could see her clench up. "My stories were accurate."

"I know they were. About the last two years of her life. About the period after she blew out her knee playing volleyball and had surgery and was prescribed oxycodone and got hooked on it during her rehab. About the period when the pharmacies started keeping track of how many pills she got and so she had to go find heroin so that she could feed her addiction. About the period when her husband was so focused on working and so inattentive to her that he believed her when she said she was tired and believed her that she was trying to lose weight and didn't realize what was happening until she was dead."

Maggie was listening.

"I want to tell you the rest of her story. About the all-state volleyball player for Carrefour South who was amazing on the piano. About the girl who got an environmental science degree from Michigan State and returned home to work in the woods and lakes of Carrefour. About the woman who saw her parents every week and volunteered as a reading tutor at the school. About the woman who did triathlons and loved the outdoors and never smoked pot or took any drugs until she dislocated her knee so badly that they were prescribed for her. About a woman who didn't deserve what happened to her because her husband failed her."

Maggie's drink came. It looked like some sort of pink vodka concoction. She stirred it with her straw. "If I listen to it, I'm going to write about it."

"That's what I want."

"All of it."

"They've read the bad. I'd like them to read the good."

"It doesn't change the ending."

"I'm very aware of that."

Maggie set her drink aside, hit record on her phone, and said, "Tell me about Sarah Shepherd."

So I did.

THE NEXT DAY WAS SATURDAY AND IT WAS SUNNY AND IT WAS beautiful and I took a day off work for the first time in more than a month. I went to my parents' cottage around lunchtime. When I arrived, my dad already had five of his grandkids out on the boat, which allowed me to hang out on the shore with my brothers and my sisters-in-law. Normally, there would have been something to do to help get dinner ready but that day there was a big, black smoker and a red and white striped tent and a scurrying staff that promised that all of that was going to be taken care of. Which my family appreciated because it gave Kate and Izzy time to mock me for having pale, inside-all-day lawyer skin and gave Tom and Mark the opportunity to wonder how a guy with a desk job could manage to break his hand. The splint on my right hand did allow for full movement of my fingers, which I utilized in response.

Hank had insisted that he thank everyone and my mom and dad never minded having people over so, later in the day, Danny and his wife and their little daughter showed up, and Lindsey arrived with her boyfriend shortly after. Olivia and Cade walked up with Cade literally carrying a keg of beer on his giant back and it wasn't long before Mom and Dad's friends from around the lake gravitated over so that by the time the pig was ready, there was a full-fledged celebration going on.

Around seven, the pitmaster, a short guy with a flushed face and a full beard, pronounced that the feast tent was open and I elbowed my way along with my nieces and nephews to get some apple-stuffed pork.

It was delicious. I mean it was melt in your mouth, eyes roll back in your head delicious.

I ate my first helping and was thinking about going back for a second when my phone buzzed. I wiped the juice off my hands and took a look. It was a text from a number I didn't recognize. It said simply, *I'm out front.*

I wasn't sure who that would be but I had a guess so I grabbed a couple of beers and went around to the front of the cottage. There was a decked-out black pick-up truck in the drive and, as I came up the walk, a large, bearded man stepped out.

Hank.

He grinned. "How's the pig?"

"Hank, it's delicious." I handed him a beer and he hesitated for a moment before he took it. I held out my left hand and he ignored it and gave me a big bear hug. "I'm glad. Is your family here too?"

I smiled. "All of them. On their way to stuffing themselves into a food coma."

"Outstanding."

"Are you going to join us?"

"No, no. I need to get out on the road."

"Will you be going back to the tour?"

"I don't think so. Lizzy might have me but I can't imagine that the label wants me around. Or that Smoke does." A cloud passed over his face.

"Is Lizzy still with him?"

"Yes."

I didn't want to voice my suspicions but Hank knew what I'd said at trial and he wasn't stupid. "Will she be okay with him?" I asked.

Hank drank his beer. "I don't know. But his absence was too convenient. And what you dug up about his former band." He trailed off for a moment. "Seems like something a coward might try to control his singer. I'll keep an eye on them. From a distance."

"Hank," I said my tone rising. "Have we learned from this experience?"

"Yes," he said in a tone that was as cold as his eyes. "Next time I'm protecting someone, I won't lose my temper."

"Jesus, Hank. Next time?"

"Years can stretch longer than you think, Counselor. Never say never." He smiled then and the joy came back to his face. "Oh, and, if I get in trouble, I'll make sure it's in Carrefour so I can have the best lawyer in the world save my ass." He put a massive hand on my shoulder. "I never would have survived the confinement, Counselor. Thank you."

I felt his gratitude and I felt his joy and, deep down, if I was being honest, I felt like Dillon Chase had it coming. "You're welcome. Hank, you have to join us. There's no way we're gonna finish all this pig and Cade literally just carried a keg of beer in here."

Hank smiled but his eyes were sad. "I don't think your family would appreciate having a murderer at the family barbeque."

"Is that him?" said a woman's voice. My mother stood on the front porch of the cottage, both hands on her hips.

I turned. "Mom, this is Hank Braggi."

My mom glared at me. "Nathan Shepherd, why is this man standing in my front yard?"

Hank raised a big hand. "I'm sorry, Mrs. Shepherd. I was just leaving."

My mom turned her stare on him. "You most certainly are not. You're coming back right now and helping us eat this magnificent pig you bought for us. And if you weren't a lawyer and an adult, Nathan, you'd be grounded for keeping a guest outside and away from the party without introducing him to your family."

Hank's gaze lightened.

"You're stuck now," I said. "Neither of us are going to get her off this one."

Hank smiled and I swear to God he actually lowered his head in modest embarrassment as he climbed the porch and accepted a quick hug from my mother. "I'm warning you; my granddaughters are going to want to hear all about this Lizzy Saint person."

Hank paused on the steps. "Are you sure, Mrs. Shepherd?"

My mom reached up and patted his bearded cheek. "Our family's been down this road, Hank. We just wouldn't have been as messy."

That actually seemed to get Hank, as if the acceptance and understanding was far more than he expected. He gave her a quick, quiet hug then straightened and said, "Do you think your granddaughters would like concert T-shirts? I have a whole box in the back."

My mom smiled. "Be quick about it."

Hank hustled back to his truck, pulled out a box, and then we followed my mother around back to meet the family.

# EPILOGUE

Maggie White was as good as her word. The next day, Entertainment Buzz carried a long story about Sarah. Maggie painted a picture of the person Sarah was, of the great things she did, and of the joy she was to be around before she blew out her knee. Instead of a story filled with contempt for a junkie and scorn for an overdose, it painted the picture so many other people have faced—of a woman unknowingly addicted and then left with nowhere to turn once that addiction had truly taken hold. The ending was the same of course, as it had to be, and there was a section at the end about how it paralleled the Braggi case and what it was like for me to defend it but I didn't read that part. It was enough for me that Sarah's story was told.

Sarah's mom called me later that morning. She was crying and she thanked me and she told me that she missed her and I told her that I did too.

There were things I didn't know yet that morning, things that wouldn't happen for a while. It would be another month before the police would determine that Aaron Whitsel's death was the result of operator error, a conclusion Olivia told me not to question because the cartel he had been selling for was nothing to mess with. I would have no desire to mess with it.

It would be another year before Jared Smoke died of an accidental drug overdose, apparently from a tainted batch of heroin. An exhaustive, rumor-filled investigation would reveal no evidence of foul play. I would have no idea if Smoke had fallen in with the wrong group or with the wrong man and would have no desire to find out.

And of course at that time I didn't know that the album Lizzy Saint would release after Smoke's death would be the biggest seller of her career or that I would drive my nieces Reed and Taylor to the Detroit stop of Lizzy Saint's *Runes* tour and become their all-time favorite uncle by introducing them to Lizzy backstage afterwards. And when I heard the long, cracking drum solo of her new hit "Seventeen" and the *a cappella* wail of the preamble to "Protector," well, I would decide not to dig too deep and would yell for an encore like everyone else.

I didn't know any of those things, though, on the Sunday morning after the trial. What I knew that Sunday morning was that the world, at least that part of the world that read Entertainment Buzz, had a picture of what my Sarah was like. I checked the clock and saw that I had a couple of hours before I was due back at my parents' cottage so I went to the garage and grabbed the hardware store bag that had sat on a shelf for more than a year. I took it to the kitchen, pulled out a tub of spackle and a putty knife, and began to fill the fist-sized hole in the wall.

The spackle was rough and uneven and it didn't match the existing drywall exactly, not the pattern or the depth or the color of the original.

But it was a start.

# THE NEXT NATE SHEPHERD BOOK

*True Intent* is the next book in the Nate Shepherd Legal Thriller Series. Click here if you'd like to order it or take a peek at what's inside.

# FREE SHORT STORY AND NEWSLETTER SIGN-UP

There was a time, when Nate Shepherd was a new prosecutor and Mitch Pearson was a young patrol officer, that they almost got along. Almost.

If you sign up for Michael Stagg's newsletter, you'll receive a free copy of *The Evidence*, a short story about the first case Nate Shepherd and Mitch Pearson were ever on together. You'll also receive information about new releases from Michael Stagg, discounts, and other author news.

Click here to sign up for the Michael Stagg newsletter or go to:

https://michaelstagg.com/newsletter/

# ABOUT THE AUTHOR

Michael Stagg has been a trial lawyer for more than twenty-five years. He has tried cases to juries and he's won and he's lost and he's argued about it in the court of appeals after. He still practices law so he's writing the Nate Shepherd series under a pen name.

Michael and his wife live in the Midwest. Their sons are grown so time that used to be spent at football games and band concerts now goes to writing. He enjoys sports of all sorts, reading, and grilling, with the order depending on the day.

You can contact him on Facebook or at mikestaggbooks@gmail.com.

# ALSO BY MICHAEL STAGG

The Nate Shepherd Legal Thriller Series

Lethal Defense

True Intent

12-23
d mw

Made in the USA
Middletown, DE
01 June 2023

31890919R00246